MIAMI MADNESS

Garry Gewirtzman
Sheila Gewirtzman

Disclaimer: All characters in this book are fictitious. Any resemblance to real persons (except the authors), living or dead, is coincidental.

Library softcover- ISBN 9798630596543

ALSO BY GARRY AND SHEILA GEWIRTZMAN

ADDITIONAL TITLES: CLIFF MANDICH SERIES

Deadly Combo
Deadly Countdown
Deadly Crossing

NONFICTION

Smooth as a Baby's Bottom: A Dermatologist's Guide to Your Child's Skin Care
Skin Sense: A Dermatologist's Guide to Your Family's Skin Care
From Chicken Soup to Oysters: A Doctor's Guide to Home Remedies

Dedication: To our family who anchors us to our past, who brings joy to our present, and who provides hope for our future.

CHAPTER 1

My morning routine never made it beyond step one. When I removed the plastic casing from the Miami Herald, I was planning to skip right to the Sports Section. I liked to begin my day by relaxing with my first cup of coffee and the newspaper before heading to my office. I needed to ease into the day, knowing that I would have a hectic schedule in my dermatology practice.

Brewing coffee suddenly became the last thing on my mind. Instead of pulling out the Sports Section, I found myself glued to the lead article on the front page of the Herald. So much for morning routines and relaxing.

In all capital letters, the headline of the article above the fold screamed: "DON KILLER STRIKES AGAIN!"

I practically fell into my chair. This couldn't be happening. What's going on in my city?

Until just a few months ago, Miami's most famous Don was Don Shula, the man with more lifetime victories in the National Football League than any other coach. He was also the only coach to lead a team through a perfect season that culminated in a Super Bowl win in January 1973. An avid fan of the Miami Dolphins, I knew Dolphin lore and could cite statistics like a contestant on a game show. Don Shula was a personal hero of mine.

I find it heretical to link the name of a well-loved and respected coach to an acronym for a murderer, In this instance, the acronym stood for "Dead Of Night," because the murders had taken place in the wee hours of the night. The cop or journalist who came up with this must be so proud of the acronym.

Including last night's victim, there have been three murders over the course of one week attributed to the new Don in town, the Dead of Night killer.

Not a positive beginning to the day.

CHAPTER 2

Engrossed in the article, I was startled when Lauren, my bride of four months, approached me from behind and planted a kiss on the top of my head. I really need to check out at what point I should stop calling her my bride and begin referring to her as my wife. There must be some social protocol about this.

Lauren, however, was good at reading clues, especially this morning. She could sense that something was wrong. She knew me so well. When she saw that I had the front section of the Herald in front of me rather than the sports page, she sat down across from me at the table.

"Another one?"

I didn't need her to clarify what she meant by that. We both were already freaked out by the first two murders. Murders in your own community will do that to you. Despite scouring the newspapers and watching the news intently, there were few details that had been released to the public.

According to reports, after the dead bodies were found, people living in the vicinity were interviewed to ascertain whether they had seen or heard anything unusual in the early morning hours. After canvassing the neighborhoods where the three corpses were deposited, the police compared notes and were shocked that citizens in all three locations reported hearing a howling in the darkness of the night, prior to the discovery of the bodies. What were the chances of that?

The police had purposely kept other details secret. So far, newspapers and television news outlets had cooperated. Even the names of the victims had not been released to the general public.

With little information available, speculation concerning the nature of the howling occupied people's thoughts. It was suggested that a large hound was roaming the three neighborhoods which were geographically close to each other or that a wild beast that ordinarily resided in the Everglades had taken up residence in a more populated area for an unknown reason.

No explanation was provided to either suggest that the murderer was not human or to propose that it was human. The media seemed to be grasping at straws. Or they hesitated to release the truth. Which was it?

The lack of clarification was unsettling.

People were terrorized.

The city was becoming paralyzed.

CHAPTER 3

Lauren and I departed our apartment together. When our schedules allowed, I liked to walk her to her car because I hated worrying about her in the parking garage. Today there was no question that I'd escort her to her gray Honda Accord and wait until she was safely out of the garage and on her way. The other reason I tried to accompany Lauren was that I enjoyed acting chivalrous because I knew she appreciated it. A modern woman in every sense of the word, Lauren still appreciated amenities like having the car door opened for her or having her chair pulled out for her in a restaurant. She admitted that she liked to enjoy the best of both worlds. I'm happy to oblige.

"Cliff, if you need to take care of any errands after work, today would be a good day. I've got some work to do for the reunion committee, so I may be home later than usual."

Like me, Lauren had gone to high school in Buffalo, New York. Due to her dad's job transfer, she had moved to Miami during the summer following her junior year. Although she knew no one in Miami when she began her senior year, she won over classmates quickly. With her upbeat personality and intelligence, she became the treasurer of the senior class. Guess it was foreshadowing for her career path as a CPA.

It's been ten years since Lauren's graduation from Miami Senior High School. Like her, several of the alumni from her graduating class had remained in South Florida. Lauren enthusiastically served on the reunion committee and volunteered to organize the traditional beach volleyball challenge. This event would be held on the world-famous sands of Miami. The alumni who attended the reunion would field a volleyball team and compete against the current seniors from Miami Senior High. As always, the match would be played on a Saturday afternoon; the reunion dinner and dance would be scheduled for that evening.

The reunion weekend was scheduled for the second Saturday in January. At Lauren's prodding, several of the alumni players had already begun preparing since enough of them were still living nearby and could practice together. Out-of-towners would be given a chance to compete for slots on the team on the morning of the match.

Always competitive, Lauren wanted the alumni team to trounce the current students. It was clearly a matter of pride. In order to do so, they needed to get together to plan strategies, foster teamwork, and hone their physical skills. Lauren organized the practices, helped her classmates reconnect to their old friends, and participated in playing. Although she agreed to be on the team if needed, she hoped to bow out the day of the game. She admitted to me that her hair had a lot to do with it. Why sweat profusely and ruin her hairdo just hours prior to the reunion dinner? A concern that never would have entered my mind.

Weather always played a role in the success or failure of this event. Although still months away, there was already a dark cloud looming overhead. That cloud had nothing to do with meteorology.

CHAPTER 4

After Lauren's car exited the garage, I tried to decide whether to go to Home Depot for some repair supplies I needed, pick up something for dinner since Lauren was going to be late and might not want to cook after a long day, or just take a nap after work. Not that I needed to resolve this right now, but she had put the idea in my head about doing errands in her absence. Guess I'd see how the day went and make my decision later. Putting those thoughts aside, I headed to I-95 for the daily demolition-derby drive to my office. It's no exaggeration that some of the worst drivers in the country reside in Miami. I needed all my attention focused on the road. Other distractions would have to wait.

However, when it comes to Lauren, I can't totally compartmentalize. Even at work, I think about her many times each day. Pictures of Lauren by herself and the two of us together covered all the desk surfaces and shelves in my office. Our recent honeymoon pictures, when added to the already voluminous collection, contributed to my inability to block her out of my thoughts. Not that I wanted to.

Thoughts of Lauren always make me smile. Receiving a text from her with her bitmoji makes me grin. Lauren had created the perfect bitmoji of herself, down to her hairstyle, body type, eye shape and color, and style and color of clothing she preferred. It really was adorable.

Although we rarely call each other during the workday, we text daily from our respective offices. We usually include bitmojis for fun to express thoughts or feelings, and to make the text more personal with our silly representations of ourselves. Since I was so enthusiastic about her creation of herself, of course, she wanted to recreate me. I have to say she did an amazing job. Now when I send text messages using my bitmoji, everyone comments on the cute likeness of me. How did we ever live without this technology?

After seeing my most recent patient, I was entering some notes into his electronic medical records when I heard my cell phone ring. More wonders of technology. The cell phone itself and the ability to personalize ringtones for specific people are amazing. Immediately, I knew it was Lauren calling from the distinctive ringtone I had chosen for her. The lyrics from the song "Who Wrote the Book of Love" gave her identity away.

Lauren calling me in the middle of the day meant something serious was up. My heart pounded.

"Everything okay, Hotsuff?" I used my nickname for the beautiful, intelligent, and sexy woman I had just married.

"Not really."

"What do you mean by 'not really'?"

"You know those dark clouds we talked about that were looming over the reunion volleyball game? Well, they just became darker."

Lauren's ominous statement was not the only indication that the volleyball game was just the tip of the iceberg. Her voice couldn't hide her distress.

"In what way?" I asked.

"It's not just the Miami Herald that's reporting on the Dead of Night killer. I just heard from two other members of the reunion committee that the local papers throughout the country are hyping the story. At least a dozen out-of-town alumni have already called, considering backing out of attending. I hate to say it, but as coverage continues, we expect attendance to be down significantly. Cancelling the entire reunion weekend is looking like a distinct possibility."

"I'd say that would be a safe bet."

"As we saw in today's paper," Lauren said, "the police have been very secretive about releasing details of the killings. They haven't even released the names of victims."

I had a sense that there was something more that she wasn't telling me. Sometimes with Lauren, she tends to build up to the most important part of the story. I've learned to let her control the tempo of what she wants to divulge. Interrupting is counterproductive.

Regarding the murders, I felt the same frustration as Lauren. The fact that the details were being kept hidden made the crimes seem more ominous. My uncle Brad, a detective with the Miami-Dade police force, and I have a close relationship. Without playing coy, I asked for information from him after the first and second murders, but he shut me out.

"I know where you're going with this, Lauren. I tried to get the information from Uncle Brad, but he's given me very few details, nothing more than what the papers are reporting. He told me it's on a need to know basis."

"Well *you need* to know. NOW!"

"Why the urgency?" It was obvious to me that Lauren knew something that I didn't.

"The three victims were my classmates. All were to play on the volleyball team."

"Are you for real? How would you know that?"

"I was notified by the head of the reunion committee to start searching for replacements. Their parents called to advise that they were planning their funerals within the next few days."

"I wonder if the cops are aware of that," I mused aloud.

CHAPTER 5

The report of the third murder by the Dead of Night killer seemed to be the straw that broke the camel's back. Despite dwindling newspaper subscription figures, more people seemed to read the Herald than law enforcement personnel had suspected. Once the papers hit the newsstands and people with home delivery received their copies, the phones at the mayor's office, the police commissioner's office, and the various police precincts began ringing. Nonstop.

The callers were asking for confirmation of the lead article and specifics as to the name and other pertinent details about the most recent victim. If this were a deliberate targeting of an individual for a personal reason, the callers would be less fearful. However, a random killing would make the callers petrified that at any moment, in any location, they could be next. They wanted details and they wanted assurances that the police were on top of locating and apprehending the killer. Fear made for irate and demanding callers.

To make matters worse, if that were even possible, Mayor Robert Diaz faced a challenger in the upcoming November election. Prior to the DON killer, he seemed a shoo-in to win. Now the campaign was becoming an uphill battle.

As is typical in any organization, pressure from the top requires response and action from the bottom. "The buck stops here," as popularized by President Harry Truman, no longer seems applicable to the person at the top in today's hierarchies. The person at the top of the pyramid, having various levels of management below, expects resolution of problems from the appropriate underlings. The leader takes credit for success but assigns blame for failure. A sad commentary on the current lack of accountability.

In this situation, Mayor Diaz demanded a rapid solution to the DON killer case or heads would roll. When he instructed the tier of management below him to drop everything and solve the murders, they proceeded to delegate the responsibility to their underlings. Those underlings did their own delegation of responsibility and on it went. Ultimately, in this instance, the primary detectives on the case were put on notice.

Detective Brad Mandich and his partner Detective Lew Dennison were at the bottom of the food chain. They were being chewed out by their superior, Sergeant Emilio Hernandez, in response to his unpleasant conversation with his boss, Chief Alberto Santiago. Santiago had his own unpleasant conversation with Police Commissioner Inez Vargas. Her conversation with Mayor Diaz ultimately created the intense pressure on Brad and Lew for immediate results.

To call Vargas' conversation with Mayor Diaz "unpleasant" would be a gross understatement. The fact that the police commissioner was female did not stop the expletives from spewing from Mayor Diaz's mouth. He was rip-roaring mad. Politically correct orders and conversations were the least of his concerns.

This was a classic case of "Shit Rolls Downhill." Filtered through the chain of command, the two detectives were receiving the brunt of everyone's frustration. Sergeant Hernandez came down hard on the lack of progress. The fact that the killer had struck again was blamed on police incompetence. It didn't matter that Mandich and Dennison had been doing a meticulous and competent investigation up to this point. Results were the only currency that mattered.

No sooner had the pair arrived at their desks when Sergeant Hernandez confronted them. "Where the hell *are* we on these DON killings?" demanded Hernandez. "Mayor Diaz is up for reelection soon and is in a panic. If we don't close this case quickly it could lose him the election. He threatened Commissioner Vargas who passed the buck to Chief Santiago. Santiago just came down on me like a wrecking ball on a condemned home. He's really pissed at me. So, you know where that puts you guys?"

It was a rhetorical question that neither detective chose to answer.

Brad couldn't keep the sarcasm out of his voice. He was sick and tired of being the object of many snide comments about his use of notepads and pens and personal contacts in the community rather than relying on computers and cell phone apps.

"We've been interviewing. You know, doing 'old fashioned' police work."

Ignoring the dig, Hernandez replied, "Who have you interviewed?"

"Family members, friends, neighbors, and employers of the first two victims." Brad pulled his notepad from his shirt pocket, as he began flipping pages. His wife Ellen knew not to purchase shirts for him unless they contained a pocket. In recent memory, the only time he recalled wearing what he considered a "useless" shirt was when he wore a tuxedo. At formal events, he gave into social convention, but not without grumbling.

Brad gave an accounting of the people interviewed and their relationships to the victims. "We've asked them to not reveal that they've been interviewed or to provide the names of the victims to anyone. For now, we've kept the gruesome manner of death from the public. Even the families of the victims haven't been told the full extent of the condition of the bodies of their loved ones."

Hernandez nodded in agreement. So far what he was hearing made perfect sense. He didn't want to interrupt the flow of the detective's summary.

Brad continued the history of what had been accomplished. "We believe that they've complied with our request. There have been no leaks that we know of. We even had the guys at the morgue work their magic to make the deceased look as good as possible before allowing family members to view and identify the poor souls."

"That's wise. Did you question anyone else? There's no time to waste."

"No, not yet. With this latest death, we're planning to meet with the family at the victim's house, talk to neighbors, visit his place of employment, and follow up on any other leads we get as a result of those interviews. Hopefully, we'll begin to see a trend now that we have three cases."

While he spoke, Detective Mandich was making additional notes about issues he wanted to address. At the end of the day, the pockets of his shirts were stretched and wrinkled from the constant inserting and removing of his notepad. Ellen insisted he use a plastic pocket protector for his pens, tired of trying to remove ink stains or discarding otherwise perfectly good shirts. He felt like the nerds he teased in college with their collection of pens in their pocket protectors.

Respectful of his size, no one would dare to call him a nerd, either to his face or behind his back. At six feet, four inches tall and an average weight of about 240 pounds, Detective Brad Mandich was taken seriously by most people he encountered. His petite wife Ellen was perhaps the only person not intimidated by his size. His coarse hair, once dark brown, was now mostly gray.

Like male film stars, the gray hair gave him an air of distinction. With his commanding physical appearance, he undeniably made an impression.

Realizing his height and weight could seem threatening, Brad cultivated a friendly attitude, trying to make people meeting him feel comfortable unless he needed to intimidate them for professional reasons. He was like a social chameleon, successful at sizing up how to behave as soon as he walked into a room.

Lew Dennison, his partner, was the more taciturn of the two, and the more likely to address people by their titles, or as "sir" or "ma'am." Unlike Brad, who was known to pepper his speech with crude slang and curse words, Lew restrained himself from such outbursts. Not quite as tall or heavy as his partner, Lew was still an imposing presence.

He worked out at the gym at least three days a week and as a result, he wore his clothes well. While Brad typically wore a sports jacket, long sleeve shirt with a pocket, and muted tie that coordinated with his shirts, Lew refused to wear a tie unless it was mandatory. Whereas Brad sometimes appeared rumpled despite starting the day with his clothing freshly pressed, Lew looked as if he never sat down. The creases in his slacks were always sharp. His rebellion against wearing a tie made him feel that he was dressed casually. His black-framed eyeglasses were stylish and complemented his deep-set eyes whose color could be best described as gun metal. Seemed appropriate for a police detective. He wore his coarse hair, which was becoming salt and pepper, closely cropped. If a Hollywood film crew needed extras in a police movie, he'd be an excellent choice.

Ordinarily, he allowed Brad to respond to most questions, but would interject his ideas if he felt something important had been left out. After working together for fifteen years, they covered all bases. Today he decided to jump into the conversation.

"Until this third murder, we were planning to check out the tip hotline today and go through recordings," stated Lew. "If we have enough time, we'll do that. It's a long shot, but maybe we'll catch a break."

Although Hernandez had taken a lot of flak from Chief Santiago, he trusted the instincts of his two seasoned detectives. They cleared the most cases in the department and that contributed to his looking good with the higher-ups. Although he stressed the pressure he was under from his superiors and the need for a quick resolution, he didn't want to micromanage the way in which Mandich and Dennison conducted their investigation.

"Even in horse racing, sometimes the long shot does win," Hernandez declared.

The sergeant didn't want to ignore any possible leads. The stakes, like in horse racing, were too high. "Truth is, I suspect you'll be opening up a whole box of crazy. People who call tip lines are often lonely, looking for their fifteen minutes of fame, so they make outrageous claims or confessions. They clearly outnumber tips that have merit. However, it just takes one valuable tip to crack a case, so have a go at it."

Gee, why didn't I think of that? thought Brad to himself. Hernandez had a habit of repeatedly stating the obvious. This conversation made Brad angry; the person who was insisting on results was delaying the pursuit of the investigation. You just couldn't win.

Brad was itching to get on the road. He pointedly looked at his watch, signaling Lew to wrap up the discussion. The silent message was loud and clear. Preparing to make his exit, Brad grabbed his sports jacket from the back of his desk chair. Simultaneously, Lew picked up his bottled water from his desk.

As he began walking toward the exit, Lew said, "In the meantime, Sergeant, we were about to interview some civilians who reside near the sites and claim to have heard a loud howl the evening prior to the discovery of the bodies."

Hernandez nodded his head, signaling his approval. Oddly, he interjected a surprising suggestion.

"On second thought, before you do your interviews, maybe you should visit Doc Murphy at the morgue."

CHAPTER 6

The two detectives approached the squad car. Without discussion, they entered the vehicle, Lew as the driver and Brad as the passenger. Both could be called control freaks. Both wanted to drive. Instead of a daily rush to the driver's side of the car, they long ago decided on an equable system. Seating position rotated every month. This was Lew's month to drive.

I rarely called my uncle during the day unless there was a dire emergency. Just as Lauren and I didn't make personal calls to each other during work hours, I typically contacted Uncle Brad in the evening after work. During the day, I had no idea where he'd be, and didn't want to be a distraction or a nuisance. I was hoping he'd pick up my call.

Since Uncle Brad wasn't a fan of technology, I often brought him into the current century making adjustments to his cell phone and his computer after explaining their value. For that reason, he allowed me to create ringtones for Aunt Ellen, for me, for Lauren, for specific members of law enforcement, for friends, and for relatives that merited his attention when his phone rang. After hearing my suggestions, he insisted on choosing the specific tone for each caller so he could readily identify who was trying to reach him. Then he'd decide whether to answer.

As my ringtone, I had suggested the theme song from "Hawaii Five-O," my favorite cop show. I admit that I think of myself as an amateur sleuth, and had, in fact, assisted my uncle in a few of his more unusual cases where my dermatological skills and knowledge had been invaluable. He told me he got a kick out of my choice and I got a kick out of installing it to identify me. That highly recognizable music alerted my uncle that I was calling. Usually, he took my calls rather than letting them go to voicemail.

Today was no different.

I was happy that he picked up the phone immediately because I thought I was the bearer of news he would want to hear.

"Hi, Cliff. Is everything ok?"

I heard the concern in his voice and told him that Lauren and I were fine in order to allay his worry about my making a daytime call to him.

"Glad to hear that. Lew and I just got into the car. We've barely left the parking lot. What's up?"

I understood why he announced that Lew was in the car with him. He wanted to avoid my embarrassment if I said anything without being aware of Lew's presence, even if Lew only heard my uncle's response to what I said. When I'm in the car with another passenger, I do the same thing.

"Uncle Brad, I'm so glad that you picked up. Where are you on the DON killer investigation?"

"Whoa, nephew. I already told you that I can't discuss this with you. You're sounding like Sergeant Hernandez. My butt is still sore from the whipping it got earlier today. Why are you so interested in this, anyway?"

"I just got some information from Lauren that I need to discuss with you. Can we meet?"

"How the hell does your wife have information that relates to this case? Since when is a CPA a crime investigator?"

Not to correct him, but my wife had also used her professional skills and knowledge helping him with several of his cases in the past. For now, I'd let it slide. I think it was just a reflexive comment from his frustration. Especially considering what he said about Sergeant Hernandez.

"I don't want to discuss this over the phone. Can you make time to see me? I really think Lauren's information may be a game changer."

Perhaps he heard the enthusiasm in my voice. Or maybe he wanted to listen to what he expected to be a long shot, because none of his methodical techniques were panning out.

"All right, Cliff. I trust your instincts. Lew and I will be at the morgue in about twenty to thirty minutes. Old Doc Murphy has agreed to meet with us."

"Perfect. I'll see you there."

Rather than calling, I texted Lauren to let her know that I was on my way to the morgue to meet with the medical examiner and my uncle. She'd realize that her information was being taken seriously, especially since I was included in the visit to the morgue.

I was pleased Brad agreed because Lauren was nothing if not persistent. It was unlikely that the police possessed the knowledge that she did. Without Lauren's information that the three victims were all scheduled to play on the reunion volleyball team, the cops might not connect the three crimes before a fourth murder went down. Not to mention, she had a particularly personal interest in the three victims.

Not wanting to put additional worries into her head, I was more than a little concerned that Lauren had graduated high school with the three victims. All were involved in the upcoming reunion. My anxiety level was approaching a critical mass.

Sometimes I mask discomfort with humor as a self-protective mechanism. This seemed to be one of those instances. Despite the serious nature of Lauren's information, I was anticipating telling her later about my meeting with my uncle. In my mind I pictured my head, like a plump hot dog on a fiery barbecue, being grilled by Lauren. She would relentlessly question me about every detail of Brad's response about the murder of her classmates. She would insist on knowing the conversation, word for word. She would suggest questions that I should have asked.

Putting aside my overactive imagination, I was in complete agreement with her. With her information and connection to the victims, she deserved to know.

CHAPTER 7

I wasted no time getting to the medical examiner's office. The Joseph H. Davis Center is adjacent to Jackson Memorial Hospital, where I spent my three-year dermatology residency program. Located at One Bob Hope Road in Miami, the complex occupied almost ninety thousand square feet. I knew the route well.

At great peril, I merged onto I-95 North and exited at State Road 836 Medical Center/Civic Center exit. After waiting for several light changes, I could finally see the complex. Considering the work that was performed inside, the facility was as welcoming as it could be. The building was brick and stucco, painted in earth tones. To soften the appearance of the nondescript exterior, the landscaping was replete with palms and tropical plants, keeping with a Florida motif.

I easily found a spot in the lot reserved for physicians. After parking, I walked over to the area designated for law enforcement vehicles. Uncle Brad and Lew were just pulling into a spot.

My uncle was a passenger today, so I ran to the passenger door of the patrol car. Brad and I did what my wife and my aunt always accuse us of doing. We got right to the reason for meeting with our usual no frills greeting. No hello, no handshake, no social pleasantries. We were on a mission. I had information to impart and my uncle was anxious to hear it, especially since he often credited me with thinking outside the box.

I spoke first. "Did you guys know that the three victims were all going to attend the ten-year reunion of Lauren's high school class?"

Brad checked his notepad. "That's Miami Senior High School, right?" he asked.

I shook my head in acknowledgment.

He referred again to his notes. "I do see that the first two victims graduated high school in the same year from that school."

Lew Dennison burst into the conversation. "We were about to investigate the third victim after our meeting here. So, you're saying that he was also a graduate from the same school and the same year as the other two? And that your wife graduated with them?"

Brad jotted that fact into his notes. "This is the first we're hearing about any reunion. What can you tell us?"

First, I explained that the reunion would be the second weekend in January. Then I dropped the most interesting coincidence on them. "Lauren tells me that they were not only classmates but all three were to be teammates in a beach volleyball game." That got their attention.

"REALLY" was their simultaneous reply, their intonation making their response both a question and an exclamation.

Stating what he thought was obvious, my uncle declared, "There are no coincidences." This was pretty much a mantra with him. "Can you ask Lauren to get me an up-to-date list of all the class members planning to attend the reunion as well as the other participants in the beach volleyball game?"

"She's already on it. After she got a call from the reunion committee about needing to replace players in the game, she started doing what she does best," I replied.

Truth be told, my private thoughts about that comment brought an inappropriate smile to my face. Fortunately, it went right over Lew Dennison's head.

"And what would that be? What is she best at?" Lew asked, having no idea what I'd reply. Or how the question could be taken at face value or with a more provocative angle. I went for face value in my answer.

"Spreadsheets."

Lew parroted my response, rephrasing it as a question.

" 'Spreadsheets'?"

"Yes, spreadsheets," I repeated. "You know my wife is an accountant. Very smart and extremely organized," I said proudly. "She's looking at the victims, hoping to find other commonalities."

My uncle was not the most technologically savvy person, but he was smart enough to enlist the assistance of people who had skill sets that he didn't possess. While he might never enter any data into an Excel Spreadsheet for the remainder of his life, he wouldn't refuse to look at the data analyzed by someone adept with that process.

In typical fashion, he acknowledged that he was open to her assistance. "Can't say that I know how to work with spreadsheets, but we can use all the help we can get."

He shifted his weight from his left foot to his right foot. "I'm getting tired of standing out here. Let's take this conversation inside."

CHAPTER 8

We made our way from the parking lot to Dr. Murphy's office. His secretary, Jackie Norton, sat outside the office like a sentinel, shielding her boss from unwanted or unannounced visitors. She looked the part.

With her short brown hair heavily sprayed in a style that I call "helmet-head," she appeared to be in her late fifties or early sixties. Bright blue reading glasses were perched near the tip of her nose, allowing me to take in her dark brown eyes which seemed to miss nothing as she watched our entry into her domain. A strand of pearls circled her rather plump neck. She was dressed in a crisp white blouse with long sleeves, a cardigan sweater hanging on the back of her chair. At the time I gazed at the name plate sitting on the front of her desk, I observed the black slacks and sensible shoes that peeked out from under the desk.

She had been expecting the two detectives but was a little surprised when I arrived with them. It felt as if I were being scrutinized by a TSA employee prior to going through the security checkpoint. She looked at me for what seemed an uncomfortably long amount of time before speaking. Then she got right to the point.

"And who would you be, sir?"

"I'm Clifford Mandich," I responded in my most neutral and professional voice. Since I wasn't on the guest list for this meeting, I needed to be unobtrusive. Somehow, I knew that identifying myself as a physician would make no difference to her and might come across as bragging.

My uncle read the situation differently. He jumped right in.

"From his name, you probably realize we're related. He's my nephew, a dermatologist. Cliff is here to offer some additional perspectives on the victims' wounds." Deliberately raising his wrist to look at his watch, he asked, "Can we see Dr. Murphy now? I'm sure he's been anxious for our arrival."

Well, he may not have scored any points with her for future interactions, but Brad clearly got his point across.

"Of course, Detective Mandich." Jackie rose from her desk and began to lead the way.

"No need, ma'am," said Lew. "We've been here before. Can I assume that Doc Murphy is in the morgue?"

"Yes, he is. He should be finishing an autopsy on a young girl that appears to have been a drowning. I'm sure he won't mind your interruption." She looked down at her desk, pretending to busy herself with straightening some files. As far as she was concerned, our departure could not be soon enough.

"Thank you, ma'am," said Lew.

When we got to the entrance to the autopsy suite, Dr. Cecil Murphy was already waiting for us. He must have been alerted by his secretary. I couldn't stop myself from staring at the man; he looked like the second coming of Ernest Hemingway in his older years.

The medical examiner's size, gray hair, thick eyebrows over blue eyes, mustache, and bushy beard painted quite a picture. My impulse was to ask him whether he ever participated in the annual Key West Hemingway Look-Alike contest, but I figured that was risky. It might set off the meeting on the wrong foot. I judged him to be approaching seventy years of age. His girth had obviously increased over the years. If I had to guess, I'd say he weighed over 200 pounds. He wore his white lab coat open, probably because he couldn't close it. It made me laugh to think that like other men who put on considerable weight as they age, he probably bragged that his waist size hadn't changed. The good doctor had chosen not to replace the pants and belt that were clearly too small by several sizes. He just wore these a lot lower.

My uncle had met Dr. Murphy on many previous occasions. As the Medical Examiner for Miami, he held a degree of Doctor of Medicine as well as being board certified in forensic pathology. Not all states have the same requirements. Many states and cities use coroners who lack medical degrees and some of the other credentials required in Florida since 1970 when Florida adopted the medical examiner system.

"Glad to see that you're still practicing, Doc."

"Got to."

"What makes you say that?"

"Well, I have three grandchildren, two girls and a boy, in San Francisco. If I quit work, my wife will want us to move out there to be close to the grandkids. I would really enjoy watching them grow up, but there are other considerations.

"Hell, I'm a big shot here. Jackie answers my phone and schedules my appointments, gets me coffee, and laughs at my jokes. Everybody knows me and I know everybody. In San Francisco I'd be just another old guy. As I've gotten older, I've become intolerant of cold weather. Plus, I don't like hills or sea lions." He made some interesting points.

My uncle seemed to agree with him, or at least validated his reasoning.

"I hear you, Doc."

"Enough about me." He began walking. We followed behind him. "You're here to see the bodies of the three young men."

When we arrived at the autopsy section, Dr. Murphy spoke proudly about the facility. He pointed out a viewing room for families as well as another area for spectators, often students of law enforcement. The room where he performed his autopsies as well the equipment all appeared to be state-of-the art. His pride was well-founded.

The bodies of the three men we came to see were placed on separate tables, each covered respectfully from the neck down with a cloth. Recalling my first experience with a dead body when I was a medical student and the strong odor of formaldehyde in the room in which we did our dissections, I couldn't help but notice that there was no odor in this room. Evidently, my less than subtle sniffing of the air was not lost on Dr. Murphy.

"You're probably surprised about the lack of odors, Dr. Mandich. Am I correct?"

"You got me. I don't think I'll ever forget the smells in anatomy lab and in the morgue from my medical school days. It was almost impossible to get the stench out of my lab coat or my clothes."

"The ventilation system is much improved from your days as a freshman medical student. Clean and fresh air is piped in from above. It flows down and passes near your nose before being drawn into a return vent at floor level. Your nose is never exposed to the more noxious odors."

"That's an improvement whose time has come. I envy today's students. If our teaching facility had been like yours, I would have saved a lot of queasy stomachs on lab days and tons of quarters on laundry."

By that point, I could see that my uncle and Lew were getting tired of my trip down memory lane with the medical examiner. Dr. Murphy could see that as well.

"Enough about my lab. I have work to get to and so do you. Let me show you the bodies you called about."

With great respect, Dr. Murphy removed the cloth coverings, one at a time and in the order of the dates of death. Knowing that they were from the same graduating class as Lauren, I knew that they were twenty-eight years old. I wasn't surprised that all appeared to be well-nourished, but not heavy. To the contrary, they were muscular and probably exercised on a regular basis. Lauren made me aware that they had planned to participate in the beach volleyball competition pitting alumni against current seniors as part of the class reunion weekend. Seeing them firsthand gave me a more complete picture, adding what I saw to what I already knew.

The name of victim number one was Christopher Dee. The organs of his abdomen had been removed. There were wounds resembling bite marks around the central face area. Similar findings were seen on victim number two, Tyler Dente. Victim number three, Max Shiff, was different. Like the other two young men, his internal organs had been removed. This would be a routine occurrence in a medical examiner's autopsy suite. The difference was that Max's face was spared but there appeared to be bite marks on his lower back and buttocks.

Like many young men in their age group, all three had tattoos on their left bicep. The tattoos were identical in size, location, and design, leading me to conclude that the three men probably were tattooed at the same place and at the same time. They were simple black ink tattoos of a stingray. It suggested to me that these three were buddies.

It was hard for me to read what the two detectives were thinking. They had witnessed the bizarre on multiple occasions. On the other hand, as a dermatologist, this was all new to me. I was intrigued. Also, I prided myself on my keen powers of observation. On the first day of my dermatology residency, the head of the program announced that everyone accepted into the residency was "talented in the visual arts." He went on to explain that our field relied on observation perhaps more than other medical disciplines and that dermatologists often saw what others missed.

He likened our talents to the "chicken or the egg" question. Did we choose our specialty because we had that talent, or did our choice of career hone a talent that might have been left undeveloped? Frankly, I didn't spend much time analyzing this. I just knew that I was able to recognize what wasn't noticed by others. That was enough for me.

I had already observed something that didn't make sense from a medical standpoint. Without a moment's hesitation, I questioned the medical examiner.

"Dr. Murphy, I know that you routinely remove the organs for study in cases like these, but where are the usual "Y" incisions on these victims? Isn't that a standard forensic pathology procedure so that that you can gain access to the organs?"

Not to mention that anyone who watched any of the myriad television shows dealing with forensic science and homicide was treated to the requisite scene in the autopsy room of a body with a "Y" incision. My knowledge, however, was based on medical practice, not television. Unfortunately, the public often believed everything they saw on TV.

"Excellent observation, Dr. Mandich. You *do* remember your medical school training. It pains me to admit that no incisions were necessary. The bellies of all three of these victims had been opened at time of death. The internal organs were removed prior to the bodies being found. Despite a perimeter search of the areas where the bodies were located, we never found the organs."

Evidently, this information had not been released to the media. From his reaction, it was also obvious that this was the first that my uncle had heard this. After making notes in his pad, he addressed at Dr. Murphy.

"No organs?"

"No. The killer has taken them for some unknown reason."

I was trying to make some sense of the missing organs and the fact that the third victim's face had not been mutilated. I was probably making what Lauren refers to as my "concentrating face" which she describes as a furrowed brow and a very quizzical expression. She joked that I would make a poor liar or gambler because I couldn't hide what I was thinking. Dr. Murphy recognized that I was perplexed.

"You seemed to be deep in thought, Dr. Mandich. What besides the obvious is troubling you?"

"It's the difference."

"What 'difference' is that?"

"Why was the face of victim three spared, yet he was bitten on the lower back and on the buttocks?"

"You would have made an exceptional medical examiner," commented Dr. Murphy.

Uncle Brad nodded in agreement. He used to tease me that if I hadn't decided to become a doctor, I would have made a great detective. Since I had chosen medicine for a career, he then tried to steer me into becoming a medical examiner. Guess he wanted to stack the deck with someone he could trust and who might give priority to his cases. In any event, he recognized my powers of observation.

I continued walking around the three tables, trying to see if any other anomalies grabbed my attention. "Thanks for the compliment, but what about my concerns?"

"I can only speculate." Dr. Murphy's response was very non-committal. I was hoping for a more definitive explanation.

"Okay. 'Speculate' away."

"The way I see it, I suspect that the missing organs were taken for some unusual ritual or they were eaten by some beast."

"That's frightening. But why wounds on the faces of two victims and only on the lower back and buttocks of the third? Also, why *these* men? They appear young and in excellent physical shape. They don't make for easy targets." I did another pass around the three bodies, as close to them as was physically possible.

"Dr. Murphy, is it your conclusion that these wounds are bite marks? If that's the case, who or what made them?"

"I have asked myself those same questions. I have no answers."

By now, I realized that we weren't going to get any transparency from Dr. Murphy. As a well-respected and experienced medical examiner, he sounded inept, or at the very least, clueless. Frankly, I believed that this was just an act, but I could see that nothing more was to be gained by spending any additional time with him.

I walked toward my uncle and gently tugged on his sleeve, signaling that it was time to go.

"Dr. Murphy, thank you for seeing us. We know you have work to do so we'll leave you to it," I said as I headed to the door.

My uncle seemed to have the same puzzled expression that I'm prone to exhibit. Must be a family trait. I don't think he knew what was on my mind or why I was terminating the meeting so abruptly, but he played along. "Yeah, we need to go."

Lew took his cues from us and led the way to the exit from the autopsy room. I held back for just a moment, and said to Dr.

Murphy as if it were an afterthought, “You are running a toxicology screen, aren’t you?”

“Yes. Of course.” Whether or not that was his intention, I had backed him into a corner. With the two detectives present, he needed to at least appear to be following protocol and looking into all areas of investigation.

“Then do me a favor. Look for sedatives or tranquilizers in their blood samples, and under strong magnification look for any small puncture wound that would suggest a tranquilizer dart. Pay particular attention to the posterior region of their necks as well as their left biceps, within the stingray tattoos. It’s been my experience that patients who are IV drug users often hide their injection sites within the design of their tattoos. Perhaps their killer used their tattoos to hide the injection of a tranquilizer.”

I figured that Dr. Murphy should be aware of this as well, but I wanted him to recognize that he needed to examine the bodies thoroughly in order to satisfy me.

“These were all athletic young men,” I said. “I’d appreciate a call if you find something else the three have in common that would explain why they were chosen.”

“Sure thing. I’ll run the toxicology screen with special emphasis on common and uncommon tranquilizers. I’ll keep you informed.” Dr. Murphy’s response seemed directed specifically to me. That didn’t sit well with my uncle as I soon found out.

We were barely out the door when my uncle put me through his own brand of interrogation.

“What the hell was up with you?”

“What do you mean?”

“Since when are you in charge? I let you come along to lend a hand, but you overstepped your bounds by taking over. You got us out of there before we had a chance to ask some follow-up questions, and then you practically dictated to Doc Murphy how to do his job."

"I'm sorry, Uncle Brad. I didn't mean to step on your toes." I regretted my overreach and vowed to be more careful in the future. "It's just that I don't trust Dr. Murphy," I added.

"Why the hell not?"

"My gut tells me that he's keeping things from us. With his years of experience, he should be able to say with certainty that those wounds on the face and back were teeth marks. Clearly, they were not human. Also, I noticed small puncture wounds on the back of the necks of all three victims. How did he miss that? Or did he deliberately not mention it? That's why I asked him to specifically check that area."

Lew had been taking in our conversation, listening rather than commenting. That was his usual policy. Apparently, he believed that I was leaning toward suggesting that Dr. Murphy was a person of interest. That prompted him to blurt out the obvious question.

"Cliff, do you suspect him of being the DON killer?"

"Well, most likely not, but he sure is benefitting from the work of the DON killer. And he seems to be hiding information that he should have divulged to you. Makes his behavior very suspicious, in my opinion," I said.

Part of me was still considering that Murphy could be involved in the killings because he had the training and knowledge to put together an elaborate cover-up. But I wasn't quite there yet. The police could dig deeper than I could.

"How would he possibly benefit from that?" Lew asked.

"I know this may sound far-fetched. You heard what he said earlier. His wife wants to move to be near their children and grandchildren, but he seemed truly fearful of being just another old man in San Francisco."

I was remembering his words and building my theory about his rationale for not reporting conclusions that seemed obvious to me.

"If these killings continue, he will have more than his fifteen minutes of fame as the medical examiner working this high-profile case. Think of how he could captivate listeners with stories about his contributions to apprehending the killer. This could be his swan song. He would remain a big shot anywhere he went. He could move to California to be near his grandchildren and would be more than just another elderly retiree. And the possibility exists that he might be sought after for television interviews or could write a book and achieve success as an author. Not a bad benefit to him for his involvement. The more he allows this to drag on, the more drama."

My uncle was looking at me the way you'd look at a child from a pet-free household explaining to the teacher that the dog ate his homework. I doubt that he bought into my theory as evidenced by his next comment.

"Your choice of 'far-fetched' doesn't go far enough with this elaborate scheme you've concocted."

There was silence for a minute as my uncle flipped through his notes. He took a pen and underlined some words on the top page. Something in his expression changed as he looked at me.

Just as I was about to embellish my tale further, he stated something that astonished me.

"Cliff, I've learned not to discount your intuition. I don't like the fact that you observed some obvious medical findings that Doc Murphy neglected to disclose to us. If he's such a seasoned professional, he should have seen what you saw with just your cursory observations. Makes me wonder why. Makes me think that there's more to his involvement than his being the medical examiner. Makes me sad that this could be an ignominious end to a highly illustrious career."

He shook his head, burdened by what he was about to say. He looked at Lew.

"Okay, Dr. Cecil Murphy is an official person of interest."

I could only hope that I wasn't leading him and Lew down the rabbit hole with my suspicions.

CHAPTER 9

After declining the detectives' offer to join them for a quick lunch, I returned to my office to see my afternoon patients. Among the other skills I acquired in medical school, I learned how to compartmentalize and direct my focus to the topic at hand without distraction. The afternoon with my patients was a true test of that ability.

It was all I could do to compartmentalize and not constantly think about telling Lauren about my visit to the ME's office. Leaving for home, I was anxious to share the morning's events with Lauren. I had permission to discuss the case with her, especially since she had alerted me to the connection of the three victims to her high school reunion, and more specifically, to their participation in the upcoming beach volleyball game.

I drove as fast as traffic allowed. Well, okay, maybe at five miles above the speed limit since that seemed to be the allowable threshold before a cop car would pull you over. The last thing I needed was a speeding ticket. Having an uncle on the police force was both an asset and a liability at the same time. You can see that I've picked up some of Lauren's accounting lingo, and it was appropriate in this instance. With the same last name as my uncle, my driver's license often provoked questions as to whether I was related to Detective Brad Mandich. Not something that would reflect positively on him if I got a ticket for speeding or for other vehicular infractions. So, I always drove carefully, not wanting to cause any embarrassment to our family name.

As I drove, I already had a smile on my face, anticipating coming home to my bride. It was still strange to me that we were actually married, and I really did need to know when to refer to her as my "wife" rather than my "bride." Regardless of the nomenclature, I always look forward to coming home to see Lauren. Today was no exception.

I can't say that I didn't find her physically attractive because I would be lying. The combination of her striking hazel eyes, the cheekbones of a model, and her size-six figure certainly played a role in my initial attraction to her. However, it was the intelligence in those eyes, the kindness of her soul, and her sense of humor that maintained and fostered my continuing interest in her. What can I say? She had it all.

I arrived to find Lauren in the kitchen, bending over the open freezer compartment of our refrigerator with French doors. When we were selecting kitchen appliances, Lauren had insisted on this style because she liked the fact that the refrigerator section could accommodate large platters and the freezer on the bottom was not as narrow as a typical side-by-side unit. I left that choice to her since she had a vehement opinion and I really didn't care.

Little did I know that I would often benefit from that choice, since I frequently encountered her bending over the freezer section, sorting through packaged meats and frozen vegetables. You can intuit why I felt that the location of the freezer section was an added bonus to this refrigerator style. Don't know whether the French originated this style fridge, but if they did, I say Vive la France!

Lauren often teased me that I had a sixth sense about finding her in that pose or other situations of her removing her clothes to go into the shower or arriving the exact moment when she grabbed the towel as she exited the shower stall. All I can say is that I am one lucky guy. She took all of this good-naturedly and said that she hoped that I would still find her equally as attractive when she was old and gray. I honestly believe that I will.

Hearing me behind her despite my attempt at stealth to prolong the view, she stood up with a package of chicken breasts in her hand. She turned to me and gave me a big hug. Thinking of her while driving home, catching her bending over the freezer, and the proximity of the hug were enough to make my hands start to roam. From experience, Lauren was adept at refocusing my errant thoughts. So much for the hand roaming, but that was okay. I tabled that for now, knowing that I would get back to that later.

"How did things go at the morgue?"

"Alright, Hotstuff."

That was my favorite nickname for Lauren. From my description of her, I'm sure you can understand.

"You are now part of the inner circle. Brad and Lew are okay with it. That said, you can't tell anyone else. I know that some of your classmates are aware that the three victims are from your class, but if they ask, you can't say anything."

"Consider me sworn to secrecy."

I knew that she took that promise seriously. In an age where people like to use social media to connect with friends as well as strangers and boast about their exciting lives and exploits, Lauren didn't so much as have an account with Facebook, Twitter, or Instagram. Although she was outgoing, she was disinclined to make herself the center of attention by posting her activities on social media. If she made a promise, she kept it. Often, I teased her that had she been a journalist she'd go to jail sooner than reveal her source. She insisted that she would. I totally believed her.

"Here's what I learned: all bodies were discovered the morning after a howling sound was heard nearby, all had abdominal organs missing, and all had a puncture wound on the back of the neck. For some reason, the medical examiner failed to report the wounds at the back of the neck. All three of the men had wounds at the base of the spine and on the buttocks, while only two had facial wounds. These wounds appeared to be bite marks but didn't appear to have been made by a human."

Until I looked at her face, I didn't realize the impact of my clinical recitation of the facts. Normally pale, she looked as if she might faint as the color drained from her face. Tears in her eyes reflected the compassion she felt for how her classmates had spent their remaining moments alive.

"Oh my God, Cliff, this is horrifying. Any death is tragic but what you described sounds barbaric. Do they believe that some crazed animal is responsible?"

"No one is drawing any conclusions right now. It's way too early in the investigation."

"You said something cryptic about the medical examiner. Do you think he plays a part in this?"

"I'm not sure, Lauren. It just struck me as strange that he didn't comment on the puncture wounds to the neck when he was reporting his findings to Uncle Brad and Lew. Guess I just have a suspicious nature."

"I want to help. These were my friends. The killer needs to be arrested. Their families deserve closure."

"No argument there."

"When I called you this morning, I had already begun working on a spreadsheet about the reunion attendees, with particular emphasis on the players of the beach volleyball team. I think better when I see the data charted out. To rip off an old commercial for Florida orange juice and adapt it to accounting, 'A day without spreadsheets is like a day without sunshine.' I'm going to update the information on my three deceased classmates with the information you just gave me. It'll enable me to see if anything stands out."

"Makes sense to me. Right now, I think you know every common element that I've been told about, and you have your own sources from the reunion committee. I hope we've seen the last of the Dead of Night Killer. If he or it strikes again, I'll have more info for you."

"Let's hope it doesn't come to that, Cliff. With what we have now, hopefully I can find a common denominator or some aberration that leads us to an answer."

"Speaking of answers, how are you preparing those chicken breasts you took out of the freezer when I came in?"

"I hadn't decided yet. Are you in the mood for a specific dish? My repertoire is somewhat limited to grilling or baking them in the oven. What's your preference?"

"How about that baked chicken with the corn flake crumbs and onion soup mix? That takes about an hour to bake, doesn't it?" Okay, so I had an ulterior motive.

"Did you have a late lunch?" Lauren asked innocently.

"No, I just wanted us to have some uninterrupted time while our dinner doesn't need your attention."

"Works for me."

She gave me instructions to set the table and turn on the oven to 350 degrees as she quickly coated the chicken breasts with the combination of crumbs and onion soup mix. After she popped the tray into the oven and set the timer for an hour, we headed down the hall.

Waiting for dinner had its perks.

CHAPTER 10

The hardest part of the investigation was placed in the laps of the two professional detectives. Brad Mandich and Lew Dennison had interviewed families of crime victims countless times but still found it the most difficult part of the job. Their plan for the balance of the day included visiting with the families of the three alumni from Miami Senior High.

First stop was the family of Christopher Dee. The detectives had called ahead so the door opened before they rang the bell. It was Charles Dee, the victim's father. His facial muscles were tense, and he was flushed, as if ready to explode. The expression of anger was stamped on his face.

Charles led the way to the living room where Christopher's mother and two sisters sat with slumped shoulders. The table between the two sofas held a box of tissues that was nearly empty. Each woman held a crumpled tissue, wet and balled up from wiping away tears. It was almost impossible to determine their eye color as all three had bloodshot eyes. The swelling and the redness of their skin below the eyes was more evidence of their incessant crying since learning of Christopher's death. None of the women appeared to have slept in days.

"What happened? Who did this to my boy?" sobbed Mrs. Dee.

"That's what we're trying to find out, Mrs. Dee. You have our deepest condolences. If you could answer our questions, it will give us a better picture of your son, his friends, his enemies, things that you as his family would know better than anyone else," Brad explained in his gentlest voice.

"We are sure that from all of the publicity, you know that Christopher and two other men were killed within two days of each other. It has come to light that the other two graduated with your son and were scheduled to attend the tenth-year high school reunion for Miami Senior High. Would you say that they were high school friends? Did they remain friends after graduation or did they lose touch with each other?" questioned Brad.

Charles was the first to respond. It seemed that his son had spoken to him about participating in the beach volleyball tournament and had mentioned the names of other players that his father would recognize. He was the most likely to have information of value to the detectives.

"Chris, Tyler Dente, and Max Shiff were inseparable while in high school, like the Three Musketeers. Spring Break of their senior year they went to the Caribbean together and swam with stingrays. When they returned, all had the same stingray tattoo on their bicep to commemorate their adventure. They lost contact with each other following graduation ten years ago. Recently, they reunited as teammates to practice for this volleyball challenge. It seemed to rekindle their friendship. Chris was strutting around the house bare-chested, bragging about retaining his high school physique and claiming that he and his teammates would beat the pants off the younger high school seniors. It was definitely a matter of pride for him and his peers."

Mrs. Dee nodded her head in agreement with her husband's recollection of how excited Chris was to be part of the volleyball team. For one brief moment she smiled, thinking of her handsome son and his enthusiasm.

"The boys went their separate ways after graduation when they went to college in different cities. Life happens and they drifted apart," Mrs. Dee confirmed.

"Until Chris mentioned the reunion, I hadn't thought about his friends or heard him mention their names in years. They hung around a lot together, especially since they all spent three seasons together on the high school's baseball team," Charles reminisced. "Chris was the pitcher. He threw a no hitter as a junior." The pride in his son was apparent.

Like a lightning strike without warning, the atmosphere in the room changed drastically. Clenching his fists as he glared at Brad, he asked in a strident voice, "Now, as to my wife's question, what do you know about the killer? You two are the only connection we have to my son and his last day on earth."

Without waiting for Brad to field that question, Lew jumped in. With an air of politeness, soothing tones, and his slightly less threatening size, Lew deftly defused a tense situation.

"Sir, we are working on that. You have my assurance that Mayor Diaz, Police Commissioner Vargas, Chief Santiago, and Sergeant Hernandez, our direct superior, are fully committed, as are we, to finding and arresting his killer."

Hearing the actual names of "the powers that be" often assuaged an angry person's reproach. In this instance, it was effective. Charles unclenched his fists and focused on Lew's response with a less threatening gaze.

"We have a tip hotline," Lew explained. "The medical examiner is running additional tests at the recommendation of an outside medical consultant. While our interviews are in the early stages, we expect significant results from them. From here, we will be speaking with the families of Christopher's teammates, Tyler Dente and Max Shiff. Also, we'll be checking and interviewing people in the neighborhood near where each body was found."

Hearing Lew refer to Christopher as a "body" initiated another round of crying from Mrs. Dee and Christopher's sisters. Almost simultaneously, they pulled tissues from the now empty box. Charles wanted the detectives out of his home. Immediately.

"Not to be rude, gentlemen, but I think you should leave. We have nothing else to say. I have your number and will call if we think of anything. Otherwise, please respect our privacy and allow us to grieve. When you find my son's killer, then contact us. Please don't come back until that time."

Charles Dee escorted Brad and Lew to the door. Unfortunately, they hadn't had the opportunity to question Christopher's family about any possible enemies. They were planning to lead up to that line of questioning after discussing the link to the other victims. Once Lew referred to their son as a "body," it was clear that Mr. Dee had literally shut the door on further questions. It was a subject that would have to be covered when speaking with Christopher's friends and co-workers.

Similar scenes were played out twice more that afternoon and evening in the homes of the Dente and Shiff families. This time, early in the conversation, they broached the question concerning any enemies, arguments at work, breakups with girlfriends, or any other situations that might have led to their loved one being murdered. No one could shed any light on enemies who might be responsible.

All agreed with the details that Charles Dee had provided concerning the relationship of the former high school classmates. It seemed that Tyler and Max were equally looking forward to the volleyball game and to trouncing the current high school seniors. As former athletes, their competitive natures still defined their personalities.

The day had been exhausting, not only due to the long hours, the frustrating drives to the three homes with all the typical traffic delays in neighborhoods, school zones, lane closures, and ongoing construction on I-95, but to the emotional nature of meeting with the three families. It had gotten late. Lew dropped Brad off at his house and decided to drive the squad car to his own home. He'd return it in the morning. The extra time he'd save would give him at least another hour of sleep. It proved to be a wise decision.

The pair would need their rest. Nothing could have prepared them for what was waiting at the precinct for them in the morning.

CHAPTER 11

Hoyt Stark, a backup middle linebacker for the Pittsburgh Steelers, was looking forward to making the best of a bad situation. Even in his street clothing Stark had the body of a linebacker. A large man, the muscles in his arms and legs were enormous and his clothing only served to accentuate his strength.

He would be taking a few days off in his hometown of Miami. During last Sunday's game he had been knocked unconscious. His confusion on the sidelines and medical exam given by the team physician showed that he had met the league's concussion criteria. Recent league guidelines and concussion protocol dictated that he would not be playing in his team's next game. His coach and team physician gave him permission to fly home. The permission came with one caveat: he needed to see a neurologist in Miami, or he would be under suspension for the next month. The Miami neurologist was to report his findings to the team physician. Without such proof, Hoyt would be sidelined upon his return to Pittsburgh.

Hoyt was to be met at Miami International Airport by four of his longtime buddies, men with a common history that went as far back as grammar school. Of the five, Hoyt was the only one earning a good living by honest means. He was also the smartest of the bunch. The others earned their money by selling the popular drugs of the day. It seemed as if they watched too much television or too many movies that dealt with drug dealers.

Their wardrobe appeared to be dictated by Hollywood's idea of the requisite garb for the role. They wore their clothing two sizes too big, enhanced by flashy neck chains with supersized pendants that contained enormous gemstones. Their demeanor, their choice of words, and their stylized strut seemed to come right out of central casting. They didn't put it together that their appearance always attracted the attention of law enforcement. No one could accuse them of being overly bright.

As Hoyt walked beyond the section reserved for passengers only, he scanned the people waiting as the flight deplaned to find his welcoming committee. The friend known only as Iggy was the first to see Stark. No one knew whether the name Iggy was short for Ignatius or whether it was related to some of his physical characteristics that were like those of an iguana. His jowls, his stout body which was nourished by his affinity for beer, and his double chin reminded people of the dewlap under the throat of iguanas. Whether it was deliberate or whether he simply preferred the color, Iggy often wore vibrant green shirts, like his reptile doppelganger.

"Hey, Stark. Over here."

Hearing his name called, Hoyt easily picked out Iggy from the crowd, recognizing his friend by the bald head, the sunglasses over his hooded brown eyes, and the oversized emerald green shirt opened almost to the waist, emphasizing a thick gold rope chain resting on his chest.

After a couple of man hugs, the five meandered to the parking lot. Iggy took the wheel of an older-model gray Toyota Tacoma pickup truck that was showing signs of age. While his attire screamed "drug dealer," Iggy's choice of vehicle was ordinary to enable it to blend in and not call attention to the occupation of its owner. Years before, his flashy red mustang had gotten him into big trouble with the cops as he drove from neighborhood to neighborhood. He had learned his lesson about his car. However, when on foot scouring neighborhoods for customers, he liked to make a statement with his wardrobe.

Turning to Hoyt seated in the passenger seat next to him, Iggy asked, "Monty's?" Rollo Thomas, Tony Augusta, and his brother Eddy all agreed since Monty's was the men's favorite drinking establishment.

"Nah. Not just yet," Hoyt said. "I best say hi to the old lady first."

Iggy drove to a stately neighborhood in an older section of Coconut Grove. Hoyt Stark's home was large and attractively landscaped with flowering shrubs and mature shade trees. The lawn was well manicured. Football had treated him well. The screeching of the tires as Iggy stopped short at the curb and the sight of the five men exiting the pickup truck seemed out of place in the upscale neighborhood.

Using his house key, Hoyt entered through the front door. His entourage followed. His wife Shannon had just finished putting a tray of blueberry muffins in the oven. A petite blond with blue eyes, she wore her long hair in a ponytail. If you could only use one word to describe a person that would encompass all their physical attributes, the descriptive word for Shannon would be "cheerleader." It was the perfect description since Shannon had been a high school cheerleader, and always found the jocks on the football team attractive. Hoyt had been one of those jocks.

She was startled and frightened when she heard the door open and the noise that the five men were making. Hoyt had heard the oven door close and knew exactly where to find her. He and his buddies were in the kitchen in a flash. Shannon hadn't had time to compose herself before her husband shouted, "Honey, I'm home."

She considered herself fortunate that she hadn't heard him say that in quite some time. If it were up to her, she hoped never to hear him utter those three words again. Shannon started to say something but before she could formulate any words or sounds,

Hoyt gave her a big hug. His large body pressed against her as he drew her toward him. She could feel his arousal and was grateful that the presence of his friends prevented him from acting on it. With his massive left arm around her upper body, she was pretty much immobilized and couldn't escape his grip. His right hand found its way to her right butt cheek and his thick fingers gave a hardy squeeze that was designed to inflict pain rather than pleasure. She was all too familiar with his motives.

Trying to regain her composure and appear as polite as possible in the uncomfortable and unsettling situation, Shannon asked everyone to sit down around the kitchen table. At least the shock of Hoyt's homecoming was buffered by the friends he brought with him. She knew better than to antagonize Hoyt. Making nice to his friends would work to her advantage.

"What's going on, Hoyt? I recognize your friends, but I had no idea you'd be coming home. You should have let me know," she said as sweetly as she could, despite her antipathy toward her husband. Had she known, she might have gone to visit her sister in Tampa.

For the last few months, Shannon had been working up the courage to leave Hoyt due to his abusive behavior. She hadn't taken all the necessary legal steps because he rarely came home during football season. The Pittsburgh Steelers had a good chance to play in the Super Bowl. When they weren't traveling for games, team members were practicing night and day, and trips home were frowned upon unless for medical reasons, family emergencies, or funerals. Now she wished that she had been more proactive.

"I know that you never watch my games. The team doc says that I have a concussion. I got some time off and wanted to come home and surprise you." Although he sounded sweet and sincere, she wasn't going to fall for that again.

"What did they do for your concussion? Are you being treated in any way?"

Shannon was basically a caring person and she didn't wish him ill. She just wanted out of the relationship before he caused her any irreparable physical harm.

"They confirmed I had a concussion and made me promise to see a neurologist or I can't play again. I'm going to make an appointment as soon as I can."

"Glad you're taking their advice. I have to say, if surprising me was your goal, you succeeded. I'm surprised as hell. Are your friends going to join us for dinner?" Shannon asked.

"No. We're going to Monty's in a minute. We'll grab a quick bite and a few drinks there. We won't be long. I'll be back soon for some private time with my favorite lady." While he sounded loving and sincere, he had played that card once too often. Shannon wasn't buying it.

"Hoyt, do you think drinking with a concussion is wise?"

As soon as the question came from her mouth, Shannon realized her mistake. Her comment wasn't meant as a reproach. She truly didn't want him to endanger his health. She should have known better.

"I'll be fine," was Hoyt's hostile reply.

It wasn't his words that were the problem, but the angry way he delivered them. Experience had taught Shannon to just say yes and hope for the best. She wouldn't dare contradict her husband, especially not in the presence of his friends.

During the time that Hoyt and his friends spent at Monty's, Shannon considered her options. In her heart she wanted her marriage to succeed. That was probably why she dragged her feet about leaving him. Maybe he did come home to mend fences with her. His earlier words did sound sincere. Perhaps she was being too cynical. Finally, she decided that she would give him one last chance. If his behavior didn't change during this visit home, she was done with him.

Sadly, Shannon realized her mistake in giving Hoyt another chance. The quick bite and a few drinks that Hoyt had promised lasted through most of the evening. He returned after midnight. He was loud and reeked of alcohol.

She had waited up for him and was seated on the couch when he came in. Looking at her watch, Shannon asked, "What happened to a quick bite?" Immediately, she regretted the question and wished that she had never spoken. Shannon's greatest fears came to fruition.

Hoyt's closed right fist crashed against her left jaw. She was dazed but conscious enough to sense that she was being carried to the bedroom where she was thrown onto the bed. Her dress was being pulled over her head and her panties forcibly removed. As the huge football player dropped down on top of her, his open fist struck her left cheek. Too drunk to perform, he struck her above her left eye, out of frustration. He immediately rolled over and fell into a drunken stupor beside her.

She had suffered enough.

She feared for her life.

She dialed 911.

CHAPTER 12

The visits to the families of the three victims were draining. Trying to console them about their losses also required delving into personal matters. When people sustain devastating news that their family member has been murdered, they don't want to dredge up criminal behavior, infidelity, shady business dealings, or other situations which might have contributed to their loved one being killed. It's like walking a tightrope, trying to balance sympathy with asking intrusive and difficult questions.

Despite attempting to recharge at home from the prior day, Brad and Lew returned to the station physically and mentally exhausted. Going through their normal routine, sorting through messages, and reviewing forensic reports were tasks that they found preferable to the emotional nature of interacting with the families. They hoped to have a few hours functioning on autopilot.

From the moment they arrived, they could see that the day augured a completely different scenario from what they envisioned. Sergeant Ted Mitchell, the desk sergeant, greeted them with a devilish grin. Already, they sensed a problem. Mitchell usually had an expression that looked like a permanent scowl, as if he were hoping that his facial expression might discourage citizens from filing police reports. Not the most ambitious person, he was just putting in his time until retirement. He figured that he'd be at his desk the daily required number of hours; it didn't matter whether he worked hard or took it easy. He preferred the easy route. The hourly count was all that mattered. Smiling and grinning were not his usual behaviors. Brad and Lew were already on alert.

"Hey guys, you have a visitor. She's at Brad's desk waiting for you." Mitchell looked across the room, barely able to suppress a grin that practically reached his ears.

"Who the hell is this 'she' you're referring to? Did 'she' say why she's waiting for us?" Brad was in no mood for games, and resented the fact that Mitchell was enjoying himself.

"She says that she's from Little Haiti. The rest you'll find out soon enough," said Mitchell, doing his best to keep from laughing out loud. His body shook and his hand covered his mouth, but his attempt at decorum was not at all successful. If he had to put in his time, at least today wouldn't be boring.

The desk sergeant followed the two detectives to Brad's desk. Eager to see their response to their visitor, he stayed close behind. This was going to be good.

Mitchell was like a dog nipping at Brad's heels and Brad didn't like dogs. He turned to him and glared. In a gruff voice without inflection, Brad dismissed the sergeant. "That will be all, Mitchell." At least he understood immediately that his presence was not required and clearly unappreciated. As quickly as the Road Runner trying to escape from Wile E. Coyote in the Looney Tunes cartoon series, Mitchell seemed to disappear from Brad's desk and simultaneously reappear at his own workstation. All that was missing was a cloud of dust. Detective Brad Mandich had obviously intimidated him with his terse words.

****

Seated in a chair across from Brad's desk, the woman had her back to the two detectives. She heard their footsteps, rose from the chair, and turned to face the men. Both men stopped in their tracks, obviously taken aback.

STRIKING!

That was Brad's initial reaction when the woman rose and turned to face them. It wasn't so much her individual facial features or her height and weight. It was the whole package that she presented. From head to toe the woman was a striking figure. Close to six feet tall, she had skin the color of mahogany. Full red lips, a nose well-proportioned to the size of her face, and thin arched eyebrows added to her exotic look. But it was her eyes that contributed the most to that description. Her almond-shaped eyes drew attention to pupils the color of coal.

With those ebony eyes, the woman scrutinized the two detectives, making them feel as if her eyes were scanning them as thoroughly as a full body scan with x-rays at the airport. The intensity of her gaze made them decidedly uncomfortable.

Doing their own scrutiny of their visitor, they assessed her as an unusually large woman with an ample bosom and wide hips, judging from her attire. She wore an enormous head scarf which was pure white, contrasting with her skin tones. It was wrapped several times around her head, leaving only the hair at the nape of her neck and behind her ears visible. The texture of her hair was coarse, the color somewhere between auburn and brown.

Her clothing defied comparison with the women they encountered on a regular basis. There appeared to be a blouse covering her body above the waist. Most of the blouse was obscured by a large swatch of multicolored fabric wrapped in layers from her waist to her neck. Peeking out under the patterned fabric was a white skirt pleated in thin accordion pleats. The skirt flared from a waist that wasn't much smaller than her more than ample hips. The skirt ended below midcalf. She seemed to be clothed in a bolt of fabric that was wound around her, rather than stitched. Brad was certain that his wife would be intrigued by how she achieved this unique style, and how the garment didn't unwind.

Beyond the clothing, her accessories made quite the fashion statement. If seeking attention was her goal, she more than achieved it. She was wearing dark leather gladiator sandals with thin soles and straps that tied almost to the top of her pleated white skirt. Her neck, wrists, and ears sported multiple pendants, bracelets, and earrings. If anyone wanted to choke her, all they had to do was to pull at the assortment of jewelry around her neck. The multiple strands of amulets, jewels, beads, trinkets, and one huge talisman could easily become weapons for cutting off her breath. From her ears dangled the largest hoop earrings that either detective had ever seen. Brad thought the earrings might have been bracelets originally; they were that large. There were at least five smaller hoops or stud earrings on each earlobe as well. Both wrists and forearms were covered in bracelets, more than the detectives had time to count. She was a walking jewelry display.

Still not over the shock of finding this unforgettable figure at his desk, Brad introduced himself.

"I'm Detective Brad Mandich. This is my partner, Detective Lew Dennison. The sergeant didn't give us your name. Please identify yourself and let us know how we can help you."

Brad put out his hand and she shook it. The clatter from her jewelry would make her easy to find in the darkest of caves.

"I am Priestess Julia. *I* need no help. I'm here to help you, sir."

"Sorry, but I don't follow. In what way can you help me? If you don't mind, please repeat your name. I'm not sure I heard it correctly."

"I am Priestess Julia. I am a Vodou priestess, what my people in Little Haiti call a mambo or female priestess."

Without responding verbally, Brad appeared to be on the verge of telling this priestess what he thought of her offer to help.

He didn't attempt to mask his feelings. Lew could read his partner's body language, the eye rolling and head shaking giving him away. Whatever was about to come out of Brad's mouth was not going to be politically correct.

Always the mediator, Lew blurted out, "Brad, I've heard of mambos. There are estimated to be three hundred thousand Haitians in South Florida. Many practice voodoo rituals. Voodoo is a religion and a highly spiritual way of life. Although it's thought to have originated in West Africa, many now practice it in Haiti. Here in the United States, it's big in South Florida in the Little Haiti section of Miami. There are also many followers in New Orleans due to the influx of Haitian immigrants in that area."

Brad approached his desk and sank into the chair. He pointed to the one on the opposite side, signaling his visitor to sit back down. That seemed to Lew to indicate that Brad was going to hear her out.

"Lew, you never cease to surprise me. You sound like a documentary for National Geographic. How are you able to spout this information so readily?"

"Did you forget that my wife is from Petion-Ville, a wealthy suburb of Port-au-Prince?"

"Sorry, partner. Now that you mention it, I seem to remember that she described it as a tourist mecca and an affluent area. It surprised me at the time because most of what we hear about Haiti focuses on the poverty and the horrible natural calamities that are always reported in the papers."

One thing Lew had come to learn was that when Brad was wrong or presented with incontrovertible facts, he had an open mind and could quickly change course. This was one of those situations. Lew's information seemed to intrigue Brad and made him more receptive to what his visitor had to say. He removed his notepad from his pocket, proof that he took his visitor seriously.

"Please continue, Priestess Julia."

"There is a spell. An evil spell over the city."

"You mean the Dead of Night killer." He stated it as a fact, not as a question.

"DON, you call him, Detective Mandich."

"Yes."

"He is neither man nor beast. He is a spirit."

"I'm not sure what you mean. His victims display bite marks and are missing their internal organs. How is this the work of a spirit?"

"Spirits are my world. I can end this curse."

Her statement was offered in a matter-of-fact manner, as if she were stating that it was raining when she looked outside and observed droplets hitting the ground.

Brad's open-mindedness was stretched to its limit when spirits and curses became talking points for his visitor. He needed an immediate reality check from his partner. Making an excuse for the pair to leave the room, he pulled Lew into an alcove out of hearing range from the proclaimed priestess.

"Lew, don't tell me you actually believe this woman."

"I don't know, but we can use as much help as possible from any source."

"Help, yes, but I'm not sure she's credible. Besides, Sergeant Hernandez will never go for it. We can't hide her from him. Anyone, including Mitchell, who saw her come in will be reporting our unusual guest to Hernandez immediately. I'm sure she has an angle and wants something, probably money. There's no way he'll give her a dime."

"Brad, you may think I'm crazy, but my wife tells me stories. I never used to believe in any of this spiritual stuff, but there have been a few times when there seemed to be no other reasonable explanation. Let's feel her out and see what Priestess Julia's angle is or if she even has one."

"Okay, Lew, against my better judgment, I'll go along with you for now, but I hope we don't become the precinct's laughingstocks because of her visit."

"Hate to tell you, but that ship has sailed."

Brad was bothered by that more than he cared to admit. Looking around the room, Brad noticed that most work had ceased. All eyes seemed directed at his desk. Mitchell had been busy, telling everyone to get a look at Brad's visitor. A regular town crier.

As Brad suspected, Mitchell made sure that Sergeant Hernandez was apprised of the unusual visitor seated at Brad's desk. Mitchell's sniggering laugh as he suggested to Hernandez that he check out the person speaking with Brad was enough to pique his interest. Mitchell didn't know that Brad and Lew were in an alcove and could hear the conversation.

As the partners were conferring with each other, Sergeant Hernandez attempted to inconspicuously walk by Brad's desk, pretending to need some records from the file cabinet adjacent to Brad's office. He briefly gazed at the strangely dressed woman sitting at Brad's desk and dismissed her as some kind of weirdo. No way was he going to get in the middle of this. He walked by her without comment and continued walking back to his office, thankful that his underlings would be handling whatever brought her to the station.

Back at Brad's desk, Priestess Julia was fiddling with her iPhone. She appeared to be in no hurry, waiting patiently for the detectives to return. Brad asked Lew to let him do the talking.

"Love to have your help, Priestess Julia, but we have no funding."

Brad's attempt to sound apologetic sounded half-hearted at best. He was positive that without being paid, Julia would rescind her offer of assistance. Her response was not what he expected.

"I ask for nothing. Miami is my home. I want it safe again." What she replied sounded sincere, at least enough to sway Brad to hear what she had to say.

"Okay, what help are you suggesting?"

"I need only a small strip of clothing from each of the victims so that their spirits may rest in peace. I need strips that were torn by the evil one."

"I can manage getting some small samples for you. You can pick up an envelope with the fabric from the desk sergeant in the morning. Your name will be on it."

"Excellent. I will leave you now."

As Julia walked toward the exit, her many bracelets and necklaces and assorted accoutrements clicked and clattered. If there was anyone who hadn't seen her arrival, her departure certainly attracted their notice.

As far as Lew was concerned, Brad acquiesced too easily to Priestess Julia's offer of help. Providing her with strips of the victims' clothing was completely out of character for Brad. Something didn't fit.

"Brad, I have to say, I'm shocked. You seem okay with this."

"Not for a minute. I'm very uneasy. We don't know it she is a priestess, knows voodoo, or is even Haitian as she claims. Any talk of curses makes me nervous. I still think she has an angle, some hidden agenda. Maybe it's publicity. Maybe we solve the case and she'll take credit for it. Maybe she'll claim that her work guided us to the solution. It could make her top mambo in her community. I'm extremely uncomfortable about what just went down."

That sounded much more like the Brad he knew.

Only time would tell.

The larger question was, how much time did they have?

CHAPTER 13

The good news was that two nights had passed without a report of any strange howling or additional dead bodies. The bad news was that the police were no closer to finding the man or beast responsible for the deaths that had already been reported. No one had seen anything.

The tip line had gotten annoying. Information leaked that people living near the locations where the bodies were found reported hearing what they described as a freakish howling from a large dog, a wolf, or some other beast that they were unable to identify. Speculation was that the animals they heard had possibly escaped from the Metro Zoo or came from the Everglades. Some of the tips were no more than irritated neighbors calling in to complain about their neighbors' dogs. Although nothing substantial had been uncovered concerning the three murders under investigation, the police received no new murder reports of a similar nature for the past few days.

That changed as quickly as a flash flood. Once again, television and radio stations reported breaking news of the discovery of two additional victims. The same killer or killers were at it again.

As they prepared for work, Detectives Mandich and Dennison each received an earful from Sergeant Hernandez who learned about the two new bodies at about the same time that the news hit the airwaves. Hernandez hadn't given them much information, other than to demand their immediate presence at police headquarters. Brad poured his coffee into a travel mug and ran out of the house. Lew rushed to his car with a few power bars for the road. Each decided to tune into the local news station on their car radios to follow what was being reported to the public as they made their way to work. They arrived almost simultaneously. Sergeant Hernandez was tapping his watch for effect as they entered his office together.

"What took you guys so long?"

Hernandez was rattled by the latest news and the unfavorable spin about the lack of progress by the police. It didn't sit well with him that the news was already disseminated, without adequate time for the police to investigate. Journalists posited that the killers hadn't been apprehended due to police incompetence and therefore more civilians had died. That was his interpretation of what he heard, although it wasn't stated quite so succinctly or with the same biting criticism that Hernandez read into the newscast. Clearly, he felt guilty.

Neither Brad nor Lew felt the need to respond. There was nothing to be gained by being oppositional. They waited for instructions, prepared for a degree of overreaction from their superior. When Hernandez was pressured from the top, he, in turn, applied pressure to those under him. It was just the way it was.

"Get your sorry asses out of here. See Doc Murphy at the morgue and don't come back until you have something."

Not exactly the most specific instruction, but they knew exactly what he meant. Results were the only thing that would satisfy their superior. Their track record up until this point had been less than stellar. Before Hernandez launched into a monologue criticizing their incompetence, both men rushed for the door.

"Any problem if I ask my nephew Cliff to join us? Hopefully, he'll bring a fresh set of eyes to the victims of the most recent murders."

"That's probably a good idea. After all, Cliff suggested that the medical examiner either overlooked or was holding back important findings when we visited the morgue the other day," Lew stated.

"I'm not sure he's available on such short notice, but I'll give him a call."

"Works for me."

CHAPTER 14

It was a typically busy day, and according to my schedule, I had about thirty-five patients scheduled before the day would be over. The flow was going smoothly, and unless additional patients called with an emergency, I could accommodate the scheduled patients with no problem. My staff was efficient, and the office ran like a well-oiled machine. I took pride in seeing patients punctually, yet never making anyone feel rushed once they were in the examining room.

As I was finishing up my notes on the fourth patient of the morning, a retiree with a questionable mole, my cell phone rang. It was my uncle.

"Uncle Brad, is everything ok?"

Frankly, I knew it wasn't. He rarely called me during the day unless there was a problem. But social etiquette seemed to require that I ask the question anyway.

"I don't know if you heard the news, Cliff, but two more bodies were found early this morning. Seems like a similar M.O. Lew and I are on the way to see the medical examiner. Any chance you can break away and meet us there?"

I could hear the stress in his voice. Flattered that my uncle valued my input, I was also directly involved because of the connection to Lauren and her high school classmates who had been murdered just days earlier. Uncle Brad's personal invitation was a no-brainer.

"I'll have my staff cancel my appointments until three o'clock. That should give us enough time. I'll meet you at the medical examiner's office."

I fully understood the immediacy of the situation. Cancelling the bulk of today's full schedule would become tomorrow's scheduling nightmare. In my mind, I had no choice. I'll worry about tomorrow, tomorrow. I seem to remember my mother singing words like that to me when I was young. The lyrics came from an old song from her childhood. I'll have to google that later.

After giving instructions to my staff about the cancellations and adjusting my schedule for the next day or so to squeeze in the missed appointments, I removed my white coat and headed to the back entrance of the office suite. The last thing I wanted was to exit through the waiting room and generate conversations and questions from my patients about my hasty departure.

Time was of the essence.

CHAPTER 15

Brad and Lew were not the only public servants who were feeling pressure. Dr. Cecil Murphy had two more bodies to examine, and superiors who wanted answers ASAP. What was happening in Miami was unacceptable; blame was being placed everywhere including on the medical examiner and the forensic specialists for their lack of progress in the case. The news outlets were clamoring for a suspect to be identified and apprehended. The fact that there appeared to be a serial killer on the loose created fear of epic proportions, especially as the time between killings was becoming shorter with each new incident. Patience dwindled and tempers flared.

The public outcry and the politicians eager to make a name for themselves were adding to the pressure that the medical examiner was under. He was noticeably less cordial than he was during the first visit. There was no polite greeting, no offer of a beverage, no small talk. He was all business.

"I know why you're here. The bodies are waiting for you. Understand that I have only had these two for an hour or two," stated Dr. Murphy defensively.

The presence of the detectives this early into his examination of the bodies set him on edge. My presence seemed to be putting him over the top. I guess I struck a nerve with my questions from the last visit.

"We'll take anything. Our sergeant is all over us," stated Brad truthfully. His tone was non-confrontational and elicited a calm response from Dr. Murphy.

"Okay. Here goes. Both are young men, probably in their late twenties. Early thirties at most. As you can see, both have bite marks on the face, lower back, and buttocks. Their internal organs are missing. They also have puncture wounds on the posterior neck where Dr. Mandich asked me to look last time. Incidentally, the first three victims had the same wounds in the same location. I found those after you left, Dr. Mandich."

He looked over at me as he was describing the neck wounds. I expected that he'd be upset with me because of our earlier interaction, but perhaps I was being too sensitive. He didn't seem to harbor a grudge against me despite my basically telling him how to conduct his autopsies. Since he mentioned me specifically, I figured I had been invited into the conversation.

"Have they been identified? Do you have their names?" I asked. Patience was not my strong suit.

"Identification was easy. Their wallets and phones were found with the bodies. The redhead is Mark Kalman. The dark-haired lad over there is Eli Thomas."

I wished I had gotten a list of classmates from Lauren when this whole mess started. At the time, I wasn't thinking that there would be more deaths among her peers. Or for that matter, among any other group of people. I must admit that I was rattled. These two were the right ages to have been part of Lauren's graduation class. It was a grim thought.

"Like I said, these bodies just got here. Can't tell you much more."

Dr. Murphy appeared anxious to get back to his autopsies. He broke eye contact and picked up his scalpel. Without uttering any words, he seemed to be dismissing us. But I wasn't ready to accept his limited information. I had just arrived and spent less time with the bodies than he had, but there were several observations that I made that I wanted to run by him. He wasn't getting off that easily.

"Before we leave I have just two questions."

"Okay. But be quick about it."

"First, my uncle tells me that the tip line has been receiving calls from a widespread area all around Miami, not just in the immediate vicinity of the actual murders. People have reported hearing a distinctive howling sound in the dead of night. Do you have any idea who might have leaked information to the public about that aspect of the murders?"

He paused for a split second. As I waited, I looked directly at his eyes to watch him answer my question. I knew there were some facial tics, particularly relating to the eyes, that indicate that a person is lying or uncomfortable with a question. Dr. Murphy's eyes were darting back and forth, alerting me to the fact that my question made him uneasy. I suspected that his response might be less than truthful.

"Nope. No idea at all."

"I know you haven't been able to thoroughly examine the bodies since it's only been a few hours, but did you notice that, like the other three victims, these two men had been athletes? From the appearance of their bodies, we can make an educated guess as to what sports they pursued," I stated.

"What do you mean? What do their bodies tell you?" He sounded intrigued by my comment, not evasive at all. Regarding me as a colleague, he wanted to hear my analysis.

"Mark's thumb is callused at the interphalangeal joint," I said. "That suggests to me that he was a bowler, perhaps in a bowling league."

"What about Eli? What sport do you think he played?"

"He has the classic golfer's tan. His legs are significantly darker in the area from just above the kneecap down to his ankles. Seems like he wore Bermuda shorts frequently in the hot Florida sun. Coupled with arms that are also darker beginning where a short sleeve shirt would end and the paleness of his left hand as compared to his right hand, I would bet that he was a right-handed golfer who wore a golf glove on his left hand. From the depth of the color of his exposed skin, the likelihood is that he golfed on a regular basis as part of a foursome."

I don't know if Dr. Murphy missed these physical findings or wanted to keep them hidden. Since I addressed what I saw, he didn't have any choice but to comment. What he said could have been sincere, or he could have been trying to ingratiate himself with me. I couldn't tell.

"That's impressive. If you ever get tired of dermatology, you really should consider a career in forensics."

"I'll take that under advisement. You'll excuse me, Dr. Murphy, but I have to get back to my late afternoon patients. Is there anything more you can tell us?" Already I was cutting it close to return by three o'clock and I didn't think he was offering me a job. This was no time for idle chitchat.

"Then I'll make this quick. Oh, by the way, right after we met the other day, I rushed the toxicology screen like you asked."

Now he had my attention. All I was hoping for was a succinct recitation of the results based upon his use of the word "quick." Unfortunately, that wasn't the case. Maybe I should have been an oral surgeon. Getting the results of the screening was like pulling teeth. He could have told me the results immediately, but somehow, he felt the need to drag it out to a question-and-answer session.

"I was somewhat surprised when I got the report," Dr. Murphy said.

I waited for him to elaborate, but it was clear that he was enjoying being the keeper of the knowledge, if only for a few moments. He was waiting for me to question him.

"Did the tests I requested turn up any sedatives or tranquilizers in the blood samples?"

“No. But we did find something more sinister. We found a toxin often employed by South American Indians and used on the tips of poison arrows or darts.”

God forbid that he should have named the toxin.

“Does this toxin have a name?” I was losing patience.

“We found trace amounts of curare.”

His use of “by the way” to detail the results of the toxicology screen was quite the understatement.

Uncle Brad and Lew were listening to our conversation with rapt attention. This revelation could be key to identifying the killer or killers. They, too, were mystified as to why the mention of curare was so offhand.

Just to be certain that they understood the significance of this toxin, I wanted to clarify the effects that it would have on the human body. I turned to face them.

“Not sure how much you know about the medical effects of curare, but this particular paralytic drug would stop victims’ muscles from functioning. These victims were paralyzed but they were fully aware of what was happening to them.”

Brad and Lew had seen the mutilation of their bodies.

I did not need to go into any further detail.

CHAPTER 16

Before getting into our respective cars, we compared notes in the parking lot. My uncle seemed pleased with our trip to the morgue.

"That was exhausting, but at least we now know how the victims were subdued," Uncle Brad stated. "Seems like tracking down access to curare should help us narrow down possible killers much more easily than access to weapons. You really hit a home run for us," my uncle stated. "Not sure about the importance of your recognition that the two recent victims were evidently athletes, but it can't hurt. You never know which piece of information might be the one that solves the case."

I had to laugh to myself. Uncle Brad was big on baseball analogies. Poor Aunt Ellen. Hard to imagine her having to hear him compare everything to baseball on a regular basis. But that was her problem, not mine.

Glancing at my watch, I said my farewells to Uncle Brad and Lew. We went our separate ways. It was only mid-afternoon, but the traffic was a nightmare on I-95 as I headed back to my office. Between the influx of snowbirds for the winter and the constant lane closures for construction and repairs, there was no time of day that the drive could be considered easy. Today was no exception.

I arrived at my office with only ten minutes to spare. Again, I entered through the back door, avoiding greeting patients in the waiting room. After a quick trip to the bathroom, a rapid brushing of my teeth and rinsing of my mouth with mouthwash, and slipping into my white jacket, I was ready for the onslaught of patients. The day couldn't end soon enough.

Fatigued from driving to and from the morgue, seeing the two bodies that had been brutally murdered, the visit with Dr. Murphy and his verbal gamesmanship, and the double booking of my afternoon patients, I couldn't think of anything that I'd rather do than sleep. Well, perhaps that's not exactly true, but on the ride home I spoke with Lauren and learned that she was staying late at her accounting office. Since the one thing I'd rather do wasn't going to happen, I figured that I'd just get a good night's sleep.

After a hastily prepared cheese sandwich which consisted of two slabs of some unidentified cheese between two slices of bread which I didn't want to take the time to toast, I stood at the center island munching on my sandwich. Following that gastronomic treat, I headed to the bathroom where I took what would have been touted by environmentalists as the perfect shower to save water. I spent more time undressing than I did showering. Brushing my teeth was another exercise in questionable hygiene. I had no energy to waste.

Ordinarily, I would have waited up for Lauren, but my body wouldn't cooperate. Instead, I left her at note expressing my love but explaining that I was exhausted and was going to bed. I fully expected that I'd hear her come in and, at the very least, kiss her goodnight. But as she told me in the morning, I was dead to the world when she got home. She admitted to banging her drawers shut and leaving the door to the bathroom open, thinking that the light or the toilet flushing might wake me up; a category five hurricane wouldn't have been enough to rouse me out of my sleep. It had been that kind of a day.

It's amazing what a good night's sleep can do for one's mood. Not to mention, waking up to the smell of waffles, my favorite breakfast, served by the most beautiful woman in the world. I was one lucky guy, and I knew it. My wife excelled at everything, at least according to me, her biggest fan. But I defy anyone to say otherwise.

Lauren knew my work schedule and how long it took me to get ready in the morning. She could calculate down to the minute the exact time that I needed to get up to have breakfast and still get to work on time. I heard water dripping and assumed it was her pouring water into the Keurig for my coffee. When I looked outside, I saw that what I was hearing was another South Florida early morning downpour that would probably end by the time I left for the office. Lauren had retrieved the morning paper despite the rain. We both enjoyed reading the Herald before setting out for work. She deposited a plate with waffles, a steaming cup of coffee, and the newspaper at my seat at the table. It was a winning breakfast trifecta.

Since I hadn't seen her at all last night, I grabbed her hand before she sat down in her seat, pulled her onto my lap, and planted a kiss on her lips. Another winning combination. Her million-dollar smile in response was the perfect start to my day.

I bit into my blueberry waffle and took a sip of coffee to wash it down. Then I tackled the newspaper, pulling out the sports section, and handing her the balance of the paper. We were so perfect together, never competing about the important things in life.

I almost dropped my coffee mug as I looked up at Lauren.

"Did you see this?"

"Something on the sports page? You already know the answer to that."

Other than handing it to me, unless she used the sports section to protect breakable items in a package she was preparing for mailing, she never touched that section of the paper

"You know Hoyt Stark," I began. I figured that everyone knew about Hoyt Stark. I found out I was wrong.

"That would be a no."

"He's a Miami native. He plays football. He lives in the Gables."

After these three simplistic sentences came out, I hoped that Lauren didn't think I was talking down to her. I was still amazed that she hadn't heard of him. But then again, if she mentioned famous designers, I probably would not recognize their names either.

"Okay, but I'm not familiar with *his* name. So, a lot of players live down here. I am only semi-clueless when it comes to sports. I know that the Miami Dolphins and the Miami Heat play down here. I suspect many live here as well," Lauren said.

I couldn't argue that she could name the teams. The fact that "Miami" was in their names was a dead giveaway, but I suspected that she couldn't name more than one or two players and might mix up the sport that they played. There was nothing to be gained by quizzing her about players. It was beside the point that I was trying to make.

"Right, but this guy is different. He grew up here. He played high school football down here and played his college ball at University of Miami. He got drafted into the National Football League by the Pittsburgh Steelers. Even though his professional career wasn't playing for a Miami team, he's a local hero, a hometown boy that made good."

"Got it. So, what's the story you're reading? Why do you seem so rattled by it?"

"He's been released by the Steelers. They kicked him off the team. Seems that he has a history of domestic abuse. Teams now have a zero-tolerance policy for players like that."

"It's about time. I never thought I'd say this, but I will. Hooray for sports. I've got no sympathy for someone like that."

"You and me both."

I couldn't imagine a man abusing a woman for any reason whatsoever. How did so many couples start out loving each other and end up in abusive relationships or in divorce? How did intense love turn into hate? Why was hate a more powerful emotion? I couldn't answer any of those questions.

Lauren was picking up her car keys, signaling that she was about to depart. It was time for me to leave as well. I had to marvel how couples with children managed to get their kids ready for school and still make it to work on time. We had trouble enough getting ourselves out the door.

The newspaper article had distracted me, and I hadn't had the chance to tell Lauren about my day yesterday at the morgue. There was no time this morning. It would have to wait until later.

"Forgive me, Lauren. I meant to tell you about yesterday, but it would take too much time now. I'll tell you all about it over dinner."

"Sounds like a plan. And by the way, there's nothing to forgive."

"Great. How's this for an idea? On my way home, I'll get takeout from Joe's Stone Crab."

I figured that if I got us an order of stone crabs, it would prolong our meal. Eating stone crabs is labor intensive, cracking the stubborn shells and carefully removing the meat from the crab claws. Clearly, it would be more time consuming than just cutting into a chicken breast or a steak. The additional time at the table would give me ample opportunity to catch Lauren up with the visit to the medical examiner. Plus, we both loved stone crabs and the delicious creamed spinach and onion rings that were signature side dishes of the restaurant.

Even though I had just consumed breakfast, my mouth was already watering for dinner.

CHAPTER 17

Somehow, I got through the day having seen fifty-two patients. My schedule was packed since I had taken off nearly five hours yesterday to lend a hand to my uncle. I was young, but I wasn't invincible. Although I prided myself on my stamina and my energy level, I came to the realization that working at the office and working with the police was taking too much of a toll.

I'd have to admit to Lauren that I wasn't the "Young Dynamo" that I had named myself several years ago. She claimed that despite my presenting myself as such, my need for naps and a solid eight hours of sleep a night disqualified me from that title anyway. Frankly, I guess it wouldn't come as much of a shock when I told her what I'd been planning. That was my hope.

Trying to give my professional practice my complete attention was at odds with my desire to assist my uncle. In the last few days, I had to instantly drop everything and complicate the lives of my patients and my staff to accommodate Uncle Brad's request for help. It wasn't fair to continue to wreak havoc on everyone else's schedules, particularly since it appeared that police were stymied, and I had valuable skills to contribute.

Plus, I honestly enjoyed the ability to use my skill set to assist the police. Even as a child, I devoured detective books; Sherlock Holmes was my absolute favorite. On Halloween, I prevailed upon my family to get me a cape, Sherlock's distinctive style hat, and, of course, a huge magnifying glass.

Uncle Brad was the one who indulged me the most. As a detective, he seemed flattered that I was so enamored with Sherlock Holmes, perhaps the most famous fictional detective. Guess my uncle took it as his being a role model or mentor to me, which was the truth. The investment in the costume was worthwhile since I must have worn it at least five years. Luckily, the cape was huge. I grew into it.

In recent years, I was no stranger to assisting the police. They acknowledged that I was instrumental in uncovering clues that would have gone unnoticed if not for my dermatology skills and attention to detail. That was the greatest high for me. If questioned or interviewed, I would describe myself as a professional physician/dermatologist and amateur sleuth. They were not mutually exclusive.

Currently, with what appeared to be a serial killer on the loose, I speculated that my energies would be better spent away from my practice in order to dedicate my entire attention to assisting the police. My thoughts tossed around in my mind like clothing in a washing machine. My ideas entered the machine, circled around in a pool of water, and confronted the agitator. Dirt and debris flowed down the drain. Considering all ramifications, I completed the spin cycle as all excess components of the process were wrung out. What I had been considering was finally clear; I would assist the police with the case. Surely Lauren would agree with the logic of my plan. My washing machine analogy would convince her. She'd love the imagery.

Of course, I'd arrange for coverage. Most of the local dermatologists know one another from professional meetings and conferences. It wasn't all that difficult to find someone who agreed to be on call for any emergencies.

During short vacations when I missed only a few days of work, I tried to reschedule appointments that could be delayed until my return. Some patients agreed to be seen by one of my physician assistants if they didn't want to wait until I got back. However, there were those that were angered by the inconvenience to them. If they insisted on being seen by a physician while I was away, they could contact one of the dermatologists taking my call.

My mind was made up. Since I expected to be out of the office for at least two weeks, I decided to try to arrange for a locum tenens physician for that time period. This is a fancy Latin name for a temporary substitute. There are physicians who are available on a short-term basis to take over a medical practice during the absence of the doctor in charge. My plan was to first contact the doctor I hired when Lauren and I honeymooned in Hawaii. If he didn't pan out, I'd widen the search.

Ideally, a local retired dermatologist might want to work for a few weeks or months to keep his skills sharp and to generate income. During the winter, it's easy to find a dermatologist to come to Florida for a few weeks of well-paid employment. Between locals and out-of-state physicians, it didn't seem to me that it would be much of a problem. My patients would be in good hands regardless of which option they chose in my absence.

The entire city of Miami was desperate and would remain fearful until the Dead of Night killer was found. Although the detectives on the case were competent, there clearly was a medical component to the case that required someone they could trust. From our interactions with Dr. Cecil Murphy, the medical examiner, the issue of trust was problematic. My observations of the bodies and the questions I posed to the medical examiner called into question the veracity of the information that Dr. Murphy provided to the police. The fact that he was handling every corpse with little or no oversight alarmed me because of what he seemingly missed.

It was doubtful that Murphy had suddenly become incompetent. I worried that he was hiding something. There was no explanation that I could come up with to justify his lack of candor. During my first visit to the morgue, he never mentioned the puncture wounds on the back of the necks of the three initial victims. No medical examiner with his level of expertise should have missed these.

While I hoped I was wrong, my only conclusion was that these wounds were not overlooked; they were deliberately not reported. If not for my presence, Brad and Lew could easily have been misled or duped.

I knew what Dr. Murphy had done, but not why.

CHAPTER 18

Now that I made my decision and formulated a plan, I looked forward to discussing it with Lauren. Knowing her as well as I do, I didn't doubt that she'd be supportive. Her encouragement was always a constant.

Thinking about her, I drove to Joe's Stone Crab. The place is a gold mine. Locals and tourists alike willingly tolerate long waits to get a table to savor the restaurant's famous service and cuisine. But today, my plan was to take our dinner home. Although the line was long, it moved quickly and efficiently.

I returned to my car, inhaling the delicious aroma of the onion rings that seemed to waft from the bag that I placed on the passenger seat. Lauren would kill me if I came home without them, and once I started, I knew I could consume the entire portion single-handedly. That would not be a good opener to the conversation I needed to have with her. It took all my self-control to ignore the allure of the bag.

The closer I got to home, the more I wondered what Lauren would say when I broke the news about taking a hiatus from work to assist with the police investigation of the Dead of Night killer. Basically, I was foregoing my medical practice and my income from it to play at being an amateur detective. There was no expectation that I'd receive any monetary remuneration for working with the police, and it hadn't even been suggested to me by my uncle that I undertake this role. Would Lauren see this as a harebrained idea?

Despite a miniscule degree of trepidation, I figured she'd understand. Lauren already knew that I was no ordinary guy. Time and time again I proved that I had a penchant for doing the unusual. Fortunately for both of us, she shared that same quirk, if that's what it was called. Not only did she go along with some of my more outlandish ideas, she even embellished upon them. Others might consider what we occasionally did as peculiar, but it all depended on who was doing the commentary. Sometimes our ideas were described as sensible, other times idiotic. In this instance, with Lauren being the one to hear me out, I was hoping for the former, not the latter.

She must have heard me insert my key into the lock, because she was walking toward me as I entered the kitchen. The table was set, and I figured she must want to eat right away to have "The Conversation." Since I fell asleep before Lauren came home last night, I was anxious to tell her what happened yesterday. Equally as important, I wanted to discuss my decision about work.

Her reaction to my arrival was everything I could wish for. She threw her arms around me and gave me a big hug, followed by a lingering kiss. Wasn't sure where she planned to go with this, but I was more than willing to follow, no questions asked.

She then shoved the bag containing our supper to the side of the table. That seemed promising. However, her next words dispelled my expectation that she was going to lead me to our bedroom. Instead she said, "Talk first. We'll eat later."

"Fine by me. I was hoping you'd say that." That was far from the truth, but I figured that I'd go along since my goal was to get her to agree to my plan.

"I missed you last night, Cliff. What happened yesterday that exhausted you to such an extent that you fell asleep before I got in? I can't believe you slept through all my attempts to interrupt your sleep. Wish I had that ability to sleep through everything."

I was grateful for the uninterrupted sleep. It was a skill I'd learned during my internship when I tuned out everything to catch even the shortest of naps.

"It was a combination of things."

"Like what?"

"At the start of my day, I got an urgent call from Uncle Brad to meet him at the morgue, so I had my staff move some of the morning patients to the late afternoon. As a result, my day was brutal. Plus, there's something going on with the medical examiner. He's either grossly incompetent, or he's hiding something. I'm leaning toward him hiding something and I want to know why."

Lauren looked at me with her beautiful hazel eyes that could see right through me.

"No offense, Cliff, but you look like shit. I mean that in only the nicest way. I'm worried about you. Hey, you're only human. Stop burning the candle at both ends."

"You're right. What you just said is the perfect segue to something I need to discuss with you. I can't keep up this pace, physically or mentally. Yesterday, I found myself worrying about my patients when I was helping Uncle Brad. Then when I was back at the office I was worrying about the murders. My focus must be on only one thing. With the escalation of the murders, it has to be helping my uncle."

Her eyes never left my face, and she could see that I hadn't completed my thoughts. She gave me the space to tell her the rest.

"There's no other choice that makes any sense to me. I'm going to take a few weeks off and volunteer my help to my uncle and the Miami-Dade police department. Mel Shapiro already said that he'd cover my emergencies until I can find a locum tenens." Slipping into Uncle Brad's frame of reference, I added, "I've got all the bases covered."

That wife of mine is no dummy. She immediately recognized my trotting out an expression that my uncle would use, and she began to laugh.

"Your uncle would be so proud. I'm just not sure whether it's because you want to help him, or because you've adopted some of his corny baseball phrases. As for me, I know you long enough to know that your mind is made up, especially since you've already put a plan together. I'm okay with your decision if you don't put yourself in danger. I'd like to make it to our first anniversary."

That was her way of granting acceptance, but at the same time giving me a warning to use common sense.

With my most coy expression, I responded by saying, "WWLD?" We have several coded abbreviations that we clearly understand from constant use. In this case, what I meant was "What Would Lauren Do?" The meaning behind this four-letter acronym indicates that I would consider how she'd approach a task and use the standard caution that she typically employs.

When I utilize this abbreviation, I understand that my initial reaction might be far less careful than what hers would be, but that I try to rein myself in. That seemed to satisfy her, so I figured that we could now eat. I'm a guy and didn't think there was anything more to discuss. Wrong.

As I began reaching for the bag of takeout food, my mouth watering as I anticipated the gastronomic pleasures of its contents, Lauren very gently slapped my hand away. Most likely I had an expression on my face like a puppy who was hit with a newspaper for chewing his owner's slipper.

"Don't give me that pitiful face, you clown."

I truly have a way of looking so helpless and pitiful that she often laughs at me and gives in. Unfortunately, not this time.

"Hold on a minute. Tell me about the case. After all, three of my classmates are dead. I have a big vested interest in this."

"Which brings up another question for you," I added. In my zeal to tell her about my intention to take time from work to help the police, I had completely forgotten to ask her about the two most recent murders.

"Remember when I said that my uncle called to ask me to meet him at the morgue? Well, there were two more murders and he wanted me to see the bodies of the victims. Do the names Mark Kalman and Eli Thomas mean anything to you?"

Lauren's eyes welled with tears. She turned pale. There was no doubt that they were her classmates.

"This can't be happening, Cliff. They were also members of the alumni volleyball team."

"I'm so sorry, Lauren. Don't do it tonight, but maybe tomorrow you could give me the names of all the students in your graduating class. It would be great if you designate the ones who signed up to attend the reunion, the ones who live locally, and the ones playing volleyball. It's horrible to say this, but your list may be invaluable to the police."

"That won't be difficult. I have a spreadsheet with the information you're looking for. Helps me keep track of the attendees and the ones playing in the volleyball tournament. Their contact information is also on the excel schedule. Just not now. I need some time to process this."

"We don't have to talk about this anymore tonight," I said, not wanting to upset her any further.

"No, I need to hear the rest of what you know about this maniac. Who could be doing this? And why?"

Without a choice, I had to recount to her the events of the last few days. In addition to my trips to the morgue and the lab results, I also filled her in on what Uncle Brad had told me about the odd visit from Priestess Julia. When I painted a picture of the woman from how Brad described her to me, I saw the color return to Lauren's face.

Between her physical presence, her clothing, her assessment that there was an evil spell over the city, and her offer to help the police, Priestess Julia captured Lauren's attention. I could see Lauren's mind working like an outboard motor revving up when she heard about Priestess Julia and her visit to the station house. Even the speed of her words and the volume of her voice changed with her next comment.

"Okay. You often say that a man must do what a man must do. The same holds true for a woman. I'm going undercover."

Ordinarily, hearing that statement would make me quite happy. Thinking about my joining her undercover in the literal sense was an irresistible thought. However, I knew that there was no sexual nuance to her use of the word. But it didn't stop me from trying. It was all I could do to get that image out of my mind.

"Is that an invitation to the bedroom?"

"You know exactly what I mean. Don't pretend otherwise. I plan on going to Little Haiti to check out this Priestess Julia."

"Are you insane?"

"No more than you are."

She had me there. I was trapped. She was an adult and I couldn't forbid her from going to Little Haiti to spy on Priestess Julia. In fact, it might be interesting to get her take on the woman. However, my concern was her safety.

"Please grant me one concession."

"What would that be?"

"Call me overprotective, but at least let me speak to Uncle Brad and see if he can assign a policewoman to accompany you. It probably won't be a hard sell. It seemed to me that he wanted to check out this woman claiming to practice voodoo. This might be perfect. The policewoman can be undercover as well. If he gives it a go, is that okay with you?"

"Deal. I'd probably feel better not going alone," Lauren admitted. Energized at having a tangible plan to help find the killer of her classmates, Lauren moved the takeout bag to the center of the table and put a napkin on her lap.

"Bring on those stone crabs," I said as I tore at the takeout bag.

In all the previous times that we had hammered at our crabs, I don't think we ever pulverized the shells like we did that evening. Each of us was probably more tense than we'd admit.

CHAPTER 19

Lauren was up before 7 a.m. the next morning. When she had something pressing on her mind, she needed to alleviate stress by taking action. Although she had spoken briefly last night with Eve Simms, her partner in their accounting firm, Lauren needed to pay Eve a visit.

Unsure how long she'd be away from the office, Lauren asked Eve to shoulder the workload. However, it was Eve's dog, Teacup, that Lauren required in her undercover scheme. Purposely vague about what role she had in mind for Teacup, Lauren relied on her long-term friendship with Eve. With Lauren's promise to keep her canine companion safe, Eve was willing to entrust Teacup to her care.

Expecting Lauren's visit, Eve had been up for hours. Although still dressed in the T-shirt and gym shorts that she wore to bed, she had run a brush through her short brown hair, streaked with blond highlights. Her green eyes, the color of jade, looked out from behind her tortoiseshell glasses as she watched her security camera for Lauren's arrival.

When Lauren rang the doorbell, Eve immediately opened the door with her miniature yorkie in hand. It soon became clear to Lauren that Teacup was full of idiosyncrasies and Eve expected Lauren to cater to all of them.

"Lauren, I typed out things you should know about Teacup. She can be very temperamental, especially if you deviate from my instructions," Eve stated seriously.

Eve presented Lauren with a small wicker basket, painted pink, with a personally monogrammed padded pillow.

"Teacup does not like being carried in a purse. I tried that once, and she kept struggling to escape. Guess it was too confining," Eve hypothesized.

Lauren knew from experience that Eve thought of her yorkie as having human traits and emotions. She sat through the "Teacup 101" lecture with equanimity.

"Since you're taking her in the car, I'll give you her special car seat. Make sure that you strap her in carefully. This striped box from Doggie Delights Baker has a container of treats for Teacup. If you run out, you can bake your own with the recipe I put in the box."

There was no way that Lauren was going to bake for a dog, but she let Eve continue. She tried her best to refrain from rolling her eyes.

"In another container, I have some extra ribbons and a brush with soft camel-hair bristles. Teacup sits contentedly when I brush her beautiful tan and gray fur, looking so happy. She enjoys being groomed and wearing her ribbons. Today she's wearing a pink leather collar embellished with Swarovski crystals. It's her favorite. She likes bling."

She likes *bling?* Did Eve ever hear herself when she spoke about the dog?

Eve went on.

"Teacup is a high-strung dog. Fortunately, I've found a sure way to calm her down. She loves listening to country music. It works every time."

Lauren formed a visual image of the dog, this time wearing a pink western hat, a brown leather vest with fringes, and tan suede boots on all four paws. She was afraid to ask whether Eve had such an outfit for Teacup. The likelihood was that she did.

This was too much to take. Eve was the epitome of an overindulgent pet owner. The idea that a dog had a musical preference was over the top. Not a big fan of country music herself, Lauren was glad she had Sirius XM Radio in her car, and Cliff had a few Kenny Rodgers, Randy Travis, and Garth Brooks CD's at home.

After all the pampering that Eve so willingly and enthusiastically gave to Teacup, Lauren thought to herself that in her next life she'd like to come back as a spoiled canine. This dog's life had its appeal.

"I can't thank you enough for entrusting Teacup to me. Don't worry about a thing, Eve. I promise she'll be in good hands. And I really appreciate your heads up about taking care of her. You've covered everything."

Notwithstanding Lauren's assurances, Eve was still uneasy about how Teacup would react to being taken from her home and familiar routines. Eve was like a parent seeing off her first child boarding the school bus for kindergarten. She picked up Teacup and cradled her tightly to her chest, holding her as if she would never see her again. She spoke quietly in the singsong cadence that parents use when speaking to newborns. It wasn't clear whether Eve was trying to comfort Teacup or herself as she crooned softly to her. Lauren knew her partner well enough to recognize that Eve was on the brink of changing her mind.

"Thanks, Eve. I've got to go. Cliff is having his uncle send over a policewoman to our home. She'll be arriving any minute, so I need to be there to let her in."

Eve quickly gathered all the paraphernalia she assembled for her precious Teacup. Grabbing a quilted pink backpack hanging by the front door, Eve put the brush, ribbons, premium dry dog food, treats, an extra studded collar, and two leashes in it.

It came as no surprise to Lauren that the backpack was embroidered in fuchsia with Teacup's name.

Eve meticulously installed the doggie car seat in the back seat of Lauren's car on the passenger side. Not surprisingly, the car seat had a plush fabric cover with a pattern of pastel ribbons and dog bones, and her name in large embroidered pink letters.

With Teacup securely fastened in her wicker basket on top of her cushion in the personalized doggie car seat, Lauren left with her canine passenger and all her accoutrements. Tears sprang into Eve's eyes as she closed the passenger door. Teacup became fidgety. Quickly, Lauren turned on Sirius and selected a country music station. The music was effective. Teacup calmed down.

Lauren just shook her head in amazement.

Once her car and treasured passenger were out of Eve's sight, Lauren sped home. She didn't want to be late for her first meeting with the policewoman who was due to arrive shortly.

CHAPTER 20

Eve's extensive instructions had taken so long that Detective Amanda Banks was already parked and waiting for Lauren's arrival. Not a promising beginning to working together. A great respecter of other people's time, Lauren was mentally preparing her apology as she exited her car and released Teacup from the complex restraints of the car seat. Fortunately, Detective Banks glossed over Lauren's delay when she saw her carrying the adorable dog. No apology was necessary.

Carrying Teacup in her basket, Lauren approached the white Suzuki that was parked outside her building. Brad told Lauren the evening before that he assigned Detective Amanda Banks to work with her and that she would be driving a white Suzuki Swift Sport. Not familiar with that vehicle, Lauren did a Google search so she could recognize the car. The diminutive detective recognized Lauren in a more unusual manner.

"You must be Lauren. I've been to your husband's office and have seen your pictures plastered all over the place. I feel like I'm familiar with your entire wardrobe from the quantity of pictures on display." Another woman might have said that with a degree of cattiness, but Amanda Banks was just being forthright. Lauren was not offended in the least.

"Oh, I feel like an idiot. I'm Amanda Banks. I know I'm early. I always am. When Detective Mandich asked me to meet with you, I was thrilled, especially since I owe your husband big-time. He spotted a melanoma on my boyfriend, who fought me tooth and nail about having it looked at. Stubborn as he is, he finally agreed to a biopsy after Dr. Mandich scared him sufficiently. Frankly, your husband saved his life."

Detective Banks smiled at Lauren, who never tired of hearing from patients about her husband's clinical skills. She couldn't help but like the attractive redhead with her short-layered hairdo with relaxed waves. Her hair color complemented her emerald green eyes, making Lauren wonder whether she had Irish ancestry. Lauren guessed that she chose that hairstyle because it was probably something she could wash and then let air dry. In her occupation, saving time with a short low maintenance haircut was probably important. Plus, it was very flattering on her. A small woman, Amanda Banks would have been overpowered by a hairdo that was too bouffant or too long. The style suited her.

"Lauren, Detective Mandich told me that you wanted to go to Little Haiti to meet with a woman identifying herself as a voodoo priestess. Both your husband and his uncle are concerned about your safety. When your husband called me earlier this morning, I made a promise to him to protect you. Kind of like returning the favor for what he did for my boyfriend. I hope you're not offended."

It was such an honest explanation that Lauren took it in stride. Frankly, she liked the idea of partnering with the policewoman for security, companionship, and what Lauren expected would be her professional way to appraise the situation. It was a win-win situation as far as Lauren was concerned.

"Works for me," Lauren responded with a smile.

"We don't want to advertise our connection to the police department, so I brought my undercover vehicle. Like me, it appears small, but packs a big punch. Don't let size fool you. Under the hood you won't find your standard engine. It's been modified just in case we need to get out of a sticky situation quickly or need to give chase to any criminal activity we encounter. Trust me, if necessary, I can also kick some ass."

"That's reassuring. Detective Banks, did Brad fill you in on everything regarding the DON killer? Do he tell you about the connection to my high school classmates?"

"So far as I know, I've been updated through early this morning. Everyone at the precinct has been following the case. Lauren, what's your game plan? Why do you want to meet this woman? What approach do you want to take? Somehow, I have a feeling that you've given this a lot of thought."

"Well, as you know, after the third murder, this woman calling herself Priestess Julia went to the station and requested pieces of fabric from the clothing of my three classmates who were the victims. It was more than just giving her material from clothing in their closets like you'd give hunting dogs to recognize the scent of the person they were to find. She wanted fabric from the garments that the victims had been wearing when they were killed. More specifically, she asked for swatches that were already torn because the torn areas had been touched by the killer, whether the killer was man or beast. She claimed that she needed the torn fabric so that the victims could rest in peace."

"Makes sense, I guess, if you believe in voodoo," Amanda said.

"I think there's something more going on with this lady who refers to herself as Priestess Julia. I checked her out on her website. Her contact information is an email address only. A list of spells and testimonials from satisfied customers make up the bulk of the site. There's no way to tell whether these are real or bogus without further investigation," Lauren said.

Still holding the wicker basket with Teacup in her arms, Lauren expressed her further concerns to the detective. "I'm not sure that I do believe that Julia is a priestess or even Haitian. I'm more than a little suspicious that the only address on the site is a mailing address for a post office box so believers can mail checks for her services. Of course, along with her email address, there are instructions for making credit card payments. How do her customers meet with her?"

"That's an interesting question, Lauren. Something tells me you have a plan to find out."

"You got that right," Lauren told her, the pride in her voice apparent to the detective.

"OK, spill it. And what's up with the pooch?"

"Well, here goes, Amanda. May I call you Amanda?"

"Please do."

"Great. We're going to Little Haiti posing as friends. This little dog in the basket is a big part of my plan."

Relieved that the dog had a purpose and that Lauren wasn't just a neurotic owner who couldn't separate herself from her pet, Amanda's curiosity was aroused.

"How does the dog fit in?"

"My arms are getting tired from carrying this basket. Let's get in the car and I'll tell you more on the way," Lauren suggested. "We need to find out more about the so-called voodoo priestess. Teacup is an integral part of the plan. She'll be playing the role of a dog that's been put under a spell. Take us to Little Haiti."

After removing the car seat from her Honda and reconnecting it in Detective Banks's white Suzuki's Swift Sport, Teacup was once again strapped into her doggie car seat behind the driver's side, enabling Lauren to check on her. Detective Banks was anxious to hear Lauren's ideas and further explanation about the dog's role. She was totally unprepared for Lauren's next request.

"Oh, by the way, Amanda, can you play some country music? Teacup would really appreciate it."

The list of oddities about the case just got longer. Detective Banks was beginning to have second thoughts.

CHAPTER 21

Walter and Vivian Raines, retirees from New Jersey, decided to beat other tourists and visit South Beach before the winter holidays began in earnest. A massive influx of people fleeing the cold weather would soon be descending upon South Florida. Celebrating forty years of marriage, they decided to do it right and booked a luxury suite at the Loews Miami Beach Hotel – South Beach. Located on Collins Avenue, this beachfront hotel is in the heart of South Beach; from the hotel, it's an easy walk to the Lincoln Road Mall, a famous pedestrian mall with shopping, restaurants, and nightlife. When Walter was researching hotels, he wasn't certain whether the shopping and dining on Lincoln Road or the beach access and spa at the hotel would thrill Vivian more. After forty years of putting up with him, Walter figured that Vivian deserved a wonderful vacation.

Uncharacteristically, Walter decided that cost was no object. But old habits die hard, and Walter planned the second part of the trip with a small degree of his typical frugality. As proof, he booked a Caribbean cruise leaving from the Port of Miami after their stay in South Beach in order to avoid additional travel expenses to fly down a second time. The combination vacation would be his way of saying thanks to his wife and sweetheart of four decades.

He sprung for a suite with a king-size bed and a balcony that allowed them to enjoy a view of the beach and the sparkling aquamarine water of the Atlantic Ocean. As the taxi from the airport approached the hotel, he saw that the website's description of their location was accurate. Access to South Beach's night life and the Lincoln Road Mall was just a few footsteps away. If not for wanting to unpack, Vivian would probably have asked to be dropped off on Lincoln Road.

Upon entering the suite, Walter couldn't have been more pleased with himself. Vivian's reaction was exactly what he'd hoped it would be. After letting out a joyous scream, she was speechless for a few minutes. Very atypical behavior for her. But then, she wasn't used to Walter spending money this frivolously. She could easily get used to the new Walter. If she didn't trust him implicitly, she might have thought that he was having an affair and was acting out of guilt. To her, that idea was ludicrous.

Being married for forty years was a milestone, and he was behaving accordingly. Once again, she reaffirmed that she made the right decision to accept his proposal so many years before. Walking over to her husband, she smiled and put her arms around him. They didn't reach as far as they did forty years ago, but despite the added pounds, she still found Walter attractive. She couldn't imagine being married to anyone else.

"I love you, Walter. This is beyond my wildest expectation."

To prove the point, she began exploring the suite, taking in its many amenities. It took her several minutes to regain her composure as she discovered all the luxurious accoutrements provided for guests. When she entered the larger of the two bathrooms and fingered the plush Turkish terrycloth robes and slipped her feet into the waffle-weave bath slippers, she declared that she wasn't sure that she was ever leaving the suite.

"Not even to go shopping on Lincoln Road?" Walter teased.

She had taken out her cell phone and was photographing everything, as she chuckled at Walter's comment. He knew her well. Like a realtor working with a prospective client, she was pointing out the unique features of the suite to her husband.

"Walter, look at this. There's a second bathroom off the living room area. The one connected to the bedroom has a tub with jets. Come over here and see the wet bar. You won't believe the view from the balcony. It's amazing. And the color of the ocean..."

As she spoke, she walked out onto the balcony, drinking in the sunshine, the beautiful ocean breeze, and the waves breaking gently onto the shore.

Strolling the entire length of the balcony, she photographed the scenery from every possible angle with her cell phone. "The kids will never believe this. I'm not sure that I even believe it."

After beginning the day at 4 a.m. for their early morning flight, Vivian couldn't resist the lure of the lounge chair on the balcony. She closed her eyes but was still smiling, a cat-that-ate-the-canary smile.

"I feel like I died and went to heaven," she remarked.

Ironically, she had no idea how prophetic that comment was to be.

CHAPTER 22

A white Suzuki Swift Sport with an undercover police detective, a full-time accountant trying her hand at investigation, and a pampered miniature yorkie headed south on I-95. It sounded like the lead-in to a joke, but what they were doing was serious. Their destination was Little Haiti, their mission to uncover the true story of a proclaimed voodoo priestess whose motive for offering to help the police seemed dubious.

Lauren had never driven in any Suzuki, let alone this model, and she was pleasantly surprised. As promised by Detective Banks, the car had more power than Lauren anticipated, a definite bonus when several crazy Florida drivers zigzagged across lanes, requiring Amanda to rev up her engine to avoid what could have been two fender benders.

Fortunately, the drive to Little Haiti was a short one. This section of the city is a stone's throw from the popular tourist destinations of Wynwood and the Design District of Miami. The street art on the buildings in Wynwood have defined the area with their colorful graffiti-like murals. It's difficult to determine the underlying color of the buildings, as the murals fill all exposed surfaces. Restaurants, galleries, and a pulsing street life characterize the area.

The neighborhood is also becoming a popular destination for visitors. It has a colorful history and is a unique blend of Afro-Caribbean culture. Haitian exiles have gravitated to the area, their influence apparent in the restaurants, grocery stores, the language spoken on the street, and other cultural aspects that originate from their homeland. The neighborhoods previously known as Lemon City, Little River, and Edison became designated by Miami Commissioners in 2016 as Little Haiti, now the official name.

"Okay, Lauren. I think it's about time that you tell me your plan. Not that I don't find her adorable, but how does Teacup fit in?"

"Teacup is going to be the ruse for our search for Priestess Julia. Depending on how the visit goes, we may have to improvise a bit, but I have a few fallback ideas."

"Always good to have a Plan B." Detective Banks was beginning to think that Lauren's training in accounting might prove helpful in thinking logically and methodically. It couldn't hurt.

"My goal is to find out whether Priestess Julia is a mambo or voodoo priestess from Haiti as she claims," Lauren explained. "We'll go into one of the voodoo shops and tell them that Teacup has been cursed. After I lay it on thick about Teacup's problems, I'll explain that I was told to ask for Priestess Julia to remove the spell. When I mention the recommendation, I'm sure that someone here will point us in the right direction. That is, if Priestess Julia is what she says she is. Let's see if anyone here knows of her."

Lauren sounded certain that her plan would work. She was positive that Teacup would elicit sympathy and the information about Julia would be forthcoming without difficulty.

Amanda knew better.

"Sheer genius. What could go wrong?" Lauren didn't detect the sarcasm in the detective's voice.

****

Amanda drove past the Monument of Toussaint L'Ouverture, the man considered the leader of the Haitian Revolution. Atop a large pedestal with a plaque in English, Haitian Creole, and French paying homage to his accomplishments, the seven-feet-tall bronze statue of the revolutionary hero stands at the corner of North Miami Avenue and 62nd Street in the center of the community. Having done some searches online, Lauren directed Amanda to their destination, the Botanica Healing Store, the most popular of Little Haiti's voodoo and Santeria shops. Fortunately, it was easy to park. The two women exited the vehicle, releasing Teacup from her restraints.

The threesome entered the doors of the store, with Teacup perched like royalty on her cushion in her custom basket. You can treat a dog like a human, but ultimately, it behaves like a dog. Evidently, something unpleasant caught Teacup's attention. Her ears perked up and she started barking in short staccato barks. The volume was increasing and the intervals between the barks were decreasing. Not well-versed in decoding Teacup's articulations, Lauren wished that Eve had given her some lessons in dog language. However, Teacup's reaction and incessant barking might just turn out to be a good thing; the dog might be able to do a convincing act as being cursed by a spell.

Lauren scanned the selves, walls, and tables in the shop. She was struck by the mix of scents and colors. There were multicolored scarves and bolts of fabric displayed neatly on a table. The pottery seemed primarily utilitarian, featuring mostly mortars and pestles. Lauren surmised that these were probably used for mixing potions.

The scents came from the many oils, plants, herbs, and candles used in various rituals. One cabinet mounted on the wall contained hundreds of small bottles of spiritual oils, labeled and sorted by type, with a chart underneath explaining the benefit of each type of oil. A huge table contained a collection of roots and herbs, arranged in long rows that were aesthetically pleasing. Again, there was a chart identifying these items with their names and medicinal or magical properties. The next table that Lauren observed contained a mosaic of candles. The entire top of the table was covered with various colors and shapes of aromatic candles, some of which were burning, contributing to the indefinable aroma in the shop. Fortunately, although no one aroma overpowered the others, it was a combination that she found pleasant. Maybe it wasn't pleasant to Teacup. No way to tell.

The product line was interesting, to say the least. The next collection that caught Lauren's attention was a wall on which an assortment of brooms was mounted. There were broom handles in a rainbow of colors, handle lengths, and bristle types. The way the brooms were mounted appeared deliberately artistic. In Lauren's opinion, removing a broom would destroy a work of art.

Again, a sign identified the preferred broom for a specific need. Not only utilized for sweeping a person's home clean of dirt, these brooms had the power to rid a person's home of evil spirits. If you believed in this stuff.

Lauren seemed thoroughly engaged in looking around the shop, but Amanda was becoming impatient. Frankly, she was beginning to wonder whether this was a wild goose chase. She was starting to resent being sent along as Lauren's babysitter because of her relationship to Detective Mandich. It didn't help that Teacup was continuing to bark without taking a break. The dog was getting on her nerves. Honestly, the yorkie was too prissy for Amanda's tastes. She'd prefer a dog that liked getting down and dirty.

Finally, Teacup's bark brought Marie, the shop's owner, out from a back room to great her potential customers. A brass meditation-bell wind chime was mounted over the door so that the bells gently tinkled when she opened the door and entered the retail portion of the building.

"How may I help you ladies? I'm Marie, the owner of Botanica Healing."

Lauren judged Marie to be in her early fifties. She was a slim woman, approximately five feet, three inches tall, and probably weighed no more than 105 pounds. Her skin was the color of coffee with just a touch of milk. She wore a pair of glasses that fit the shape of her face perfectly. It was obvious from her appearance that she was the one who arranged the displays. Wrapped around a simple rust colored round-neck T-shirt, Marie had draped one of her beautiful scarves with a pattern of gold, orange, and brown leaves. The colors set off the rust in the T-shirt perfectly, and the way it was draped made Lauren envious of the woman's sense of style. From the way she accessorized her own attire, Marie was the perfect person to sell the merchandise in her store.

"Hello, Marie. I'm Lauren and my friend is Amanda. And my little princess is Teacup. Your shop is amazing. Your website doesn't do it justice. I certainly won't leave without buying one of your gorgeous scarves, as long as you show me how you draped it. It looks amazing on you," Lauren's stated enthusiastically.

Marie gave her a big smile that revealed a set of perfectly aligned white teeth. The lipstick color she had chosen also enhanced her appearance. She headed toward the display table with the scarves, intent on helping Lauren select something that would complement her coloring. Before she got that far, Lauren mentioned another item that she wanted to purchase.

"I also think I need one of your cleansing brooms. But first, I need help with a sensitive matter," said Lauren.

Marie responded with compassion.

"I often deal in matters of that nature. How can I be of service?"

"I hope you can help poor little Teacup."

Lauren glanced at the dog who had not stopped barking, although she had reduced the volume and the frequency. Whatever had set her off in the shop continued to bother her. She was wearing herself out.

"Is she not well? I sensed something in her bark."

Putting all her theatrical skills to good use, Lauren recounted a fabricated story about her unfortunate dog. Lauren felt guilty deceiving Marie, but it had to be done.

"My neighbor hates her. To punish my sweet Teacup, she put a curse on her. The woman insists that Teacup's barks keep her up at night. I can tell you that there is no way she can hear Teacup. The walls are insulated and Teacup only barks when she's provoked by something. At night, we're inside and she rarely makes any noise at all. She cuddles with me and falls asleep in my arms. Personally, I just think my neighbor has it in for dogs," Lauren stated.

"Ever since the curse, Teacup's taste buds no longer work. I bake little Teacup special homemade doggie biscuits, her favorite snack. She can't even enjoy *them* anymore. This crazy woman cursed her and bragged to me that she did. What kind of person puts a hex on a dog?"

Lauren was really laying it on thick. Amanda had to walk away because she worried that she'd burst out laughing. Fortunately, Marie had a kind heart. She was buying everything that Lauren was selling.

"We have many potions to remove such things. Let me show you."

As Marie began walking toward the appropriate display in the store, Lauren stopped her in her tracks.

"Please forgive me. I don't mean to insult you, but my Teacup deserves only the best. My husband works closely with the Miami police. According to him, they are using Priestess Julia for help in their cases. That says to me that she must be the best, and that's what my little Teacup deserves. I need to meet Priestess Julia face-to-face."

Without taking offence, Marie asked, "What makes you think that I can arrange this?"

"I was hoping that you'd know her. My attempts to try to speak with her have failed. She has a website that provides her phone number, email address, and post office box address; I've tried contacting her by all three. When I called the phone number multiple times at different hours of the day, I never reached anything other than a recording. Despite leaving messages, I never received a call back. The website advises that clients can ask questions only after they share their credit card information via email with Priestess Julia. It made me a little uneasy."

"But how can I help?" asked Marie.

"When I asked around, I was told that your store has the best reputation in Little Haiti. I was hoping that Priestess Julia shops here. Or perhaps, that you might know her. Have any of your clients mentioned using her services? Do you think that she is legitimate? Can you help me? I'm desperate. Poor Teacup isn't herself. Is there a way that you can you get Priestess Julia to meet with me?"

Amanda waited for Lauren to finish her spiel and jumped right in. "I know my friend. Lauren won't rest easy until she meets with Priestess Julia herself. Please help her. She's driving herself and me crazy. Seriously, if you could set up a meeting with Priestess Julia, not only would you be helping Teacup, but you'd be helping me retain my sanity," added Amanda, playing along with Lauren's ruse.

Lauren nodded her head in agreement. Amanda appealed to Marie's compassion for Lauren, for the dog, and for Lauren's supportive friend. If Marie knew Priestess Julia, she surely would offer to contact her on their behalf.

"I'm afraid that I cannot help you. I know pretty much every priest or priestess in Little Haiti even if they aren't customers. Since I don't know her and haven't heard her name mentioned by my customers, I have serious doubts that she is what she says she is."

Lauren wasn't overly surprised that Marie hadn't heard of Priestess Julia. She trusted that Marie had no reason to lie or to cover for the woman. In fact, it confirmed what Lauren expected since she doubted that the woman calling herself "Priestess Julia" was a priestess. Moreover, her name might not even be Julia.

Lauren's ploy to find Julia using the tale about Teacup and the spell was to no avail. Time to get Eve's pampered pet back to her owner. All Lauren accomplished was to realize that she had no desire to be a dog owner. Certainly, not if it required all the attention that Eve lavished on Teacup. *Not my cup of tea,* thought Lauren.

Then Lauren laughed to herself for that thought; the yorkie's name was so perfect. Already Lauren's mood lightened.

With the attitude "When in Rome, do as the Romans do," Lauren proceeded to the table with the colorful scarves. Marie's assistance in choosing a scarf and teaching her how to drape it in a unique manner did not disappoint.

Lauren was a firm believer in retail therapy.

CHAPTER 23

Walter and Vivian Raines, the tourists from New Jersey, were ecstatic with their decision to take a Florida vacation followed by a Caribbean cruise. They planned to celebrate the milestone of their forty years together in style. Getting out of the northeast in the winter was a bonus. From mid-December until after New Year's Day, they would bask in sunshine and mild temperatures. They selected the departure date of their cruise so that they would celebrate Christmas, New Year's Eve, and their anniversary on the ship. What could be better?

The stay in South Beach, part one of the vacation, would have qualified as a spectacular celebration, even without the cruise to follow. The trip of a lifetime was getting off to a promising start.

Still seated on the balcony in the lounge chairs, they both scrolled through the news on their respective iPhones. It appeared that they left from Newark Airport just in time. Hours after their flight departed, the airport was shut down due to blizzard conditions.

When they watched the video feeds of the storm hitting the east coast, they found even more reason to congratulate themselves on their impeccable timing and on money well spent. Photos of homes and businesses blanketed with snow, reports of dangerous road conditions, and announcements of the sub-freezing temperatures up north gave them cause to celebrate and pat themselves on the back.

"Not only am I glad to be out of New Jersey, but you picked an incredible hotel," gushed Vivian. "This is what I'd have to call living in the lap of luxury."

She pointed to the beachfront below with the enormous swimming pool flanked by a pool deck with what appeared to be hundreds of beach chairs. Cabanas, daybeds, a children's pool, as well as a hot tub occupied a portion of the pool deck area. Hotel guests in bathing suits sat on barstools at an outdoor bar that served the sunbathers.

"If you think this is something, I reserved a special spa suite with an ocean view for the two of us tomorrow morning," Walter informed her. "We'll be relaxing in our own spa suite with massages, soft music, champagne, and even a butler to tend to our needs. It'll be like the lives of the rich and famous for two hours."

"Wally, I've never seen this side of you before, but I'm loving it!"

"You deserve it, Viv. I mean that sincerely. Forty years being married to me hasn't always been a picnic. I planned this second honeymoon to show you how much you mean to me. Money is no object. The sky's the limit."

Vivian resisted the urge to walk over to Walter and place her hand on his forehead to check whether he had a fever. This was such atypical behavior for her husband. Instead, she decided to take his words at face value and just enjoy the new Walter. Maybe the next forty years, if they were fortunate enough to live that long, would continue with his new attitude.

Instead of placing her hand on his forehead, she walked over to him and placed her hand on his heart. She then kissed him on the lips and declared, "I love you."

Making her happy was Walter's goal for this vacation. His next suggestion would achieve that objective as well as satisfy one of his immediate needs as well.

"I don't know about you, Viv, but I'm starving. That crummy sandwich we picked up at the airport had almost no meat at all. It was basically a bread sandwich with mustard and lettuce. Let's put on some shorts, take a quick look at the pool area, and walk over to the Lincoln Road Mall. We'll find some food for me and shopping for you."

"Sounds like a plan. Let's eat before we shop," Vivian suggested. From forty years of experience with Walter, she knew that if he were hungry, he'd have little patience for shopping. With food in his stomach, he'd be content to let her indulge in one of her favorite pastimes. It worked every time.

They walked through the lobby to the massive pool area. It was more beautiful than any they had ever seen before, even more impressive than at the hotels in Hawaii. There were people lounging on beach chairs, loads of children in the kiddie pool supervised by parents sitting on the pool coping, and others soaking in the hot tub.

"Maybe after eating and shopping we can rent a cabana, big spender?" joked Vivian. She was in vacation mode and wanted to see if Walter was serious about "the sky's the limit" philosophy.

"If you're up to it when we get back from Lincoln Road, it's fine by me. Let's get going. My stomach is growling," Walter replied.

Not wanting to spoil the mood and knowing that Walter could get cantankerous when hungry or tired, Vivian quickly pulled a pair of shorts and a top from her suitcase and was ready within five minutes. The Lincoln Road pedestrian mall was within walking distance. Behaving like newlyweds, they held hands as they strolled. Not until they sat down at one of the outdoor Cuban cafes did they release their clasped fingers. They sat under one of the large pastel umbrellas and perused the menu.

Like tourists who had done some research about their destination, they selected the Cuban sandwich made the authentic way. You couldn't visit Miami without experiencing this signature sandwich which included sliced ham, Cuban-style roast pork, Swiss cheese, mustard, and dill pickles on buttered Cuban bread. Typically, the sandwich was prepared on a Panini press to make it hot and crispy. Their mouths were watering even as they read the description.

After taking his first bite, Walter moaned with pleasure. Before the vacation, Vivian promised herself she'd watch her caloric intake so the clothes she packed would continue to fit. However, after smelling the platter set in front of her, she decided to enjoy herself. Once she bit into the sandwich, she informed Walter that this was a creation that was well worth the calories.

"My new motto for this vacation is 'You only live once' and I'm going to enjoy everything to the fullest."

As they devoured their sandwiches along with the beans and rice on the platter, they took in the unique sights of the area. Due to the foresight of developers, the mile-long street had been converted to a promenade allowing no vehicular traffic. It was a haven for pedestrians as well as their pets. Many stores had bowls of drinking water for animals placed on the pavement outside their entrances. People seemed to parade their well-groomed dogs as if they were being exhibited at an American Kennel Club show.

Normally, Walter tended to avoid animals that were strangers to him. He tolerated his children's pets, but just barely. At first, he was taken aback by the people who sat their pets on chairs at the outdoor tables or kept them at their feet while they dined. Seeing dogs in clothing that probably cost as much as his own, Walter was astounded by the animals who seemed so nonchalant at being in human-style apparel. What really cracked him up were the dogs who wore sunglasses and visors. Only in Florida.

In addition to numerous dining establishments featuring a multitude of ethnic foods, traditional brand-name stores alternated with local specialty shops along the walkways. Several art galleries, souvenir shops with T-shirts and beachwear advertising Miami, and both colored and white lights illuminating the fronds and the trunks of the palms on the tree-lined streets added to the unique South Florida flavor of Lincoln Road.

People watching seemed to be an activity enjoyed by tourists as well as locals. Back home, Vivian often engaged in a game of "fashion police" with friends; they found a bench at a mall and commented on the clothing of other shoppers as they passed by. In New Jersey, this didn't interest Walter too much, but it was entirely different for him on Lincoln Road.

Fortunately for Walter, it was a warm December day that required minimal outer wear. Pretending not to be looking, Walter enjoyed some of Florida's beautiful women strolling or roller blading while wearing bathing suits or skimpy shorts and revealing fabric tops designed to cover only the most essential body parts. These predominantly young and nubile specimens strutted down the street, looking as if they were about to participate in a fashion photo shoot.

As Walter was paying the bill, Vivian spotted a women's clothing store with an enticing window display. In her coquettish way, she led Walter, who was again holding her hand, into the store. In a matter of minutes, she selected a lightweight shawl that was artfully draped over her shoulders. She twirled and modeled for her husband.

"What do you think, Wally? You know the temperature change here is unpredictable. It may be warm in the sunshine but freezing in the air conditioning. It has all the colors I love, and the cost is so reasonable. This is perfect, plus it fits in my purse. I know I'll get lots of wear out of it."

Vivian didn't need to justify the purchase to Walter. Glad that such a trinket could make his wife happy, Walter gave an enthusiastic approval and insisted that he buy it for her.

"Wally, I love this vacation and I love you. I am so happy. Thanks for going the extra mile."

"Just so you know, I love you more."

He often made the same retort to her declaration of love, but it always touched her, regardless of how many times he said it. While shopping invigorated Vivian, it wore Walter out. Taking pity on him, she readily agreed to his next suggestion.

"How about we go back to the hotel now? You can go for a swim while I nap in our poolside cabana. I decided to act on your earlier suggestion and reserved one while you were going through the clothing racks."

If Walter hadn't been with her, she could have shopped until dinner time. However, he had been so loving and generous, she wanted to please him. Probably why they stayed married for forty years.

"I think a swim sounds great. After that Cuban sandwich platter, it wouldn't hurt to work off some calories."

Not surprisingly, Walter fell asleep in the cabana. Vivian swam for a brief time and then read a novel as she relaxed next to him. What was surprising was that she fell asleep as well. Now they would be on the same schedule, both having recharged their batteries with a nap. The rest gave them more incentive to plan an evening that would keep them out until the wee hours of the morning. After all, they were in the Magic City.

Wanting to experience everything that they heard or read about South Beach, they planned to check out the nightclub scene. Walter suggested that they walk, find a place to dine, and afterwards visit a club.

Vivian was thrilled to have a chance to put on her nicest outfit. Before the trip, she had splurged on a new "little black dress" which the saleswoman assured her was the height of fashion. Although, like most women, she had a collection of "little black dresses," this one was a cold shoulder style. When she slipped into it in the dressing room of the store, the dress made her feel pretty and sexy. Two excellent reasons to spent more than usual.

She had no regrets about her purchase. Paired with a new pair of black strappy sandals and glittery silver jewelry, Vivian was pleased when she saw her reflection in the full-length mirror. Seeing how she was dressed, Walter quickly changed into nicer pants and a collared shirt. Jeans would have been more comfortable, but Walter knew it would make her happy if he dressed up as well.

Even after forty years, Walter was still sexually attracted to Vivian. Her new dress certainly pleased him. He was already imagining helping her remove it later in the evening.

The hotel concierge suggested several restaurants in an area near some of the more popular clubs. He then signaled to one of the valets call a cab for them. Their excitement mounted as they slowly traversed the streets that were bogged down with traffic. "It looks like Times Square on New Year's Eve," Walter commented.

After exiting the cab, their ears were assaulted with deafening noise and the pounding beat of electronically generated music from within the clubs; that was just what they heard from the street. They could only imagine what it must be like inside. They were unwilling to find out.

Their earlier excitement turned to disappointment with the realization that they were out of place. The people entering the clubs appeared to be decades younger than they were. The clothing showed blatant generational differences. When Vivian looked at the club patrons, she felt as if she were dressed like a Puritan. The revealing tops that showed more breast tissue than they covered, and the short Lycra skirts and dresses that hugged the derriere, leaving nothing to the imagination, contrasted with Vivian's dress with the cold shoulder top that Vivian had considered as "sexy" earlier. Vivian's strappy sandals couldn't compete with the at least six-inch stiletto heels worn by the young women. The prevalence of tattoos covering entire arms, the heavy kohl eye makeup, and the hair color in all shades of the rainbow contributed to the couple's decision to forego the club scene.

Gazing at each other, they shook their heads as they simultaneously verbalized, "Not for us."

Walter reached for Vivian's hand. They decided to walk until they found a quieter location to dine. According to the concierge, there were several fashionable restaurants in the area where the cab had dropped them off. Making the best of the evening, they entered a restaurant that didn't have loud music emanating from the interior, and from whose window they noticed cloth covered tables set with candles. Even better, it wasn't filled to capacity with patrons half their age and even younger. They lingered over their dinner, enjoying each other's company.

The next morning, a couple from New Jersey was found murdered behind a nightclub on South Beach, apparent victims of the Dead of Night killer.

CHAPTER 24

Carmen Gutierrez, an assistant to Miami City Councilman Kyle Griffin, was anxious for her boss to arrive. The councilman was ambitious, hoping to depose Mayor Robert Diaz in the next mayoral election. With ambitions of her own, Carmen hoped to ride Griffin's coattails.

Griffin was skilled at avoiding work while giving the impression that he was a tireless worker. In fairness to him, he was the master of delegating assignments to the right person. Unfortunately for that person, Griffin then took the credit. Based upon his track record of successes, he had high aspirations of being elected mayor.

In the past, Carmen had proven herself to be an asset to Griffin in his quest to garner publicity and create name recognition. Both abilities would be indispensable if he were to run a successful campaign against a popular incumbent. One of Carmen's daily tasks was to read, print, and sort his emails in order of priority if she determined that they would further his goal. One email this morning caught her attention as being of special interest. She printed in and placed it at the top of the pile.

At 8 a.m. sharp Councilman Griffin entered his office. Although he dressed at home and went directly to his office, he created the impression that he had already put in hours on the job. In his mid-thirties, Griffin had a full head of sandy brown hair which usually appeared tousled, as if he had run his fingers through his scalp as he contemplated serious issues of government. Carmen always found it amusing that Kyle's standard mode of attire included a solid-colored long sleeve shirt with the top button unbuttoned, his tie loosely knotted, and the cuffs rolled up to reveal his muscular forearms. His public relations people had once suggested that this look made him appear both sexy and hard working. That was the image that he sought. Being both trim and young, he easily pulled off the look. Young female voters were especially drawn to him.

Carmen greeted her boss with his daily tiny cup of Cuban coffee, an acquired taste for him. The first time that she served it to him in a cup that he judged to be about the size of a thimble, he practically gagged on the strong and syrupy brew. He mistakenly drank it all at once, like a shot of alcohol. It was so much stronger than American coffee that he quickly understood why it was specifically served in such a small cup. Carmen explained that the demographics of his district called for him being seen drinking Cuban coffee.

Image was everything. He drank his Cuban coffee each morning in the customary small espresso cup, deliberately leaving the cup on his desk should any constituents visit his office. He made it a point to be photographed often in local Cuban restaurants while holding this caffeine-laden drink in his hand. Every effort was made to endear him to the heavily Cuban population.

Depositing the cup on his desk, Griffin noticed that Carmen seemed unusually keyed up this morning. After delivering the coffee, she poked her head into his office several times already, the heels of her stilettos clacking on the floor with each approach. Her excitement was almost impossible to suppress.

"Carmen, what's up with you this morning? You seem like a kid on Christmas morning, ready to tear into the gifts under the tree. How many Cuban coffees have you already had?

"Just one. It's not the coffee. It's one of the emails that's got me wired. It's the top one on the pile."

"Now I'm intrigued." He beckoned for her to enter his office. "Let's take a look."

Griffin's thoughts and his words were at odds with each other. The news in the email presented him with the ammunition his campaign needed, but he had to maintain a façade of sympathy and concern. Trying to hide his glee, the councilman said, "This is terrible. Two tourists are dead. Has this hit the papers yet?"

"No, sir. Their bodies were found only hours ago."

"Call a press conference for this afternoon. With these additional two murders added to the others and the increasingly negative publicity for Miami, Mayor Diaz is going to have a hard time with his re-election bid. My chances are looking better and better."

Carmen wasn't at all surprised by Griffin's reaction. When she read the email earlier, she predicted his reaction. Oddly, she hadn't recognized the email address of the sender, especially since the information related to a crime. That struck her as unusual. She acted on her curiosity.

"Sir, I see that the email came from an iCloud account from 'graysquirrel305,' an e mail I'm not familiar with. Who is that? And why did he send it to you?"

Griffin wasn't about to reveal his source. He cut her off from asking further questions in an abrupt tone as he said, "Sorry, some things are private."

****

With a podium, an audience, and an agenda, there was no one was better than Councilman Kyle Griffin at stirring up support for his cause. His agenda was clear. He set out to embarrass Robert Diaz, the current mayor of Miami.

Griffin painted a grim picture. His description of the victims was graphic, providing more information to the public than was typical from someone outside the chain of command of the police department. He did not hesitate to divulge that when the bodies were found, the internal organs were missing. This information had not previously been disclosed to the media, partly to keep some information from the crazies who might present themselves to the police with false confessions. The other reason was to avoid the mass hysteria that Councilman Griffin had so eagerly created.

After providing this gruesome visual image, Griffin elaborated on other issues that would inflame the public. If the current mayor couldn't keep the city safe for residents and tourists, every business would suffer. Economic woes would affect everyone.

The rhetoric was not lost on the press or the widespread television audience. All the local news channels picked up the press conference. The segment of Griffin's speech in which he elaborated on the gruesome murders and his warning of the dire consequences for the local economy was recycled every hour on the hour. The press conference was a blatant attempt to foment further dissatisfaction with the current mayor. No one in the community could have avoided watching his performance. "Performance" was truly the operative word.

Even those in the hierarchy of the police department had caught at least one cycle of the news with the staged outrage of Councilman Griffin. They all awaited what they knew would be sharp criticism from their superiors. Surely, Mayor Diaz wouldn't take this obvious rebuke of his handling of the murders sitting down.

As expected, the mayor was displeased with the unmistakable attempt of Councilman Griffin to turn this into a campaign issue. Prior to the recent murder of the two tourists, the mayor had already come down hard on the police commissioner to apprehend the Dead of Night killer. With or without this additional negative publicity from Griffin, Diaz would take decisive action. He immediately placed a call to Police Commissioner Inez Vargas, demanding investigation and results.

That call instigated other communications down the chain of command. After filtration through the police hierarchy, the problem ultimately landed in the laps of Detective Mandich and Detective Dennison. They caught clips of the press conference and anticipated that when Sergeant Hernandez tasked them with extra responsibilities and hours, they'd be subject to a lecture full of colorful expletives that would not be G rated. Hernandez didn't disappoint.

Returning to their desks, Brad and Lew compared their opinions concerning the purpose behind Griffin's press conference. Lew expressed his disgust, saying, "Kyle Griffin isn't doing anything to *solve* this problem. He's just turning it into a way to make the mayor look bad. He just got a free campaign rally from a tragic situation."

"You got that right," responded Mandich. "How the hell do you think he knows as much as he does? Who told him about the missing organs?"

"I was wondering that myself."

"Doesn't make me happy. Seems to me that he has someone inside the department feeding information to him."

Lew shook his head in agreement. There was clearly a leak in the department. Both men were disturbed by this.

"I'm going to run this by Cliff and see if he saw the press conference," Brad stated. "I'd like an unbiased view. Maybe as cops, we're too suspicious."

As he spoke, Brad pulled out his cell phone. He heard the word "hello" immediately.

"Hi, Cliff. By any chance, have you been watching TV this afternoon?"

CHAPTER 25

I have always been a believer in telepathic communications with people in my family. Sometimes Lauren and I communicate from afar without verbally contacting each other. There have been numerous times that as soon as she arrives at home, I suggest eating dinner out. She swears that she put the idea in my head just by thinking about it during her drive.

Today I felt that my uncle was part of this nonverbal communication network. I had just caught the tail end of Councilman Griffin's press conference. No big fan of his, I thought that today he had sunk to a new low. Using the death of two tourists to further his career was unconscionable. I was about to call Uncle Brad to get more details about the murders when my cell phone rang.

"Hi Unc," I said, instantly recognizing the caller. His ringtone, the theme music from "Miami Vice," played loudly. "You're not going to believe this, but I was just about to call you."

Without waiting for me to say another word, he jumped right in.

"Did you happen to see the shitty press conference that asshole Griffin just gave?"

"That's why I had the phone in my hand when it rang," I stated. "Griffin seemed emotionally detached from the fact that two more people tragically lost their lives. They only mattered to him as a PR opportunity. A real humanitarian," I said sarcastically.

"This isn't the first time that he's tried to grab the spotlight."

"Did the police notify his office about the murders with the degree of detail that he described on the news? Is that normal, or is it just that I can't stand the man and I'm suspicious of anything he does?"

I found it strange that Griffin was privy to so much information. Furthermore, it was disgusting that he didn't filter what he said while speaking on television. He appeared to be deliberately creating panic for nothing more than personal gain.

"Well, Cliff, your instincts are right on target. There is no way he should have been able to call a press conference that quickly and disseminate information that we don't want released at this point in our investigation. That's why I was calling you. Lew and I wanted your take on things."

Brad and Lew had valid reasons to distrust the councilman. If what my uncle said was accurate, and I had no reason to think otherwise, then Griffin had to be getting information from someone on the inside.

I considered a few possibilities, some of which seemed far-fetched even to me. Either Griffin had a mole in the department, was in cahoots with the killer, or was the killer himself. When I proposed these scenarios, Uncle Brad didn't contradict anything I said. He had considered similar explanations. Before I could ask how I could help, he quickly terminated the phone call.

"Gotta go. Sergeant Hernandez is beeping into my phone. It's gonna be a long day."

I turned up the volume on the TV and watched a few sound bites from the press conference. The newscasters were focusing on the killing and mutilation of the unfortunate tourists. There were multiple clips taken from Griffin's speech.

Then I turned off the volume completely, wanting to focus on Griffin's facial expressions and body language. There was no empathy or sadness apparent when he discussed the deaths, but his diatribe against the mayor seemed to invigorate him. He waved his hands as he pointed furiously into the camera. Shaking his head vigorously, you could see the anger in his face.

Griffin was a master at utilizing publicity to his advantage. It was a sickening display of a politician profiting from a horrific crime. I returned to my suppositions as to how he knew so much, so far in advance of the normal notification process. My three choices all included activities that were not within the boundaries of the law.

Not one of those alternatives was comforting.

CHAPTER 26

Katrina Bell, one of Tiffany & Company's fastest rising executives, should have been sitting contentedly in her New York Fifth Avenue office, but she was not. Sales from her division were several percentage points ahead of her predecessors and it was only mid-December; the last-minute Christmas sales just prior to the holidays were not even part of the statistics. Based upon the period beginning with Thanksgiving and Black Friday, the revenue projections for the holidays would translate into a huge end-of-the-year bonus for her. Sales were expected to go through the roof.

Due to her position in the company, her speaking ability, her professional demeanor, and her sales figures, Katrina had been selected to go to Miami to deliver the Super Bowl trophy that would be presented to the winning team on the first Sunday in February. At work, Katrina wore her natural auburn hair in a chic bun with a few loose tendrils framing her face. In her mid-thirties, she ignored faddish clothing trends and was always stylishly dressed in tailored clothing, frequently in various shades of green, which was flattering to her coloring. She accessorized with pumps and handbags that complemented her attire without making their own fashion statement. A simple strand of signature Tiffany pearls was often her only piece of jewelry. Her tailored and understated appearance reflected the taste of many longstanding Tiffany's customers. She was the perfect candidate to represent the iconic jewelry maker whose patrons reached back many generations within families.

Television interviews would be scheduled at the stadium for the Friday night before the game. An articulate speaker,

Katrina would then deliver the trophy to the Tiffany & Company's store in the posh shops of Bal Harbor on Saturday morning for a viewing by the public. The prestigious jewelry company had been supplying the Super Bowl trophy ever since 1966 when Tiffany & Company's Vice President Oscar Riedner sketched the design during lunch with Pete Rozelle, the reigning National Football League's commissioner. In 1970, as a tribute to the memory of National Football League icon Vince Lombardi, the trophy became known as the Vince Lombardi Trophy.

Normally, Katrina would have been counting the days until she could transport the trophy to Miami where this football season's championship game would be played. It was a fantastic opportunity for her on so many levels. Acknowledgment of her success within the company, the faith entrusted to her because she had proven that she was worthy of the level of responsibility this job required, and being the face of Tiffany & Company on the world stage made her proud of all she had achieved.

Delivering the trophy had personal benefits as well. Getting out of New York during the winter would have been more than enough of a reward. However, that was only a small part of what she regarded as subsidiary benefits. Premium seats at a Super Bowl game was enough to impress even a person with little interest in football; she was entitled to two such seats as part of the perks of this task. All the hoopla and excitement surrounding the game more than made up for her basic lack of interest in the sport. In addition, she'd be able to bring her boyfriend as her guest. If that didn't earn her points with him, nothing would.

Katrina hated to admit to herself that her boyfriend, Steve, was a guy with serious commitment issues. Although they had been sharing an apartment for the last seven years, and despite periodic hints on her part about marriage and children, he seemed more than happy with their current arrangement. There was no talk about taking their relationship to the next level.

In her mind, this trip would be a turning point, one way or the other. While she didn't relish rocking the boat, her biological clock was ticking. Katrina pushed aside thoughts that she might have to deliver an ultimatum to Steve, hoping that the excitement of the Super Bowl and her role in transporting the trophy and securing VIP seats would make him see her as a trophy in her own right.

Since being selected to bring the trophy to Miami, Katrina had been fantasizing about Steve's reaction. Perhaps the experience would seal the deal. Maybe the Super Bowl rings wouldn't be the only rings in play.

With less than two weeks until Christmas Day, Katrina had little time to daydream. The Christmas season in a huge retail operation like Tiffany & Company created the same time pressure as that experienced by an accountant in early April counting down the days until April 15th. A missed deadline could have significant monetary consequences for her and her co-workers and repercussions for subsequent sales in the months and years to come.

Head of Corporate Sales, Katrina was tasked with ensuring that all purchases requiring engraving and personalization would be completed, shipped, and delivered by the dates indicated on the purchase orders of the customers. At the latest, all holiday merchandise needed to arrive by the afternoon of Christmas Eve.

Her concentration was broken when her secretary entered her office. The pressures from deadlines at work and the anticipation of being at the Super Bowl with Steve suddenly became unimportant.

The New York Times dropped onto her desk by the secretary changed everything.

The Miami murders had become national news. Katrina was scared to death.

CHAPTER 27

Unlike the reaction of Katrina Bell, the negative news stories out of Miami brought a smile of satisfaction to the face of Hamilton Davies. Currently a resident of Dallas, the attorney still subscribed to the Miami Herald, as he had done when he attended law school at the University of Miami and while he resided in the city. Unlike many people who retain an interest in the news from their former town to keep up with local politics, read about newsworthy residents, or maintain a positive connection to a place that holds fond memories for them, Hamilton didn't read the Herald for any of the above reasons.

Basking in perverse pleasure at the plight of Miami, Davies felt justified in holding a grudge against the entire city. At one time, he had a perfect record as a lobbyist and enjoyed the reputation as the best pitchman in the business. He was like King Midas – everything he touched turned to gold. Due to his flawless record, only a few years before he had been chosen to lead the promotional team for the city of Dallas in its bid for the Super Bowl. The city elders were convinced that it would be a slam dunk. Dallas had one of the most modern and beautiful domed stadiums in the league. The Dallas cheerleaders, the charisma of the owner, and the Cowboy's reputation as "America's Team" seemed to make those in Dallas feel like their city was a shoo-in to be selected to host football's most watched and prestigious event. If those weren't enough credentials to sway the choice of locations, Hamilton Davies was their secret weapon. Unfortunately, he was unable to secure Dallas as the venue for the upcoming Superbowl. He took his failure personally, feeling that his lobbying skills had been discredited and his reputation damaged. He placed blame on a past indiscretion rather than on his present inability to be sufficiently convincing to sway the selection committee. He blamed Miami for publicizing that indiscretion.

Regrettably, there was a secret from his past that haunted him. Just before his fourteenth birthday, he had done something stupid and he lived to regret it. Flattered that some older boys from his school invited him to join them, he didn't want to refuse the invitation. The youngest of the group, he succumbed to a dare. It was Halloween night. Alcohol was involved. One of the boys said he was bored knocking on doors for candy and thought it would be fun to break into the Texas State Capitol building in Austin. Once inside the building, they defaced the statue of the legendary Sam Houston. The prank ended badly, and they were caught.

It was the first time Hamilton had been in trouble, and his parents breathed a sigh of relief that he had not yet reached his fourteenth birthday. The judge was sympathetic to his parents who promised strict curfews and financial restitution to repair the statue. Hamilton had to perform community service in Austin, where he resided. He was promised that his juvenile record would be sealed.

When he failed to secure the Super Bowl game for Dallas and it was instead awarded to Miami, Davies was furious. Without proof, he believed that it was because someone in Miami investigated his past and advised the selection committee of his prior scrape with the law. Ever since then he harbored a hatred for the city of Miami.

He felt especially betrayed since he was a University of Miami Law School graduate, who, at one time, had worked for the office of the State Attorney. He still maintained his license to practice law in the State of Florida, although he had been living in Dallas for many years.

Texas suited him, with his larger-than-life presence. His stocky body, loud voice, extra-long Cuban cigars, and Stetson hat covering his bald pate made him impossible to ignore. He was a figure who could never be missed, even in a crowd. Being recognized was extremely important to him. He was a firm believer that *any* publicity was good publicity, and he often expressed outrageous views to garner attention.

Most people found him obnoxious. This was especially true of his all-female staff. Hired more for appearance and sex appeal than for competency, his staffers were noticeably young and voluptuous. Hamilton did not understand or chose to ignore the concept of "political correctness." His sexist remarks, directed to his female staff and about them to clients, were cringeworthy. Like his cigars and cowboy hat, the women he employed created an image that he liked to cultivate. They were his showpieces and gave him the illusion of being a magnet for beautiful women. The women endured his sexist remarks because he paid well. Very well.

"Hey, Lorna," he shouted. "Bring me a scotch on the rocks. Go easy on the rocks. I don't wanna mess up getting my rocks off later. Maybe you can help me with that."

He smiled at his own joke, realizing that he had probably grossed out his employee. Putting her in an uncomfortable position enhanced his enjoyment of having power over her.

Lorna was used to his vulgarities and ignored his innuendo as usual. Despite her wavy blond hair, Lorna Campbell was anything but a dumb blonde. Not that Hamilton noticed or cared. When she applied for the job, Davies hired the statuesque blond beauty without a glance at her resume.

With a degree in psychology from the University of Texas at Dallas, Lorna had taken the job in the law office because it paid far better than any other job for which she was qualified. It was only a first step to being able to support herself and start repaying student loans. Her long-term goal was to one day start her own clinical practice.

This morning she was curious as to why her boss circled a story in black magic marker on the front page of the Miami Herald. Also, he requested an alcoholic beverage. His crude language wasn't uncommon but drinking at 9 a.m. was atypical.

"Are you celebrating something special this morning?" she asked sweetly.

Hamilton folded the newspaper and then lifted it from the desk and tossed it in the air to her. She caught it on the fly and focused her eyes on the portions that had been circled in the black ink.

"This is horrible," she exclaimed. "Those poor tourists from New Jersey. Did you know them?"

His response was offensive. "No, I don't know who the hell they are, nor do I care. I'm only interested because it happened in Miami. For all the positive hype about Miami and the Super Bowl, they just got their comeuppance. It's about time. Who would go to the game now?"

"Why the negativity about Miami? I've seen your diploma from the University of Miami Law School."

"None of your damn business," Davies screamed. "Just get me my drink like I asked and get your pretty little ass back to work. Girls like you are a dime a dozen, so if you want to keep your job, enough with the twenty questions."

Smiling all the while, she poured the scotch and inserted ice cubes that she intentionally dropped on the floor in the kitchen area before adding them to the drink. Lorna felt a small measure of revenge as she served Hamilton his drink.

She'd keep her responses short and sweet. Something about Hamilton Davies and his hatred for the city of Miami had her spooked.

CHAPTER 28

The death of the two tourists from New Jersey started up the frenzied news cycle about the Dead of Night killer once again. Investigations of the prior murders yielded no tangible results and were replaced in the public conscience by headlines of other more current crimes. The recent murders of Vivian and Walter Raines dredged up all the stories of the other victims since the rampage by the Dead of Night killer began.

The timing of the murders couldn't have been worse. Christmas and New Years were just around the corner, the most lucrative time of the year for the tourist trade. Contrary to the philosophy that *any* publicity is good publicity, the Miami news reported throughout the country immediately impacted airplane flights and hotel reservations, and would ultimately affect restaurants, retail stores, entertainment venues, and taxi drivers in an adverse manner. And those were just a small portion of the industries that would suffer.

To make matters worse, the anticipated revenue from being the host city for the Super Bowl in February was astronomical, a tremendous boon to the local economy. Unless the killer was caught prior to that event, the ramifications would be debilitating to a city that depended on tourist dollars. No one wanted to publicly express this fear, but it was uppermost on the minds of the mayor and the city council. Money from the Super Bowl that would end up in the city's coffers had already been designated for various projects that weren't covered by annual budget allocations of money from Tallahassee. They were counting on the additional funding or couldn't proceed with several important commitments they made to contractors and the residents of Miami.

Hotel reservations and car rentals for Super Bowl weekend in February had plateaued in November, with little growth in December. Some prior reservations were even being cancelled. Not surprisingly, sales for game tickets for out-of-towners were also stagnant. Locals were taking advantage of the greater availability of tickets and were making lemonade out of lemons.

****

Mayor Diaz was incensed regarding the negative publicity about Miami throughout the country and abroad since the killings began. The city could no longer depend upon the expected revenue that tourists usually generated for the city, especially at this time of the year. He was taking flak from the Chamber of Commerce, the Greater Miami and the Beaches Hotel Association, the owners of the local malls and restaurants, the airlines, and all ancillary businesses that worried about a substantial drop in income.

Worse even than the impact on tourism, the long-range ramifications were more than troubling. The Miami Association of Realtors was on his back, worrying about a decrease in home sales and rentals at a time of year when many tourists decided to purchase property or rent for the season. Savvy realtors were scrambling to close deals, anticipating a glut of property that they wouldn't be able to move because of the damaging publicity. They hoped that prospective buyers from South America, Europe, or Asia weren't fully aware of the mass hysteria troubling Miami. Unfortunately, social media and the internet connected all parts of the world, and the news travelled very quickly across the globe. Each murder reported was inversely proportional to the sales revenue generated by the realty industry.

Like a ripple that spreads in ever widening circles when a pebble is tossed into a lake, the impact on other businesses was already becoming discernible. Sales of appliances, home furnishings, carpeting, flooring, and window coverings were down; if property didn't change hands, renovations came to a halt. New construction was also at risk. Service industries that provided roofers, carpenters, painters, plumbers, day laborers, and all other workers on resales as well as new construction projects found the demand falling short of what was typical in prior years.

The mayor recognized the possibility that things would get worse before they would get better. He had no expectation that any speech or verbal communication on his part would satisfy the citizens of Miami. He was up to his eyeballs in complaints about the police. Diaz recognized that it was time to do whatever it took to catch the killer, whether that required demands, threats, or ultimatums to his underlings. The police commissioner and the entire police force had been expecting a stern lecture from the mayor, both because he feared for the welfare of the city of Miami and its citizens, and of equal importance, for his own political future.

Mayor Robert Diaz emanated an aura of power. Well over six feet tall with perfectly coifed black hair, his physical presence was not the only characteristic that caused people to respect, and sometimes, fear him. He didn't look at you – he looked through you. It seemed as if he could divine a person's thoughts without any verbal communication having taken place. The intensity of the stare from his cobalt blue eyes was enough to instill fear in anyone subject to his unblinking inspection. The riveting color of his eyes was mesmerizing, but they were as hard as marbles, not unlike the hardness of his unrelenting demands.

Police Commissioner Inez Vargas thought she was prepared for a call from Mayor Diaz when the news broke about the tourists from New Jersey. She was wrong. Nothing could have prepared her for his tirade. Without any greeting, Mayor Diaz commenced his attack once she answered her phone.

"Police Commissioner Vargas, I regret to say that you are a major disappointment to me. Maybe this job is too much for you."

Not a good beginning to a conversation that became incrementally worse as Mayor Diaz continued to heap insults and outrageous demands on the police commissioner.

"I can only assume that you've seen the television coverage of the two middle-aged tourists from New Jersey. It's all over the airwaves. For some reason, their age and the fact that they're from New Jersey celebrating a second honeymoon for their fortieth anniversary seems to resonate with the media. Wish they had been college students on Spring Break. Probably would have generated less of an outcry, like they had been partially responsible for being attacked."

That callous remark wasn't the worst of it.

"Vargas, get your act together. I don't care how you do it. JUST DO IT! This killing spree by the Dead of Night killer has gone into overtime. END IT NOW! As far as I'm concerned, shoot first and ask questions later. It's the only way you're going to get results. Let *me* deal with the fallout."

The phone was slammed in her ear before she could respond. The mayor dropped his bomb and didn't care to listen to any excuses, suggestions, or opposition from her. Commissioner Vargas poured herself a cup of coffee from the carafe on her credenza, needing to process the monologue. It certainly couldn't have been described as a conversation.

The mayor's rudeness wasn't unexpected. He wasn't her greatest fan, and he let her know it in ways that were less than subtle. What seemed to bother her equally as much was his reference to the Dead of Night killer, a name that rankled with her. In her opinion, giving murderers catchy names diminished the seriousness of their crimes and made the deaths of their victims seem inconsequential, merely sound bites repeated around water coolers, in bars, and at cocktail parties.

The names also attracted copycat killers, a small portion of the population that was attracted to these horrific acts. The appeal of being named with a clever nickname by the media took on an importance well beyond that of their birth names. Most people remembered the killer known as the Son of Sam but didn't necessarily remember his birth name was David Berkowitz.

Ever since assuming the role of police commissioner, Inez Vargas felt like a bug on a glass slide in a science lab. As a female, she was a rarity to have risen to the rank of police commissioner. A few chauvinistic male politicians, including the mayor and several disgruntled male law enforcement personnel passed over for promotion, were waiting for her to fail. Comments about how she dressed or wore her hair seemed to be open to public scrutiny. As a result, she wore muted colors and avoided clothing that was form-fitting despite her slim size-four body. She wore her brown hair short because she felt that long hair or a ponytail would make her appear too youthful and not adequately serious for her position.

The hell with the mayor's criticism and the negative media publicity, Inez decided. She had more than earned her job as police commissioner and realized that, as a female, she had to outperform her male counterparts. It might not be fair, but it was what it was. No more pity party.

Despite the current climate of fear in her city, she had a following of supporters who recognized her dedication to the job. With her use of twitter and email she was always available to the public. Her adept use of social media kept the citizens abreast of what was happening in the police department. She never hid from any press conference on issues that concerned the public. She responded to the questions of reporters without sugarcoating her replies. Born and raised in Miami, she was proud of her city and vowed to hold herself and her hometown up to the highest standards possible.

The décor of her office reflected the personality of the woman who occupied it. The photos of her predecessors and plaques dedicated to officers who lost their lives in the line of duty were hung on the wall behind her desk, so that a visitor would see them when seated across from her. The fact that these mementos were displayed in her personal office spoke volumes about an individual who respected the contributions of others and wanted them to be acknowledged for their service and their sacrifice. Unlike other people whose walls were filled with photos of themselves with celebrities, she had only her diplomas on the wall that faced her desk. The few personal photos in her office were those of her husband and their two boys, both of whom were in high school. Her office appeared uncluttered and organized with nothing appearing to be out of place.

Approaching fifty, Inez Vargas gave the impression of being at least a decade younger due to her exercise regimen and a little hair coloring that she applied to her short-cropped brown hair.

The mayor might not have realized it, but he helped recharge her batteries. His dressing down motivated her more than praise would have. She'd make him eat his words and would prove to him that she was up to the task; it was time to brainstorm with all those involved in investigating the murders. Punching the intercom button on her office telephone, Inez instructed her secretary to place calls to Chief Santiago, Sergeant Hernandez, Detective Mandich, Detective Dennison, Detective Banks, and Dr. Cecil Murphy. From the instructions she dictated, it was obvious that she meant business.

"I want you to speak with them personally. Do not leave a voicemail. Stress to them that this is not an invitation. They are being summoned. They are to report here at 1 p.m. sharp today with a progress report on where they stand with the investigation and any leads they're planning to pursue. Attendance is mandatory. No excuses accepted."

CHAPTER 29

There was no question that the police commissioner's secretary accurately conveyed the tone of her boss's directive to her underlings. They, in turn, had their secretaries or receptionists reschedule appointments for the afternoon. It was clear that Commissioner Vargas wasn't inviting them for afternoon tea. They expected no social amenities, nor would she provide any if history was any indication of future behavior.

The phone rang sequentially three times in the bullpen as Detectives Mandich, Dennison, and Banks received their calls from the police commissioner's secretary. Just a moment earlier, Sergeant Hernandez also received his notification. As he walked toward Brad Mandich's desk, he heard the phone ring and saw Brad's face. Brad evidently received the same curt instructions as he had. He waited for Lew and Amanda to get their calls, certain that their phones would ring as well.

"Was that a human or a robot? I've never heard so many words spoken so rapidly or tonelessly," commented Sergeant Hernandez. "What the hell kind of meeting are we getting ourselves into?"

The three detectives felt some of their tension dissipate based upon the sergeant's response to the phone call. They also sensed that they were going to be called on the carpet at the police commissioner's office. At least their sergeant was including himself as part of the group that was heading into a shit storm.

"No use wasting gas, so we might as well drive together," Hernandez suggested. "We've got a good hour until we need to leave, so gather all your notes, files, and reports from your desks. Review them thoroughly so that when Vargas asks you a question, you're at the top of your game. I'm going back to my office. Come get me in an hour."

"Let's go one step further," Brad recommended, "and brainstorm about what we've learned from our individual interviews and investigations."

"Can't hurt," agreed Lew.

"Works for me," added Amanda.

By the time they stopped in front of Sergeant Hernandez's door, they felt prepared for the "command performance" ordered by Police Commissioner Vargas.

Brad volunteered to drive so Sergeant Hernandez could outline his strategy for the onslaught he was anticipating. While his detectives had been brainstorming, Hernandez was doing his own preparations for the confrontation with the police commissioner. The plan was to stand firm, present the facts, and demonstrate to the police commissioner that progress was being made.

****

Fortunately, traffic on I-95 was flowing and there were no cones or barricades narrowing the lanes and causing delays. They took that as a good sign. Punctuality was demanded by Inez Vargas. It demonstrated that you valued another person's time and that they valued yours. Although they arrived twenty minutes early, Commissioner Vargas was ready for them and ushered them into the conference room. She took the seat closest to the door at the head of the large oval mahogany table and motioned them to their chairs, crafted from matching mahogany wood with black leather seats and brass upholstery tacks.

The conference room created an impression of both utility and taste. Leather blotters were set in front of each chair, and a wooden tray with a carafe of ice water and drinking glasses sat in the center of the table. Police Commissioner Vargas held meetings in the conference room when she met with city officials or when her office didn't accommodate all the participants for a meeting.

"Please have a seat. I'm expecting Chief Santiago and Dr. Murphy, but we can catch them up when they arrive. Let's begin."

No sooner had she said that when the door opened and the secretary popped her head in, saying, "Sorry to interrupt, but I think you might want to take a call that came in for you on my line."

Irritated, Inez responded, "Can't this wait?"

"I know you're expecting the medical examiner, Dr. Murphy. He's on hold on my extension."

Abruptly, Vargas stood up and exited the conference room. There was no mistaking the annoyance in her voice as she returned to her seat. "That was Dr. Murphy on the phone. It seems that he has *other* responsibilities that require his *immediate* attention. He won't be joining us after all."

Detective Mandich muttered under his breath, "Better to hold this meeting without him, anyway."

What Brad thought was a whisper was unfortunately heard by the police commissioner. From her question, Brad wasn't sure whether she heard what he said or just the fact that he mumbled something. Looking directly at him and making him squirm in his seat, she asked, "Did you say something, Detective Mandich? Maybe you can share it with the rest of us."

Brad felt like a kid being reprimanded by an elementary school teacher. "No ma'am. Just talking to myself. Nothing important at all."

He wasn't ready to discuss with the police commissioner the suspicions that his nephew Cliff had put in his head concerning Dr. Murphy. If, in fact, he was somehow involved in the murders, Dr. Murphy's presence would only alert him that he needed to cover his tracks better. If that were the case, they certainly wouldn't learn anything from his attendance at the meeting.

Picking up as if there had been no interruption, Commissioner Vargas opened a leather portfolio that held a file folder and a pad of yellow legal paper. She removed a gold-color engraved Cross pen, a gift from her husband when she became Police Commissioner. It was her lucky pen; today she wanted all the luck she could get. Looking across the table, she took control of the meeting.

"Sergeant, I'll start with you. What the hell is happening out there? From what I've heard, it appears that young athletic men, all native to Miami, were the initial targets. Now I understand that two tourists from New Jersey, a middle-aged couple, were also murdered in what can only be described as a gruesome manner. Seems that the killer has been removing the internal organs of the victims. So, I'll ask again. What the hell is happening? Miami natives are terrified, and tourists are petrified to visit here, especially since there are rumors that the killer might not even be human."

Hernandez wasn't aware that he had nodded his head in agreement. The police commissioner possessed the up-to-date information on the victims as well as the possibility that the killer might not be human. Knowing that his next comment would not be well-received, he steeled himself for what he was about to reveal. Squaring his shoulders, he nodded to his detectives and made eye contact with his superior.

"Commissioner Vargas, I think we have a leak in our department. It appears that someone is not only feeding information to the press, but to an opportunistic city councilman by the name of Kyle Griffin. Where did he get *his* information? If you caught his press conference on TV, he knew too much too soon. What he did was disgraceful. He made a deliberate decision to alarm the public by releasing the details about the missing internal organs of the victims. That information has been under wraps within our unit. The leaks may not be slowing down the investigation, but they've caused citywide panic."

As she listened, Vargas was jotting down notes on her legal pad. She looked up at Sergeant Hernandez and then glanced at the three detectives. None of them seemed surprised by what Hernandez said. Judging by their body language, they all seemed in agreement about a leak in the department.

"Don't leave me hanging here. Who do you think is responsible?"

"We can't prove anything just yet, so I'd rather not say. But, trust me, we're working on it," Hernandez replied.

Brad, Lew, and Amanda remained silent. They were grateful that their sergeant was on the hot seat instead of them. Their turn came momentarily.

Directing her gaze at the detectives, Vargas said, "The public is losing faith in the police department. What's the holdup? How close are you to putting an end to this? Can you give me a time frame? These killings must stop. Beyond the grisly deaths, the reputation of Miami is at stake. Need I remind you that the height of tourist season is just around the corner. If tourists cancel their Miami travel plans and choose alternative vacation spots, the economic repercussions for our citizens will be catastrophic. I'm counting on you to see that doesn't happen. Every day puts us in further jeopardy. FIX THIS!"

Defending his detectives, Sergeant Hernandez replied on their behalf. "Commissioner Vargas, these three are working round the clock. You don't need to remind us of the importance of apprehending this killer. We live here and have our own families to protect. I can only say that we're closer than we were days ago."

Fortunately, Vargas didn't press him to explain further. Their time would be better spent working the case.

"If you assure me that you have tangible leads, I'm not going to ask you to go into specifics. Just don't disappoint me. I have a long memory and I've been known to hold grudges. You've got two more days before I go outside the department, despite my reluctance to do that," Police Commissioner Vargas warned. "That would be humiliating to you and embarrassing to me."

Hernandez felt as if they had been granted a stay of execution. However, they all realized that her patience with them was tenuous. Two days was better than nothing, but not by much.

"Is Chief Santiago on board with this?" Hernandez asked.

"He will be. Rather than making you wait, when he arrives, I'll fill him in on our discussion. We *should* be able to contain the problem within the Miami-Dade police force, but your performance to date leaves me unconvinced. If you don't resolve this within two days, I might have no choice but to ask for assistance from the US Marshals Service."

Police Commissioner Vargas let her statement sink in. As the group rose to leave, she stated, "You can consider that a threat or a promise, whichever you prefer."

CHAPTER 30

Clearly, Dr. Cecil Murphy was aware of the bite marks on the first three victims. He hated to admit it to himself, but he had never seen bites like these before. From his years of experience, he only knew that they were unlike any human bites that he had examined. He lacked the dental expertise to identify them. Once the bodies of the tourists from New Jersey were delivered to the morgue exhibiting similar marks, Murphy could no longer delay calling in an expert.

Without question, Douglas Wirth, DDS is regarded as the foremost forensic dentist in South Florida. Fortunately for Cecil Murphy, Wirth resides in Miami. Back in the late 1970's, Douglas Wirth was enthralled by compelling testimony from Dr. Richard Souviron, a forensic odontologist, in the infamous Theodore Bundy murder trials in Tallahassee, Florida. The case of Bundy v. State of Florida remains the most famous case involving bite marks and forensics in the United States. The evidence presented by Dr. Souviron led to Bundy's conviction.

That evidence presented by Dr. Souviron also led to Douglas Wirth's decision to pursue further training in the field of forensic odontology, more commonly known as forensic dentistry. Already interested in this facet of dentistry, the trial cemented his growing passion for the specialty. He found his niche.

Beyond his reputation in South Florida, Wirth is considered one of the premier experts on bite marks in the world. His work and contributions continue to be at the forefront of forensic odontology.

In demand as a lecturer and consultant worldwide, Wirth has nonetheless chosen to limit his travels. That proved to be fortuitous for Dr. Murphy.

Dr. Wirth often lectures to dental students at the University of Miami. Still youthful at sixty-six, he is a striking figure with his almost full head of snow-white hair and thick dark-black bushy eyebrows. Some of his students find the contrast of his hair and eyebrow color disconcerting. Both are natural and Wirth is not inclined to mess with Mother Nature.

His manner of dress contributes to his somewhat odd appearance as well, particularly because he resides in Miami. Regardless of the temperature in Florida which exceeds seventy degrees throughout most of the year, he regularly wears a long-sleeve button-down white shirt under a caramel-colored tweed wool jacket with brown suede patches on the elbows. He's been dressing the same way since his college days, emulating of one of his favorite professors.

From the months of May through October, his attire seems particularly out-of-place in Florida due to the heat and humidity. Despite temperatures in the upper eighties and low nineties, he continues to wear his signature uniform, seeming impervious to the temperature.

Blessed with a booming voice that captures and holds attention when he lectures, he captivates his audience who respond to either his appearance or his voice – or both. A cartoonist's dream, artists attending trials at which he serves as an expert witness have a field day sketching him, their drawings like caricatures due to Wirth's unusual appearance. Yet his somewhat odd appearance belies his knowledge and stature in the forensic community. Those familiar with his work consider him an icon.

During the first year of his dental training, Wirth took an intense interest in bite marks to demonstrate that they could provide incontrovertible proof of the guilty party. He learned that there was absolute documentation from the Salem Witch Trials that bite marks had been used as evidence of criminal behavior in the United States. He was hooked. Reading about the earliest recorded case in the United States using bite marks in a trial, he learned that it wasn't just females who were tried and convicted during the Salem Witch Trials. That was a piece of information about which he had been ignorant.

Reverend George Burroughs was convicted of witchcraft during the Salem Witch Trials in 1692, almost three hundred years before the world ever heard of Ted Bundy. The people of Salem believed that he was trying to recruit some local women to witchcraft. In order to do so, it was said that he bit them, somehow using his powers to effect their transformation. During his trial, the prosecution pried open his mouth and compared his teeth with bite marks on some of the victims who were seated in the courtroom. It was determined that his teeth matched the bite marks on the skin of the young women he was accused of biting. Found guilty, Reverend Burroughs was sentenced to death by hanging.

There was no time in his long career that Douglas Wirth regretted his decision to forego private practice in lieu of research, teaching, and serving as an expert witness. While in his office preparing a lecture that he was scheduled to deliver the following week to a group of second-year dental students at the University of Miami, he heard his phone ring. The call was from his colleague, Dr. Cecil Murphy.

Assuming it was a work-related issue, Wirth asked the medical examiner, "So, Cecil old friend, whaddya got for me?"

"Several bodies. The first three are Miami's own

homegrown high school alumni. At first, there seemed to be a pattern. All three graduated ten years ago from the same high school. All three were athletes. All three were planning to attend their ten-year reunion. However, now we have a married couple from New Jersey who are neither athletes nor part of the same graduating class."

Impatient, Wirth asked, "Where do I come in?"

"All of the victims appear to have bite wounds."

"Sounds like what I've been hearing described as the DON killings."

"You got that right. For the time being, we're lumping them together as part of the DON killings, but I'm hoping that you can help prove or disprove that. Either way, I need your expertise."

"Okay, Cecil, you've piqued my interest, and of course, I'm happy to help. Give me forty minutes and I'll be at the morgue. It's best that I see the victims."

****

When Douglas Wirth arrived, he was glad he wore his tweed jacket. The temperature in the morgue was cold, as always. Cecil Murphy led him to the portion of the room that held the stainless-steel refrigerated spaces for individual bodies. He pulled the handles of the doors that contained the bodies of the victims of the DON killer, wheeling them out so that Douglas could examine them.

"At first," Murphy explained, "we thought that we had a pattern when we examined the initial three bodies. All were male. All had been athletes. All had gone to school here. All had bite marks. All were missing abdominal organs. All had puncture wounds which might explain how they were immobilized before they were killed. It seemed as if they were targeted for a specific reason which remains unknown. That is, until the bodies of

Walter and Vivian Raines, the couple from New Jersey, were found. That makes me wonder if they were random victims or whether a copycat killer utilized the techniques he heard about on the news."

Douglas was familiar with most of what Cecil divulged. Impatient to get back to his office to complete the lecture he was preparing, he asked, "What is it that you want *me* to do? Do you have a suspect?"

"Nope. That's why I need you."

"This isn't how I usually work," Douglas stated, his annoyance obvious in his next comment. "What you're asking is, as they say, ass backwards."

"Isn't that a little harsh?"

"Look, Cecil, usually I'm called in on a case when a suspect is *already* in custody. At that point, I'll take a model of the suspect's teeth and compare it to the bite wounds. We call this the direct method. I've also had some success with an indirect method where I prepare a transparent overlay of the suspect's teeth pattern and try to match it to photographs of the bite pattern on the victim. This method of bite comparison is reserved for cases in which a suspect isn't found until the body of the deceased is no longer available or badly decomposed."

"I understand what you're saying, but as long as you're here, just look at the bodies."

"Cecil, you're not giving me a model, a transparency, or the actual suspect to make any comparisons. I'm not sure how much I can help, but I'll give it a try. Start with the first victim and proceed chronologically. At least I can see the bite pattern and take photos of the marks to compare to the teeth of any suspect who is found later."

Dr. Murphy identified the dates of death of the victims and confirmed their identities from the toe tags on each of the bodies.

As he located the corpse of Christopher Dee, the initial victim, he explained that he was under pressure not only from the police department, but from the families of the victims. They deserved to be able to put their loved ones to rest, and it was his responsibility to determine when they would be able to do that.

"I need some sort of answer soon. As you can imagine, the families are pressuring us to release the bodies for burial."

"I'll do my best," responded Douglas.

The appearance of Dee's body came as a total shock to the dentist. Backing away from the table, he confronted Cecil, the hostility in his words evident.

"Are you kidding me? Any medical examiner or first-year dental student would recognize that these bites aren't human. Stop wasting my time. You must have recognized this. Why did you keep it from me?"

"I didn't want to influence your evaluation."

"Well, Cecil, you got the wrong guy here. If it were me, I'd get a wildlife expert from Miami Metro Zoo. Look at the penetrations here. The canine teeth have penetrated more than one inch. The shape of the jaw is clearly elongated. It's not the more semicircular pattern that we see in our own species. Am I telling you something you didn't know?"

Waiting for Murphy's response, Wirth tried to contain his anger. Looking at Cecil's face when he berated him, Wirth felt sorry for his outburst. Then his scientific curiosity took over. Dr. Wirth was clearly intrigued by the Dead of Night case. Also, it didn't hurt that the media attention would only increase his already glowing reputation as an expert in the field of forensic dentistry. Known primarily in academic circles, Wirth's connection to the investigation might catapult him to his fifteen minutes of fame. The idea was enticing. Speculating further, he imagined that his contribution would develop into a new paper for publication or, at the very least, to a fascinating lecture for his students and the public at large.

Not intending it as a pun, he couldn't help but think that he wanted to sink his teeth into the project. To that end, Douglas took digital photographs of every bite mark on each of the victims. Alongside the marks he included a metric ruler for size comparisons in his photos. Wirth recognized that his meticulous attention to detail would vastly benefit law enforcement.

After photographing the corpses, Wirth visually examined all the bodies several times to confirm his observations. "The bite wounds are remarkably consistent. I'll go out on a limb and tell you that all the bites marks are from the same creature. Cecil, take DNA samples from each victims' wounds, and put a rush on it."

"What are you thinking?"

"I have a hunch. Get the DNA results. Then we'll talk."

CHAPTER 31

Ever since I made the decision to help the police department with the DON killer, I had been scouring the newspaper and watching the television incessantly. Strangely, the media often released information before I heard anything from my Uncle Brad. It was the weekend and no additional bodies had been found within the past twenty-four hours.

I took that as a sign from the universe that I could spend the weekend, or at least part of it, with the woman I adored. It was only 7:30 a.m. When I exited our bedroom to bring in the Herald and flip channels on the TV, Lauren was still dead to the world. Just seeing her sound asleep with her dark hair splayed on the pillow and her face with her high cheekbones (probably from her Russian ancestry), I felt like the luckiest man on earth. I couldn't wait for her to open her large hazel eyes with their small brown flecks and smile at me in a way that I'm certain could melt at polar icecap. What can I say? I'm completely and utterly captivated by her.

Today would be a great opportunity to spend the day together, just the two of us. Already the wheels were turning in my head as I considered Lincoln Road, Coconut Grove, Bayside, and several other options. Since it didn't matter to me what we did, I'd leave the choice to her. Being together was my goal.

When I returned to the bedroom, I found Lauren awake, rummaging through her dresser drawers. Hearing my footsteps on the tile floor, she turned, smiled at me, but immediately returned to her quest. When she didn't find what she sought in the top drawer, she bent down to the second, and finally the third. I was in the right place at the right time!

My tentative plans no longer seemed so pressing. First things first. As Lauren reached for her watch on her nightstand, I put my hand on her waist and pulled her back into the bed. She turned my fantasy into reality. Too bad that every morning didn't start this way, but I wasn't complaining. I'll take what I can get. Today was off to a great start.

A pleasant lethargy overtook us and neither Lauren nor I felt like getting out of bed, but the sun coming through our bedroom window was becoming annoying. Perhaps even more annoying was my stomach which began to rumble. Lauren put her ear to my stomach, pretending to have a conversation with this deprived body part.

"How about I prepare some eggs and a low-fat café latte?" she said, speaking into my belly button. It was ridiculously funny, and I decided to play along.

Pretending to be my stomach, I attempted to speak in a completely different voice, having no idea what a stomach would sound like, but it clearly didn't sound like me. I could barely get the word out without laughing, and she was laughing so hard that she told me later that her cheeks ached.

"Sounds great but forget the low-fat," my stomach responded. Then I patted what I considered was my trim stomach and my stomach-voice added that I had no need to pay attention to the fat content of the milk in the latte. Fortunately, Lauren agreed with me, and ran her hand on my stomach to confirm the six-pack abs that my tummy had also bragged about. At this rate, I'd never get any food, if you get my meaning.

Having breakfast together was a treat that we liked to indulge in on the weekend. During our normal work week, our schedules didn't allow the luxury of more than grabbing a cup of coffee and perhaps a bagel for me. Taking advantage of our time together, we made a conscious decision to leave our cell phones on vibrate, as we had done when we had gone to bed the previous evening. We didn't want to break the mood and decided that there would be no checking phones or emails until after breakfast.

Breakfast was perfect. We ate on our terrace and had some classical music playing softly in the background. It was a chamber-of-commerce type of day and we wanted to make it last. Even doing the dishes together turned a chore into a cozy domestic scene. We stood side by side at the sink as Lauren rinsed the dishes and handed them to me to load into the dishwasher. She rightfully said that my spatial perception was superior to hers, and I could fit at least twenty percent more dishes inside the machine than she could.

Since we couldn't delay the inevitable any longer, we both simultaneously turned our cell phone ringers to the on position and checked for emails, voicemails, and text messages. Aside from the usual emails about discount coupons, special sales, charitable solicitations, and political surveys, nothing was urgent. I can't say how relieved I was. My plans to spend some quality time with Lauren were looking good.

That was until I looked up at Lauren. Her face told me that her phone alerted her to something that required her attention. With her furrowed brow and brisk pace as she headed toward her office, Lauren began typing on her phone, her fingers in constant motion as she walked. She must have been responding to a text or email. I had the feeling that she wanted some privacy, evidenced by her closing the office door. About fifteen minutes later she emerged, still appearing concerned by the email she received.

"What was that about? Are things okay?" I asked.

"It's this business with the reunion committee. Lately, it's always something with them. Back in the day, I wasn't a jock or a nerd, so I wasn't pigeonholed into any specific category. Since I treated everyone with respect, I became popular. That's how I got elected to student council my senior year. Somehow, that led to me being asked to be on the reunion committee.

"By tradition, there's always a volleyball game put together for the athletes. As you know, I agreed to organize it. With the murders of three of the players, my heart hasn't been in it. On top of that, it now appears I might have offended the more studious of my classmates. No good deed goes unpunished." She shook her head and sighed as she reflected on that saying.

"I don't get it. What are you talking about?"

"I'll give you more details later, after I digest the contents of this email. It feels like I'm being backed into a corner, and not because of anything that I did deliberately. It never occurred to me that by arranging the traditional volleyball game for the athletes, I'd offend other classmates by making them feel excluded. That wasn't my intent."

Handing me her phone, Lauren pointed to the email and its subject line, "Nerds Are People, Too." There was no doubt that the game had ruffled some feathers. I gave the phone back to her.

It didn't surprise Lauren that the sender of the email was Charlie Post, the class valedictorian. It had been ten years since she last saw Charlie Post at graduation, standing at the podium and addressing his classmates. His speech was articulate and inspiring, a valedictory address that brought everyone to their feet at its conclusion. A champion debater, he could write and speak in a way that was both factual and convincing.

Charlie had not lost his abilities in the years since graduation. His email made a strong case for an additional reunion competition. He proposed an event that would involve the academic stars of the school.

Lauren reread the contents of the email:

Dear Lauren,

It's been 10 years since graduation. I'm still in contact with several other alumni and we've been receiving the class reunion updates. Your name was on the short list of reunion organizers, and you were mentioned as being responsible for arranging the traditional volleyball game. My friends and I take issue with an activity that's primarily directed to the class jocks, a group that doesn't include us.

How about our class making a politically correct statement by recognizing not only the athletes, but also those of us that pursued academic excellence? In school, we were the bookworms, yet we also were involved in competitive endeavors.

I've contacted three like-minded classmates who loved to study, but still made the time to compete in debate club, chess club, mathletes, and spelling bees. Just like the members of the football, basketball, and baseball teams, we represented our school and brought home trophies. I don't know if you recall, but after we won the State of Florida Mathletes Competition based upon individual as well as team scores, there was a school newspaper article comparing the number of trophies added to the display cases by the mathletes as compared to the athletes. For all us nerds, that article validated our dedication to scholarship.

While the athletes compete in their volleyball match, we would like to compete in a team chess competition against the four best chess players from this year's senior class. Each player can play in two matches. At the end of the eight matches the total scores will determine the winning team.

I don't want you to be burdened by additional work. We all appreciate your contributions to the reunion committee. You don't have to recruit any alumni to participate. I've already spoken with Elliot Cook, Jaclyn Struzer, and Ronald Martella.

They are on board and have agreed to join me as the alumni team. If you need any help speaking to the chess players from the current senior class or the school administration to assign us a room for the meet, I'd be glad to take this on.

I hope I've made this as easy for you as possible. Please understand that we'd like our fifteen minutes of fame just like the athletes from our class. I look forward to your reply.

Your Classmate,
Charlie Post

I followed Lauren back into her office and headed for my favorite cushioned swivel chair. When we set up her office, I suggested the location of the chair, and threw out the words "feng shui" when I recommended where it should be placed. Frankly, I had no idea about this Chinese concept, but I made myself sound authoritative on the subject; Lauren went along with my suggestion. The truth is, I just wanted to be able to sit in the chair and face her as she worked at her computer. Whenever I plop down into the chair, I mention that I'm seated in "the chair of adoration." That's not a concept that I made up out of thin air. I truly adore Lauren.

From her facial expression, I could see that she was still distracted. Her eyes were glued to the phone as she scrolled down the contents of the email with her index finger.

"What's going on? Are you still disturbed by the email? You seem so deep in thought."

"It's so strange. With all the news about the DON killer, Charlie didn't mention a word about our three classmates who were killed. He'd have to be living underground or on a remote mountain to not know what's been happening. Instead, our class valedictorian is entirely focused on a chess match. That's disturbing in itself," she said.

"What really upsets me is that he makes a great argument for the chess match. It's almost embarrassing that the reunion committee didn't consider the feelings of students other than the jocks. He pointed out something that should have been obvious to me."

"Lauren, don't beat yourself up about this. Move forward and set his idea in motion. Is there enough time for you to be able to arrange it?"

"It shouldn't be a problem. I'm guessing that we can use the school library on the morning of the reunion. Who knows? Maybe it will become another tradition. It would be nice to be known as the class that initiated a tradition."

"Sounds like your mind's made up."

"Frankly, it's a terrific idea, but I just wish the circumstances were different. My thoughts have been occupied with the tragic deaths of my classmates and with the pragmatic issue of having to replace three players. It all seems so surreal."

Lauren replied to the email in the affirmative. Certain that seniors on the school's current chess team would welcome the idea of competing against the alumni, she would clear the event with the school administration. Also, she advised Charlie that she'd secure the venue. The library would probably be the best location, but she'd let him know once she spoke to the school officials.

Giving him credit for the idea, Lauren expressed her opinion that the chess competition would enhance the reunion experience, offering a second challenge to pit the alumni against students ten years younger than themselves. Supporting one's peers against opponents always brought people together. Lauren thanked Charlie for his innovative concept and for putting together the alumni chess team.

"There, I've sent Charlie an email. I'm excited by this. What could go wrong?"

CHAPTER 32

When Sergeant Hernandez and the three detectives exited the building after their meeting with Inez Vargas, they were relieved to have bought themselves some time, albeit only two days. The sergeant had somehow placated the police commissioner; his department was given a short reprieve before she would possibly reach out to the US Marshals Service.

His assurance to her that they were homing in on the perp was so convincing that his underlings believed he had some additional information that he hadn't yet divulged to them. The three hastily left the building, not wanting to be called back. Once on the sidewalk, Brad Mandich spoke.

"Do you really believe we're getting closer? What haven't you told us?"

"Nothing. Nada. Zilch. Nothing at all that you don't already know. Maybe I should take up poker. Seems that I can tell a blatant lie with conviction."

"You sure had me fooled," admitted Amanda Banks. "Frankly, I was beginning to feel good about this case, hoping that you'd made some real progress."

"No such luck, I'm afraid. Before the murder of those tourists I thought we had a pattern. Now I don't see that anymore. I just wanted us to get out of the commissioner's office in one piece."

"Good thinking. I felt my makeup melting under the police commissioner's laser-like glare," Amanda stated, trying to add some levity to the situation.

"Maybe Doc Murphy or my nephew Cliff will come up with something concerning the latest victims," Brad volunteered. "The other thing we need to figure out is the identity of the mole in the department. I hate to think that someone is leaking information, but it's the only explanation for Councilman Griffin having a press conference with information that hasn't been disclosed to the public or the media."

"It's awful if someone we work with is subverting his or her responsibilities to the force. Guess you never fully know another person," Lew said sadly.

To Lew, what had been done was unimaginable. The police culture usually created a united front, kind of an "us against them" mentality. Thinking that one of his peers had gone over to the other side made him upset and angry.

"I couldn't agree more," stated Brad.

There was little conversation in the car on the way back to the station. Each person was mentally reviewing details of the case and planning how to proceed. For Brad, ferreting out the source of the department leaks seemed to be of the utmost importance.

Sergeant Hernandez had another goal that was uppermost in his mind. As they entered the elevator in their building and arrived at their floor, he addressed the three detectives, letting them know his priorities.

"The clock is ticking regarding what the police commissioner told us. Knowing her, I believe she's serious about the deadline she gave us. None of us wants the US Marshals Service working in our backyard. It's demeaning."

With that, Hernandez poured himself a cup of coffee and headed into his office. Brad, Lew, and Amanda made their way to their desks to begin checking for new messages or emails that might have arrived during their absence. Within moments of parting ways with Sergeant Hernandez, he burst into the squad room shouting.

"Everyone in the briefing room. Now!"

Anyone within earshot of the sergeant stopped what they were doing. Chairs scratched against the floor as people rapidly exited from their desks. The path leading to the briefing room resembled an indoor track with lanes for speed walking. Some of the younger personnel were running, passing those they considered human obstacles in their attempt to have first pick of seats in the room. No one wanted to be stuck sitting up front. Each attendee was hoping to be obscured from the sergeant's view by the unfortunate latecomers who would have no choice but to sit in the front rows.

As patrolmen and detectives jockeyed for position, the sergeant entered and approached the podium. His clenched jaw and hands that gripped the podium so tightly that his knuckles turned white foreshadowed the seriousness of what he was about to discuss. He pointed to empty seats as latecomers arrived.

"Welcome people. I hope you're comfortable now because none of you will be comfortable again until this Dead of Night killing shit has ended. I'll be watching every person who is in this room today. If you think that microscopes are only found in a lab, I'm telling you that you'll be under my microscope in this office. Should it appear to me that you are relaxing, resting, or taking it easy, I assure you that there will be hell to pay."

Subconsciously, everyone altered their posture, now in their chairs like a platoon of soldiers sitting ramrod straight. Their eyes widened, unblinking, staring intently at their sergeant. They didn't know what triggered their superior's tirade, but all awaited the bomb to drop.

"I just got word that the medical examiner has been able to identify specific toxins in the bloodstreams of the victims. Up until the murder of the vacationing couple, every victim was immobilized by curare. They were all young residents of our fair city. Curare was administered to them to induce paralysis of their motor systems, leaving them awake and aware of what was happening to them; however, they were unable to speak or to move. Although the curare didn't kill them, the other wounds administered by the killer brought about their deaths. The killer left them awake until their bodies failed. While they watched, their internal organs were ripped out of their bodies. There was no way for them to protest or escape. I imagine that they probably prayed to bleed out quickly. A very inhumane way to die."

Sergeant Hernandez painted a disturbingly graphic picture in the minds of his audience. More than their initial outrage and anger, their faces reflected a determination to catch this madman before he subjected other innocent victims to this treatment. But the sergeant was not finished.

"Interestingly, the medical examiner notified me that the Jersey couple was immobilized with carfentanil. This drug can bring down an elephant. In a way, use of this agent is somewhat kinder. The victims were quickly rendered unconscious. They wouldn't be awake to watch the subsequent mutilation of their bodies."

He let that fact sink in. Looking down at the rows of police officers, he could see puzzlement. *Why the change in how the victims were immobilized? The inability to get enough curare? The lack of desire to taunt the older victims by making them watch their own deaths? Or was there a different killer?* Each of these scenarios was a possibility Hernandez was certain they entertained.

"So, I challenge you to find out whether our DON killer has tired of the effects of curare and become kinder, or whether we are now dealing with a second killer. It's possible that the killer is changing his methods or that he has a protégé working with him who has his own favorite way to sedate his victims. A more likely possibility is that the killer of the couple from New

Jersey was a copycat killer. The method of administering the drugs to the initial three victims was with blowguns or tranquilizer guns. If a copycat murdered the tourist couple, he might not have known the specifics of the tranquilizing agent used in the deaths of the earlier victims."

It wasn't necessary for the sergeant to stress the importance of what needed to be done. Working normal nine-to-five hours was no longer an option.

"One last thing, overtime pay has been approved. Now get outta here and earn your paychecks."

Apparently, it was the possibility that the city might have a second killer that caused Hernandez to lose his cool. They hadn't found the first one yet.

A sea of blue flowed toward the exit. Cell phones materialized from pockets as calls were made to advise spouses and significant others not to hold dinner for them. About to call his wife, Ellen, about his extended hours, Brad felt the unmistakable grasp of the sergeant's hand on his shoulder.

"Mandich, I need a minute. In my office. NOW."

Without removing his hand, he pushed Brad down the hall and into a chair. Not that Brad had any intention of disobeying the sergeant, but this was ridiculous. Being singled out from the crowd was never a good thing when it came to how Sergeant Hernandez operated.

"Detective, I respect you and frequently give you leeway because your instincts are often right. However, I'm not so sure that you have a good handle on our current situation. It's come to my attention that you did something that not only was foolhardy but might be a problem when we arrest the perp and the case comes to trial."

"What is it that I did that's got you bent out of shape?" There were several things that Brad thought might be considered questionable. He wanted to know the specific incident that had his sergeant on his back.

"I know that you put yourself out there with this so-called 'voodoo priestess.' You even gave her swatches of clothing from the earliest victims. What on God's green earth were you thinking?"

"Oh, you're talking about Priestess Julia. Looking back on it, I admit it may not have been my finest hour."

"No shit, Brad. I want to see this priestess or mambo, whatever you call her, in my office by five o'clock sharp this evening. Also, get your nephew's wife down here. I understand that she also had some doubts and went on an undercover investigation with Detective Banks with your approval. Between you and me, that decision is like going out on a limb while being pursued by someone with a hacksaw. Can only make you fall on your ass."

There was no way to argue with the reprimand. Brad had taken some liberties with the evidence and with allowing a civilian like Lauren to participate in an investigation with a detective. He had to give it to the sergeant. Nothing that went on in the precinct escaped him.

"On second thought, in addition to Lauren Mandich and the dubious priestess, inform Detective Banks to join us in my office later. Might as well have the whole gang together and see what shakes out." Finished with his instructions, Hernandez pointed at the door.

With no choice but to do what he was told, Brad responded, "Sure thing. I'll get right on it."

In his mind, the only sure thing that Brad could anticipate was that the upcoming meeting would not end well.

CHAPTER 33

Detective Banks had an uncanny ability to sense people's arrival even before they were completely within her range of vision. Regarding Brad, that wasn't such an unusual feat; a man as large as Brad was hard to miss. Out of the corner of her eye, Amanda saw him long before he arrived at her desk. She recognized him by the way he walked. It's a known fact that individuals have a distinctive gait, kind of like their personal fingerprint, making their characteristic walk identifiable.

"Hey, Brad. Can I help you with something?"

"Actually, you can. What are you working on right now?"

"Whaddya think? The Dead of Night Killings, of course. I've decided to try a different approach."

"And what would that be?"

"I'm checking for crimes and crime reports that have been coming in over the last week just in the city. Then I'll expand the search into Miami-Dade and surrounding counties. Frankly, we may have neglected or pushed aside other reported crimes because we've been so focused on this case. It's possible that I might turn up something that may connect to the DON killings, even in the most tangential of ways."

"Can't hurt. Even the slightest connection might be the one that pans out. Ironically, I need you to set that plan aside temporarily because I've got something more pressing."

"No problem. What do you need me to do?"

"Hernandez called a five o'clock meeting today with you, me, Priestess Julia, and Lauren Mandich. I know I can count on you to get the priestess here. It will be interesting to see whether she deserves the title. I'm afraid if she doesn't show, Sergeant Hernandez will come down on me like a wrecking ball."

"Do you want me to contact Lauren or have you already spoken with her? You know, at first, I was skeptical of her, but I have to say that she had some good instincts the day I spent with her in Little Haiti. Seems she has a very fertile imagination. Strange as it was, she came up with a plausible scheme for needing assistance from a voodoo priestess."

Brad looked relieved. One less chore on his never-ending list. For sure, Amanda was a team player.

"I'd appreciate your handling it."

"No problem, Brad. I'll call Lauren. The trick is to get Priestess Julia to come. Lauren found an email address and cell phone number listed for her, but she didn't respond to texts, voicemails, or emails when Lauren tried to arrange a face-to-face meeting. That's why we had to go to her home turf in Little Haiti to speak with her. Unfortunately, no one there seemed to know her."

"Not what I wanted to hear. If she doesn't respond to calls, texts, or emails, how in hell am I going to get her here by the five o'clock deadline? I'm screwed."

"Not necessarily, Brad. I bet that when she first came to the station, she left contact information since you gave her those clothing swatches from the victims. It's doubtful that she gave you her home address or we could send a car out there to get her. If you give me her contact information, I'll try to reach her. Maybe we'll have better luck with her today. At worst, I'll leave messages that we need her expertise immediately. I'll lay it on thick. Maybe that will entice her to come."

"From your mouth to God's ear," Brad said.

Working from the paperwork Julia filled out, Amanda sent an email, a text message, and left a voicemail on her cell phone.

In addition, the contact sheet had the phone number for an answering service. That might be the best way to reach the elusive priestess. Amanda left word with the service that Julia's assistance was required immediately by the police and that her presence was requested for a five o'clock meeting.

Typing "Priestess Julia" in the Google search box on her keyboard, Amanda checked the webpage of the priestess. It listed her email address and cell phone. Underneath a huge photo of a woman in colorful garb and a large turban wrapped around her head, the words "Priestess Julia, Proprietor" were printed in large typeset. The products and services she provided were listed below her picture. As Amanda was perusing the website, her phone rang. Priestess Julia was the caller.

Guess she's more responsive to her answering service than to other means of communication, thought Amanda. Somewhat surprised by Julia's willingness to comply with the police request, Amanda reported her success to Brad.

"Today must be your lucky day, Brad. Just spoke to Julia. She'll be at the precinct at five."

Brad looked up and said, "I'll believe it when I see it."

CHAPTER 34

The Pittsburg Steelers played their next to last regular season game. Their lopsided victory guaranteed the number one seed for the AFC (American Football Conference) playoffs. The outcome of their final regular season game in two weeks would hold no significance.

In addition, the Steelers were the one contending team that would be entering the playoffs relatively intact. The other AFC teams had key injuries to either their starting quarterback or another star player. Most of these injuries occurred during the prior weekend, prompting Las Vegas odds makers to call it Black Sunday.

When the team members suited up for the game, Hoyt Stark was not among them. He was missing from the Pittsburgh lineup because he had been released from the team due to spousal abuse and was back home in Miami; Stark was easily replaceable. Bookies didn't even factor in his absence when figuring the point spread or odds making on the upcoming game.

Clinching the number one seed was cause for locker room celebration. With the players and coaches wearing safety goggles, champagne corks were popped. Players doused each other and their coaches with the foaming liquid. Champagne sprayed everywhere.

Despite the celebration there was an undercurrent of grumbling and arguing among the players. The dismissal of teammate Hoyt Stark for domestic abuse turned into a divisive issue. Some argued that as a first-time offender who confessed to beating his wife, he deserved suspension for the regular season games and for the playoffs. However, they asserted that he should be permitted to participate if the team qualified for the Super Bowl.

That argument didn't hold water with the current commissioner. His zero-tolerance policy for domestic abuse heralded the termination of Hoyt Stark's playing days in the NFL (National Football League). The Steelers players were taking sides, and their once cohesive team was bickering constantly. The conflict among players was getting ugly. As adamant as those who thought the dismissal from the league was excessive, there were others who backed the decision of the commissioner. The morale of the team was in jeopardy.

Mike Grover, head coach of the Steelers, had his finger on the pulse of his players. He attributed their success to more than the skill of individual members or to the well-choreographed plays. Their winning attitude came in large part from the camaraderie of a unified team. Sensing that his team was coming apart, Grover made an executive decision.

With no game scheduled for next week, the Steelers wouldn't play again for fourteen days. It was the perfect time to schedule a "bye week." The time off would cool the hotheads who were the most vociferous, egging on the others to take sides.

"Listen up," Grover said. "We don't have another game scheduled for two weeks. I'm giving everyone the next eight days off. Go home, rest, and have fun. You all earned it. Come back a week from tomorrow for our game-planning session for our final regular season game."

Like students in elementary school, the teammates had the joyful look children experience when they close their books and head outside for recess, often their favorite school period. Everyone could get on board with the idea of the "bye week." The team hadn't been this unanimous in their reactions since Hoyt had been discharged.

Cells phones replaced champagne bottles in the players' hands as they made travel arrangements and notified family members. Smiling members of the Pittsburgh Steelers were going home. One player was headed to Miami.

CHAPTER 35

It was 4:45 p.m. Detectives Brad Mandich and Amanda Banks were working at their desks when Lauren Mandich arrived, Brad greeting her with a hug and Amanda thanking her for her punctuality. They confirmed that the purpose of the meeting was to confront Priestess Julia. Lauren's trip with Amanda to Little Haiti explained why she had been invited.

Priestess Julia had not yet arrived. Neither detective spoke once they resettled at their desks, pointing to an unoccupied chair for Lauren. Both detectives worried that Sergeant Hernandez would criticize them for what he might deem "social chitchat" due to Lauren's arrival.

Their silence wasn't the only indicator of the tension in the room. Even from a distance, Lauren recognized Brad's anxiety. He kept running a ruler through his hair as though it were a comb. If he kept that up, she worried that his scalp would start bleeding. In addition, he had been perspiring profusely. When Brad hugged her, Lauren instinctively pulled away from the sour odor of his sweat. The large perspiration stains under the armpits of his shirt confirmed his nervousness.

Lauren wasn't surprised that Brad was stressed. Amanda informed her during their phone conversation that Sergeant Hernandez berated Brad, considering Priestess Julia solely Brad's problem. Since Brad had brought the woman into the investigation, it was his reputation that was on the line. Hernandez didn't fail to reiterate each time the priestess was mentioned that enlisting the help of someone claiming to be able to lift a curse (from a city, no less) could prove embarrassing to the department. What Hernandez really meant was that it could prove embarrassing to Detective Mandich. Somehow, Hernandez would manage to absolve himself of any involvement.

At 4:55 p.m. there was still no Priestess Julia. The two detectives and Lauren made their way to the sergeant's office. Like a child caught in the open while playing hide-and-seek, Brad tried the impossible. He attempted to achieve invisibility by walking behind the women. Like a jack-in-the-box trying to shrink its accordion neck to return to its container, Brad was stooping and positioning his head as close to his shoulders as possible, trying to shorten his neck.

Not only was it not working, but he looked ludicrous. The insanity of the scheme did not escape his superior's attention.

"Mandich, are you kidding me? Do you think I can't see you? What I don't see is the priestess. Where the hell is *she?*"

As he spoke, the volume of his speech became incrementally louder and his tone of voice became increasingly accusatory. Seated when the trio first entered his office, Hernandez was now half-sitting and half-standing, elevating his body to a stance that appeared threatening. He slammed his hands down on his desk with a thwack that could be heard throughout the squad room. The skin on his face took on the deep red color of a person who sat outside for hours in the sun without sunscreen. Veins in his neck and face protruded from under his skin. Lauren imagined his veins as balloons filling with air, concerned that like an overfilled balloon, he was close to exploding.

At that moment, a commanding figure appeared, heading for the sergeant's office. The four occupants of the room turned to look at the woman in the corridor. She wore at a colorful fabric head covering, at least five patterned scarves draped around her neck, chest, and waist, a blouse in a reddish-brown color, and a full ankle-length skirt with vibrant prints that resembled numerous animal hides. The sounds of her jewelry announced her arrival before she reached the doorway. Dangling earrings tinkled, several layers of metallic chains around her neck clinked against each other, and bracelets that covered both wrists up to her forearms jingled as she walked. Sergeant Hernandez didn't think it possible, but he believed that she was wearing even more jewelry than when he first walked by her in the squad room days before.

Fortuitously for his blood pressure and for Brad Mandich's ego, Sergeant Hernandez began to calm down. Easing himself down into his chair, he invited Julia to take a seat across from his desk. Then he glared at Brad, mumbling under his breath, "You're a lucky bastard."

Julia's arrival made Brad feel somewhat fortunate both because she showed up and because he figured that he wouldn't be subjected to the sergeant's derogatory comments with their guest in the room. Clearly, Brad wasn't certain that he had entirely escaped the wrath of Sergeant Hernandez, but for now, he would take what he could get.

"Priestess Julia, I am Sergeant Hernandez. Thank you for coming on such short notice." Pointing to Brad, he said, "I'm aware that Detective Mandich gave you samples of swatches from the garments of the three initial victims of the Dead if Night killer when you offered your assistance to our department. Detective Amanda Banks, seated next to Detective Mandich, is one of our younger rising stars. Next to her is Lauren Mandich, a civilian who is married to Detective Mandich's nephew. The first three victims of the DON killer were classmates of hers, so Lauren has a special interest in this case."

"Thank you for the introductions, but let's get to the point. I know this isn't a social visit. Just why am I here, exactly?" asked Julia.

"When you initially suggested over a week ago that you could help Detectives Mandich and Dennison, we were never introduced. From what I understand from Detective Mandich, you've been kind enough to offer your services to the department to help with this case."

Priestess Julia shifted in her seat and bent to retrieve her oversized purse which sat on the floor next to her. After rearranging her voluminous skirt, she pulled out a bottle of Evian water from the large handbag. She took a few sips before responding.

"I see your concerns, Sergeant Hernandez, but there's a misunderstanding concerning my abilities. First, I don't solve crimes. However, I do deal with curses. I can say with certainty that there is a curse on the city of Miami. I can provide help with *that*, but you will need to find who or what is responsible."

This was a far cry from what Sergeant Hernandez wanted to hear. While he didn't believe in psychics or voodoo, part of him hoped that this enigmatic woman could lead the police to the perpetrator of the murders. She destroyed even the modicum of hope he harbored on that score. The idea of the city of Miami being cursed was not well received by any of the participants of the meeting. It sounded like a lot of hogwash, especially to Sergeant Hernandez. His look of incredulity almost gave him away.

Uncharacteristically, Hernandez then decided to hedge his bets by not dismissing the idea of a curse outright. He feared that his skepticism of Priestess Julia might prove ill-advised, especially since the investigation was going nowhere. Frankly, both Brad and Amanda were shocked by his response to the priestess. It was so out of character.

"Please," Hernandez said, "clarify something for me. If what you say is true, it seems like Miami is still under this curse.

More people have died since you took the clothing swatches from the original victims. What did you do with the swatches? Were you trying to use them to stop the murders? If that's the case, can you explain why there have been more deaths?"

There was resignation in Julia's voice. It seemed as if she were also frustrated by her inability to lift the curse and prevent additional victims from dying. Absently, she transferred her bottled water back and forth from one hand to the other.

"With the cloth Detective Mandich gave me, I had everything I needed from the police to help you, as I offered to do. Rest assured; I've taken the necessary steps and performed the proper ceremony to lift this death curse. If you were more familiar with the nature of what I do, you'd understand that it takes time, usually several weeks, to see results. Sometimes it even takes longer."

"That's not good enough," blurted Sergeant Hernandez. His patience wearing thin, he grabbed the letter opener on his desk and began cleaning his nails. Brad feared when he saw Hernandez pick up the pointed metal object, he might stab someone with it out of sheer frustration.

"I'm sorry to hear that," responded the priestess, "but these spells can't be rushed. They're not an exact science like your lab tests and the other procedures *you* use to solve crimes. I've done all I can do for you."

Lauren could remain silent no longer. As she looked over at Hernandez, she asked, "With your permission, may I say something?"

"Sure. Why not?" Sergeant Hernandez was intrigued by what she might say, especially since Detective Banks spoke highly of her.

Looking directly at the priestess, Lauren expressed some concerns about the woman's authenticity. She knew she was treading a fine line between calling Julia a charlatan and sincerely looking for explanations as to why she was unable to verify Julia's identity as a legitimate practitioner of voodoo.

"Julia, pardon me if I seem skeptical, but I am. I went to Little Haiti seeking your help. No one there had ever seen you or knew of you. At the time I researched your webpage and the webpages of several other priests and priestesses in Little Haiti, I was surprised to see that many provided the same email address, phone number, and even post-office address as you. My attempts to reach you via email, text, and phone were unsuccessful. You never replied to me. If you have a legitimate business, I'd expect that you would respond to potential clients. Your lack of response and the shared contact information puzzle me. Can you explain that?"

If Lauren believed that she was putting Priestess Julia on the spot, she was wrong. Without hesitation, Julia had a credible explanation that she rattled off without nervousness or anger in her voice.

"There's a simple explanation. I don't open texts if I don't recognize the telephone number of callers who aren't in my contacts. As far as the shared information, we practitioners of voodoo function like a single unit to share expenses and keep down costs. We all use a service that screens phone calls and emails for us. For some reason, your inquiries were never forwarded to me. I'll be talking to a supervisor about that." Julia added the last comment to give her response more legitimacy, attempting to sound outraged that she hadn't been given her messages.

The answer seemed too smooth and too prepared, like a theatrical performance. The comment about the supervisor didn't achieve its intended effect either. Unconvinced, Lauren had more weapons in her arsenal, additional questions to throw Julia off balance and get at the truth. The look on her face spoke volumes.

With his uncanny ability to size up a situation, Hernandez cut off what might be considered "interrogation" from Lauren before things could escalate. "Well, I guess that explains things," he said. "You two civilians are excused with my thanks for coming. Detectives, please remain in my office for a few moments. We have some police business to discuss."

Confused by the abrupt dismissal, both women stood up to leave. Julia was glad to be on her way while Lauren wanted to stay and ask her more questions. Upset that she had been dismissed like a child at a party for grownups, Lauren was insulted that Sergeant Hernandez didn't value her input. Trailing behind Julia, Lauren was too angry to even say goodbye. For her part, Julia wanted no further contact with the police or Lauren. She was happy that Lauren remained silent.

Before starting her car in the parking lot, Lauren reached into her purse to check her phone for voicemails, emails, or text messages. During the meeting, she had her ring signal turned off. Whenever the phone was on silent, it seemed that she received more important time-sensitive communications than at any other time of the day. A true Murphy's Law phenomenon. Today appeared to be no different.

Typically, she rated text messages as first, voicemail messages as second, and emails as third in the hierarchy of their importance to her. In the short time that she was at the meeting, ten new emails, two voicemails, and one text message had been left on her phone. The text message got her immediate attention. It had arrived just moments before. Sergeant Hernandez summoned her back to his office.

Lauren exited her car and returned to the building, somewhat annoyed, but also baffled by being asked to rejoin the meeting. The two detectives were still seated in their chairs. They were now joined by Detective Dennison who had been suddenly dispatched to a crime scene just prior to the meeting.

"You texted me, Sergeant Hernandez?"

"Yes, I did, Mrs. Mandich. I'm sorry for the charade earlier. It's obvious that you don't trust this Priestess Julia any more than we do. From the conversation we just had after you left, none of us are convinced that she is what she says she is. I was afraid that any further pointed questions from you might make her think that we were hatching a plot against her. If it makes you feel better, during our meeting, I had a tracking device placed on her car. Now we'll be able to monitor her comings and goings. We'll know where she eats, shops and lives."

Lauren was impressed by Sergeant Hernandez. His apology, his forthcoming explanation, and his willingness to tell her about the tracking device dispelled her earlier anger. What he said more than justified why she had been asked to depart. She acknowledged to herself that sometimes she allowed herself to become angry before knowing all the facts. This was one of those times. The sergeant's decision to dismiss her along with Julia made perfect sense. It put the two women on equal footing. Furthermore, it demonstrated that Lauren wasn't a tool of the police. That might prove helpful in future interactions.

Lauren nodded her head in understanding, giving the sergeant one of her most charming smiles. Perhaps that influenced his decision to fill her in on another trap for Julia they put in place. He pointed to where she had been sitting.

"See that bottle of Evian over there? Lucky for us, Julia left it behind when she departed. Now we're able to have her fingerprints analyzed. Like you, I doubt her story. I wouldn't be surprised if she's not what she claims to be. In fact, I'd bet on it."

CHAPTER 36

I pulled the Miami Herald from its plastic wrapper at the kitchen table while depositing my coffee mug at my seat. Like always, I rifled through the paper and opened the sports section, covering my placemat and napkin. Today the news in the sports section also made the front-page headlines.

What was it with the Pittsburgh Steelers? The suspension of Miami native Hoyt Stark from the Steelers was now considered yesterday's news. Today, above the fold, was the story of another Miami native who was also a Pittsburgh Steelers player. His dead body had been found in an unusual location. The supposition was that he was possibly a victim of the DON killer.

According to the article, the body of Sam McKay, a Pro Bowl player and leading running back for the Steelers, was found in the center of the field that would host the Super Bowl game in less than two months. A graduate of Miami Central High School, he maintained a home in Miami-Dade County. He had taken his coach's advice and went home for the bye week for a little rest and relaxation. For both Sam and his family, who anticipated seeing him on the field at the Super Bowl, this would have been a dream come true. The killer had a cruel sense of irony, depositing the body on the football field; the dream turned into a nightmare.

McKay's death was not a tragedy only for his family. It shook up the local community who gloried in his successful career. The ramifications of his death stretched across the country. Las Vegas odds makers were scrambling to recalculate their numbers. The people of Pittsburgh were no longer certain that they would see their team in the Super Bowl. Without Sam McKay, the team's chances of success in the playoffs was iffy.

I reread the article, noting with surprise the location of the body; it was found on the field on which the Super Bowl would be played. My gut told me that it was a message, but I couldn't figure out its meaning. Up until this point, all the bodies that were considered related to the Dead of Night killer were found at the locations of the actual killings. It made no sense to me that Sam McKay would have been at the stadium at the time of his death. There was no reason for him to be there nor would he have had access to the stadium or the field of play. The obvious conclusion was that he had to have been killed elsewhere, his corpse relocated. *Why him, and why was his body placed there?* I had no answers, not even theories.

It was more than morbid curiosity. Something nagged at me, but I couldn't dredge up any connections to the other deaths, although I was positive that there was a piece of the puzzle that I was missing. I called Cecil Murphy, the medical examiner, hoping that I could sweet-talk him into approving my attendance at the autopsy.

"Dr. Murphy, it's Cliff Mandich. I'm sure you saw the headlines today."

"I certainly did. The body is here."

He didn't even mention whose body, but we both knew we were discussing Sam McKay.

"With your permission, I'd like to come down and check him out."

"Okay by me. Why don't you come around three this afternoon? I should be ready for you by then. Just so you know, at the suggestion of my friend Doug Wirth, a forensic dentist, I called Metro Zoo. I've got a guy from there coming to look at the bodies."

"That sounds pretty odd. Why'd he suggest you call *them?*"

"Dr. Wirth suspects that the bites aren't human. He wanted a wildlife expert to view the bodies and give an expert opinion. Unfortunately, the head guy is on a photo safari in India. Just my luck. An underling agreed to stop by this afternoon around three. Since I'm rather busy, it would be most convenient if the two of you could visit at the same time."

****

Upon arrival, I was greeted by Jackie, Dr. Murphy's secretary.

"Oh, Dr. Mandich, go right in. He's expecting you."

"Thanks, Jackie. I know the way. Oh, by the way this is for you."

I handed her a pink bag designed specifically for my office. We often send patients home with samples of sunscreen, moisturizers, and other skin products. The package for Jackie was full of sunblock with moisturizer.

Surprised, Jackie smiled and said, "Thanks. I love surprises."

She peered into the bag, examining it like a kid on Halloween looking through her loot bag upon returning home. Only her goodies were skin products.

"They're for you. Your boss seemed a little testy on the phone the last time we talked. When I asked him about it, he told me that these murders were getting to him. He said his stress was compounded by your upcoming vacation next month, cruising to the Caribbean out of the Port of Miami. It's obvious how much he relies on you based upon his concern about your absence.

"I, however, am concerned about your skin. Can't help myself. For sure, you'll be getting more sun than usual. Frankly, I'd like to avoid seeing you in my office with painful sunburn after your trip. Beyond the short-term discomfort, sunburn can have lasting effects. So, make sure you pack the sunscreen and reapply it throughout the day, especially if you go swimming."

"Dr. Mandich, that's so sweet of you. I'm going to put it with my vacation stuff when I get home, so I don't forget to bring it."

Happy at her response, I continued down the hall toward the morgue. When I got there, another visitor was already with Dr. Murphy. He heard me enter and signaled me over to the stainless-steel tables.

"Dr. Mandich, this is Pete Ward. He's an assistant wildlife expert working with Dr. Adam Crowe at Miami Metro Zoo. Dr. Crowe has a doctorate in wildlife and zoo management, and according to Mr. Ward, is a wonderful mentor. I believe I told you that Dr. Crowe is currently in India, but Pete has graciously volunteered to fill in for him."

Walking toward the examining tables, I deposited my car keys and my cell phone on the Formica shelf by the refrigerator that was used for samples. As I extended my hand to Pete, I took a critical look at him. He wore his sandy brown hair in a long shaggy style, practically covering his eyes. His trim, athletic body was dressed in a khaki safari-style shirt with the logo of the Miami Metro Zoo on the pocket. His Bermuda shorts were made from the same fabric as the shirt, and brown leather sandals completed his attire. Not that I consider myself old, but Pete seemed like a teenager to me. I couldn't help but wonder when I crossed over from a kid to an adult. I never saw it coming.

"Glad to have your help, Pete" I said. "Have you already viewed the body of Sam McKay?"

"Not, I haven't. Dr. Murphy tells me that I don't need to examine McKay since his corpse doesn't have any bite marks. I'm basically here to help interpret bite marks on the other victims' bodies to see whether I recognize an animal that could have left them. If I understand this correctly, all victims *except* McKay have bite marks. I realize the urgency since families are clamoring to have their loved ones returned for final burial."

It was news to me that McKay hadn't been bitten. I was curious about other ways in which his death deviated from the prior killings. Maybe Pete didn't need to see the body, but I did. It wasn't enough to hear about the differences; I wanted to see for myself. Fortunately, Dr. Murphy was amenable to my request.

He walked us to the table with Sam McKay's body and removed the sheet which covered it. McKay had the body of an athlete. He was quite muscular, yet trim. Dr. Murphy reviewed the physical findings relating to all other victims; he then focused on specific differences between McKay's corpse and the other bodies. Engrossed in his explanation, I barely looked up from the table. When I did, I glanced at Pete Ward who stood on the opposite side of the table from me.

Earlier, when introduced to him, I noted that his occupation as a wildlife expert explained his deeply tanned skin color. He probably spent a good deal of his time outdoors. Looking at Pete Ward now, I observed that the color had drained from his face. In addition to his pallor, he was holding both hands below his chin in the shape of a cup. He was about to puke, his queasy stomach ready to explode like the eruption of a volcano. He began gagging.

Without missing a beat, and with only a few seconds to spare, Dr. Murphy jumped into action. He grabbed a stainless-steel pan and thrust it into Pete's hand. Not a second too soon. Ward heaved up the contents of his stomach into the pan, mortified. Heading for the nearest bathroom, he gratefully accepted the canister of Lysol disinfecting wipes that Dr. Murphy also provided. It was obvious that this wasn't Murphy's first rodeo with a newbie in the morgue.

Pete Ward's response was no doubt common among visitors without medical training when they viewed a dead human body that had been autopsied. Several moments later, he returned from the restroom, having recovered his composure. His color returned to normal. Without hesitation, he indicated that he was ready for Dr. Murphy to resume his discussion about Sam McKay.

"You sure you're feeling well enough, Pete?" asked Dr. Murphy solicitously.

Frankly, I sensed that he was hoping that one mutilated dead body would have been enough for Pete. Dr. Murphy was giving him an out. Most likely, Murphy was wishing that Pete's supervisor could have been the one to examine the bodies. Pete, however, was not about to wimp out. He acted as if the last few minutes had never happened. Partly from embarrassment and partly because he hoped the two physicians wouldn't tell his boss about his humiliating vomiting episode, he felt the need to demonstrate his professionalism and his stoicism.

"Sure, let's continue with Sam McKay as Dr. Mandich requested. Then, I'd like you to show me all the victims with bite marks," Pete said. Not only did he sound convincing, but Pete proved that he successfully controlled his gag reflex.

"There's a lack of a puncture wound at the back of his neck. This suggests that no tranquilizer was used," explained Dr. Murphy. "Also, the hyoid, a small bone at the anterior aspect, or front of the neck, was crushed. As you can see, the tiny blood vessels in the eyes have hemorrhaged. This suggests strangulation. If I may speculate, I think that Mr. McKay might have known his killer; it appears to me that the killer was able to approach his victim without alarming him. What is extremely odd is that although his internal organs were removed, his body exhibits no bite marks."

Dr. Murphy's final statement struck me as the most perplexing. Attempting to synthesize all of the information he provided, I stated, "We're dealing either with the Dead of Night killer changing his pattern to deceive or because he requires different ways to satisfy his lust for murder. The other possibility is that there's a copycat out there. I don't these scenarios."

****

Once Dr. Murphy highlighted the differences between Sam McKay and the other victims, he walked over to the first of the bodies with bite marks for Pete to examine. There were several more corpses placed on the parallel stainless-steel tables in the autopsy suite.

Other than his footsteps as he walked from table to table, and the rustling sound of the coverings of the victims pulled down to reveal the bodies, there was no other sound in the room as Pete surveyed the cruel damage done to the victims. The mutilated condition of the bodies was appalling. Pete Ward focused on the wounds of the victims, studying the bite marks first. Concentrating on the wounds allowed Ward to forget about his surroundings and the horrible nature of the crimes. He scrutinized the abdominal regions as well.

Finally, he looked at the medical examiner, needing an answer to a question that would confirm what he suspected.

"Dr. Murphy, did you remove the organs during your autopsies or were they missing at the time that the bodies were found?"

"They were missing at the scene, including the organs of Mr. Sam McKay."

With a sense of professional and personal pride, Pete Ward announced his conclusion. No preparatory remarks, No detailed explanation. He uttered just two words.

"Canis rufus."

That was a new one on me. I never heard this term and had absolutely no idea what this meant to the case. When I don't know something, I don't pretend that I do. There's no point in that. Immediately, I asked, "What is 'Canis rufus'?"

Being the "answer man" evidently appealed to Pete Ward. When he saw our baffled expressions and heard me ask for an explanation of Canis rufus, he seemed to grow in stature, becoming more self-assured than he had been earlier. There was no doubt that he was enjoying being the fount of knowledge.

"Canis rufus, also known as the red wolf or Florida wolf, did this. Take note of the shape of the jaw that must have made these marks. Also, look at the depth of the bite marks. No human could have inflicted bites like these. The only logical explanation is that canine teeth made these distinctive marks."

"Did anything else lead you to this conclusion?" I inquired.

"Actually, yes. When Dr. Murphy indicated that the organs were missing when the bodies were found, I immediately thought that a wolf might be involved. We humans consume animal flesh and muscle but tend to toss away the internal organs such as the stomach. By contrast, the stomach is a delicacy to the wolf. If you watch wildlife shows you've probably noticed the body parts animals begin consuming after capturing their prey."

Dr. Murphy was as fascinated as I was by Pete Ward's response. However, true to his nature as a scientist, the medical examiner was still somewhat skeptical and required further information. If he hadn't started speaking, I would have come up with a similar question for the wildlife expert.

"That's impressive, young man," said Dr. Murphy. Again, Pete was practically beaming from the praise. He was like a balloon, filling with helium and soaring to new heights. But the subsequent question tempered some of his pride in identifying the culprit as a wolf.

"Did you see anything that disturbs you and would make you question your conclusion?" Dr. Murphy asked.

That inquiry served as a pin, piercing the wall of the balloon, and releasing the helium within. To his credit, Pete hesitated before responding, wanting to consider all other possibilities. He looked at us earnestly as he cited several inconsistencies that came to mind.

"There are a few things that I find peculiar. Red wolves are an endangered species. Although native to Florida, they no longer are found here in the wild. I guess someone could capture one in North Carolina where a small number of them still roam free and transport it to Florida. Also, it's rare for a wolf to attack a human. If we accept that it *was* a wolf, it's strange that the early kills seem to have been selective. It's hard to understand why a wolf would choose athletes."

Ward's statement impelled me to share my theory.

"Wolves wouldn't know the difference between an athlete and a plumber. They don't use tranquilizers. If we accept that a wolf *ultimately* carried out the killings, a human would have had to set up and direct the plans. That makes the Dead of Night killer one impressive puppet master. Who would have guessed that the elusive DON killer employs a wolf as a murder weapon?"

I'm not sure that Dr. Murphy and Pete Ward shared my theory. They stared at me, their expressions a cross between disbelief and credence. *Had either of them postulated what I just suggested but hesitated to put it into words?*

Picking up my key fob and my cell phone, I shoved them into my pocket. Then I prepared for the perfunctory handshake prior to exiting. Focused on my upcoming Google search about Florida wolves, I was barely paying attention when Dr. Murphy cleared his throat and asked me for the second time, “Anything else you need from me before you leave, Dr. Mandich?”

“Yes, I know that you are or will be testing for traces of DNA that the killer or killers left behind. Please check the bite wounds.”

Then I added what I thought would be the most consequential finding of the test results.

“I’m curious whether they’ll show wolf DNA.”

CHAPTER 37

The following morning, I began my daily routine as always. Coffee mug in hand, I tore the yellow plastic bag from the Miami Herald, and began reading the paper. Interestingly, the lead news in the sports section and the featured story on the front page reported the identical event – the death of Sam McKay. Same as yesterday's paper. Reminded me of the movie "Groundhog Day."

When I saw the headlines all I could think was that fear sells papers; though readers might be horrified, they still eagerly pore over articles about murder. A scandal about sex or pornography is also an attention grabber, appealing to the prurient interest of readers. Stories about celebrities garner more interest than reports on local budgets or the day-to-day operations of government. Knowing this, newspapers cater to headlines and stories that titillate people. Sales were probably up the day before.

I'm fairly sure that Sergeant Hernandez and my uncle Brad were thinking the same way about news coverage as I was. If the police can't get the killer or killers off the streets, it's imperative to prevent gruesome details from being leaked to the press. The fear these details engender in local residents and the subsequent loss of visitors and related revenue from tourist spending has an enormous impact on the city. A classic example of the ripple effect.

So far, no one was reporting the possibility of a wolf being used as a murder weapon. If that got out, there would be pandemonium in downtown Miami. Beyond mass hysteria, the tourist flow would come to a screeching halt, immediately resulting in cutbacks to staff at stores, hotels, and restaurants that catered to the tourist trade. And that would be just the beginning of the economic fallout.

To the best of my knowledge, other than me, the only ones who knew about Canis rufus, the Florida wolf, were Dr. Murphy and Pete Ward from the Metro Zoo. After returning from the morgue the prior evening, I pondered about Pete Ward's suggestion of a wolf involved in the killings. I didn't want to sit on this information any longer. It was essential that the police be informed so they could pursue this lead. Without hesitation, I called my uncle and he scheduled to meet with me in two hours.

Killing time before my meeting, I read the story in the Herald which was none too favorable about Mayor Robert Diaz and his lack of progress in apprehending the DON killer. The shocking death of Sam McKay compounded the anxiety of an already frightened public. People wondered if anyone was safe. The killing of Miami's own pro football star, Sam McKay, was the tipping point. Mayor Diaz was taking the brunt of the blame, accused of poor leadership.

By contrast, the day could not have been going better for City Councilman Kyle Griffin as he strategized about his mayoral campaign. He was a hot topic in both the Herald and on the local television broadcasts. The derogatory comments about Mayor Diaz in the media fueled Councilman Griffin's confidence in his chances to unseat the mayor.

Out of curiosity, I turned on the television to the local news stations to see what they were reporting. My kitchen television was set to WPLG Local 10 news, but I also flipped to WTVJ on channel 6 and WSVN on channel 7. Photos of Sam McKay filled the screen each time I changed the channel. His death was the biggest story of the day, overshadowing all else.

The local news was suddenly interrupted by a "Breaking News" announcement. The station cut away to what was staged to appear as an impromptu interview with Councilman Griffin as he exited City Hall. No doubt someone from the councilman's office alerted the station that the councilman had some choice comments about Sam McKay's death and the ineptitude of the current administration. The reporters arrived en masse, expecting some memorable quotes. The timing seemed prearranged. The event was too seamless to appear coincidental.

Griffin was very much at home with a microphone in front of his face. He acted as if he had been caught unaware, rushing from City Hall with briefcase in hand to handle vital city business. He looked at his wristwatch, a dramatic pause to give credence to his next statement.

"I can only give you a minute. If you want a statement, I'll make it brief. The murder of Sam McKay is the final outrage. Like the others, McKay was missing his abdominal organs when the police found his body. A vicious killer is on the loose, mutilating bodies. This *cannot* continue. What Mayor Diaz has allowed to happen to our city is atrocious. I know that our fine police officers are working as hard as they can, but they are hampered by inadequate resources. Because of his mismanagement, Mayor Diaz hasn't given the police the tools they need in this public crisis. There is no excuse for his incompetence. Now please pardon me. I really have to go."

Once again, he consulted his watch, a gesture showing how busy he was and how attentive he was to keeping to his schedule. I couldn't help but recognize how slick the councilman was with his contrived statement meant to appear spontaneous. His dramatic pauses and emphasis on words specifically meant to criticize Mayor Diaz and his handling of the murders belied the spontaneity of his speech. I doubted that Griffin really cared about the police lacking resources. His eye was on the next mayoral election. For him, the murders gave his campaign an unanticipated advantage as he ripped into his opponent. Not once did he mention how he would successfully apprehend the killer and bring peace to the city. His "impromptu" press conference was all smoke and mirrors.

Miami had enough troubles. Mayor Robert Diaz was a decent man who went into public service for all the right reasons. Watching what I could only describe as a "performance" by Councilman Griffin, I was scared for my city. With residents in a panic that a killer was still running amok in Miami, Griffin's disparaging comments about Mayor Diaz might be enough to get him elected. If that happened, Miami's next mayor would be far less ethical and far more self-serving. A dangerous combination.

Dictating into my phone, I had a few ideas I wanted to remember for my meeting at the police station. My concentration was interrupted when my phone rang.

It might sound stupid, but I literally felt my jaw drop.

A bombshell had just landed.

CHAPTER 38

It wasn't easy, but I fought the urge to exceed the speed limit. Didn't seem like a good idea to get a ticket on the way to the Miami Police Headquarters or having to explain to Uncle Brad any delay a traffic stop might cause. My uncle's job as a police detective seemed to be my primary guardrail against speeding.

Two hours earlier when we scheduled our meeting, I informed my uncle that I uncovered a significant piece of information. My plan was to inform him of the wolf theory.

That was before the shocking phone call. The wolf theory paled by comparison with the revelation from the caller.

Trusting that my findings were credible, Brad alerted Sergeant Emilio Hernandez that important new evidence was on its way. The desk sergeant, Ted Mitchell, was given instructions to send me directly to the conference room.

Unexpectedly, a crowd awaited me. In addition to my uncle and Sergeant Hernandez, Lew Dennison, and Amanda Banks were part of the welcoming committee. As this was an APE (Acute Political Emergency) situation, Police Commissioner Inez Vargas and Chief Alberto Santiago were also present. It didn't take a degree in rocket science for me to deduce that if the police commissioner and the chief of police were present, there was no doubt that stopping the Dead of Night killer was akin to putting out a raging inferno. No doubt the flames were fanned by Sam McKay's death and the media coverage of it. The inflammatory press conference of Kyle Griffin on the news added fuel to the fire.

I was greeted like the pizza delivery guy in a frat house. Everyone was waiting for my arrival and ready to pounce on the product I was delivering.

Police Commissioner Vargas assumed the role of chairperson. She pointed to a seat at the head of the table in the conference room. All the assembled players were seated, waiting eagerly for my arrival. Guess Uncle Brad prepped them. Once I was in my chair, she wasted no time.

"Doctor Mandich, you have our full attention."

"Thank you, Commissioner Vargas. I'd like to start chronologically with what I learned during my visit to the morgue late yesterday and then finish with some blockbuster news that I received not more than an hour ago."

I had everyone's attention.

"Okay. Do it your way, but just get on with it."

Police Commissioner Vargas was unable to disguise her impatience both in her tone and in her words. She wanted answers, not theories, and wanted them now. Guess it came with the territory. I began my delivery of the facts as I knew them.

"The killer first stuns or paralyzes his victims with a dart from a blowgun or tranquilizer gun. In his earliest cases, he used curare which paralyzed the victims but left them conscious. In a later case involving the tourist couple, he used carfentanil which would have rendered the couple unconscious. Except for the most recent victim, distinguishing bite marks were found on all the bodies."

That's when I explained that Dr. Murphy called in a wildlife expert to help identify the source of the bites at the suggestion of a forensic dentist.

"The wildlife expert indicated that the configuration of the bite marks and their depth indicate that the bites were delivered by a non-human. His familiarity with animals led to his conclusion that the Florida wolf was the culprit. Further confirmation that an animal was responsible for the fatal wounds is the fact that the abdominal organs of the victims were missing prior to autopsy. The wolf feasts first on its prey's abdominal organs.

Looking at my audience, I waited for someone to gag, but instead of making them sick, that last detail seemed the most convincing. So far, so good. While I still had their attention, I continued.

"Obviously, a wolf didn't administer tranquilizers. That was done by a human. If not for the body of Sam McKay, the most recent victim, it could be concluded that the Florida wolf was somehow involved in all other killings. The evidence from the autopsies, except for Sam McKay, was consistent. However, the findings concerning Sam McKay ran contrary to the pattern," I explained.

"No bite marks were found; no tranquilizer was used. McKay was rendered unconscious via strangulation. Per Councilman Griffin's press conference and subsequent newspaper reports, one of the signature links to the Dead of Night killer is the missing abdominal organs. The disparate details concerning McKay's death suggest a copycat killer. It makes sense that the killer removed the abdominal organs, attempting to tie McKay's death to the other murders. It's my opinion that you should be looking for at least two killers."

"Excuse me, doctor," interrupted the police commissioner, "but regarding the wolf, just how much do you trust the wildlife guy?"

She had a good point. Frankly, I also felt a degree of hesitation concerning Pete Ward's explanation and accepting it as 100% accurate. *Where did the killer get the wolf? Where did he keep it? How did he train the wolf?* I'd need further confirmation to convince me completely.

"Let's just say, I'll be more comfortable when his superior, the director of wildlife at Miami Metro Zoo, returns from India. I believe he's photographing animals there, probably tigers."

"All right. For now," Vargas stated, "we'll accept his theory until the director returns. Now, what about the groundbreaking news you mentioned?"

Her tone and choice of words told me that Police Commissioner Vargas was probably thinking, *this had better be good.* She seemed less than impressed with my source of information about the Florida wolf. What she wanted was for me to provide a revelation that would crack the case wide open. I figured my next statement would do just that. At least, I hoped so.

****

"You've all suspected there's a mole who's been leaking information. I can identify him. We all......"

I was interrupted by a buzzing of conversation in the room and the voice of Inez Vargas, impatient for answers.

"Who is it? And what does this person have to gain?" she asked.

"As I was starting to say, we all know that Councilman Griffin has been the conduit to the press."

"Where is *he* getting his information?" demanded Vargas.

At this rate, we'd be here all night.

"From Cecil Murphy, the medical examiner." Another buzz of conversation from this surprise disclosure. I felt like a magician, mystifying children by pulling rabbits out of a hat.

"But why? What's their connection? Why would Murphy leak evidence and details of his findings to the city councilman?"

It pained me to respond to her question. We doctors tend to stick together and watch each other's backs. But Murphy had crossed the line; I was obligated to tell her what I learned.

"He did it out of obligation, and fear of reprisals from Griffin if he didn't cooperate," I explained. "Dr. Murphy was appointed when Dr. Meacham retired three years ago. Kyle Griffin used his political influence to help Murphy secure the post. Seems that Griffin believes his favor entitles him to information he can use to his advantage in the upocoming mayoral election. Insider information could help him sway the voters."

This time Vargas seemed satisfied with my explanation. You could almost see the wheels turning in her head as she digested what I said. Also seemed that she didn't hold a high opinion of Griffin.

"That explains a lot. Councilman Griffin must have sifted through the information Dr. Murphy gave him, picking out the most disturbing elements of the autopsies. His release to the press from the steps of City Hall of previously undisclosed information regarding the missing organs of the victims caused panic and massive dissatisfaction with the current mayoral administration." She shook her head and sighed as she said, "No consideration of the impact on the public. All for his personal gain."

Sergeant Hernandez, not wanting to be caught with his pants down, addressed his concerns.

"Dr. Mandich, I'd like to know how you came upon this information. Do you believe your source is trustworthy? We can't afford to make accusations and come off half-cocked."

I did trust my source. It was Dr. Murphy's secretary. What she revealed explained a lot, including why Dr. Murphy originally missed the puncture wounds on the victims' necks. Griffin put Murphy under intense pressure. Being a victim of extortion, it would be normal to lose focus. I suspected that Griffin also pressured Murphy to anonymously leak information to the press.

"I understand where you're coming from, Sergeant Hernandez. Jackie Norton, Dr. Murphy's secretary, contacted me about several conversations she overheard between her boss and

Councilman Griffin. It bothered her that the councilman was extorting information from Dr. Murphy. She became incensed when she saw that Griffin then used the information to deliberately whip up fear and incite criticism of Mayor Diaz."

Addressing all attendees at the meeting, Vargas declared, "It will give me great pleasure to speak to Griffin myself. I'll make it abundantly clear that his disclosure of any information the police was keeping under wraps can be traced back to him or Dr. Murphy, I'll bring charges against them. His actions have compromised our investigation and are probably responsible for the specific actions of this copycat killer."

Her next commented was directed specifically to me. "By the way, Dr. Mandich, your analysis made a credible case for a copycat killer."

"Thank you, Commissioner Vargas. Beyond wanting to help the police, I have an extremely personal stake in this investigation. My wife, Lauren, graduated from Miami Senior High School with some of the victims. She is on the committee for their upcoming ten-year reunion. Lauren is worried that the gathering might provide more targets for the killer. I worry about Lauren's role in the reunion and whether the killer has taken notice of her involvement."

Although Police Commissioner Vargas initially struck me as a no-nonsense bureaucrat, my explanation of my fears concerning Lauren seemed to bring out her softer side. Once she understood why this was so personal for me, she seemed less curt, more human.

"In case I haven't already told you, Dr. Mandich, you've done a great service for us with your information about the Florida wolf, and by suggesting a copycat killer. I trust we can continue to count on your help."

From the inflection of her voice, I realized that she meant it as a question. Without a moment's hesitation, I responded, "Of course."

Since she requested my help, I figured I could ask a favor of her. It was worth a shot.

"What Jackie told me about Dr. Murphy was in confidence," I said. "She was concerned he might find out that the information came from her. I assured Jackie that I'd make sure her name wasn't mentioned to him or to the press as the source. I'd like to be able to count on you to leave her name out of it. She's worried about losing her job, or that Dr. Murphy could make her life a living hell if he found out."

"Not a problem, Dr. Mandich. I see your point. This will be our secret."

If I didn't know better, I'd swear she winked at me. I had a good feeling about Inez Vargas keeping her word. Call it instinct or a gut feeling, but I think Jackie's secret would be safe.

The police commissioner then outlined how she would handle the councilman. Her ultimate goal was to insure the re-election of Mayor Diaz.

"After I read Councilman Griffin the riot act, I plan to contact Mayor Diaz. We have worked together harmoniously through the years and along the way, Bob and I have become friends. Rest assured, I'll let him know what Griffin has done and the underhanded way he secured his ammunition. Turnabout is fair play. If Griffin still chooses to run in the next election, Diaz will squash him like the insect that he is."

I liked her attitude.

Forewarned is forearmed.

CHAPTER 39

After the meeting at the police station, I couldn't wait to share the news with Lauren. As I told Police Commissioner Vargas, I worried constantly about Lauren's safety ever since the murders began. I wanted to confirm for myself that she was okay without seeming obvious. It's not easy to get something by Lauren. Most of the time, I think she knows exactly what I'm doing. Calling from my car, I had the phone on speaker. Lauren picked up on the first ring.

"Hi, Cliff. How'd your meeting go?"

"Just driving back from the police station. Yours truly has a new friend at the highest level. With the information I provided to her, I'm in the good graces of Police Commissioner Vargas. No small feat, I might add."

So, I was bragging, but I *was* impressed with myself, and wanted Lauren to be equally impressed. She didn't disappoint.

"That's terrific, Cliff. From what I hear, she's very reserved and keeps a distance. I've heard your uncle say that several times. Good for you. But I'm not surprised," Lauren said. That statement alone told me just what I wanted to hear.

"What have *you* been up to?" I asked.

"Reunion business, what else?"

"Could you be more specific? Where are you taking care of this business?"

"Believe it or not, I'm still home. Every time I think I can leave to take care of some errands, I get another email or phone call from someone wanting reassurance that it's safe to come to Miami for the reunion. I should just make a recording. The truth is, I'm not sure that I'm being entirely truthful with my classmates considering what's been happening. It's beginning to bother me."

What I wanted to ask was whether she was fearful for her own safety, as a high-profile member of the reunion committee. But I held back, hoping she'd say something that would allow me to segue into that topic. No such luck. I held my tongue, glad she was at home and safe.

"Maybe I'll run out to Publix and pick up some salmon for dinner," Lauren suggested. She knew I loved how she prepared it, with a delicious ginger dressing. However, I would forego dinner at home if it meant she had to go anywhere alone. Instead, I suggested eating out and going to the movies, not necessarily in that order. Guess that idea appealed to her because she instantly agreed.

"You pick the movie, Lauren. Depending on the theater it's playing in, we'll decide where to eat. I should be home no later than three thirty, so if there's a movie that starts around four o'clock, we should be able to make it and eat afterwards. Otherwise, we can reverse the order. I'm completely flexible," I said.

"You got that right," she replied. It was as if I could hear the smile in her voice. No doubt she was referring to bedroom activities, and I had to smile as well.

"Okay, Cliff. Get going so you'll be back somewhere between three and four o'clock. I'll start looking at what's playing. Date night should be a nice diversion from all the stress we've both been under. Lately I've been glued to the TV set. Going out with you will stop me from obsessing about the news.

I reiterated her words, "You got that right."

CHAPTER 40

True to her word, Police Commissioner Vargas placed a call to Kyle Griffin after the meeting broke up and she was back in her office. He was blindsided by her call. When his secretary announced that the police commissioner was on the line for him, Councilman Griffin was expecting congratulations on his "impromptu" press conference with the reporters. In his mind, he had been articulate, poised, and informative. He deluded himself into thinking that he had performed a tremendous public service to the people of Miami. The smile on his face was short-lived.

With her measured tone, Vargas accomplished more than she would have had she screamed at the councilman, although it took all her self-control to contain her anger. "Councilman Griffin, for future reference, I don't *ever again* want to see you on television divulging information that hasn't been released to the media. You were showboating and should have known better. It just so happens that I'm aware that the source of your information is none other than our medical examiner, Dr. Murphy. I know you've been extorting him to reveal details of his autopsies."

The councilman was stunned. Had she shouted at him, he would have responded defiantly. Unable to mount a defense for his actions, he listened passively. He didn't want to escalate the situation any further. As Commissioner Vargas continued, things worsened for Griffin.

"I'm considering bringing you up on charges, Councilman Griffin. The nature of the information you released to the news media is compromising a murder investigation. Consider this your last and only warning. You're on notice." Again, her calm tone, as she warned him matter-of-factly of potential consequences he could face, hit him with the force of a tsunami, likely swamping his candidacy for mayor.

Before Griffin could make any response, he heard the phone slam down in his ear. He acknowledged to himself that his earlier euphoria about his press conference was *totally eclipsed* by his fear of her warning. He was too upset to realize the juxtaposition of those two words.

Dr. Murphy was the next person to have his day upended by Inez Vargas. As angry as she had been at Kyle Griffin, that degree of anger was minimal in comparison to her fury at Dr. Cecil Murphy. Griffin was a politician through and through; shoddy behavior and taking advantage of a situation for his own political gain was something that came with the territory. The same was *not* true regarding the standard she expected from a respected medical examiner. A person who held that title typically epitomized professionalism and extreme discretion. Releasing sensitive information regarding an ongoing police investigation was a breach of ethics; that breach could lead to criminal prosecution.

This time, rather than masking her anger, Police Commissioner Vargas attacked the medical examiner for his malfeasance. Her anger simmering when she spoke to Griffin, it was now boiling over.

When Cecil Murphy answered the phone, he had no inkling that anyone knew that he was the councilman's source of information for his press conference. Murphy was grossly mistaken. Police Commissioner Vargas shouted at him, barely pausing to breathe. Her speech pattern was staccato; she seemed to enunciate every word of criticism in a loud voice that accentuated the condemnation she heaped on him. When she got to the part where she warned him that he was on thin ice, he felt as if he had already cracked through the thin surface covering the pond, close to drowning.

"Do you have any idea how you've compromised this investigation?" Vargas asked him. "What got into you? Should I be concerned that other cases have been tainted by your inappropriately supplying information to Councilman Griffin and possibly others? You are dangerously close to being reported to the district attorney's office."

With that warning, the Police Commissioner abruptly terminated the call. She purposely did not allow Dr. Murphy time to reply with some poorly concocted explanation.

Dr, Murphy replayed the conversation in his mind, analyzing both what Vargas said and what she didn't say. Her rebuke was devastating to him. Never before in his professional career had he strayed from doing everything by the book. Just his luck to have made a terrible decision that came back to bite him in the ass. The irony of this thought was not lost on him, especially since bite marks seemed to be a common theme of the murders he had been investigating.

Murphy rebuked himself for not having resisted Griffin's pressures. It could cost him more than his job and all the concomitant benefits that went along with that, including his health insurance and his pension. He was terrified that Vargas was giving serious thought to asking the district attorney to bring charges against him, the most serious being obstruction of justice. Even worse, he feared that his reputation could be forever tarnished. He treasured the sterling reputation that he worked so long and so hard to develop.

All his accomplishments could come crashing down in an instant. *How could he have been so stupid as to allow Kyle Griffin to pressure him into revealing information that he used in such a self-serving manner?*

Within minutes of mentally berating himself for compromising his principles and imagining all the repercussions of what he had done, he was startled by the jingling of his phone. He couldn't bear another reaming out by Police Commissioner Vargas. Steeling himself for more invective, he grabbed the phone. His response was intended for Vargas.

"Any more warnings from you that I should be aware of?"

Instead of Vargas, Kyle Griffin shouted at him. His tone was hostile. "Don't communicate with me anymore. I've got Inez Vargas breathing down my neck about bringing charges against me for what I told reporters based on the information *you* gave me. That woman is such a bitch. I can't take this crap."

"Who the hell do you think *you* are, telling *me* not to communicate with *you*? You're blaming *me* for giving *you* information that *you* chose to leak to the press? Because of you, my entire career is in jeopardy. Where do *you* come off acting like the injured party? You've got more nerve than brains."

Councilman Griffin was in a panic about the impact that being brought up on charges would have on his candidacy for mayor. That was his preeminent goal and he had come so close to achieving it. In his mind, the speech he gave about Mayor Diaz's incompetence should have closed the deal. His earlier smugness at providing information damning to the mayor didn't seem like such a good idea now, but only because it backfired. It hadn't entered his mind that Dr. Murphy would also have to deal with the consequences. Nor did he care.

The only reactions they had in common about their calls from Police Commissioner Vargas were their shared anxiety about how she found out about their clandestine connection. The source of her information would remain a mystery to them. As promised,

Commissioner Vargas kept the identity of the whistleblower secret. They would never know that Jackie Norton, Dr. Murphy's secretary, supplied the details of their relationship.

More importantly, they worried about how far Vargas would proceed with her threats. "Don't worry, Griffin. If I never speak to you again, it'll be too soon. I could lose my medical license because of you. Vargas might investigate all my past cases to see if any of those have also been tainted, thanks to you. Now, run along and crawl back under that rock of yours. I've got more important problems than you."

With that, Dr. Murphy closed his eyes, took a few deep breaths, and used some meditation techniques to calm down from the two disturbing conversations. He needed all his focus to deal with the intense pressure to release the bodies of the victims to their respective families. It wasn't that he couldn't empathize with their need to bury their loved ones and try to have some closure, but he felt stressed, nonetheless. A meticulous individual, Dr. Murphy still had additional tests that he would have liked to conduct to be sure that his findings were 100% accurate. It didn't appear that he would be afforded that luxury.

The family of Christopher Dee, victim number one, had been waiting the longest for the release of his body. Believing that there is strength in numbers, Christopher's family contacted the other Miami families and together they hired attorney Lambert Elkington to facilitate a more rapid release of the remains of their loved ones.

When Elkington contacted Lily Raines, the daughter of Walter and Vivian Raines of New Jersey, he learned that Lily was also an attorney. She provided invaluable professional input. Her personal stake in the matter fueled her zeal for release of the bodies from the morgue of her parents as well as those of the other victims. Both attorneys applied pressure to the medical examiner for his immediate compliance.

Under different circumstances, Cecil Murphy might have attempted to stall the families. Ordinarily, he would perform examinations and re-examinations until he satisfied himself that he hadn't overlook anything. Today was different. He didn't have the stomach to delay further because of his own predicament. Dr. Murphy yielded to the entreaties from the families, convincing himself that the bodies had been studied and photographed enough. The forensic dentist, Dr. Doug Wirth, had carefully taken pictures of the bite marks from every angle imaginable, and recorded measurements down to the smallest degree of accuracy possible. Before sending them to Dr. Murphy, Dr. Wirth first wanted to work with them on his photo enhancing programs for further detail and documentation. Also, Dr. Murphy had DNA samples and toxicology screens for all victims. No more delay could be justified.

Empathetic to the families, he also acted to avoid unflattering publicity that might come his way if the attorneys chose to sue for release of the bodies on behalf of their clients. It was more important than ever before to stay out of the limelight.

He called out to Jackie to come into his office. Earlier, she heard his raised voiced while he was on the phone. She was reluctant to deal with him when he was that upset. Dr. Murphy sensed her hesitation and signaled to her to enter.

"Jackie, please call Lambert Elkington and inform him that we're ready to release the bodies. We can place calls regarding the pickups if he provides the names of the local funeral homes the family members have chosen. When he contacts Lily Raines, the daughter of the couple from New Jersey, he can advise her to have their bodies transported to a local funeral home for preparation for final transport back to New Jersey. If Elkington advises us the names of both funeral homes, I'll contact them with information regarding transport and final interment."

This would leave the one remaining body in the morgue to work with, the body of football star, Sam McKay. McKay's family hadn't exerted pressure for release of his body, allowing Dr. Murphy to scrupulously gather evidence from the corpse, the victim's clothing, and other items found at the scene. Even the smallest piece of evidence might enable Dr. Murphy to identify the killer by a strand of hair, skin scrapings under the fingernails of the victim, fibers from clothing not belonging to the victim. There were myriad tests and methods that he used in the painstaking process of his examination of a dead body.

Unfortunately, the corpse that remained for study was very possibly the work of a copycat killer and not the work of the Dead of Night killer. But regardless of whether the findings related to the bulk of the murders or not, the killer needed to be identified. Dr. Murphy's work was still part of an ongoing investigation.

CHAPTER 41

Very much aware of the deaths of some of their classmates as their reunion weekend approached, the "nerd chess team" decided to practice from the safety of their homes. They played cyber chess in front of their computers with webcams fully operational, taking no chances of getting together in public locations. Since no one volunteered the use of their home for practice sessions, the webcams seemed like the best solution. The Dead of Night killer had them all spooked.

Charlie Post, who first contacted Lauren to set up the tournament, was the self-appointed captain. In high school, he manifested many symptoms of obsessive-compulsive disorder and took lots of flak because of it. He was working hard to keep it under control. Since graduation he also made strides in modifying his physical appearance. Anyone looking at his photo in the high school yearbook would do a double take upon seeing him ten years later. All throughout his high school career, the girls all but ignored him unless it was to snicker at his scrawny arms or legs.

The once skinny kid, often picked on by the "jocks" in high school, had deliberately undergone quite a physical transformation since graduation. In addition to membership in a health club where he worked out daily, he also installed a home gym in his spare bedroom. Whereas a woman might think that you could never be too thin, he thought you could never be too buff.

His workouts accomplished their desired goal. Now that he rigorously pursued a regimen to give him sculpted biceps and the much desired six pack abs, there was no question that he seemed attractive to the opposite sex. He couldn't wait until the reunion to show the girls who snubbed him and the jocks who ridiculed him how he had become one fine looking specimen of masculinity.

Charlie's newfound self-confidence carried over to his wardrobe as well as the way he comported himself. He didn't walk; he swaggered. To keep his hair in its deliberately messy style, he used a lot of hair products, but blamed the messiness on the intensity of his workouts.

His clothing reflected the new image he sought to develop after his countless hours in the gym. Previously, he used to ridicule girls who seemed to follow the mantra "If you've got it, flaunt it," but now he saw the merit in that attitude. A trip through his closet and dresser drawers would reveal a collection of tight-fitting sleeveless T-shirts to showcase his arms and abs in addition to more traditional but form-fitting slacks and slim-fit oxford cloth shirts for business.

One evening at a bar he met an attractive brunette who was so complimentary about his physique that she convinced Charlie to get a tattoo of a small barbell on his left shoulder. At the time, he had a few too many drinks, but he didn't regret getting the tattoo. It became quite a conversation starter when he deliberately wore shirts that drew attention to the artwork. He couldn't get enough positive feedback about his appearance.

With so much focus on his appearance, it seemed logical that he would gravitate to a career where appearance was paramount. With financial help from his family and three years' experience working as a manager a local Gold's Gym, he purchased a franchise in the company.

Now that he had the physique that aspiring customers envied, he was a perfect "poster child" for his enterprise. With a working knowledge of all the equipment, an outgoing personality bolstered by the self-confidence that his appearance gave him, and a degree in business administration, he had customers signing up in record numbers. When he pitched his spiel to prospective customers, his appearance in his athletic wear was the feature that always seemed to close the deal. His business was hugely successful.

The ten years since graduation hadn't been as kind to Jaclyn Struzer if one were to judge her solely from the standpoint of appearance. Typical of most of her female classmates, she wore her brown hair long and straight in her graduation photo. There was nothing exceptional about her facial features that made her stand out as either particularly unattractive or especially beautiful.

Her interests in high school separated her from the bulk of the female members of the class. Unlike the cheerleaders, or the members of the drama club, or the participants in the high school quasi-sororities, or the other cliques that attracted girls, Jaclyn excelled at activities that were more scientific or cerebral. A member of the mathletes team, she was a driving force who contributed to the multiple trophies that the team won during the years she participated. Chess club was another activity that she dominated with her ability to utilize logical thinking skills and anticipate the moves of her opponents.

Not terribly popular with the girls in her class because she didn't share their interests in fashion, in pop culture, or in dating, she had many male friends who treated her like one of the boys. If questioned about her appearance, their description would depict someone who was quite ordinary. Most likely they might say she was of average height and on the thin side, but beyond that, they wouldn't have been able to point out her eye color as hazel or describe much more about her appearance. She was their friend rather than a girl they considered dating. Possibly, they might have remembered that she wore her hair long, but that might be no more than a guess; long hair was the prevailing style at the time for most of the girls in their graduating class.

Jaclyn had always been thin. Ten years later, she looked gaunt, almost sickly. The long brown hair in the yearbook photo appeared to be lustrous, but not so anymore. It was as if the vitality of her hair was gone. Now the color would probably be described as mousy brown. Adding to her frail appearance, she currently sported an easy to manage pixie haircut. It wasn't a flattering style, accentuating the fact that her face was almost skeletal. There didn't seem to be enough flesh to cover the bones

It wasn't as if Jaclyn was deliberately dieting, or that she cut her hair short because she thought it fashionable or flattering. Her successful career as an architect was the cause of her gauntness and her choice of hairdo. Never comfortable with delegating, she ran her own architectural design company with only one employee. She entrusted her secretary with the performance of only clerical functions. Everything else fell on Jaclyn's shoulders.

As her business grew, she found that there weren't enough hours in the day. Somehow, eating and sleeping became luxuries that she could barely afford. When she had a deadline for filing blueprints or obtaining permits, she sacrificed all personal considerations to meet the time constraints under which she found herself. Her hairstyle had to accommodate to her schedule. Washing and blow-drying long hair required more time than she was willing to devote to grooming. Her short haircut was a wash-and-wear style that might not have been the most flattering, but it saved her at least a half hour each day. When she was already working upwards of fourteen hours daily to keep up with the demands of her clientele, every moment counted. Skipping meals and allowing herself no more than six hours of sleep impacted her health, making her appear gaunt and tired.

Those seemed to be sacrifices Jaclyn was willing to accept because she watched her bank account growing and found her name becoming known for her creative designs and her professionalism. Showcased in a recent issue of "Architectural Digest" as a promising up-and-comer, Jaclyn reveled in this recognition that she never thought possible. After the issue was circulated, her business increased beyond her expectations.

Of the four members of the "Nerd Chess Team," Ronald Martella had become the most financially successful of the bunch. He lived up to his nomination as the person in their graduation class "Most Likely to Succeed." Back in high school, he always had his eye on opportunities to make money. Some of that resulted from the untimely death of his father, during Ronald's sophomore year. An accountant by profession, his dad had been diagnosed with leukemia; his health began to falter. Cutting back on his hours, burdened with medical bills, and finally having to resign his position, Ronald's dad saw all his savings rapidly disappearing.

As the eldest of three children in the family, and the only male child, Ronald felt responsible for helping his mother. Her husband's death left her with unpaid bills and insufficient income to simultaneously pay them and to run the household. Ronald immediately got a job after school bagging groceries and worked weekends mowing lawns or doing any other available jobs he could find.

To his credit, Ronald wasn't angry that he had to fulfill this role in his family. It was something he accepted willingly. He felt an intense surge of pride that he had become "the man in the family."

Recognizing that the type of jobs he took to supplement his mother's income would never lead anywhere, he figured that employment in the professional sphere or as an entrepreneur would earn him the most income. The latter choice appealed to him more than pursuing both college and graduate degrees that would require long years of education and significant monetary outlay that he didn't have. Owing hundreds of thousands of dollars in student loans after graduation was equally unappealing to him.

What he did love was computer games. He astutely recognized that there was significant money to be made in that field. Combining his interest in playing the games, a degree of talent in graphic design, and lots of creativity, Ronald decided to develop some computer apps. Much to his surprise, his initial attempt met with great success. Although he created a second successful app, he was particularly proud of "Thundering Herd," one of the most popular computer games among millennials. Since it was the first one he developed, he tended to think it was "beginner's luck." When the second app also became a success, he accepted that he had a talent that was worth pursuing.

Although his apps and games appealed to the young, he didn't look like the creative talent behind them if one judged him by his appearance. Rather than wearing jeans and T-shirts with slogans or graphic designs like other creative talents in his field, he tended to dress like a businessman. He didn't find it necessary to appeal to the young by dressing like them. His thick brown hair looked as if it were glued to his scalp; no errant strands would dare to be out of place. The dark frames of his eyeglasses called attention to his piercing gray eyes. Often, people took him for an attorney or an accountant. When he mentioned the true nature of his work, people then commented on his "retro style." His clothing choices of shirts with white collars, color-coordinated ties, French cuffs, and chunky cuff links were his connection to his father. This was how Ronald chose to honor the memory of his dad who always dressed in a formal manner when he went to his office.

The fourth and final member of "Team Nerd," Elliot Cook, had changed the least since graduation. He had always been somewhat withdrawn and reclusive in high school. Despite all the activities available to the student body, Elliot had few friends, shied away from athletic sports, and never once asked a girl out on a date. At the insistence of his parents, Elliot joined the chess club because they felt that he needed to participate in a school activity that would bring him some degree of self-esteem. As a child, he played against his parents and his older brother and rarely lost a game. In his spare time, he devoured books about chess and the chess grandmasters. With his eidetic memory, he was able to quickly recall and utilize moves that he studied in his books When he competed, it gave him a significant advantage over his competitors who hadn't devoted as much time to their research of the game as he had. Chess was a lifeline that filled the time during which his peers were engaging in sports, dating, and hanging out with friends. For him, chess was a necessary distraction which motivated him to develop his skills. It wasn't surprising that all the time he spent analyzing and playing the game paid off – he was on his way to becoming a grandmaster.

After graduation from high school, Elliot earned an online degree from the University of Phoenix. The whole college experience of living on campus held no appeal for him. With a major in accounting and a minor in business administration, he was hired as an accountant/bookkeeper for a local construction company upon earning his degree.

During his job interview, Elliot indicated that he would only accept the position if he didn't have to work in the office. His employer arranged a schedule for pickup and delivery of the various documents needed to prepare budgets, tax returns, and other financial reports. Elliot would pick up his work from the company trailer and complete his tasks in his home office. As a person averse to engaging in face-to-face meetings on a regular basis, Elliot found this arrangement the perfect solution. Often, he waited outside the trailer until most of the employees left for lunch, and then he would carry out the paperwork exchange. It was a system that appealed to him on so many levels.

Today, during the practice chess session with his teammates, Elliot continued to foster his air of reclusiveness. Even in the seclusion of his home office while web chatting with his friends from the chess club, he had much of his face hidden under a long-brimmed baseball cap. If the others thought he wore the cap because he had gone bald, they would have been wrong. He had the same wavy black hair that he had in high school. For him, the cap was part of his identity; he hid behind it as a self-protective measure. Jaclyn tried to catch a glimpse of his eyes under the brim of the cap, but she was unsuccessful.

If the other three members of the team could have seen Elliot's face under the hat, they would have seen that he was enjoying himself. This was for the first time in years. The members of the chess team were the closet thing he had to friends, but in the truest sense of the word, he didn't allow them to be close enough to him to deserve that title. However, in his mind, this group represented the only friends that he made in the four years of high school, the only people who made him feel accepted.

Catching each other up on the ten years since their graduation, they shared funny stories from high school and amusing tales from the years since they graduated about some former classmates. Behind the humor and the laughter, it was obvious that all had emotional scars from how they were treated by some of the most popular and successful members of their class. All four were anxious to kick the butts of the current seniors in the upcoming chess match, both for the honor of their reunion class and to excise their own demons from their high school days.

It wouldn't be an exaggeration to say that they all had an ax to grind. Like many high school nerds, they were among the most successful of their graduating class. What better way to make their tormentors regret their behavior than to flaunt their accomplishments and laud them over some of their least favorite classmates at the reunion. They couldn't wait for their chance.

Charlie Post, who had taken it upon himself to be the team captain, seriously wanted to win this tournament. He was not alone in that goal. He had already formulated a strategy for the reunion tournament. After their practice session on the computer, he would analyze the moves and rate the skill level of his team members. Then, he'd put his team's number one ranked player, probably Elliot, in the first match against the number one player representing the senior class. He was hoping that an early victory would demoralize the younger, less-experienced players. It sounded good in theory.

Before signing off their respective computers, he ordered each team member to hold up a chess piece - the king - in their right hand. They were to raise their king high in the air, and like football players in a huddle before a game, shout the mantra of encouragement that they used before each high school chess tournament.

Four voices chanted in unison "NERDS RULE."

CHAPTER 42

During my drive home I had been anticipating spending a relaxing evening with Lauren, grabbing a bite to eat, and going to a movie. When we spoke on the phone earlier, she seemed to agree that we both needed some stress relief. My plan would do the trick. Somehow, between the time that we spoke and when I walked through the door, I could sense that Lauren was on edge. Before going anywhere, we needed to talk.

Evidently, she heard me open the door because she greeted me by throwing her arms around me but remained completely silent. Not typical behavior, by any means. She then led me to the kitchen and the words began flowing.

"Cliff, I'm feeling like I'm dodging bullets. Each day I'm hearing from more and more alumni, asking about the possibility of cancelling the reunion because of the news out of Miami. What they're hearing and reading isn't encouraging out-of-town classmates to return to a place where glaring headlines make the city seem like Chicago during Prohibition. Reports of murders aren't conducive to enticing alumni to put their lives in jeopardy. Especially since some of the murder victims were members of our graduating class."

Rather than interrupting her, I just nodded my head in agreement.

She continued, "Graduates who still live here are also hesitant to attend the reunion. At this point, no one wants to offer themselves up for target practice."

I wasn't sure whether I should voice my fears about her safety, but I thought that the alumni who were contacting her were exercising good sense. If the police couldn't catch the killer, attending the reunion wasn't worth any more lives. Especially my wife's.

As I considered whether to segue into that discussion, Lauren then mentioned one specific classmate who was ready to attend with no hesitation. That struck her as odd.

"Interestingly, Charlie Post seems immune to the fear that's overtaking the other alumni. Despite all the communications from other graduates anxious to cancel the reunion, he sent me a text confirming his intention to participate in the chess match. I think that maybe it's a manifestation of his OCD. He may feel compelled to participate in the chess tournament since he's dedicated lots of time preparing it. To see it to its end. During high school he was teased mercilessly that he was a textbook case of obsessive-compulsive disorder. Winning the tournament seems more important than his personal welfare or that of his teammates."

Lauren's assessment of Charlie Post seemed reasonable to me. However, her lack of concern for her own safety seemed unreasonable. Not once had she mentioned how she felt about whether to proceed with the reunion based upon her own safety. It may not have entered her mind, but it was pressing on my brain like a malignant tumor.

Just as I was about to interject my concerns, she cut me off before I could say boo. Maybe that was a good thing. I hadn't rehearsed how I would approach the subject and might possibly blurt out something that would sound condescending to her. Better to think it through.

"And it's not only calls from my classmates that are driving me crazy," Lauren added, "Eve is calling me multiple times a day. She's been sounding distraught and I feel so guilty leaving my partner alone to run our accounting practice. I'm not exaggerating when I say that she calls or emails me at least four to five times a day. She's got questions about handling various clients, tax filings, and negotiating Offers in Compromise with IRS to establish payment plans for taxpayers who can't fully remit payment of their tax liabilities."

"That's not surprising," I said. Of the two, Lauren was far more experienced in dealing with IRS, and seemed to enjoy that aspect of their accounting practice. She had a feel for how far she could push the IRS and how to arrange a plan that would allow her clients to pay the rent, put food on the table, and still satisfy their tax debt. Eve had no such skills and was floundering when clients approached her to negotiate with IRS.

"Do you think that Eve is trying to tell you indirectly that she wants you to return to the office? Maybe, Eve's increasing frequency of contacting you and the frantic nature of her calls and emails are the equivalent of her saying *Come Back to Work. NOW!*"

"You're probably right, Cliff. While I do feel guilty leaving Eve holding down the proverbial fort, I'm not ready to end my participation in the case. After going to Little Haiti with Detective Banks, I'm convinced that Priestess Julia is a fraud. But I feel that she holds the key to tracking the DON killer. I've been doing some research on my own about other practitioners of Voodoo in Little Haiti, and general information about the types of services a Voodoo Priestess provides. This Julia doesn't fit the mold. I've been wanting to reconnect with Detective Banks to tell her what I've found out."

I felt the same way about being kept in the loop when it came to Uncle Brad and the police investigations.

"Unfortunately," Lauren said, "for the past few days the phone's been ringing ceaselessly with calls about the reunion or our clients, so I haven't had the time to connect with the one person I'd liked to have heard from. After our trip to little Haiti, we both questioned the credentials of 'Priestess' Julia. Maybe I read too much into it, but I expected to hear from Amanda Banks after what seemed like the start of a good relationship."

If I didn't know better, I'd think that Lauren felt as if she'd been rebuffed like a one-night stand. No way would Lauren accept that status. *Never had, never would.*

As if confirming what I'd been thinking, Lauren grabbed her cell phone from the kitchen table and typed the detective's name into the search box of her contacts. She said to me, "I'm sick of waiting for her to call me. I'm going to call Amanda's cell number rather than the line at the precinct. Better to reach her directly. I don't have the patience to be transferred all over the place."

Somehow, I knew this wasn't going to be a short conversation. Going out for dinner was no longer in the cards. Starving, I headed for the kitchen to forage for a snack. Maybe I live here, but the truth is, I often have no clue as to where anything is kept. At work I notice everything, at home, not so much. I left Lauren making her phone call, hoping she wasn't disappointed by the detective's reaction.

"Detective Banks, it's Lauren. Lauren Mandich. I've been hoping to hear from you. Anything you can tell me?"

"Funny, I was just about to call you. We must be on the same wavelength. After our fun together in Little Haiti, we agreed that you'd call me Amanda."

Lauren could hear the warmth in her voice and appreciated being on a first-name basis with the detective. Maybe she had been overly sensitive about not being contacted since their undercover operation.

"Is it about Priestess Julia?" Lauren asked.

"Let's just say that she's as much a Voodoo Priestess as I'm a Benedictine nun."

Lauren attempted to envision Amanda as a nun, but just couldn't cull up that image. It was too ludicrous. She had to suppress her laughter before continuing.

"Obviously," Lauren said, "you found out something to confirm that she's a fraud. What is it?"

Amanda grabbed her notepad and began flipping pages. "Our friend Priestess Julia is not who she'd like us to believe. Her following of clients has been equally misled."

With her usual impatience, Lauren interrupted. "Can you be more specific?"

"Whoa. Hold your horses. I'm trying to find my exact notes about her identity. Oh, here it is. After searching several fingerprint databases, we got lucky. It turns out that she'd been printed and booked in Georgia for fraudulent check writing. The only real part of her identity is that her first name is Julia - Julia Marlowe. She entered the United States only three years ago from Manchester, England. Despite identifying herself as Haitian, the woman has never even been to Haiti. Review of her passport history shows no entries at all for that country."

Lauren let that sink in for a moment. She couldn't help but wonder why Julia Marlowe adopted that specific identity. Her first conclusion was nothing more than stating the obvious.

"Well, if she's never been to Haiti, she certainly is NOT a Haitian Voodoo Priestess."

"No kidding. Basically, she's a fraud who uses her website to fleece naïve victims. It's amazing how much stock people put into psychics, fortune tellers, readers of Tarot cards, and other prognosticators."

"Are you going to arrest her?"

Lauren had no idea what specific legal action could be taken against Julia. In her mind, what Julia did was wrong and deserved punishment for preying on weak and frightened people who were gullible enough to trust in her. But Lauren didn't know the law.

"We won't arrest her just yet. We know that she's a fraud, but we don't know if she's connected to these killings. It's clear that she's benefited from them. I took another look at her webpage after getting back the fingerprint results. 'Priestess' Julia includes in her rather sketchy résumé that she's a police consultant. Guess that was part of the purpose of her visit to the station. Now that we're on to her, let's see how things play out. Sorry, but I gotta go. My sergeant is texting me and I can't keep him waiting."

Not entirely satisfied with Amanda's response, Lauren had no choice but to accept the detective's decision. That didn't mean that she was any less perturbed. To help deal with this frustration she chose to engage in an activity that she was comfortable with. True to her profession, Lauren attacked problems in a logical and systematic manner. She was at her computer reviewing the data on the spreadsheets she had designed. She was in control.

With each subsequent death, she updated her database and added new columns for characteristics of the killings that were unique. Seeing everything organized into categories describing the victims in the chronological order of their deaths allowed her to view and analyze the facts in a thorough manner. She was hoping for an epiphany. She just wasn't there yet.

Although she hadn't come up with the identity of the Dead of Night killer, she had formulated an independent conclusion. The pattern of target selection may have changed as subsequent bodies were discovered. First it was her classmates on the beach volleyball team, then an older New Jersey couple, and most recently a renowned football star. The choice of victims was puzzling.

To Lauren it was clear that Sam McKay was a victim of a copycat based upon the data on her spreadsheet. Regarding all previous victims, Lauren was convinced that none of the other deaths were random. The police had just not identified the motive.

At dinner that evening, Lauren convinced me. Her theory made sense. Why those victims? What was the killer's motive?

CHAPTER 43

Deciding to sleep on the turbulent thoughts going through her mind, Lauren awoke unusually early the next morning, resolved to speak to Detective Banks again. The results of her conversation with Amanda Banks would determine Lauren's strategy in speaking with Eve to try to placate her partner.

Knowing Lauren as well as I do, I recognized that she was on a mission and wasn't in the mood to explain her course of action to me yet. When she was ready, I knew that I'd hear all about it. For now, I was willing to make myself scarce.

Taking a disposable cup, I prepared a coffee to go and pointed at the front door. She barely looked up, but acknowledged my departure by saying, "Have a good day, Cliff. I'm hoping to have a good day, too. Tell you all about it later when I get things arranged."

Taking a chance that Detective Banks might find her argument convincing, Lauren called the detective with her evaluation of the victims and her suspicion that there was more than one killer. After hearing Lauren state her case that none of the targets had been random, Detective Banks decided that Lauren's theory had some merit.

"Listen, Lauren, you may be barking up the wrong tree, but just in case you're right, I think we need to pursue your line of thinking further. Frankly, I've been puzzled about how the tourist couple fits into all of this. They're considerably older than the other victims and they reside in New Jersey. If you can come up with some connection to the other murders to explain why this tourist couple was targeted, I think that would move us forward. Right now, we're spinning our wheels."

Had Amanda Banks seen Lauren's face, she would have seen a smile forming. The detective was giving serious consideration to her assessment of the murders. The next words brought a silent *YES!* to what Lauren was hearing, as she raised her hand in a victorious fist.

"Lauren, I don't know what your schedule is like, but would you consider taking a more active role in the investigation? We had good chemistry when we went together to Little Haiti. A fresh set of eyes and your wizardry with spreadsheets could be invaluable. It'd be another weapon in our arsenal, like King Arthur's sword Excalibur. Whaddya say?"

Weaponized spreadsheets! Excalibur!

Lauren almost burst out laughing, the concept was so hilarious. Most people saw accountants as stodgy and boring; this characterization of one of the prime tools of her profession captivated her fancy. *Wait until she shared Amanda's reaction with Cliff!*

Without hesitation, Lauren gave Amanda her answer. "Amanda, wild horses couldn't stop me from working with you. You've made my day."

The truth was that there was one wild horse she'd need to tame. She had all but promised Eve during one of her panicked calls that she would return to work shortly. Lauren could have handled all the calls about the reunion at work or delegated some of them to her secretary. She had almost convinced herself that it was time to return to her normal schedule. Otherwise, her partner Eve might have a breakdown, worrying that Lauren would leave her holding the bag during tax season which was approaching rapidly. It was time to resume her responsibilities in her accounting firm.

But that was before the conversation with Amanda. Lauren would do her best to balance her responsibilities at work, her reunion duties, and her assistance to Amanda Banks. But Eve would have to understand that her return could not be fulltime.

The day in Little Haiti with Amanda and her subsequent research concerning "Priestess" Julia as well as her analysis of the victims and the nature of their deaths had Lauren hooked. She needed to see this through.

Two cups of coffee later, Lauren still didn't have the plan for her conversation with Eve fixed in her mind. She was concerned about how Eve would deal with the news that, temporarily, her return would be part-time. What she needed was some physical activity to help her think more clearly.

It was a typical day for this time of year, perfect for a long walk. The sun was shining, the sky was blue, and there was no humidity. Dressing in a tank top, leggings, and sneakers, Lauren applied sunscreen, put on a baseball cap, grabbed her sunglasses, cell phone, and Bluetooth headphones. She headed for the park, only a five-minute walk. When she reached the entrance, she set her alarm for an hour, the amount of time she typically liked to walk daily. From her music playlist, she hit shuffle and began walking on the concrete path to the tempo of the music. Each time the song changed, she noticed a subtle shift in her pace to match the beat of the song. For that reason, she fast-forwarded through all the ballads because they slowed her down.

Lauren prepared herself for a tough sell to Eve, who had acquiesced to shouldering the burden of doing Lauren's work as well as her own. In retrospect, Eve probably didn't know what she had agreed to.

As always, while Lauren was doing laps around the small lake in the center of the park, thoughts of how to best approach Eve were tumbling around in her brain, like raw gemstones in a mechanical rock tumbler, undergoing the process of becoming smooth and polished. Her thoughts coalesced into the points she would make when speaking with Eve.

After her alarm signaled her hour was up, she headed back home, showered, dressed, and made another cup of coffee. Taking a deep breath, Lauren picked up her phone, located Eve's name in her contacts, and pressed the FaceTime mode. She didn't want to go through the office telephone and subject herself to questions from Luisa Martinez, their secretary.

Plus, she wanted to see Eve's face since they hadn't worked together for some time. She missed her partner, the camaraderie, and their silly banter. She was certain that Eve missed her even more because of her increased workload in Lauren's absence.

While Lauren was still composing her last-minute thoughts, Eve's face appeared on Lauren's screen. Maybe it was her guilt, but Lauren thought Eve looked more tired than usual.

"Hi stranger," Lauren said. "It's good to see your face. Just want you to know how much I appreciate the way you've been dealing with my absence. I know it's a lot for you to handle, and I'm forever grateful."

"Why are you buttering me up? Somehow, I have the feeling that you want something from me. You better not be telling me you're leaving me on my own for the entire tax season."

Lauren could see Eve's pursed lips and hear the anxiety in her voice. There was no time to waste. Lauren immediately tried to allay her fears.

"Not to worry, Eve. I've decided that it's time for me to come back to the office, but not full-time yet. I'm thinking in the neighborhood of about three or four days a week."

"Well, Lauren, it's better than you not being here at all, but the neighborhood I'd like to live in would have you here *at least four days*, especially since January is almost upon us, and we both know what *that* means."

With that, Eve walked over to a stack of files on her desk that she was preparing for the quarterly payroll tax returns, for the year-end reports, and for both personal and corporate tax returns that would soon be top priority. The months of January through April are the crunch time of a CPA's calendar. Eve liked to get the prep work done before clients began inundating them with thick envelopes and boxes full of tax records.

"As you can see, Lauren, we're in good shape for now. You know that I still like to keep paper records for some of our clients even though we have everything backed up on the computer. I've prepared files for your clients as well. Call me crazy, but I always like to have Plan B in case the computer crashes."

Lauren had no argument with that. "I'm grateful for all the extra time you've been putting in to cover for me. I know it's a lot to ask, but Detective Banks asked me to take a larger role in the investigation of the Dead of Night killer. I'll do my best to squeeze my assistance to her into one day a week, but this is something important to me. I went to school with some of the victims and I must see this through. Please understand," explained Lauren.

"Okay, I've got your back. But you'll owe me one, partner." Eve tried to sound stern, but she couldn't say no to her partner. She understood how deeply Lauren cared about her dead classmates and how much she needed to help the detective. Just knowing that Lauren would be at the office working again, albeit with reduced hours, was enough to assuage her anxiety.

But she'd make Lauren sweat it out just a bit longer. It was part of their relationship. They liked to tease each other for effect. Eve delivered her next comment in the most deadpan voice she could muster. "Listen, Lauren, do you think we should revise our partnership agreement? I can look it over tonight to see about the current terms and what revisions we need to make."

Unable to keep up the pretense, Eve began laughing. Lauren immediately joined in. "You really had me going there, Eve. Frankly, I wouldn't blame you."

"You know I wouldn't do that, Lauren. But you should have seen your face. It was priceless!"

They spoke for a few more minutes about office issues, and about Teacup, Eve's spoiled dog. Eve's demeanor already seemed less stressed. More than just business partners, the two women were close friends. The conversation with Lauren lightened Eve's mood.

Despite Lauren promising four workdays per week, which Eve somehow expected might be only three, she was pleased. Compared to running the whole show alone, Eve felt as if she had been thrown a life preserver.

CHAPTER 44

As soon as my mobile phone rang, I heard upbeat music and the lyrics "who wrote the book of love." I knew it was Lauren from the unique ringtone I assigned to her cell number. She didn't see my face when I answered the phone, but I can assure you that I was smiling. She had that effect on me.

"What's up?" I asked.

Lauren tried to not make a habit of calling too frequently during my working hours, especially since I was often doing a biopsy or other surgical procedure. Although I cut back on my hours, I was back at work and had been for weeks. The locum tenens physician I hired had a personal emergency and I didn't try to replace him. Keeping my schedule light allowed me the luxury of helping the police without having to make major adjustments to work hours. I relied on my staff to reschedule patients at different times if necessary.

From her response, I knew that everything was okay. Whatever preyed on her mind earlier had been resolved. No doubt, she was ready to confide in me.

"Cliff, I'm feeling great but there's a lot I want to talk to you about. Don't worry, it's all good. I'd rather not cook tonight, so I can focus on what I want to discuss. How about going out? I was thinking of Las Vegas in the Grove."

I didn't need further convincing, Las Vegas is our favorite restaurant for Cuban food; everything we've eaten there is consistently good, the portions large, and the side dishes delicious.

"Sure. You know I can't say no to you. Your timing is great. I'm not far from there now. Do you want me to meet you or should I pick you up?"

"Come home first. I plan to celebrate. I just may drink the entire carafe of sangria myself. You can be my designated driver."

"Boy, Lauren, you *are* in a good mood. I'm putting the pedal to the metal. I'll be home soon."

When I arrived, I could see that the tension I noticed in her face over the last several days was gone. She appeared more energized. As she walked to the door to greet me, I could swear that even her gait was different. She gave new meaning to the phrase "a spring in one's step."

My curiosity got the best of me, and I couldn't help myself. Her body language was making me impatient to find out what made her so excited.

"Honey, I can't wait to hear the news."

"Let me grab my purse, and I'll tell you in the car. All day I've been craving churrasco with chimichurri. Let's go before the restaurant fills up."

(For you gringos, that's barbecued meet, most often steak, with a sauce made of finely chopped parsley, minced garlic, olive oil, oregano, red pepper flakes, and red wine vinegar. Some people say the sauce is the Argentinian version of pesto.)

Usually, I was the one who needed to eat as soon as I had a hunger pang. Lauren's insistence on leaving immediately was out of character, but far be it from me to cause my bride to starve.

"Love the way you rolled your r's when you pronounced churrasco and chimichurri. Say that on Calle Ocho and you'll be mistaken for a Latina."

Lauren rewarded me with a smile. She enjoyed speaking Spanish and had a flair for languages; in college she minored in

Spanish. Living in Miami, she listened to the various Spanish accents of people from Cuba, Puerto Rico, and from various Latin American countries to get the accents right. Sometimes, I'd catch her engrossed in a Spanish telenovela on TV. Her fluency was impressive.

We headed to the car, with Lauren sounding like an ad for Las Vegas Cuban Cuisine. She could literally sell me anything. After hearing her rave about what she planned to eat, I intended to have the same dish as her.

"Good choice about the food, Lauren. I'm already salivating, thinking about my churrasco with black beans, rice, and plantains."

As we walked to my car, I declared, "Your chariot awaits." She belted herself in, put on her sunglasses, and turned off the radio. As soon as I merged into traffic, Lauren began to share her excitement with me. I love how enthusiastic she is.

"Okay, here goes," Lauren began. "I've been on the phone a good part of the day, trying to integrate my accounting work and my desire to help the police so I can do both, and not shortchange either. I spoke with Detective Banks and with Eve. Remarkably, both seem happy with my proposal.

"Amanda and I got along well on our Little Haiti caper. In her words, we had 'good chemistry.' In fact, she thought I had good instincts and wanted me to take a more active role in the investigation of the Dead of Night killer. Coming from her, I was flattered. You *know* how much I want this killer found. Plus, get this, she *loved* my spreadsheets. Can you believe it? She'll keep me informed if there are any tasks I can do to help the investigation. I assured her that I'd make myself available whenever she needs me. In the meantime, I'm going back to work. Eve suspects that I might have to pick up and leave at any given time, but for now, she's tickled pink to have me back. I've been feeling guilty leaving her to run the office, handle emergencies for my clients, and get her own work done. She's been a trooper, but it's time for me to carry my own weight."

"Sounds like you've figured out how to keep everyone happy. I can see how happy this is making you. I'm really proud of you, Lauren."

With that last comment, she put her hand on my thigh and gave it a little squeeze. The squeeze meant as much as any words she could have said.

"The best part is once I'm back at work, I'll reroute my calls to Luisa, our secretary. Since I've been away from the office, I've been inundated with calls about the status of the reunion because of the situation down here in Miami. It's been driving me crazy. I don't know why I didn't think of it before, but I'll direct the calls to Luisa. Believe me, she's more than capable of dealing with them. She'll probably enjoy all the talking and the drama. Sometimes I think she'd make a great character in one of the telenovelas she enjoys so much. I've been watching some and have become hooked on one series in particular. She'd be perfect in it."

As she spoke, Lauren pulled down the sun visor and flipped open the mirror. Digging into her purse, she pulled out a lipstick and began to apply it. Without missing a beat, she continued speaking.

"Luisa's instincts are usually spot on. I'm certain if there's anyone she feels requires my personal response, she'll let me know. Just making this decision and delegating much of the responsibility makes me feel invigorated. I've taken my life back."

I was happy that Lauren was so pleased with her decision. And speaking of being pleased, when we arrived at Las Vegas we were immediately recognized by the restaurant's owner,

Edmundo Santana, who greeted us like old friends. A genial man in his late fifties, he made a point to acknowledge our arrival. While I'd like to think that we were treated specially, I tend to think that all customers were treated with the same degree of warmth. The food brought people in, but it wasn't only the food that brought them back. Edmundo and his entire staff were engaging, accommodating, and knowledgeable about the dishes and their preparation. They all seemed fortunate to be working at the restaurant and enjoyed their interactions with the customers.

We made good time to the restaurant and since it was early, our favorite booth was available. Although it was designed for four, we preferred being able to sit next to each other in the booth. Plus, the additional room alleviated the crowded feeling of a table for two which lacked the space for all the serving plates and glassware that inevitably accompanied our dinner. Edmundo also knew that we liked to sit in a quiet section of the restaurant so we could hear ourselves speak.

"Senor Mandich, not only do I have your favorite table tonight, but I also have your favorite waiter, Geraldo." When he smiled at us, I'm not sure which was brighter, his wavy snow-white hair or his gleaming white teeth.

"That's great. We're celebrating this evening."

"Wonderful. I will send over Geraldo immediately."

Geraldo Diaz was a hardworking young man who was attending the University of Miami on a partial scholarship. To supplement his income, he worked as a waiter at Las Vegas and had several other part-time jobs. Lauren and I both admired his work ethic and deliberately over-tipped him. When he spotted us, his smile widened. Immediately, he headed into the kitchen, his longish black hair pulled into a rubber band to keep hair out of the customers' food.

Several minutes later, Geraldo arrived at our booth with a large glass carafe of Sangria and two glasses on his tray.

"Compliments of the house. Edmundo tells me you're celebrating."

"Gracias, Geraldo. No need to bring menus. We know exactly what we want. I believe my bride wants the churrasco with chimichurri sauce." I forgot about the sides. Since I never deviate from the way the chef prepares the food, I often forget that Lauren always likes to have it her own way. Honestly, I can't remember the last time that she placed an order without asking for a different side or an alternate way of preparing the meal. Tonight was no different. She was quick to clarify her order.

"Could you please substitute broccoli for the plantains? I'm watching my carbs," Lauren chimed in.

"Of course, Mrs. Mandich. What would you like, Dr. Mandich?"

"I'll also have the churrasco with the *standard* sides of rice, beans, and plantains. I just love those sweet bananas."

As always, the dinner plates were barely visible, as the food covered every inch of space on them. Neither of us could even contemplate dessert, although we did love their Tres Leches cake, another specialty of the house. Maybe next time, but not tonight. However, no meal at Las Vegas is complete without some café con leche.

Geraldo returned with the delectable brew, enticing us with its rich coffee aroma. It was prepared perfectly, with steamed milk and a generous serving of sugar, far more than we would have added ourselves, but that's what made it so delicious. After placing the coffees in front of us, Geraldo walked back to the kitchen, and then returned with two forks and a single cake plate on which sat a generous serving of Tres Leches, the very sweet three-milk cake that was the signature dessert of Las Vegas and many other Cuban restaurants.

"Geraldo, we didn't order this." But looking at it, my willpower was going down the drain.

"Again, a gift from Edmundo. He told me to say that 'No celebration is complete without dessert,' and I was to make sure that you ate it."

"Well, who am I to argue with Edmundo? Looking at this cake, there's no way that we're not going to enjoy Edmundo's gift. Neither of us is hungry, but somehow, we'll make room. Thanks so much. Please don't let Edmundo disappear before we get to thank him as well."

With one plate and two forks, I was up to my old tricks. I asked Lauren a series of inconsequential questions, encouraging her to talk while I consumed ninety percent of the delightful dessert. There's no doubt that Lauren knew exactly what I was doing but she played along. As always. We'd been re-enacting this scenario for the entire time that we've been together as a couple. Sometimes she credits me with helping her stay slim by my obvious ploy.

When the bill arrived, I left an especially generous tip, since neither the sangria nor the cake had been added to the total. When we found Edmundo, I thanked him for his generosity, and he pulled me toward him and gave me a huge hug.

"I've been watching the two of you since you first began dating," Edmundo said. "You've been here so many times and each time I see the love and respect you have for each other, and the kindness you show to my waiters. When you choose to eat at my restaurant, I feel honored. I hope there will be many more celebrations that will bring you back here."

Lauren had tears in her eyes, and the embrace she gave Edmundo was full of emotion. Neither of us expected the evening to have brought us as much joy as it had. Walking hand in hand to our car, I turned to Lauren.

"I've been thinking that I should resume my normal schedule at work. My staff has been fielding complaints from patients who are unhappy with having to wait too many weeks for an appointment with me. I don't want to jinx it, but things seem to have quieted down in the city. Maybe the killer has moved on. At worst, Uncle Brad can always reach me it something comes up."

"That makes sense," Lauren said. "We could both use a return to normalcy."

"Yeah, one can only hope. But first, I need to run something by my uncle."

CHAPTER 45

Recovered from his concussion, but not from his suspension from the National Football League, Hoyt Stark was looking to let off some steam. Complicating his anger was the restraining order which kept him away from his wife Shannon. What he resented even more than having to keep away from her, she was the one still living in their house. Frankly, he was furious because it had been paid for with *his* money. That just didn't sit well with him at all.

Instead of their luxury home with every top-of-the-line appliance and every conceivable amenity, including a home theater which enabled him to enjoy watching replays of his games, he was renting a small one-bedroom apartment that was not too far from his 24-foot Sea Ray Laguna fishing boat. At least, Shannon had no interest in his boat, and had never accepted any of his rare invitations to go on the boat with him. He had it docked at the Rickenbacker Marina on Key Biscayne.

The boat was a center console model that was popular with fishermen. A small blue sunshade protected the person in the captain's chair. The boat's size and design allowed anglers to quickly access all portions of the deck and prevent fishing lines from tangling. Twin outboard Mercury engines supplied plenty of power. Most essential to Stark were the compartments that would keep his beer chilled and his fish fresh, in that order of importance.

He would frequently go out alone at night to dangle a line in Biscayne Bay and drink his beer, adding to his sullen mood. He blamed his situation and fall from grace on the actions of others. It still infuriated him that Shannon called 911 on him and now *he* was paying the consequences for *her* actions. In his mind, he was the victim. After five beers and extensive anger directed as his wife, his team, and the NFL, Hoyt needed a diversion from his self-pity. He vowed to call Iggy in the morning.

****

"Hey Iggy, get the guys together. Meet me at my boat. It's docked at the Rickenbacker Marina. I'm taking you guys fishing."

"Fishing? I don't know shit about fishing. Sure, I'm in. Do I need to bring anything special?"

Iggy's response was so typical of his personality, and just what Hoyt needed today. Hoyt laughed to himself that Iggy knew squat about fishing and didn't care to learn anything, but without hesitation, he was literally on board with the idea. No matter what Hoyt proposed, Iggy was usually supportive. For that reason, he was always Hoyt's go-to guy.

"Nah, I've got you covered. I'll have the bait and tackle."

"You're serious about this fishing thing. I'll give fishing a try if it makes you happy, but just so you know, I'm not touching any slimy worms," Iggy stated. "Maybe we could go to the track instead. Does that work for you?"

Hoyt wasn't surprised by Iggy's naive response. His friend was ignorant about many things. They would not be using worms offshore in a saltwater location. But just like Hoyt knew how to bait a hook to lure a fish, he knew what lure would work with his friend.

"Listen, how about I stock up on some Pabst Blue Ribbon? That's your favorite beer, isn't it? A man can get mighty thirsty out there."

"Now you've got my attention. Where'd you say this boat of yours is?"

"Cross the Rickenbacker Causeway, and you'll find the Rickenbacker Marina on the left side of the road. Remember, the name of the boat is 'Tight Lines.' There's a blue canvas canopy in the center. I'll be the guy with a Pabst in each hand and a cooler full of plenty more."

"Ok, Hoyt. I'll drink to that. Hey, that's pretty funny, right? Listen, I'll round up the guys. I figure we should be able to meet you in about an hour or so."

"The sooner the better if you want your fair share of the beer. I'll be getting pretty bored and plenty thirsty out there by myself."

****

His plans made, Hoyt Stark stopped at the local 7-Eleven where he stocked up on beer and ice. Before boarding his boat, he visited the marina's bait shop. Fishing had always been an activity that he enjoyed. As a kid, his dad had taken him fishing, leaving before dawn to get out on the water before other fishermen and before the heat became intolerable. From his father, he absorbed all kinds of information about the type of bait to use to attract specific fish, and which waters were rich in the variety of fish he sought. Determined to show his buddies a good time, Hoyt wanted them to feel the excitement of catching their dinner or maybe even landing a trophy-quality fish they could mount and display on their walls. *Wouldn't that be something!*

With those goals in mind, Hoyt spared no expense. He purchased live goggle eyes which many considered premier bait in the waters of South Florida. These small puffy fish with eyes that bulge at the sides of their heads were a delicacy to larger fish. He also hoped to catch dolphin, which is marketed on restaurant menus as mahi mahi, not dolphin, the mammal.

Hoyt's father taught him that dolphin fish also enjoy a meal of cut bait such as ballyhoo and shrimp. The marina had both types of baitfish frozen in bags. Hoyt purchased several.

Hoyt Stark was well known in South Florida because of his football success. As a result of his suspension, he was even better known in and around the marina where he spent a good part of his time since the NFL suspended him. Every visit to his boat began with a visit to the bait shop, and a conversation with Oscar Clayton, the one employee of the small enterprise. While no one was certain of his age, it was obvious from his sun-darkened and lined skin that he spent too much time in the sun without any application of sunscreen. His skin was the least of his problems.

Oscar's appearance was a parody of an "old salt" cast in Hollywood, with all the characteristics of such a character. It wasn't a stretch to envision Oscar as an aging sea captain from another era who spent too much time at sea. Because of a drinking problem, he neglected nutrition and personal hygiene. He had only five teeth remaining in his mouth. That impaired his nutrition as well.

A friendly and talkative guy, Oscar liked to engage Hoyt in conversation. The problem was that Oscar was difficult to understand. Any speech pathologist can attest to the fact that teeth are required to articulate properly; five teeth are inadequate for clear pronunciation.

One day an inebriated tourist asked if anyone ever called him "Mumbles." Oscar always hated his given name and took no offense. Oddly, he got a perverse kick out of being called "Mumbles" and reveled in his new nickname. His self-deprecating humor earned him respect.

On that day, the legend of "Mumbles" was born.

****

The football legend and the bait shop legend were shooting the breeze since Hoyt had some time to kill before Iggy and the guys made it to the marina. Among other topics, they covered a recent shark attack at Haulover Beach, Portuguese Men-of-War washing up on Fort Lauderdale Beach, and dangerous rip currents in Miami Beach. Oscar had a small television in the bait shop and was always the voice of doom and gloom after watching reports about dangers at the local beaches. He liked his customers to stay safe; he considered his news updates a public service.

Hoyt appeared to listen politely but was lost in his own thoughts. Abruptly, he removed his wallet from one of the numerous pockets in his khaki cargo shorts, signaling that he needed to leave.

"Well, Mr. Stark. No matter what fish are running, with all the bait you have, looks like you're prepared."

"I got some buddies coming and I plan to show them a good time. We should catch plenty of dolphin or anything else that's biting. If not, at least we'll enjoy getting drunk trying."

"Sure sounds like a good time to me."

Mumbles was in awe of Hoyt despite his suspension from the league. He had followed his career in the NFL because of Stark's Miami roots. Plus, Hoyt had been hanging around the marina frequently lately and had been friendly and patient. Mumbles was infatuated with the thought of spending time with this football hero. Today he finally got up the courage to approach Hoyt with a proposal.

"Maybe someday I can go out with you. I'll supply the bait and chum."

Hoyt's response, if he meant it, was more than Mumbles expected. Part of him was waiting for a polite brush-off, thinking Hoyt would make an excuse that would cover all future time beginning today until the world came to an end. Instead, Hoyt seemed open to the suggestion and sounded sincere in his reply.

"We'll make a date. Sorry that I gotta go now, but my buddies should be arriving at any time. This is gonna turn out to be a day to remember," he said prophetically.

CHAPTER 46

Sometimes an offhand comment creates a life of its own. When Hoyt mentioned that the day would be memorable, neither he nor Mumbles had a clue as to the chain of events that would begin that afternoon. Certainly, Hoyt had no expectation that his afternoon's fishing expedition with his friends would spiral into an outcome that would unravel what was left of his life as he knew it.

Hoyt Stark hauled his bags with the purchases from the bait shop to his boat and immediately stocked the two coolers. When he looked up, he noticed a noisy old gray Toyota pickup backing into a parking space at the marina's parking lot. The lot was crowded, and the spot was tight, but, nonetheless, the driver persevered. It took several maneuvers, but the truck was successfully backed into the parking space.

Recognizing the parking maneuver, Hoyt knew it was Iggy driving. Regardless of the difficulty in backing into parking spaces, Iggy never pulled into a spot with the vehicle facing forward. It was a deliberate tactic, born of necessity. In Florida, vehicles have only one license plate which is displayed on the rear of the vehicle. Iggy or his truck had been the subject of so many searches by the police or the repo man that, out of habit, he backed into all parking spaces. As an additional precaution, he preferred to park in a space with thick or spiny vegetation behind it. The likelihood of someone taking the trouble to check the plate of a vehicle concealed in a thicket cut down on the risk of being identified.

Unless someone was specifically targeting his vehicle by searching for the color, make, or year, his truck would be one of many that were parked with the license plate hidden from view. Just another line of defense against having his identification revealed. He didn't need any more investigations after all his prior run-ins with the cops or his creditors.

Hoyt shouted to Iggy to get his attention. Following closely behind was Rollo Thomas, another boyhood friend. Like Iggy, Rollo wore his tropical floral-print guayabera shirt at least two sizes too large; he wore it opened almost to the navel, displaying a huge gold medallion on a thick chain which rested on a chest covered with bushy black hair that masked some of the flabbiness underneath. It wasn't that Rollo was overweight, but he clearly hadn't no interest in exercise unless it was the type that was practiced under the sheets.

The two ambled down the dock, checking out the boats they passed on the way to the "Tight Lines," the one owned by Hoyt. One boat immediately caught their attention. Based on its size and amenities, it probably warranted being called a yacht, rather than a boat. However, it wasn't the boat that interested them. Sunbathing on the prow of the expensive vessel were several bikini-clad females. The ladies were wearing oversized floppy hats with decorative ribbons dangling down the back, large Prada sunglasses, and fabric sandals in shades to match their perfectly pedicured toes. Their jewelry included earrings, rings, and bracelets in colors chosen to accessorize their manicures, which included one nail on each hand decorated with a custom design.

The yacht was owned by one of Miami's most prominent plastic surgeons. The figures on these women were a testament to his excellent work. The two friends appreciated the skimpy bathing attire on the well-endowed sunbathers. They weren't particularly interested in the rest of their attire, what they considered "window dressing."

Whether or not the yacht's owner was impressed by their appearance, Iggy and Rollo found it hard to take their eyes off these magnificent women. As far as Iggy was concerned, things were looking up. Hoyt's invitation might prove to be just what he needed. Taking their sweet time, Iggy and Rollo finally appeared at the dock where Hoyt was preparing his boat for their fishing expedition.

The luxury yacht gleamed with polished brass railings, a staircase that led to the flying bridge which contained upholstered pilot chairs mounted on metal pedestals, as well as navigation equipment that could probably allow the yacht to circumnavigate the globe. In comparison, Hoyt's boat seemed like the nautical version of an inexpensive car with only the essentials, stripped down to little more than the engine, the steering wheel, the tires, and an interior that even teenagers would find uncomfortable for the purpose of making out. Hoyt's boat was designed specifically for fishing: i.e., no luxuries.

Plus, the yacht had something that Hoyt's boat did not – it had nubile young women. Iggy and Rollo would end the day with stiff necks if they continued to contort their bodies to gawk at the yacht's passengers. Hoyt tried to redirect their focus back to his boat and fishing.

"What's up guys? It's just the two of you? I was figuring we'd have a little reunion now that I'm back in Florida."

"Sorry, Hoyt. We tried to round up some of the guys we knew you'd want to see. I found out from their sister that the Augusta brothers are being detained by the cops. It's something about a gas station incident, but she wasn't clear on the details from Tony or Eddy. Since they couldn't come, I texted Brandon Walker, but never heard back from him."

"That's not surprising," said Hoyt. "Walker never responds unless you mention that money is involved."

"Guess I only mentioned you asked us to go fishing," Iggy said. "My bad. Anyway, I gave up trying to reach anyone else after that since you sounded like you were anxious to get started."

"Not your fault. Guess we should look on the bright side - more beer and fish for us," said Stark, trying to hide his disappointment. He'd been looking forward to showing off his boat and fishing prowess to *all* his buddies.

He did his best to appear upbeat, but the split with his wife was always simmering below the surface.

CHAPTER 47

Hoyt's temper was well known to both Iggy and Rollo. Not wanting to insult Hoyt or his boat, Rollo attempted to compliment his friend.

"Sweet boat, man, even without the girls we just saw." The proper term would have been "ogled," but that was well beyond the scope of Rollo's education and intelligence.

How much did it set you back?" asked Rollo.

The three friends shared more personal information with each other than with their wives or girlfriends. Shannon never asked about the cost of the boat, so Hoyt never discussed it with her. In his mind, it was *his* boat, and the information was on a need-to-know basis, and *she* didn't need to know, particularly since he figured she'd have found what she considered a better use for the money. New appliances, replacing the worn carpets, redecorating the family room were all on her agenda of worthwhile expenditures of *his* money. Not that he bought the boat out of spite, but it might have played into his decision.

"About sixty grand."

"Geez, football has been good to you."

"*Had* been good, you mean. The emphasis is on the word '*had*.'"

The bitterness in Hoyt's voice was unmistakable. Even his buddies, who were no Einsteins, could tell that Hoyt was not going to get over what he felt was a bad deal from the NFL and his wife Shannon.

"How about we get onboard? Show us how fast this sucker can go," suggested Iggy, sensing the need to distract Hoyt before he exploded like a volcano that had lain dormant for years and suddenly blew its top. Revving up the engines and racing through the waves would be a good release of Hoyt's pent-up frustration and anger.

"Good idea. Enough talk."

The motley crew boarded. Hoyt tossed each man a beer. He steered the boat out of the bay with minimal wake, observing the regulations concerning speed limits and boat wakes. No sense in starting the journey by breaking the rules. Coast Guard and Shore Patrol could ruin your day. When they got further out, he could pick up the speed.

"Where we going?" shouted Iggy over the noise of the engine. He had already finished his first beer.

"Probably somewhere between eleven and eighteen miles offshore. That's where we should find the most dolphin."

After getting into open waters and increasing the speed, Hoyt allowed Iggy to take the wheel. Hoyt's friend was clearly delighted, enjoying being at the helm out on the open water. It was exhilarating. By way of instruction, Hoyt offered the following directions.

"Just keep us on a straight course. See that tall building behind us? Keep it at your back."

Iggy turned to see the building that Hoyt mentioned. Crushing the first beer can in his hand, he asked Rollo to grab him a second one from the ice chest. Hoyt said nothing to discourage this request. With his second beer in his right hand, Iggy's steering was one-handed, and not entirely safe.

With his polarized sunglasses, a must on sunny days on the ocean, Hoyt kept a lookout. He was okay with letting his buddies steer, despite their inexperience and increasing inebriation. However, he was still conscious of at least a degree of safety issues and would take over if his friends became too drunk to function appropriately. Also, Hoyt was searching for birds circling the area to feed on bait fish. When they swooped down into the water, their presence would indicate larger fish below. Those larger fish were the ones Hoyt hoped to catch.

Rollo asked for his turn at the wheel. Like Iggy, he had been instructed to keep the tall building at his back. Taking his cue from his friend, Rollo also used only one hand on the steering wheel and the other around his beer. It was his third.

"Whoa, slow down," shouted Hoyt. Not waiting for Rollo to respond, Hoyt grabbed the wheel and throttled down both engines.

"Okay guys, we'll anchor here. Can you see that floating weed line and all the floating debris? Did you notice the birds hovering above? I guarantee that there are small baitfish below. Where there are baitfish, there are bigger fish. My guess is we'll catch us some dolphin."

Hoyt was adept at setting up the bait and tackle. Since the boat had several rod holders, the guys could rest their rods in them, making fishing easy for his crew of two. He assigned two rods per person and set out lines near the floating weeds. He used his smorgasbord of baits: live goggle eyes, frozen ballyhoo, and frozen shrimp that thawed quickly once in the warm water. Since all the tasks related to fishing were handled by Hoyt, the only activity that Iggy and Rollo engaged in was to open and drink additional cans of beer.

Seating was at a premium on the Sea Ray Laguna boat model. Usually Hoyt went out alone, so there was no problem. Today, Stark let his two buddies alternate sitting in the seat by the center console where the controls were located because it was the only shaded place. Hoyt was content to sit on a cooler, drink his beer, and wait for the fish to bite. It didn't take long for the first dolphin to take the bait. The tip of one of Iggy's rods dipped noticeably and the scratching of the rod against the rod holder indicated that a fish was fighting strenuously to release itself from the hook. In his excitement, Iggy spilled his beer as he ran to see what he caught. Hoyt instructed him to "play" with the fish awhile before reeling it into the boat.

Dolphins are a strange breed of fish. If a member of their school is hooked while feeding, it excites the others to feed. Once Iggy's fishing rod successfully lured and caught the first dolphin, a feeding frenzy came over the school of fish.

"Reel them in boys," yelled Hoyt. "Now you know why I chose the name 'Tight Lines' for my boat."

"I don't get it," Rollo stated, clueless.

Feeling sorry for his alcohol-impaired friend who probably wouldn't have understood the boat's name even if he were functioning at his one hundred percent mental capacity, Hoyt gently explained. "You just saw what happened. A fish took your bait and your fishing line tightened."

"Okay, okay. Now I get it," replied Rollo.

Female dolphins comprised the bulk of their catch, but there was a large bull dolphin with its distinctive blunt square head and its brilliant green, yellow, and blue color. Without question, they would have enough fish for supper for the next few weeks.

The feeding frenzy may have ended for the fish, but the beer drinking continued for the men. With all that beer in their bladders, both Rollo and Iggy felt nature calling.

"Hey, Hoyt, where's the head?" they asked almost simultaneously, sounding like an echo.

With a huge grin on his face, Hoyt pointed to the ocean. "You're lookin' at it."

Unfazed by Hoyt's answer, they relieved themselves over the side. It beat the trees, alleys, and stops by the roadside they had no problem using over the years. When you gotta go, you gotta go.

After the beer ran out, Hoyt saw the interest of his fishing buddies start to wane. To rejuvenate their enthusiasm, he told them they'd troll for bigger game on their way back to the marina. The boat headed home with lures dropped into the water at the back of the boat from two fishing rods. After about twenty minutes, one of the lines tightened and dipped. Iggy and Rollo both jumped to hold the rod. Somehow the novice fishermen managed to reel in a large wahoo, considered by many as one of the fastest swimmers in the ocean.

Everyone was elated, drunk, and sunburned.

At the dock Hoyt showed off his impressive skills with his boning knife. He cleaned and filleted their enormous catch. Each friend got a huge bag of fish. When Mumbles saw the boat arrive, he offered to rinse it down with freshwater, cover it with the protective tarp, and perform other miscellaneous tasks to leave it in pristine condition before its next sailing. For his troubles, Mumbles received a generous share of their catch.

The three friends staggered to the parking lot. Iggy and Rollo thanked Hoyt for what turned out to be a great day. None of the men should have gotten behind the wheel of a car in their inebriated states, but that didn't stop any of them.

Hoyt waved goodbye to his friends and yelled that he would call them tomorrow. Still feeling euphoric from the excitement of the day, he loaded his car and headed to the house where he once lived. He wanted to show off his catch to Shannon, to impress his estranged wife. If she acted nice, maybe he'd give her some of the fish. In his mind, he congratulated himself for his impending generosity. Maybe he could sweet talk her into letting him come home. His idea sounded reasonable to him. *What could go wrong?*

Not for one moment did he consider that (a) he was drunk, (b) he smelled like fish, and (c) there was a restraining order against him.

There was no way that this could turn out well.

CHAPTER 48

For the first portion of his photo safari, Adam Crowe, Miami Metro Zoo's wildlife expert, refused to respond to the growing number of emails and text messages that were building up on his phone. Crowe was tall, lean, tanned, and possessed chiseled features that in another era would have been described as belonging to a matinee idol. His body fat index was like that of an Olympic swimmer. He wore his dark hair, which was slightly graying at the temples, slicked back. His week-old beard gave him a rugged look.

Over the last two decades his photos of wildlife from every corner of the world were featured multiple times each year in acclaimed nature and photography magazines. Admirers of his photos naturally questioned him as to his preference in camera equipment. Even prior to becoming a spokesperson for Canon, he found that their equipment was superior to their competitors. When the upper echelon of Canon learned of his unpaid recommendation of their products, they offered to sponsor many of his photographic trips, if he would continue to use their equipment. For him, it was a win-win situation. In addition to financing many of his expeditions, Canon supplied him with the latest and greatest products to use in his travels. This current trip was paid for on Canon's dime.

His commitment to photography motivated him to travel extensively to capture magnificent animals on film. The time he spent researching these animals prior to his trips and the hours he devoted to observing them in their native habitat during his photo safaris vastly contributed to his expertise. His experiences enhanced his knowledge about many of the animals at the Miami Metro Zoo where Crowe was the preeminent wildlife expert. Due to his unique and potentially hazardous encounters with animals in the wild, he was also a sought-after lecturer.

Sadly, this trip proved to be more dangerous than he anticipated. His expedition to photograph the Bengal tigers of India took its toll when he watched one of his porters being mauled by the powerful carnivore. It was a horrible sight. The camouflaged predator hiding in the grass seemed to lunge from nowhere. Before Crowe's experienced guide could get off a rifle shot, the porter had been mortally wounded. The powerful jaws and teeth of the tiger, along with its claws, mercifully made the kill a quick one.

Since the death of one of his party, Adam Crowe planned to return to Florida. He regarded the tiger attack as an omen, signaling it was time to go home. No longer in vacation mode, he tackled his emails and text messages, transitioning to his normal life. One of the emails from Pete Ward alarmed him. Wanting to put what he regarded as Pete's embellishment of his participation in a police case in actual context, Crowe read several current stories coming out of Miami. The headlines from the Miami Herald's digital edition about the Dead of Night killings frightened him. What he found shocking was Pete's involvement in the investigation and the credibility given to his conclusions.

He reread Pete's email once he familiarized himself with the stories in the Herald. Pete sounded quite proud that he identified the bite marks on the victims as those of a wolf, probably a red wolf once indigenous to Florida - the Florida wolf or Canis rufus. Crowe was more than a little worried. So far as he knew, no red wolves remained in the wild in Florida. Pete's email to his boss (which Pete also copied to other recipients) bragged about his role assisting the police, presenting himself as an expert in his identification of the bites. As Adam Crowe realized, a mistake in identifying or reporting or revealing anything in this high-profile case could be disastrous. Adam needed to return to Miami ASAP.

Gathering his crew, Crowe informed them that he was terminating the photography expedition. Fortunately, they had enough exceptional pictures to satisfy his sponsors. He could already envision an outstanding photo spread in National Geographic. As part of his farewell message, he assured everyone involved that any future exhibit or display of the photos he had taken with their assistance would be dedicated to Duleep, the porter who lost his life to a tiger.

The members of the expedition, while disappointed by the abrupt ending of the adventure, understood Crowe's motivation. They mourned their comrade but took solace in Adam Crowe's intention to dedicate any use of the photos to their friend.

Because of the urgency to return to Miami to either verify or refute Pete Ward's identification of the bites, Crowe hurriedly packed his camera and a few personal items should he encounter any delays. With the number of plane changes required to get home, he avoided checking any baggage. Anything he couldn't bring as a carryon could be sent to him by his second in command. Time was of the essence.

CHAPTER 49

Something seemed off about Pete Ward. Although the young man oozed confidence at the morgue, I wasn't sure how trustworthy he really was. Evidently, Brad and Lew had some concerns about his qualifications. They readily agreed to meet me at the zoo's entrance gate first thing in the morning.

The three of us were all anxious to get down to business and to coordinate our concerns and questions before meeting with Ward.

In the deaths prior to that of Sam McKay, tranquilizers or paralytic agents were used. A tranquiller gun or blow gun was the most likely tool for delivery. I did some research and learned something interesting. Carfentanil is the tranquilizer of choice to bring down elephants. I reasoned that Ward had access to both the tranquilizer and a tranquilizer gun. I wasn't sure yet where one would obtain curare, the paralytic agent. I addressed these issues with Brad and Lew before our meeting with Ward.

Per Brad's call, Pete Ward met us at the gate. In his khaki-colored shirt and shorts, and a broad-brim hat with one side snapped into an upright position, he looked like he'd been to the Australian Outback. Either that or he bought out the safari collection of Columbia Sportswear or LL Bean, attempting to look authentic. That is, his concept of how someone on safari should dress.

"Let's talk in the office where the air conditioning is working. Even though it's December, it's still hot for this time of the year. You can probably tell from my hat that I try shielding myself from the sun as much as possible. It can take its toll over the years, you know."

Of course, I knew. *I'm a dermatologist for crying out loud and this guy is lecturing me about the dangers of the sun.* My uncle and Lew seemed to find this as amusing as I did, because they could barely maintain eye contact with Pete.

The office that he took us to obviously belonged to his boss, Adam Crowe. The first giveaway was the quality of the photographs on the walls of the office; it was obvious that they were taken by a trained photographer, as good as anything I'd ever seen in a gallery or in a magazine.

In addition to these stunning wildlife photographs, the wall across from the desk was filled with numerous awards, diplomas, certificates, photos of Crowe with various dignitaries, and family photos with his wife and children.

Crowe would be returning to work shortly. He was on his way back from his photo safari in India. Yet, it didn't stop Pete from putting his stamp on his superior's office. I spotted two pictures that appeared to be out of place. Both photos featured Pete Ward in exotic locations. And of course, in his safari-style attire. At least he got his money's worth.

Wanting him to feel comfortable before we got to the real reason for our visit, I commented on the two personal photos that he chose to display on his boss's desk.

"Pete, I recognize your location in the photo on the left. If I had to guess, I'd say it's a great shot of you in Machu Picchu in Peru. Am I right? I was there two years ago with my then fiancée, Lauren. Regarding the other one with the monkeys in the background, I can't say for sure where it was taken. Help me out. Where were you?"

"You're right about Machu Picchu, Doc. The second one was taken a few days later when I was on a river cruise through the Amazon."

"I'm envious. When we visited Machu Picchu, we didn't have enough time to do the Amazon. Someday, I'd like to cruise there with my wife."

Brad lost all patience with this idle conversation. On the job he was like a heat seeking missile, focused only on the target.

"Let's cut to the chase. We need to know more about these agents, curare and carfentanil," Brad said, testily.

"Well, you came to the right place, Detective Mandich, at least regarding the carfentanil. Curare isn't something that we have on hand, but we use carfentanil all the time, especially for our larger animals."

"How would you go about administering it to an animal? I'd like a step-by-step explanation, so I can understand the process," Brad stated in his most authoritative voice.

"Sure thing. I have the agent and the tranquilizer gun under lock and key. Follow me."

Like newborn ducklings trailing a mother duck, we followed Ward to a back room. I have to say that I was impressed. The tranquilizer pistols and rifles were secured in a wall-mounted cabinet that was padlocked. Brad and Lew were noticeably impressed as well by the security measures, as they communicated their approval with eye movements, head nodding, and gestures to each other. Pete indicated that he and his boss Adam Crowe were the only ones with access to the cabinet. He then led us to a refrigerator/freezer that also had a padlock. Again, he and his boss were the only employees with access.

Medications and their administration are more my bailiwick, so I was the most eager of the three of us to find out the proper use of the carfentanil with an animal. Pete explained the importance of adjusting the dose of the carfentanil based upon the animal's weight. Then he used a pressurizing syringe to prepare a dart with a dose of tranquilizer. I had no idea what he planned to do with the filled syringe. I soon found out.

"Once we prepare the dart correctly," Pete explained, "we can choose from a blow gun, rifle, or pistol to put the animal out. It all depends upon how safe I feel based on the behavior of the target. That determines the proximity I'm comfortable with. Each case is different. If I can get close to the animal, I choose the tranquilizing pistol. If I'm at a greater distance like we will be today, I'll use the rifle. Let's go out to the elephant habitat and I'll demonstrate."

Frankly, I was horrified by his eagerness to tranquilize an elephant. For the moment, however, we played along with him, feigning our desire to witness his demonstration.

We exited the building where he brought us to a modified golf cart that he used to traverse the zoo grounds. Looking at the vehicle, I had my doubts that it would fit all four of us. Certainly not comfortably.

"It's a long walk. It's better to ride," Pete said. By the time we got to our destination, I couldn't say that I agreed. Only one of my butt cheeks rested on the seat. The other one was unsupported as my uncle took up most of the seat that we shared.

Once at the elephant habitat, we practically jumped from the golf cart, not because we were so eager to see Pete's demonstration, but because we were cramped in the cart. Ward deftly loaded the dart into the rifle. He was no stranger to this process. It was clear that he was about to shoot.

I quickly touched his shoulder and interrupted him. Brad and Lew appeared relieved.

"You know, Pete, we get the idea. No need to bring down the animal to demonstrate your accuracy with the rifle and the dart. How about shooting at the bale of hay of over there? Oh, wait, there's an apple sitting on top of the bale. Could you hit that?"

"Not a problem."

It seemed important to him to be able to show off his marksmanship. Like the legendary William Tell, Pete Ward struck the center of the apple.

"How's that for accuracy?" Pete smiling face reflected his obvious pride.

Had he known my reaction to his skill, the smile would have left his face.

CHAPTER 50

"So, Doc, I told you that hitting the apple would be no problem. It's a smaller target than I'm used to, considering the size of the animals that we need to tranquilize, but the technique is the same."

Unfortunately for Pete Ward, he didn't realize that observing his technique provided me with the confirmation of my earlier suspicions about him.

Anxious to terminate the visit, I began walking toward the golf cart so that Brad, Lew, and I could discuss how Pete fit into the DON killings.

"Thanks, Pete," I said. "You've shown us exactly what we needed to see. Would you mind driving us back to the entrance gate now? I suspect that zoo patrons should be arriving shortly and won't want to be kept outside waiting. Plus, we've got jobs to get to ourselves."

"No worries. Hop in. Glad I could help. Maybe you could let my boss, Adam Crowe, know what I've done when he gets back."

"We'll do that, all right," Lew answered.

I'm not sure if Lew intended his words to be ironic, but I saw them that way.

The ride back was equally uncomfortable. Again, we practically jumped out of the golf cart when we reached the zoo entrance. Before driving off, Pete shouted, "I hope you learned something helpful."

Little did he know.

I wasn't sure how much Brad and Lew zeroed in on my suspicions concerning Ward. My uncle did, however, recognize that once I saw Pete shoot the apple so adroitly, I was anxious to part company with him. Brad knows me so well.

Outside the zoo's gates Brad began picking my brain. "That was an abrupt exit. Why so anxious to leave?"

"I saw all I needed to see," I said cryptically. Guess I thought back to all the times he played Twenty Questions with me, making me draw out information from him, piece by piece. Now the shoe was on the other foot.

"And what was that? What exactly did you see?"

"Mr. Ward is proficient with mixing and delivering the tranquilizer carfentanil. The autopsies of the tourists from New Jersey showed it in their bloodstreams. Seems like more than a coincidence," I replied.

"Yes, that's true," Brad agreed, "but what about the curare? Doesn't seem like he has a source for that. He told us that the zoo doesn't use it on the animals. If you recall, Cliff, curare was used on all the other victims of the DON killer."

"Call it a hunch, Uncle Brad, but I think he may be lying. You saw his pictures. He's been to Peru and the Amazon. Curare is commonly used by the native people in South America. All he needed to do was take home some of the plant material and he'd be able to manufacture his own."

It was a stretch, but it wasn't out of the range of possibility. Lew was listening to our discourse and offered his opinion.

"Pretty interesting idea, Cliff. You might be right, but for now, it's just conjecture. We'd need a helluva lot more proof before we could sell this to Sergeant Hernandez."

My uncle saw the merit of presenting this idea to his sergeant. Once he had Hernandez on board, he could dig deeper.

Brad needed to present Pete Ward as the primary person of interest to get the green light to investigate Ward further. Even if my theory didn't pan out, at least it would buy them some time because the screws were tightening, beginning with the police commissioner and down the chain of command.

It took less than a minute for Brad to make up his mind. For now, he was going to sell my idea to his boss. His motivation was clear from what he said to his partner.

"Lew, this could work. Cliff may be right about Ward. We just don't know. But even if what Cliff suspects is wrong, it might just get Sergeant Hernandez off our butts for the time being. We have a suspect. He'll see that as progress."

Maybe. That was the unstated word we were all thinking.

Lew conceded that it was worth a try. They had nothing else. He agreed that Brad should pitch the idea to Hernandez.

"Now we have suspect number one," declared my uncle.

I hoped like hell that my suspicions were correct. If they were wrong, I might have thrown my uncle under the bus.

CHAPTER 51

About fifteen miles from the Metro Zoo, a concerned neighbor called police to report a possible break-in. Since daybreak patrol cars had been swarming the neighborhood in a normally quiet section of Coral Gables. When Lamont Wilson went out early to walk his dog, he noticed that the front door of the residence of Palm Drive's most famous couple was battered and left partially open. Seeing the condition of the door, he became suspicious and frightened. Wilson yelled from halfway up the driveway not wanting to get any closer, hoping that someone inside would hear him and come out. That didn't happen.

Fearing that the person who had apparently broken into the house might be still inside, Wilson called Miami PD. The home belonged to Hoyt and Shannon Stark. Everyone in the neighborhood knew that they separated under acrimonious circumstances. Ever since Hoyt Stark was forced to move out, the home had been peaceful. Evidently, something untoward happened to dispel that peace.

A crime scene barrier had been set up. The street in front of the home was a scene of flashing lights, police cruisers, a Crime Scene Unit van, and what had become a growing mass of humanity. People were bustling around like bees buzzing around a hive. The news media had helicopters in the sky and vans with satellite hookups on the ground.

Speaking with the police at the scene, Lamont informed them that the broken door in the open position had drawn his attention to the house. He assured them that he had not entered the premises and hadn't heard anything from within. From the amount of time the police spent speaking with Wilson, the reporters figured out that he was the one who alerted the police to the break-in. They zeroed in on him like vultures picking at a carcass.

With the police remaining silent with the pat response of "No Comment," Lamont Wilson found himself the most sought-after individual in this ever-increasing crowd. A recent retiree in his late sixties, he hadn't formed too many friendships with the neighbors due to his prior arduous work schedule. He spent most of his spare time with his wife, his kids, and his grandchildren, and of course, with walking his dog, Flip. When people commented on the odd choice of the name for the pooch, Wilson laughed, reminding them of one of his favorite old-time comedians, Flip Wilson. Seemed like a fitting name. At least he didn't name any of his children Flip.

With microphones in his face coming from what appeared to be every direction, Lamont remained pretty much closed mouth as instructed earlier by the police. Their directive was unnecessary since he knew little about the Starks, beyond what was written in the tabloids and what made the evening news. Even if he were privy to any personal information about the couple, he would have kept it to himself. Gossiping wasn't in Lamont's nature. Being in the limelight also made this shy individual uncomfortable.

Doubting that he'd be able to give any further information to the police, he did inform an officer that he'd be available if they wanted to speak with him again. That being said, he retreated to the privacy of his home across from all the chaos. As he crossed the street to his house, several reporters followed him, intent on keeping the ongoing story alive. When Lamont all but ran into his home and slammed the door in their faces, they got the hint.

A large percentage of the reporters chose to remain at the crime scene, because the house belonged to Hoyt Stark. The name recognition in the community and on a national level merited their time, even if all they were doing was waiting for something to unfold. Their wait was rewarded several hours later after CSU finished processing the crime scene.

From their den, Lamont Wilson and his wife Chloe periodically peered out at the commotion. It seemed to be taking an exceptionally long time for the police to exit the home. Gawkers were still on the scene, and reporters were interviewing some of them, just to have some footage for the news. It didn't matter that the onlookers had no information and were just hanging around because Hoyt Stark was a famous football player. The interviews were just fillers, giving the reporters a reason to remain at the scene.

Finally, the atmosphere changed. Something significant was happening. Two employees from the Medical Examiner's office came through the front door, wheeling a gurney. On the gurney, a body bag encased the victim who had been found in the house. As the gurney was wheeled down the driveway, the reporters sprinted to the van that was identified as belonging to the Medical Examiner's office, attempting to take photographs and solicit information. The police waved them away, irritated by their relentless interference which impeded their investigation.

Ultimately, the reporters gave up their vigil. The gurney was loaded into the van and driven away. The crowd began to disburse. There was nothing left to see at the house. The reporters began loading equipment and moving their trucks.

For Lamont, the worst was confirmed. From the moment he spotted the door that morning, he knew that something horrible had happened in that house. He had no doubt that one member of the Stark family was the corpse in the body bag, but he had no way of knowing the exact details of what happened inside.

Had Hoyt returned home, ignoring his restraining order? Had one of them killed the other? Had a stranger entered the house?

Lamont Wilson couldn't stop the crucial question that cycled through his brain in an endless loop.

Whose body was in that bag?

CHAPTER 52

Adam Crowe was still fatigued from his photo shoot of the Bengal tigers of India. The long flight home with multiple layovers and plane changes was physically exhausting. The sickening image of his porter dying in the mouth of a tiger continued to resurface in his mind. The combination left him physically and emotionally drained.

In an ideal world, he would have spent his first day home acclimating to the time zone change, taking care of piles of mail that accumulated in his absence, emptying all the clothing from his duffel bags into the washing machine, and restocking his bare refrigerator and pantry. Finally, he would have slept.

But this was not an ideal world. Aware of the newspaper headlines, he cut his photo safari short. Fearful about the condition of the zoo and the level of panic sustained in Miami during his absence, he knew that he wouldn't be able to rest until he saw for himself. After being dropped off at his home shortly after 1 p.m. by an Uber and depositing his bags and equipment in the hallway, he headed for the garage. He said a silent prayer that his car would start after not being driven while he was in India. The sound of the car's engine proved to be the highlight of his next few hours.

When he landed in Miami, Crowe immediately texted his assistant that he'd be returning to work that afternoon. Fortunately for Pete Ward, that heads up gave him enough time to clear out of Crowe's office, which he improperly used to impress the police and other visitors with his importance.

The return of his superior brought him back to reality. Pete removed his photos and nameplate, making sure that he didn't leave anything out of place. Reluctantly, he looked back at Crowe's office as he retreated to his desk in the cubicle that didn't even have a full wall to afford him privacy from the other occupants in similar setups. His regular station was utilitarian, a euphemistic way to describe a desk facing a half-wall just inches away, surrounded on two sides by other half-walls that barely allowed his swivel chair to travel more than two feet in either direction. A broom closet probably was larger than his cubicle.

Shortly after Pete finished his lunch, the director of wildlife, Adam Crowe, walked into the area where Pete's cubicle was located. Tall, lean, and dressed from head to toe in khaki-colored clothing, the boss made his entrance. No one at the zoo had ever seen him dress in anything other than clothing that made him look like he was either returning from or going on his next safari. The biggest change in his attire was a seasonal one. He would exchange the dual-pocket khaki short sleeve shirt for a dual-pocket khaki long sleeve shirt during cold weather. He always wore long pants, never shorts. When he attended any formal even, he made sure that his khaki shirt had long sleeves. It was his only accommodation to the formal nature of an event.

"Hey, Dr. Crowe, welcome back. I'm surprised to see you today. Figured you'd need a day to chill. How ya doin'? You must be exhausted."

"I'm fine, Pete, other than the fact that I need to catch up on some sleep. More importantly, I need to catch up on what's been going on here in the zoo and with these murders. Seems like when I go away, and all hell breaks loose."

"Not to worry. I've been taking care of things."

"Did I hear you say, '*not to worry*'? Pardon me, Pete, but there's no way I can say this that doesn't come across as insulting. From what I've read in the digital version of the Herald, your presumed expertise is way above your pay grade."

Not exactly the response Pete was expecting, and certainly nothing remotely close to what he wanted to hear. To diffuse Crowe's anger, Pete at least had the good sense to agree.

"Of course. That's why I sent you emails so that you'd be aware of things and advise me if you felt it was necessary. Now that you're back, let me fill you in on the latest developments."

Crowe had no patience to hear anything further. Without looking back, he headed to his office. Ward followed behind, hoping to continue the conversation.

Crowe made his way to his desk and settled into his chair, looking over the files and sticky notes on his desk blotter. The files were stacked precariously high and make him think of a Jenga game. If he pulled one file from the bottom or middle of the stack, he envisioned that the entire group would topple over.

Uninvited, Pete pulled up a folding chair that had been resting against the wall and sat across the desk from his boss. He waited until Adam made eye contact with him. Pete still felt the need to try to impress Crowe with his contribution to the police investigation.

"As you can imagine, I'm rather busy, first day back and all. But if it'll get you off my back, just say what you came to say, Peter."

Crowe often called him by his given name, particularly when he was about to admonish him. Trying to lessen the impact of any criticism, Pete attempted to present himself in the best light possible.

"I don't want to brag, but I think I pointed the police in the right direction with the case that everyone calls the Dead of Night or DON killings."

At that point, what Crowe wanted to say was that people who say that they "don't want to brag" clearly *do* want to brag.

This false humility doesn't fool anyone. He kept that thought to himself, and merely said, "Explain yourself."

"Well, the medical examiner called in a dental expert to analyze the bites on all the victims. I understand that he took meticulous photos and said the bites were not human; it was his opinion that they were made by another mammal."

"So, what did you say?"

"I knew right away that they were made by a wolf, probably Canis rufus. That would also explain the howling that people have been hearing at night. That's what I told them." As he recounted his involvement to Crowe, Pete insinuated that his analysis was indispensable to the police. Crowe shot down Pete's conclusion with a single question.

"Do you realize that it has been decades since a wolf of that genus and species has been seen in the wild in Florida?"

"I guess so, Dr. Crowe," replied Pete sheepishly.

Pete thought quickly about what he should say next to get back in the good graces of his boss.

"I guess maybe you'd be interested in the tranquilizer darts."

Exasperated by Pete's response, Crowe slammed his fist on the desk, stood up abruptly to enable him to peer down at Pete, and leaned forward into Pete's personal space.

"Did I hear you correctly? 'Tranquilizer darts'? When were you going to tell me about those?"

"I was getting to it. Two cops and a dermatologist were here this morning. They asked me........."

Before allowing him to complete his explanation, Crowe interrupted.

"Two cops and a dermatologist walk into a zoo. It sounds like a joke," commented Crowe sarcastically.

"Believe me, it's no joke. They asked me about carfentanil, so I explained how we use it to tranquilize the animals. I showed them how we prepare the medication, and then I loaded the tranquilizer rifle. We went out to the elephant habitat so I could demonstrate the efficacy of the tranquilizer, but the doctor stopped me before I took a shot."

His honesty was appalling. Pete had no idea that he was skating on ice so thin that it was about to crack, and he would soon be submerged in the water below the surface. Crowe's only thought was how in the hell could his underling he even consider shooting an elephant with a tranquilizer rifle solely for the purpose of showing how it was done. It was unthinkable.

"At least the doctor showed good sense. What the hell were you thinking? Were you seriously considering tranquilizing an elephant just to show off? This conversation is far from over."

"I was just trying to be helpful," whined Pete.

"Did you *help* them with anything else?"

"Yeah, they asked about curare, but I told them that we don't keep that on hand."

"Curare? That's very strange. It's time that I visit the medical examiner. My understanding from what I read is that an autopsy was recently performed on the body of a football player. Evidently, he wasn't bitten like the others, but there seems to be some connection to this case."

Telling Crowe about the inquiry concerning curare turned out to be a blessing in disguise for Pete. His boss seemed both intrigued and puzzled by the interest in the paralytic agent. He was determined to follow up immediately. For the moment, that got Pete off the hot seat.

With his phone in his hand, Crowe signaled to Pete that he should leave. Pete walked away, considering what he could do for damage control. Not only did he need the money, but he enjoyed his work. He was under no illusion that Crowe would forgive and forget his lapse in judgment. *If only he hadn't tried to show off.*

Walking toward his cubicle, Pete heard Crowe place a call to Dr. Cecil Murphy, the medical examiner. Seemed as if his request to visit the morgue to see the body of the football player was answered in the affirmative because Crowe indicated that he was on his way. What Pete didn't hear was Dr. Murphy's last statement before ending the phone call.

"Another body arrived at the morgue this morning."

CHAPTER 53

Welcome Home.

That was all that Adam Crowe was thinking on his drive to the medical examiner's office. It wasn't the homecoming he anticipated. Pete Ward's attempt at being a big shot in front of the police and the medical examiner was beyond ill-advised.

It had been years since Adam Crowe had been to the medical examiner's office. Although he was no stranger to the complex, he was a stranger to the new ME. Crowe assisted Dr. Meacham, Dr. Cecil Murphy's predecessor, on a case seven years earlier.

Crowe's drive was short. He was pleased to see that Jackie retained her position as secretary to the ME. He didn't recall her last name, but her first name came to him immediately upon seeing her. She greeted him with a smile, flattered that she recognized him after all this time as well. Jackie previously impressed him as both pleasant and efficient. Since she also worked for Dr. Murphy's predecessor, Crowe sensed that she had probably become indispensable to the smooth operation of the office.

Also, she seemed to have an exceptional memory. Her greeting as Crowe walked to her desk proved it. "Dr. Crowe, you haven't changed a bit," she said as she looked him over.

Adam Crowe took this as her way of being kind, but it was true. In the seven years since he had seen Jackie, there were no significant differences either in his appearance or in his wardrobe. He remained fit; his weight was probably within two pounds of what he weighed seven years ago, and more remarkably, he managed to keep his full head of hair, although now he was graying at the temples. As always, he wore the same style khaki outfit with dual shirt pockets and long pants.

Although Jackie put on a few pounds since their last encounter, social graces dictated that Adam should reply in the same vein. He knew enough about women to know that any mention of weight gain was inappropriate.

"Thank you, Jackie. You know, I recognized you immediately as well. You haven't changed in the slightest either. Your friendly greeting always put me at ease when I visited this office. The same still holds true today. I get the feeling that you make everyone who walks through these doors feel like a long-lost relative. No doubt Dr. Meacham advised your new boss that he'd be smart to do whatever was necessary to keep you on."

If it were possible, the wattage of the smile she flashed at him after these effusive compliments was double that of her initial greeting. Her eyes shone.

"Thanks for saying that. You're right about Dr. Meacham. He and I were close. I think Dr. Murphy wanted to bring in his own secretary, but he yielded to Dr. Meacham's advice. The best part is that Dr. Murphy has told me numerous times that he's glad that he listened."

"Well, Jackie, it really is good to see you. As much as I'm enjoying this mutual admiration society, I'd better get to the task at hand."

"Dr. Murphy is just down the hall in the morgue. I'll buzz him to let him know you're here."

When he heard footsteps at the door, Dr. Murphy looked up from the autopsy table. Approaching his visitor, he removed the latex glove from his right hand and extended it for a handshake. Adam Crowe extended his hand as well. The two men looked each other straight in the eye, trying to take the measure of each other. They both responded positively to the firm handshakes and to the eye contact which neither wanted to be the first to break. It seemed almost competitive, a male power thing. As the visitor, Adam Crowe let Murphy win this round. He began speaking.

"Dr. Murphy, I appreciate your agreeing to meet with me. I've been out of the country have gotten spotty news about the DON killings. Today my assistant, Pete Ward, briefed me on his involvement with a police investigation and indicated that a dental expert identified *animal* bite marks on some of the deceased. Pete gave me his rendition, but it seems exaggerated to make himself a hero. I want to hear from you what you found as it relates to animal involvement in the DON killings. I trust you to tell me what's what."

"Seems like we can both profit from our collaboration, Dr. Crowe. Your visit will help me out considerably. We have some conflicting problems that require the expertise of a wildlife expert like yourself. In your absence, I met with Pete. He did his best, but to put it bluntly, he lacks your knowledge and experience."

"What can I do to help?"

The question seemed clear-cut. Yet Murphy stared at the examining table, avoiding eye contact with Crowe, ruminating much too long over his response. Something was going on.

"Dr. Murphy, what's the problem? Just spit it out."

"I'm ashamed to admit it, but I created part of the problem," replied Dr. Murphy, his eyes downcast.

"You're losing me. What problem are you talking about, and why do you think you created it?"

Murphy shook his head, let out a sigh, and this time looked directly at Crowe.

"The problem is I don't know how many killers are out there. I suspect at least two, but there could be a third, for all I know. This isn't doing much for my self-esteem, I can tell you."

"Why do *you* feel responsible for the problem you're having?"

"I'd rather not go into details, but the basics are that I leaked information to a city councilman. Under pressure from him, I even leaked some things anonymously to the press. My actions may have led to more deaths."

Hearing his confession, the first thought that popped into Crowe's mind was the quote "Loose lips sink ships" from history class when studying World War II. Crowe wondered how bad the consequences were of Murphy's imprudence.

"Dr. Murphy, why do you think you're responsible for these additional deaths?"

"Some of the specific details about the condition of the bodies could have been used by a copycat killer who read the papers or watched the newscasts. I can't help but feel that their blood is on my hands."

"Does anyone else know what you did?"

"Police Commissioner Inez Vargas knows. She let me know that I'm on thin ice. Now, I'm doing everything by the book."

"At least it's out in the open, Dr. Murphy. What's the problem now, and, more to the point, what I can do to help you resolve it?"

"I'm fairly certain that we have *at least* two killers."

"Why?"

Dr. Murphy began a chronological history of the victims and the autopsies he performed. Yielding to the desires of the families, once he completed the autopsies, he had no valid reason to delay the release of the bodies for burial or cremation, per the instructions of the family members. With the arrival of the two most recent bodies in the morgue, he wished that he still had the initial victims' bodies available for further study and comparison.

"Unfortunately, the families of the earlier victims have already taken the bodies. Upon autopsy, we found those bodies had bite marks that looked alike to me. Another similarity we found was that every one of them had the mark of a tranquilizer dart on the posterior neck. Most disturbing to the family members was the fact that all the internal organs were removed from the abdomens of the victims. These findings made me certain that all were victims of the same killer; I therefore felt comfortable releasing the bodies to their families," Dr. Murphy explained.

"Dr. Murphy, you appear to be differentiating between the earlier killings and the two bodies that are currently in the morgue that you just alluded to. What makes you think that an additional killer is responsible?"

"There are significant differences in the findings upon autopsy. Like the other bodies, the abdomens of the two recent bodies were opened and the internal organs were removed.

"However, the strange thing is that, unlike the others, these two have *no* bite marks and *no* markings from tranquilizer darts. The other difference is that these two most recent bodies have fractured hyoid bones at the front of the neck, suggesting strangulation. I'd like you to take a look."

"Let's get to it," said Crowe. In the abstract, this was fascinating, a complex puzzle to assemble.

Had he been aware how he would react to viewing the bodies of both victims, he might have been considerably less eager.

CHAPTER 54

Dr. Murphy crossed the room, explaining in advance what he was about to show his guest. "The first body that you will be viewing has been here for a few days, but I was able to convince the family that the autopsy hadn't been fully completed. I wanted to retain it because my findings were different from those of the original victims. Understand that the second body only came in this morning. There was only time to do a preliminary investigation."

"Not a problem. We'll take it from there," Adam replied.

Dr. Murphy pulled the handle of the drawer that stored the first body. As he unzipped the body bag, the room felt even colder, as if they had just entered a meat locker. Although he read about the football player's murder, he wasn't prepared for viewing him in the flesh. Crowe immediately recognized the face. It belonged to Sam McKay, hometown football hero. Looking at a dead body was bad enough, but Crowe knew Sam McKay personally. McKay had been most generous with charitable contributions to the Miami Metro Zoo, often participating in fundraising events at the zoo that Crowe orchestrated. His personal connection to the victim made it worse. Adam took a deep breath, closing his eyes for just a moment. He needed to organize his thoughts before speaking.

"I followed this guy's career from high school through college and into the pros. Sam was an outstanding football player. I was anxious to see him play in the Super Bowl. He was also a good person who gave back to the community. What a waste. You said that the hyoid bone at the front of the neck was fractured and the abdominal wall opened. I wanted to see if there were bite marks that you might have missed.

"Looking at this body, I can assure you that there is no way that a wolf or any wild animal could have done this. An animal would feed at the belly and would tear at the contents. That would leave teeth marks, but I see only a clean wound, probably from a knife. You agree, don't you, Dr. Murphy?"

What Crowe asked was clearly a rhetorical question. A question that made Dr. Murphy uncomfortable, considering he divulged information about the autopsy findings to Councilman Kyle Griffin.

Dr. Murphy was pleased that Crowe agreed with his assessment about a copycat killer being responsible for McKay's murder. Simultaneously, he was terrified that Miami had a second killer in its midst.

Crowe continued discussing his observations. "Based upon the borders of the wound, the incision in the abdomen appears to have been made by a serrated knife. No animal uses a knife. Also, no animal could break a bone in the neck and not leave teeth marks. Without question, what you're looking at is the work of a human."

"I thought that you'd say that. A second body arrived this morning with similarities to Sam McKay's manner of death. The hyoid bone was fractured. Comparable wounds mark the body. I'd appreciate your evaluation as well."

"Of course."

After pushing Sam McKay's body back into the drawer that housed it, Dr. Murphy walked over to the autopsy table. He had been working on the second body when Adam Crowe arrived but hadn't completed his examination. The body was delivered to the morgue only hours ago. When he uncovered the body, he again stated that his findings were still preliminary.

Dr. Crowe again recognized the victim, Shannon Stark. Both she and her husband had been featured prominently in the Miami Herald before Adam left for his photo safari. Their domestic disputes and Hoyt Stark's suspension from football because of domestic violence had been big news. With Dr. Murphy at his side, Crowe carefully viewed the body, searching for bite marks or other evidence of animal involvement. He could find none.

"Dr. Murphy, I can't understand how a person could do this. It's beyond horrendous. A serrated knife appears to have slit open the abdomens of both victims. I'm ashamed to say this but the only animal capable of this cruelty walks on two legs."

Dr. Murphy was now convinced that a copycat killer *was* responsible for the deaths of Sam McKay and Shannon Stark.

Both men were certain that the fractured bone in the neck and the wound pattern on the abdomen were made by the same individual.

"Okay," said Murphy. "We're in agreement that there are two killers: the Dead of Night killer and a copycat killer."

Still feeling responsible for what he divulged to Griffin and the media, Murphy revealed his concern.

What worries me is the possibility of a third murderer. What do you think?"

CHAPTER 55

This was becoming more complicated by the minute. Crowe hadn't anticipated being Dr. Murphy's sounding board. All he expected was to examine the bodies for evidence of animal involvement in the killings. However, he was intrigued by the ME's question.

"Why do you think that there may be a *third* killer?" asked Crowe.

"I'm not sure whether Walter and Vivian Raines, the couple visiting from New Jersey, were killed by the Dead of Night killer or a *different* copycat from the person responsible for the deaths of Sam McKay and Shannon Hoyt."

"Are you considering that possibility for a specific reason?"

"Their autopsies," Murphy explained, "showed that the couple was tranquilized with carfentanil. They would have been unconscious, unaware of what was happening to them and how they were killed. The other victims were paralyzed with curare. Therefore, they would have been helpless but fully aware of the horrible mutilation the killer perpetrated on their bodies and their imminent deaths. It was unimaginable cruelty. With Police Commissioner Vargas already breathing down my neck, I can't afford to make another mistake."

Crowe fully understood his dilemma. If the ME didn't consider a *third* killer, he'd be judged incompetent if that turned out to be the case. But if he delayed reporting his findings to enable further investigation, he'd be accused of stonewalling, negatively impacting the city's ability to put the matter to rest.

It was a catch-22 situation.

"Well, I think I can solve this for you," Crowe offered. "You said that other than the drugs used to subdue the victims, all other autopsy results were the same. That would include bite marks, wouldn't it?"

Murphy nodded his head in agreement.

"I see that you had a forensic dentist take photos of the teeth marks from the faces and backs of the victims. If you get me all his photos, I'll study them to determine whether the same animal is responsible. If it was the same animal, then they were all victims of the Dead of Night killer. The sooner you get the photos to me, the sooner I can perform the comparisons. Then we'll know conclusively."

"Dr. Crowe, that's an excellent idea. But why do you think you're better able than Dr. Wirth, the forensic dentist, to compare the bite marks?"

"If an animal other than a man did the biting, *I* am your expert, not Dr. Wirth."

"I'll call Dr. Wirth immediately and get those photos sent to you. He was working with them using some photo-enhancing software program. He should be done with them by now. Leave your contact information with Jackie. And get back to me as soon as you know anything."

After Adam Crowe left the medical complex, Cecil Murphy placed two calls. The first was to Dr. Wirth who assured him that he'd speed up his work. He would send copies of everything to both Murphy and Adam Crowe.

The second call was to Detective Brad Mandich to advise him that there were at least two killers terrorizing Miami.

Upon Adam Crowe's review of Dr. Wirth's photos, it would be determined whether the two New Jersey tourists were killed by a third madman.

An enormously frightening prospect.

CHAPTER 56

I had given my uncle what I thought was a more than reasonable link between the curare, the trip to the Amazon, and Pete Ward. For the moment there was nothing more for me to do regarding the police investigation. Uncle Brad was going to pitch my idea to his sergeant. Until then or until another dead body turned up with a similarly disfigured body, I resumed my actual day job on a full-time basis.

My return to the office was not the homecoming that I hoped for. My absence put a strain on my staff and my patients. Molly Daniels, my receptionist, who fielded the bulk of the calls to the office, and Blythe Ingram, my physician assistant, were at their wits' end.

Typically pleasant and accommodating when scheduling appointments, Molly had been taking the brunt of the anger from patients when she advised them that they'd have to wait several weeks to see me. Often, I'd kid her that she'd been appropriately named. When Molly had to schedule a patient appointment no less than two weeks from the date of the call, with her kindness and good humor she was able to "Mollify" that person into accepting the delay. However, some patients were becoming frustrated and confrontational. Hearing their angry voices and unreasonable complaints began to affect Molly's attitude each time the phone rang. The more assertive patients decided to bypass her apology and would ask to speak with Blythe, thinking she had more authority to squeeze them into my schedule. My office staff was close to mutiny.

Although I hadn't been physically present, during my absence I communicated with my staff daily. They were aware that I trusted them to recognize what was urgent. Had a crisis arisen, of course I would have returned to my office to treat a patient requiring my immediate attention. Short of beaming me up like in the old "Star Trek" series, my team was trying to please the patients as best as they could. Molly attempted to appease the callers by offering to have Blythe see them. The preponderance of patients who accepted this offer knew, from seeing her working with me, that Blythe was a qualified PA. She teased me that some of them might book future appointments with her rather than me once she treated them. I wouldn't have been surprised.

Ordinarily, my office runs like a well-oiled machine. I guess you'd say that I'm bragging about this, but patients frequently comment on how we pretty much run on time, unusual for a medical office. They seem to enjoy the entire experience of their visit and often express their appreciation for the friendliness of my staff. I've tried to impress upon them that we are treating people first and disease second. The personal touch goes a long way.

The primary thing that can jam the smooth-running office paradigm is the emergency work-in or walk-in. Today started with a walk-in, a patient who arrived without an appointment.

A man who had never been to the office was waiting at the front door well before 7:30 a.m. when we open the door to the waiting area. Although we don't begin seeing patients until 8 a.m., we realize that people arrive early. Sitting comfortably is preferable to standing outside in the hallway.

At 7:30 sharp, Molly opened the door. When she asked the patient about the time of his appointment, he indicated that he didn't have one, insisting that he needed to be treated this morning. Despite her explanation that my schedule was already full since it was my first day back from vacation, the argumentative man shouted that he wasn't interested in my scheduling problems. He yelled that he was in pain and needed to be seen. Making a scene, he screamed that he wasn't leaving without being treated.

As the waiting room began to fill with other patients also arriving before their appointments, Molly tried to do some damage control. She took the easiest course of action and handed the man a clipboard, a pen, and a slew of forms to fill out concerning his personal information and his complete medical history. She made copies of his driver's license and insurance cards and asked him to take a seat. Occupied with the paperwork, he settled down. Not only did he calm down, but the walk-in emergency patient's paperwork was processed by 7:45 a.m. How's that for efficiency!

As always, I used the private entrance to the office to avoid being bombarded by patients in the waiting room. Anticipating a crazy day, I was at my desk by 6:30 a.m. which was earlier than usual; I knew that in my absence there would be a mountain of messages and biopsy reports piling up on my desk. Boy, did I get that right.

Ordinarily, I leave my office door open, allowing the staff to poke their heads in with questions and permitting me to keep tabs on how the front desk was dealing with the patient flow. This morning, I deliberately closed my door upon arrival, wanting to clear away the accumulated paperwork before seeing the first patient.

Once I waded through the clutter, I could actually see the mahogany wood on my desk, whereas before the desktop could have been made of brick, metal, or fabric for all that was visible. Relieved, I would be able to see my first patient early and get a jump start on the busy day ahead.

I didn't know yet that the morning's first patient was new to the office. It was the man who moments before caused the disruption in the waiting room; he was a celebrity who had fallen from grace.

CHAPTER 57

Blythe grabbed the newly created patient chart from the front desk and opened the door to the waiting room. Looking down at the folder, she called out the name on the tab; it sounded familiar to her, but she saw from the paperwork that he had never been to the office before. *Why was his name so familiar?* She waited for him to rise from his chair slowly and deliberately. It seemed like a painful process for the man.

"Good morning. I'm Blythe, Dr. Mandich's PA. I'll be escorting you to the examining room. Please follow me."

In the short walk, she already noticed two things and that was before any actual examination began. The first thing was his awkward gait. He exhibited stiffness in the way he was moving, making his pace unusually slow. It was as if he were trying to ambulate without flexing any joints for fear of pain. The second thing was his face. The degree of sunburn was appalling. People should know better.

Suddenly it hit her. The sunburned man was Hoyt Stark, the man whose estranged wife Shannon was recently found dead in her home. Stark was a suspect in her murder.

The newspaper covered the story on the front page. There was an unflattering photo of him unsuccessfully trying to hide his face with a baseball cap as he left the police station with his attorney.

Blythe wasn't comfortable having Hoyt Stark as a new patient. Not with the news reports about his dead wife. Mustering all the self-control she could manage, she escorted him to an exam room. She addressed Stark as she would any other patient despite her discomfort.

"I'm going to let Dr. Mandich know that you're waiting to see him. Please change into these paper shorts. The doctor will be in shortly. While you wait, if you want some reading material, there are some magazines in the rack on the wall."

I was just about to walk out of my office to see the first patient when Blythe practically accosted me. She hastily closed my office door, unusual behavior for her. I followed her lead and sat back down in my chair.

"Dr. Mandich, the guy in the waiting room who intimidated Molly into working him into today's schedule is none other than Hoyt Stark," Blythe said breathlessly.

Then she asked whether I knew who he was. That almost made me laugh. Unless a person was living under a rock, everyone in Miami had heard of Hoyt Stark. You couldn't escape hearing about him.

"What's he doing here?"

"From the look of it, I'd say he's had so much sun exposure that he's gotten his quota of vitamin D for the next decade. Frankly, I was so anxious to give you a heads up on his identity that I didn't ask him. My guess is he'd like some relief from his sunburn."

I was very much up to speed regarding the details of the case, including the background stories of the animosity between the Starks. As a fan of football, I also knew that Sam McKay, also recently deceased, had been one of Hoyt Stark's teammates. I headed to the examining room and grabbed the file that Blythe had deposited into the plastic holder outside the door.

Two things surprised me when I entered the room. Unlike most patients, he disregarded Blythe's request to change into the light-blue paper shorts that she had given him. It's much easier to thoroughly examine male patients when they wear these shorts. Secondly, Mr. Stark was standing with his legs spread several inches apart and his arms extended out from his body, not touching his sides. His posture intrigued me, making me wonder whether he was doing a meditation technique, a yoga position, or practicing something he learned in a tai chi class. I was anxious to find out.

As I customarily do, I introduced myself, asked how I could help him, and extended my hand expecting that he would do the same. Immediately, he explained his failure to shake my hand in return.

"Pardon me, Doc, but it's painful for me to move, even to shake hands. My arms and legs are spread apart because when skin touches skin, it's agony. Just walking is painful. I took a chance and parked my pickup truck in a handicapped parking spot. Even if I get a ticket, it's worth the risk."

"I can imagine how uncomfortable you must be," I said sympathetically. "You do have that boiled lobster look. That's one helluva sunburn. Didn't my assistant offer you the disposable shorts?"

"Yeah, not to worry. She did her job, but there's no way I'm removing my clothes and then putting them on again when I leave. Getting dressed this morning was bad enough. I'm not gonna repeat the procedure."

All I could think was *this guy was a football player.* The injuries he must have endured from the tackling and other stresses to his body had to have been far worse than his sunburn. I would've expected him to be more stoic; seemed to me that he was making a big deal out of this.

"Frankly, I'm surprised to see *you,* though," I said.

"Why? You *are* a dermatologist, aren't you? Says so right on your diploma." He pointed at the wall for emphasis.

"Yes, rest assured, I am a dermatologist. What surprised me is that you live here. Most residents of Florida know how to protect themselves from the sun. It's almost always the tourists who get sunburns like you. What happened?"

"I strayed from my usual routine. Usually, I fish alone. My boat has a center console and small canopy. You know the kind of boat I'm talking about?"

"Sure, I've been on that type of boat. It offers little if any shade."

"Well, this time I invited two friends. Each wanted to take turns at the controls. Since you know this type of fishing boat, you know that the area with the controls is the only one in the shade. I should've lathered up on sunscreen throughout the day or used sun protective clothing, but I didn't. Now I'm paying the price for being such a nice guy."

"Well, I hope you caught a lot of fish at least."

"Sure did. I cleaned and filleted them right there at the dock. I keep everything I need to do the job in my pickup truck."

"Better than having to do it at home. Sounds like you're a rather good fisherman, Hoyt."

"I am," said Stark proudly. "Maybe you'll come out with me some weekend. I keep the boat at the first marina you come to after you cross over the Rickenbacker Causeway. Someone with no imagination named it the Rickenbacker Marina."

"You know, I just might take you up on your offer. What's your boat called?"

"Tight Lines."

"Nice name," I commented.

Now that we bonded in typical male fashion over a shared interest, the time had come to discuss the deaths of Sam McKay and Shannon Stark with him.

Because he knew them both, the amateur sleuth in me wanted to question him. Guess you could say that I was on a fishing expedition.

CHAPTER 58

"Hoyt, I hope you don't mind me mentioning it, but you've been in the news a lot these last several weeks. In my opinion, you've been getting a raw deal."

I pretended to take his side. He nodded in agreement when I said he had gotten a raw deal from the media. The papers had written about his domestic abuse charges. It was also big news after Shannon's death when he was questioned at the police station and then released.

"You got that right. But why do you think so, Doc?"

"In my experience, domestic abuse charges always have two sides. For some reason, your own team managers and teammates failed to support you. Shannon's tragic death added more fuel to the fire. The article in the paper has a photo of you leaving the police station with your attorney. There's no question that the police jumped to conclusions. It's still a far leap from domestic abuse, even if true, to a murder charge. What you deserve is compassion, not humiliation."

"Thanks, Doc."

I could see that he appreciated my sympathy and support. That gave me the perfect opportunity to segue into the death of Sam McKay. I had to tread carefully.

"Also, I suspect that you're grieving over the death of your former teammate, Sam McKay. Two such losses in such a short time can't be easy for you."

"In truth, McKay and I were never close. But I do feel bad for his family," he added.

For a moment I thought I detected a sense of sadness. I wondered if he felt remorse or guilt. The time had come to shake him up just a bit. Whereas before I addressed him by his first name, I became more formal now, hoping he'd recognize the seriousness of what I was about to say.

"Mr. Stark, do you know that my uncle is a detective for the Miami-Dade police?" I was guessing that he had no clue, and I was looking for his reaction.

Stark's pupils widened noticeably, his eyebrows raised, and his facial muscles tightened. He began clenching and unclenching his fists. He cast his eyes downward, as if watching something very entertaining on the floor beneath his feet. Clearly, he was becoming uncomfortable.

"Sometimes I consult on cases, Mr. Stark," I stated. "My uncle is the lead detective on this case the media has been calling the Dead of Night killer. Also, he tells me that both Sam McKay and your wife were killed by the same person."

"Holy shit! Are you sure?"

"Without going into all the details, the police have determined that both were strangled and then cut open by a knife. The wounds on the bodies appear to have been made by the *same* knife."

"That's scary," Hoyt declared.

He still hadn't looked up since I mentioned my connection to the police department. Since he became so uneasy with my revelation, I continued, hoping to make him so nervous that he'd blurt details that would implicate him in the murders.

"If I were you, I'd be plenty scared, Mr. Stark."

"Why should *I* be scared? I didn't do anything. Do they have evidence against me?" There was a tremor in his voice.

"The killer has targeted two people pretty close to you, Mr. Stark." In my most serious voice, and slowly enunciating each word, I said, "For all you know, *you* may be the next target."

If I'd been told that I could be the next target, I'd be shaken. Hoyt Stark's reaction was just the opposite. He relaxed noticeably when I told him that he could be a target, not a suspect. Clearly, he was unconcerned about being a target. That would certainly be a reasonable reaction if *he* killed McKay and Shannon.

"Listen, Doc, I appreciate your sympathy about my wife and all, but I didn't come in to discuss my problems with the law. This sunburn is a bitch. What can you do for me?"

"Judging by the way you're walking and standing, we need to make you more comfortable immediately. Make sure you drink lots of water to get you hydrated internally. As far as external hydration, go to any drug store and look for over-the-counter colloidal oatmeal bath products. You'll find them very soothing. Take a nice long bath, and immediately after bathing, you can trap in the moisture by applying an over-the-counter moisturizer lotion. Most people find relief with products containing aloe. I suggest storing the lotion in the refrigerator. It will feel cool and give you some instant relief when you slather it on your skin."

"That's it? I've been waiting for your office to open since the crack of dawn, and you're giving me over-the-counter solutions? I could get the same advice for free at the drug store," Hoyt complained.

"Mr. Stark, you didn't let me finish. First, we tackle your discomfort with hydration and the oatmeal bath. In addition, I'll write you a prescription for a topical cortisone spray which you can use to cover large areas of your body. I'll also give you a prescription for a potent cream commonly used in burn centers across the country. Your skin has already blistered. Once the blisters have broken, use the burn cream in those areas of the skin."

He listened attentively, satisfied that he was leaving with prescriptions. Like the large percentage of my patients.

"Anything else I should do?"

"Since this may be uncomfortable for several days, you might want to try aspirin, to alleviate some of your discomfort."

"Do you need to see me again?"

"It depends upon how you're doing. Schedule an appointment for three days. If you're doing well, you can call to cancel, but at least you'll be on the schedule."

"Thanks, Doc. Oh, and don't forget, I meant that invitation to take you fishing on my boat."

Looking at him, I laughed as I answered. "Maybe we should wait a few months to let your skin recover. But I'll keep it in mind. Thanks."

Stark stopped at the front desk and scheduled his appointment before leaving. I watched as the massive football player lumbered out of the office. His gait was so awkward that my first thought was since he had tanked his football career, he could easily land a part as the monster in a Frankenstein movie.

Then it hit me that the police already suspected him of being a monster. A monster who committed two horrific murders.

CHAPTER 59

No sooner had Stark left the office that I got on the phone with my uncle. I had a great deal to report to him from my interaction with Stark. Hopefully, he would be as impressed with my detective skills as I was.

"Uncle Brad, I've learned that Hoyt Stark owns a boat and a pickup truck. You should probably search both since I think you'll find the knife that eviscerated both Sam McKay and Shannon in one of those places. He does a lot of fishing and likes to fillet the fish he catches. If the knife isn't on the boat, check his tackle box. It's probably in his pickup truck. Oh, the boat is at the Rickenbacker Marina, the first one you come to after you cross over the Rickenbacker Causeway."

Before I could finish, Uncle Brad interrupted me.

"Did you get the name of the boat?"

"What do you think? It's called 'Tight Lines.' I was just getting to that, you know."

"Sorry, Cliff. I should've known. You know, for a civilian, you make a surprisingly good detective. What you found sounds promising. I'll get right on it."

Interestingly, my uncle never asked me how I knew so much about Hoyt Stark. Not sure whether he figured Stark was a patient and he didn't want me to compromise patient confidentiality or because he wanted to get on with the investigation without extraneous background information. Either way, for the rest of the day, I had a big smile on my face.

I returned to patient care, the true area of my expertise.

As my uncle's area of expertise didn't include computer research, he enlisted the help of the much younger and computer savvy Detective Amanda Banks. She did a quick search on the department's CLEAR (Citizen Law Enforcement Analysis and Reporting) database, a powerful research tool utilized by law enforcement investigators. Within seconds she was able to confirm that Hoyt Stark was indeed the registered owner of a boat, "Tight Lines," a Sea Ray Laguna, and a black 2019 Ford Ranger pickup truck.

Solving the rash of murders had become an APE (Acute Political Emergency) situation. Consequently, the process of obtaining search warrants was expedited.

Within the hour, with a search warrant in hand, Brad Mandich and Lew Dennison headed for the marina. They stopped at the bait shop, figuring that the employee who ran it would be the best source of information about the boat owners. They encountered the semi-toothless Oscar, better known as Mumbles.

"Morning. I'm Detective Mandich and this is my partner, Detective Dennison. Maybe you can help us. We're looking for the boat owned by Hoyt Stark."

Over the years, Oscar had had his share of interactions with the police. None of these had been pleasant. What was foremost in Oscar's mind was that during his last encounter with Hoyt Stark, he walked away with two weeks' worth of fish dinners. It was understandable that he'd be somewhat hostile to the cops and protective of his benefactor.

"Whaddya want him for?" mumbled the man nicknamed Mumbles.

"We don't want him. We just need his boat. Where's it docked?" Brad walked closer to Oscar, using his size as silent intimidation.

Oscar stood his ground. "That's just it. It's Mr. Stark's boat. Not yours."

"Are we going to have a problem?" asked Lew in an authoritarian voice. Without identifying it, he waved the search warrant at Oscar. It could have been a flyer for a store opening for all Oscar knew. However, it had the intended effect.

Not wanting to get into trouble with the detectives or charged with obstruction, Oscar chose to cooperate. Exiting the shop, he pointed in a vague direction, having no intention of walking the detectives to the boat. That would have been too much cooperation, he figured.

"That's Mr. Stark's boat over there. The one with the name 'Tight Lines' painted on the stern," he said begrudgingly.

"That's better," said Lew.

While the two detectives headed toward the fishing boat, Oscar returned to the bait shack. Immediately, he placed a call to Hoyt Stark.

"Listen, Mr. Stark. It's Oscar, you know, Mumbles from the marina. Two detectives are here, asking about your boat. You should get down here right away. I'm sorry but I had to point out where your boat is docked. I can't afford trouble with the cops. You understand."

"No worries. I appreciate the heads up. Thanks."

Stark trudged to his pickup as fast as his painful sunburn would allow. He was in a rage. *Goddamn cops. Why the hell are they checking out my boat?* One wouldn't think that his face could have gotten any redder after the fishing trip, but it did.

In the time it took Stark to reach the marina, the two detectives had already completed their hunt for the knife. After all, a twenty-four-foot boat has only so many places to hide a weapon. While they found several items that could do severe damage, including a spear gun and grappling hooks, they didn't find a knife aboard.

The men were about to leave when they noticed blood in the crevices on the deck. It was likely this was fish blood; in a normal situation, they might have ignored it. However, this was anything but a normal circumstance.

"This guy Stark isn't going to be happy when we declare his boat a possible crime scene," snickered Lew.

"No, he sure won't. I've got some crime scene tape in the car. I'll get it while you call CSU to go over this boat with a fine-toothed comb."

Brad was heading to his car in the unpaved lot when he heard the deafening roar of Hoyt Stark's pickup truck. It sounded like he had revved up the engine to its maximum speed, as if he were competing in the Indianapolis 500. Seeing the detective, Stark brought the vehicle to an abrupt stop. Pebbles crunched and tires screeched as he angled the truck close to where Brad stood. He didn't bother with a parking space.

Outraged, he flung open the door of the truck. His ire would have been more impressive had he been able to jump out, but his sunburn prevented anything more than a careful exit. The red-faced man began shouting. Sunburn didn't inhibit his ability to yell.

"What the hell do you cops think you're doing? Stay away from my boat, or you'll regret it," Stark screamed.

When Lew heard the truck's thunderous arrival in the parking lot, he joined his partner. It was obvious to him that Hoyt Stark wasn't going to cooperate willingly. As always, he had Brad's back.

"You need to calm down, Mr. Stark." Lew stated as he waved a paper in the air. "We have a search warrant for your boat and your truck. They're both crime scenes until we say they aren't."

In a show of defiance, Hoyt spat on the ground. "You guys are out of your minds. You want a real crime scene? I can make one happen right now, if you don't get the hell outta here and leave my property alone." He balled his fists to make his point. Used to intimidating people with his sheer size, Stark didn't get the reaction he was expecting.

A big man himself, Brad wasn't intimidated in the least. "We're not leaving. In fact, you've just threatened two police officers and given us cause to take you in. Turn around and slowly put your hands behind your back."

As Brad was speaking, Lew placed his hand on his holstered gun. The gesture did not go unnoticed by Stark, who realized that he was outmanned.

Stark turned his back to the men and placed his hands behind his waist. Ironically, he had no choice but to follow the instruction to *slowly* put his hands behind his back because of his sunburn. Then Brad placed a plastic handcuff tie around both of Stark's wrists, eliciting a wince of pain because the cuffs cut into his already painful flesh.

Lew called for backup. The undercover vehicle they were driving didn't have a secure cage separating the back from the front seat. Also, there were no anchoring brackets in the vehicle to secure the suspect. They were taking no chances.

Within minutes of Lew's call, a police prisoner transport vehicle arrived. Brad and Lew had already read Stark his Miranda rights.

As the transport officers were securing their prisoner, Brad opened the door on the passenger side of Stark's pickup truck. On the floor sat a fishing tackle box. Putting on gloves, Brad opened the tackle box. Among hooks, lures, fishing line, and other fishing gear, he spotted a serrated boning knife. It was still bloodstained.

"My nephew is a genius," he commented to Lew. "He knew exactly where the knife would be."

If he were a betting man, Brad would have bet the farm that they had just found the murder weapon that killed Sam McKay and Shannon Stark.

Lew was pulling out an evidence bag from his kit when Brad walked over to the transport vehicle. Before he said a word, Brad taunted Hoyt with the bloodied fishing knife, turning it over several times, and passing it from hand to hand.

"You're under arrest for the murders of your wife and Sam McKay. I hope you know a good lawyer."

CHAPTER 60

Dallas attorney Hamilton Davies had been closely following the news from Miami on his digital subscription to The Miami Herald. Still bitter about his embarrassing failure to bring the Super Bowl to Dallas, he sought revenge.

Like most of the nation, he followed the Dead of Night Killings and other Miami headlines as well. Hoyt Stark received significant media coverage in recent weeks. The Hoyt Stark domestic violence incident that sparked a restraining order against him as well as the photo of Stark and his attorney leaving the police station after the discovery Shannon Stark's dead body intrigued Davies. An arrest had been made in what might be the Dead of Night Killings or at least two copycat killings.

The attorney representing Hoyt Stark, the suspect, was Patrick Maloney. Everything you wanted to know about Patrick Maloney was on his social media page. He had a wife, two daughters, and a beagle.

Always a schemer, Hamilton Davies saw an opportunity to embarrass the city of Miami if he could utilize his legal skills to win Stark's freedom. The trial of Hoyt Start would be a high-profile event. Already, he devised a plan to replace Patrick Maloney. He wanted this case so badly he could taste it.

The overweight, cigar-smoking attorney grabbed his Stetson hat from the mahogany antique coat rack in his office. In his typical demanding style, he stopped in front of his secretary's desk. He recited a list of instructions to her in his clipped tone, never once mentioning her by name. The names of his long string of frequently replaced secretaries weren't important enough to him to register in his brain.

"Book me an early evening flight to Miami, nothing that's leaving earlier than six o'clock. Also get me a suite at the Intercontinental Hotel in downtown Miami near Bayside. I'll need it for a week at a minimum. Reschedule my appointments next week and push them into the following week."

Since Davies gave her no explanation, she asked. "What do I tell your clients if they ask why? What if they say it's an emergency that they see you?"

"Don't you worry, little lass. I'll have my computer, cell phone, and email capabilities and the hotel will have a fax if needed. I don't have time to stand here and explain this to you. Just do what I say. Let me know the airline, the time, and the flight number when you've made the arrangements. I'm going home to pack, but don't call the house line. Text or call me on my cell."

Experienced enough not to argue, his secretary made the hotel reservations and began checking into flights. One of these days, she'd up and quit. She hated his condescension and being called "little lass."

Davies headed for the parking garage under his building. He deliberately gave himself enough time before his early evening flight to implement his plan.

He drove to Houston and found an Internet café. Leaving his Stetson in the car so he wouldn't be remembered, he sat down at a terminal. With a large cappuccino, a chicken Caesar wrap, a bag of chips, and a blueberry muffin by his side, he began typing. When satisfied with his communication, he pushed send. With his business completed, he paid cash. No paper trail.

Then he drove back to Dallas. He stopped at home, packed a suitcase, and called an Uber to take him to the airport for his flight to Miami.

****

In the morning Hoyt Stark received a surprise visit from Patrick Maloney, his attorney. Stark was in jail being held without bond, having been deemed a flight risk. Since Maloney's visit was unscheduled, Hoyt was hoping that maybe he was being released. He got up from the bed and walked toward the bars to the cell.

Sadly, for him, nothing was further from the truth.

"Hey, Patrick. I'm so glad to see you. Are you getting me outta here?"

"Sorry, Hoyt. No can do. In fact, I have some bad news for you. I have to resign as your legal counsel."

"What? You can't! I'm up a creek without a paddle. What the hell happened? What's going on?"

"I'm really sorry. I just can't represent you. I can't." Maloney sounded regretful.

"You owe me some explanation," Stark said. He walked to the interior of the cell and dropped down onto the cement floor, cupping his face with his hands.

"All I can say is that if I represent you, none of my family is safe. I'm afraid that you may have difficulty getting any attorney in Florida to represent your interests. Especially one that has a family. You can try, but it's more than likely that you'll end up with a public defender."

"What the hell are you talking about, Maloney? I'm a celebrity. And I'll be on trial for my life. If you want more money, I can pay you. You're talking *public defender*? I don't understand. That's insane."

Although he wasn't the one locked in a jail cell, Maloney was beginning to feel the walls closing in on him. He needed to get out of there. Fast.

"I'm sorry, Hoyt, but I can't say more. I'm leaving now. Good luck to you."

It was obvious, even to Hoyt Stark, that Patrick Maloney was terrified of something.

****

Patrick Maloney was shaking after visiting Hoyt. Even the short conversation with Stark unnerved him. Unlocking his car door, he practically collapsed onto the seat. He could feel the sweat on his forehead, dripping down into his eyes, and onto the paper that he withdrew from the pocket of his pants.

After he printed the page from his computer the day before, Patrick folded and unfolded it countless times. The anonymous email contained a disturbing threat that he was unwilling to ignore. He read it again, certain that he had done the right thing.

The message was simple and clear.

"I will kill you, your family, and your dog if you represent that degenerate Hoyt Stark. I will do the same to any sleazy attorney who represents that scum."

CHAPTER 61

Prisoner Hoyt Stark had not yet digested the significance of Patrick Maloney signing off his case when a visitor arrived. A guard escorted him to Hoyt's cell and stepped aside as he entered.

The new visitor was a stranger to Hoyt. If they had met before, Stark would have remembered. You didn't often see someone in South Florida wearing a Stetson unless you were in Davie, Florida, a suburb not far from Fort Lauderdale. In fact, Davie had an active rodeo arena and several local businesses had hitching posts, surprising many visitors.

Hoyt didn't know what to make of the stranger. The hat made him appear even taller than what was probably his six-foot three-inch height. He reeked of cigar smoke, although he wasn't smoking as he walked toward Hoyt. However, a few cigars poked out of the pocket on his western shirt with its pearl snap buttons. It was clear that this man loved his cigars.

Stark was still assessing the situation and trying to regain his bearings, when the visitor introduced himself, his self-assurance as big as the state of Texas.

"Mr. Stark, I'm Hamilton Davies, your *new* attorney."

"Already? Hell, you don't look like any public defender I've ever seen."

"I guess I'll say thank you for that. You're damn straight, I'm not a public defender, not by a long shot. For your information, I'm a licensed attorney in both Texas and Florida. Rest assured, Mr. Stark, I'm well versed in the laws of this state."

The man oozed self-confidence.

"I don't come cheap, but you don't need cheap. You need good, and I'm the best."

"Well, I don't know that yet, but I gotta admit, you make one helluva first impression," replied Stark.

"Never underestimate the importance of a first impression, son." Davies was enjoying himself, wanting Stark to feel grateful that he was taking his case.

"You certainly don't lack confidence in yourself, Mr. Davies. You'd make a good salesman, but I'm here sitting on my ass in a jail cell. You'd best be able to convince me that you're a good lawyer."

"That's fair enough."

Hamilton Davies finally took his hat off and sat down on the flimsy metal chair that was in the cell. Stark pictured it crushing like a beer can from the Texan's weight. The thought brought a smile to Hoyt's face.

"From the look on your face, Stark, you have no idea what you're up against. So, let me give you the short version. You're in trouble in a big way. I graduated from the University of Miami Law School. I know Miami and I still have connections here. My area of expertise is criminal law, which is what you need. I'm a seasoned trial attorney with a record for acquittals that I'll put up against anyone. Feel free to Google me and you'll see that what I'm telling you isn't bragging. It's the God's honest truth."

"Okay, let's say that I believe you, Mr. Davies. Then tell me, to what do you attribute your remarkable success?"

"I'll do *anything* to win. And I stress, *'anything.'* I'm proud to admit that I play dirty."

Hoyt Stark had no idea of how dirty. He never found out that Davies was the person who sent the threatening email to his prior attorney, Patrick Maloney. Covering his tracks, Davies took the precaution of leaving Dallas to visit an Internet café in Houston to send the email. It would be untraceable back to him.

At least Hamilton Davies was truthful about one thing. He did play dirty.

CHAPTER 62

Recognizing a kindred spirit, Hoyt's spirits were again buoyed after the abrupt resignation of his former attorney. Already he liked Hamilton Davies, particularly his style. Stark also would break any rule.

"I'm wondering something," Stark said.

"What would that be?" As he spoke, Davies pulled a cigar out from his pocket, snipped the end, and inserted it into his mouth. He knew he couldn't smoke it in the jail cell, but he found having a cigar in his mouth gave him a certain gravitas.

"How'd you know I'd need an attorney? I had one up until about an hour ago."

"Let's just say that I've already given you as much of an answer as you need to know. Suffice it to say that I already told you that I play dirty."

"Okay. Okay. I get your point. Let's say that I hire you. How do you get me out of here? And what's is gonna cost me?"

"Let's get down to brass tacks, Stark. You'll pay me and pay me well. We'll work out the financial details later, but I can promise you it'll be worth every penny. Although nothing is beneath me with in my relationships with everyone else, I play fairly with my clients. You'll have to trust me on that. Besides, what's your money worth if you spend the rest of your life in prison? Or worse? Think about that."

Hearing the attorney paint the grim picture of his future, Hoyt realized that he had no alternative but to engage Davies.

"So, what's it gonna be? Are you my client, Stark?"

"Yes, I'm your client."

"Good. That's settled. Now let me answer your question about getting you out. By law, you're entitled to a speedy trial and I plan to get you one. Right now, you've been charged with two murders - Sam McKay and your wife. The police don't believe that you're the Dead of Night killer. They've decided that you're a copycat, using those killings to mask what you've done. Due to mass hysteria, the bulk of their resources are being spent on the Dead of Night killer. I want your trial over *before* that case is solved so they won't refocus their resources on you."

"Makes sense to me."

"At trial, they'll try to prove motive, means, and opportunity. I'll punch holes in their arguments. There's no evidence of domestic violence since the restraining order, is there?"

"No, I haven't been home since that stupid restraining order was issued."

Neither party was being entirely truthful. Hoyt needed an attorney badly and Davies was using Stark to advance his personal agenda.

"Okay, now that we've settled that, where do we start?" Stark asked.

"First, Hoyt, let me be clear. I don't care whether you did the crime or not. But I don't want any surprises in the courtroom. I suspect you'll go to trial unless we get a plea deal that's too good to pass up."

"I don't want a plea deal if it means time behind bars."

"Let's cross that bridge when we come to it."

Stark began pacing, clearly uncomfortable with that response. Davies continued, outlining what he knew about Stark's situation.

"I mentioned motive, means, and opportunity earlier. Let's face the facts that will be brought into evidence at your trial."

"Okay, so what's my motive?" Stark queried.

"To the prosecution, that's pretty clear. Revenge and jealousy regarding your teammate, Sam McKay."

"What the hell are you talking about.? What revenge? What jealousy?"

"All the odds makers had your team, The Steelers, as a shoo-in to play in the Super Bowl in Miami. The prosecuting attorney will bring up that your team didn't fight your suspension from football. He'd argue that you deliberately sabotaged the team's chances to play in the Super Bowl by killing their star running back, Sam McKay. Revenge on the team and jealousy that Sam McKay, not you, would get the team into the Super Bowl seems like a damn good motive."

"Shit, that don't sound good for me."

"No, it does not. Let's move on to motive in the case of your wife. Even if we can miraculously get anyone on the jury to forget the previous charges of domestic abuse, she had you kicked out of your own home. You were furious. There's your motive."

"You're scaring me. You sound like you believe those motives. So, what're you doing to defend me? Where's the good news?"

"I'm not going to sugarcoat this, Hoyt. It gets worse."

"How so?"

"Let's turn our attention to means. You're a football player with the strength to fracture the small bone at the front portion of a person's neck. The real problem is that the cops have your fishing knife. If there is DNA on it from either of the bodies, the case is a slam dunk. You'll likely never be a free man again. However, if DNA evidence is absent or inconclusive, we have a slim chance. If the knife wounds are consistent with those made by your brand of fishing knife, things can get dicey."

"I thought you're on my side, Davies. Sounds like I'm going away for life. And that's the best-case scenario. How can we beat this?"

"You've overlooked a few things. As far as we know, no one saw you at either crime scene. Your alibis for the times of death can be tweaked, if necessary."

With his freedom and his life at stake, Stark let that admission from his attorney slide. In fact, he saw it as a positive. "Anything else in my favor?"

"Sure thing. Mistrials happen all the time, if you get my drift. Remember our secret weapon. Like I told you before, I play dirty."

Hamilton Davies left the jail grinning about the success of his plan. He was now the attorney of record for Hoyt Stark. His little trip to Houston and the anonymous email he sent did the trick.

Tangible proof that he did, indeed, play dirty.

CHAPTER 63

It had been days since stories about the Dead of Night killer monopolized the news cycle. With no new deaths to investigate, the police investigation stalled. The lack of new crime scenes reduced the likelihood of finding new evidence to track the killer. Sergeant Hernandez had been making things difficult for his detectives. Only Amanda Banks seemed to escape the sergeant's wrath. Currently, she was reviewing reported crimes of all sorts hoping to find some connection, no matter how tenuous, to the DON killings.

What made things even worse was the report from CSU concerning evidence from Hoyt Stark's boat. The blood found on Stark's boat was fish blood. No one had been killed aboard his boat. Regarding the knife found in his truck, DNA samples were taken but results were still pending.

Brad needed to get out of the office before Hernandez subjected him to his daily tirade. He was literally saved by the bell when his phone jangled in his pocket.

"Detective Mandich, it's Cecil Murphy."

"Tell me you have some good news."

"If you come to the morgue, I'll show you.

"If it's okay with you, I'd like to bring my nephew, Dr. Mandich."

"Not a problem. I'd welcome any input he has."

For the first time in days, my uncle felt encouraged. Grabbing his suit jacket from his desk chair, he related his conversation with the medical examiner to his partner. As Brad and Lew walked to the car, Brad phoned me.

"Perfect timing, Uncle Brad. I just finished seeing my afternoon patients. I can meet you and Lew there in a half hour."

Surprisingly, there were no barricades or accidents on I-95. I arrived only a few minutes before the two detectives but chose to wait for them before speaking with Dr. Murphy. Chatting with Dr. Murphy's secretary, I reassured Jackie that I kept her secret. No one would ever know that she told me that her boss had furtively given information about the DON investigation to Councilman Griffin.

Ignoring pleasantries, my uncle burst into the room with Lew trailing behind.

"Jackie, is Dr. Murphy ready for us?"

My uncle didn't address me by name but acknowledged my presence with a quick head nod.

When Jackie confirmed that Dr. Murphy was waiting for us, we headed for his office. Anxious and stressed, Brad again ignored social conventions, neglecting a handshake or a customary greeting. My uncle exhibited equal opportunity rudeness.

"Hope you got something good for me," Brad began.

"Let's say the news is slightly mixed."

"From your call, I figured you had a break in the case. What's going on?"

"The police Crime Scene Unit took samples for DNA analysis from the knife that you uncovered in the trunk of Hoyt Stark's pickup. The results aren't back yet."

"Then why'd you call me?" blurted my uncle. "Do you have *anything* for us?"

"I have a knife, two bodies, and a demonstration."

The medical examiner produced an evidence bag that contained the knife that was recovered from Stark's pickup. Brad and Lew immediately recognized the boning knife they found in

Hoyt Stark's tackle box. It had been sent to the ME for comparison with the wounds on the two most recent victims.

"Observe the serrations, detectives, and the length of the blade."

Frustrated, Brad grumbled, "Okay we're looking. Explain what we're looking at."

"In order to explain, I need to show you the bodies. Follow me to the morgue, gentlemen."

Dr. Murphy yanked open the drawer that stored the body of Sam McKay. He exposed the abdomen and chest of the deceased.

"The lower abdomen was penetrated first. The cutting edge was facing up towards the victim's chest. The wound, which suggests that a serrated blade was used, was then extended upwards with the blade thrust as deeply as the blade handle and its guard allowed. Knowing that the knife guard stopped further penetration, the blade was inserted to the maximum depth possible. Examining the depth of the wounds allows us to determine the length of the blade. As you can guess, the blade length we calculated from McKay's body is exactly that of Mr. Stark's knife. As you saw, Stark's knife has a serrated blade."

"What about the knife wound on Mrs. Stark's abdomen?" I asked. Dr. Murphy's response wasn't surprising.

"I would testify in any courtroom that the same knife was used on both Mr. McKay and Mrs. Stark," answered Murphy.

"Was this also the knife that caused the wounds on the earlier bodies, the ones released to their family members?" Lew asked.

"Definitely not a match to this knife," Dr. Murphy stated.

Directing his attention to me, Brad said, "This fits our theory that Sam McKay and Shannon Stark were killed by a copycat. All signs now point to Hoyt Stark as the copycat."

Dejectedly, Brad added, “Unfortunately, I don’t think that we’re any closer to finding the Dead of Night killer than we were two days ago.”

CHAPTER 64

My uncle wasn't satisfied that Dr. Murphy told us everything he knew. Eyes blazing like high-beam headlights, Brad stared at the medical examiner as he asked, "Are you sitting on any other evidence, Dr. Murphy?"

Offended by the tone of the question, Murphy rapidly fired back.

"I'm sitting on *nothing.* For now, we're in a holding pattern, waiting for the DNA results from the bite wounds on the bodies that were released to their families and for the DNA results from Stark's knife."

Dr. Murphy's tone was anything but friendly. "Another thing I'm waiting for is a call from Adam Crowe of Miami Metro Zoo. By now, he must have seen the photographs of the bite wounds taken by Dr. Douglas Wirth, the forensic dentist."

Knowing my uncle probably had the same question, I asked, "Why the delay in the DNA findings from the bite marks of the previous victims? Shouldn't you have the results back by now?"

"Apparently the results were quite confusing," offered Dr. Murphy.

"What kind of explanation is that?" shouted my uncle. "That answer is unacceptable. What's your next step?" His exasperation with the medical examiner was growing exponentially.

Dr. Murphy could only reply that no further explanation would be forthcoming until confirmation was received from an additional lab due to the perplexing findings. He stated that the Florida Department of Law Enforcement uses multiple labs. Dr.

Murphy sent the first samples to the laboratory in Tallahassee where his long-time friend, Dr. Donald Pinkney, was the director. A cautious and thorough individual, Pinkney called Murphy and explained that he'd never seen anything like this. The initial analysis was so unusual and confusing that he wouldn't issue even a preliminary report until receiving confirmation of his conclusions from a second laboratory.

Since the DON murder case was an APE (Acute Political Emergency) situation, there was already enough panic; he hesitated to create more. Pinkney chose to err on the side of caution.

"Didn't you ask him about the confusion?" I asked. After the words left my mouth, I realized the stupidity of my question.

"What do *you* think?" snapped Dr. Murphy. "All he would tell me was that he expected to find saliva in the bite marks. And he was reluctant to divulge even that to me."

"Did he clarify his comment about the saliva? Did he say anything further?" I asked.

"His exact words were 'From the bite wounds, we expected saliva. We found none. There was DNA but the results boggle the mind.'"

All of us left wondering how bite wounds would show no residual saliva. What DNA did Pinkney find in the wounds that mystified him to the degree that he requested confirmation from a second lab?

CHAPTER 65

As we walked to the parking lot, Lew resealed the evidence bag with Hoyt Stark's fishing knife, intending to return it to the evidence locker. Dr. Murphy had no further need for it.

Mulling over the conversation with the ME, Brad directed a question to me. "What the hell do you think this means, Cliff?"

"I can only speculate. DNA is retrievable from multiple sources including body fluids like saliva. When Dr. Murphy's friend found DNA but no saliva, it made me wonder about the source or nature of the DNA in the bite wounds. I hope the problem Pinckney had wasn't a result of contamination."

We all wondered who or what had bitten the victims. None of us had an answer. With unfounded optimism, my expectation was that a conversation with Adam Crowe, the renowned wildlife expert, might give us further insight into the teeth marks.

We parted ways. Once in my car, I called Adam Crowe. Fortuitously, he was at his desk when he answered rather than in one of the animal habitats. After I identified myself, he indicated that he was not surprised by my call.

"How can I help you? Pete Ward mentioned that two cops and a dermatologist came to see him about the Dead of Night case. Now it makes sense. I recognize your name and that of Brad Mandich, a major player in the investigation. Obviously, you two are related. He's supposed to contact me if there's another victim so I can survey the crime scene personally. Is that why you're calling? Is there another victim?"

"No, fortunately."

"Good to hear. Then, what can I do for you?"

"I'm interested in the teeth marks on the victims."

"I reviewed the photographs sent to me by Dr. Wirth. For now, I can't offer any helpful comments. Anything I'd say would be no more than an educated guess. I don't deal in guessing. These photographs taken days postmortem are not sufficient."

"What would it take for you to speak with certainty?" I asked.

"I regret to say, I need to see a body, a fresh kill. Only then will I better understand what's going on. That's why I need your uncle to call me to the next crime scene. I promise to give you an answer when I get to see a recent kill. I'm sure this sounds awful to you," Crowe stated.

I ended the call praying that there would be no new bodies. Realistically, I suspected that Adam Crowe would get to see the fresh body that he spoke of. It was only a matter of time.

CHAPTER 66

Primarily tasked with investigating the Dead of Night killings, Detective Amanda Banks had been relentlessly scouring police reports from the last several months, hoping for any tangential cases that could possibly be related to her investigation.

One recent report galvanized her attention. The name "Priestess Julia" was cited as the owner of a dog who had bitten a neighbor. Veronica Adell filed a complaint citing Tutu, Julia's wolfhound, in the incident report.

Amanda, like many of her colleagues, distrusted the priestess. Amanda saw the opportunity to use the neighbor's complaint as a rationale to search Julia's home. Convincing a judge to grant a search warrant would be hurdle number one. She made a strong case that this woman, who first presented herself to the police as a priestess from Haiti, had been lying to the police. Her real name was Julia Marlowe. She came from Manchester, England, had never traveled to Haiti, and had committed check fraud in Georgia. *She* contacted the police to insert herself into the investigation of the Dead of Night killings; possibly she sought information to help cover her tracks. Certainly, she should be considered a person of interest.

The judge granted the warrant. Amanda formulated a plan that would again have her team up with my wife for another subterfuge.

"Hello, Lauren. It's Detective Banks."

"Oh, hi. It's good to hear from you. Is there a break in the case? I can't stop thinking about my classmates; I wish I could do more to help other than data analysis." Lauren clearly enjoyed being the detective's sidekick.

"In that case, Lauren, today may be your lucky day. There may be a break and I'd like you to be a part of it. We were a great team in Little Haiti. Any chance you're available today?"

Elated, Lauren shouted, "I'm yours. When and where?"

"Great. Is it convenient for you if I pick you up from your home?"

"Perfect," Lauren replied, "since that's where I am now."

"In that case, be sure to dress comfortably. Take your time. I need to stop at the butcher shop first, so as soon as I'm done, I'll be on my way. Should be there in about an hour."

"The butcher shop? Now I'm intrigued. What for?"

"I'll explain later when I pick you up." That was the only explanation she provided.

****

Amanda headed for Moshe's Meat Market. As always, Moshe was hard at work. His personality and willingness to customize his cuts for his customers explained why his place was constantly crowded.

In addition to being packed, it was always cold in the market. Amanda came prepared. Like many of the market's customers, she slipped into her sweatshirt before entering the store. She, like many detectives from the precinct, was a regular. Moshe immediately recognized her.

"Shalom, Detective. What can I do for you today?"

"Hi, Moshe, I've got a special request. I'll take two of your thickest rib eyes. Make one about twelve ounces and the other twice the size."

"Sure thing, there's never a problem at Moshe's." He said that so often, he should have it printed on T-shirts for himself and his employees. Plus, he meant every word.

While he worked on her order, Amanda observed Moshe through the eyes of a police officer. He had been a meat cutter for many years. He remained a thin man with a slight curve of the upper spine, probably a result of the many years he spent leaning forward over the chopping block. The bicep muscle of his right arm was that of a champion arm wrestler.

He wore a black yarmulke secured by a small bobby pin on the back of his head. Sadie, his wife, knitted him a supply of them. Each morning when he dressed, he couldn't help but smile at her handiwork. Not surprisingly, the yarmulke was personalized with the image of a smiling cow outlined in white. It was the trademark of his store.

Amanda marveled at Moshe's skills. He cut the meat with the speed of a gourmet chef and placed it on the scale. As usual, his estimate of weight was right on the money. He was rarely off by more than an ounce.

"Anything else I can get you, Detective? I have some beautiful veal chops on special today. Take a look."

"No, that'll be it. Thanks."

She placed the package into the cooler she brought with her. As usual, Moshe sealed the wrapper with a large sticker with the image of a smiling cow. As Amanda checked out, Moshe shouted out to her, "Have a great day. Come again."

"I will," she replied.

Moshe saw the broad smile on her face. Pleasing his customers was Moshe's goal. By the looks of it, he had accomplished that goal.

Chuckling about her plan for the steaks, Amanda was certain that her purchase would help her accomplish her goal.

CHAPTER 67

With both expert knowledge of back streets and the occasional flashing lights of the squad car, Amanda arrived at Lauren's house early.

"Wow, Amanda, you brought a squad car. Last time we went undercover."

"It's all about appearances. I thought that the squad car and search warrant would make a bigger impression. It's a greater show of force, just in case."

"Makes sense. Ever since you called, I've been wondering what we're doing. And especially, what's the deal with your stop at the butcher shop?"

Detective Banks explained that her review of police reports turned up a complaint from a woman named Veronica Adell, one of Julia Marlowe's neighbors. Ms. Adell reported that she was bitten on her thigh by an enormous wolfhound she recognized as Tutu, a dog owned by Priestess Julia.

Other reports on file showed that Veronica Adell called the station several times recently because of nighttime disturbances. Apparently, Tutu, a wolfhound, howls at night like other members of the hound family. The howling precipitated the previous calls from Veronica to the police. As a result, the two women have an acrimonious relationship. Oddly, no other neighbors complained. The detective suspected that the others might fear that Julia would put a curse on them if they contacted the police.

"What exactly are we doing today, Amanda?"

"We need to get into Julia's house. I have a search warrant granting me the authority to enter. We'll improvise to get you inside as well."

"Assuming that we both get in, then what? Don't keep me in suspense. What's with the meat market?"

"I'm getting to that. My goal is to get an impression of the wolfhound's bite. I'll explain to Julia that we're here to determine if her neighbor's complaint about being bitten by Tutu is valid. If Julia insists her dog wasn't responsible, she'll likely cooperate and let us take the bite impressions. That's the ploy that gets us through the door. My prime goal is to determine whether there's a connection with her dog and the bites associated with Miami's Dead of Night killings."

"Ingenious!" said Lauren. "Although I feel badly that Ms. Adell was bitten, her complaint gives us the perfect cover."

"I just hope that Moshe's meats will appeal to Julia's dog, Tutu."

With all the talking, the ride to Julia's home seemed to take no time. However they each imagined what a house belonging to Julia would look like, the reality surpassed all their expectations. A person on hallucinogenic drugs would have been unable to fully imagine what they observed.

Driving down Julia's street, the women had no need to look for the house numbers. This house needed no address. From the appearance of the property and the outside of the home itself, there was no question concerning the ownership.

The house clearly belonged to Priestess Julia.

CHAPTER 68

Priestess Julia's street was full of parked cars, the only clear area being the portion of the street in front of her home. Even without tire-piercing impediments on the swale in front of the house, it was as if no one dared to park there.

The lawn had no grass. Dead weeds served as landscaping. It was as if nuclear fallout rendered the area contaminated, preventing plant growth. There were scattered bones and bleached animal skulls in the front yard. Detective Banks planned to gather samples to determine whether any of the skulls appeared to be that of Canis rufus, the Florida wolf. Large boulders were painted with boldly colored geometric symbols unfamiliar to the two women. The tinkle of multiple wind chimes resounded through the air. Upon closer inspection, Amanda and Lauren noted that the wind chimes dangling in the trees from wooden poles were comprised of teeth and bones.

Each wall of the house was painted in intense hues of red, black, orange, and purple. Vivid images of flames, angel wings, skeletons, and spiders were painted on the walls. It wasn't in preparation for Halloween.

Amanda and Lauren peeked around the back, Amanda wanting to see whether Julia had a rear exit. The back was no different from the front regarding plant growth. There were no living plants in the soil. What had grown there at one time could not be identified from the leafless spindly twigs that remained. However, on the back patio a collection of ceramic pots in psychedelic color schemes contained multiple herbs. Some of these were instantly recognizable as basil, dill, and parsley. Amanda immediately identified several pots growing marijuana;

she had no intention in pursuing these plantings with Julia. Much of this herb garden consisted of plants that neither woman recognized. Without stating their judgments aloud, each thought these mystery herbs might be used in Julia's potions.

"What're you thinking, Amanda?"

"If she offers you any tea, you'd be safer if you politely decline."

"I think I'll take that advice."

Returning to the squad car, Amanda pulled out the search warrant from the glove compartment, removed the cooler from the back seat, and grabbed several evidence bags. When she and Lauren walked to the front of the house, they encountered a broken doorbell with a disconnected wire. The front door bore a large sign, decorated with snarling dogs baring their teeth, warning visitors of a "bad dog" in residence. It couldn't be more obvious that Julia was not receptive to visitors.

Lauren knocked. From within they heard footsteps.

"Amanda, does it strike you as peculiar that the dog isn't barking? In my experience, dogs typically bark or throw themselves against the door when they hear someone knocking, or when someone approaches the house."

"Ordinarily, I'd agree with you," Amanda explained, "but I did some research on wolfhounds. These huge dogs often howl at night, but they're known to be poor watch dogs, not very protective of the home. However, they do come to the protection of their owner if they sense that their master is threatened."

Her footsteps signaling her approach, Priestess Julia opened the front door. She had an expression of recognition and surprise. She greeted her guests pleasantly.

"Detective Banks and Mrs. Mandich, how can I help you?"

"We're here on police business. Your neighbor filed a police report that claims that your dog, Tutu, bit her. I have a warrant allowing me to enter your home," Amanda stated as she unfolded the warrant.

"Wait, stop right there. You didn't need a warrant. I'm a friend to the police. You may recall that I offered my assistance to help rid Miami of the evil curse over it. Won't you both come in and perhaps have some tea?" The invitation came as a surprise.

Julia couldn't help but notice the cooler that Amanda Banks was holding as she walked through the front door.

"Did you bring lunch?" asked Julia in a joking manner. "Perhaps something that would go with tea?"

"Nothing like that, I'm afraid," stated Amanda. "What's in the cooler is related to the purpose of my visit."

"And what 'purpose' would that be? I'm inquisitive by nature," said Julia.

Wanting to enlist Julia's full cooperation, Amanda addressed her by the title she used to identify herself. "Priestess Julia, your neighbor, Veronica Adell, has made several complaints about Tutu howling at night. It's been disruptive to her sleep. Most recently, she was treated at Jackson Memorial Hospital for a dog bite. She identified the dog as Tutu, your wolfhound."

"That woman is a crazy fool. I won't deny the occasional howling, but Tutu wouldn't bite anyone."

"That brings me to the cooler. We can put the matter to rest if you'd allow me to get an impression of Tutu's bite. Then we could compare it with the wounds on Ms. Adell's thigh. She has supplied us with a series of photos and detailed measurements."

"Go ahead. I don't have a problem with that. But I wish you good luck getting an impression," replied Julia.

Amanda removed the twelve-ounce rib eye from the cooler. The tantalizing scent of the meat got the dog's attention. Tutu bounded into the room. Amanda was prepared to see a large dog, but Tutu was the tallest dog she'd ever seen. When she researched wolfhounds, she learned that these tall dogs were bred to hunt wolves in Ireland. The large gray dog with its long hair was an imposing figure.

Amanda tossed the steak in the dog's direction. Natural instinct took over and Tutu caught the steak from the air and deposited it on the floor. The large jaws bit deeply into the steak.

Mesmerized, both Julia and Lauren were wondering how the detective planned to recover the steak from the enormous dog's mouth. The answer came immediately as Amanda again reached inside the cooler and pulled out a steak twice the size. She tossed this huge piece of meat into the air in Tutu's line of sight, but away from the steak on the ground. Instinctively, Tutu lost interest in the smaller steak and went for the larger one. Understanding Amanda's intent, Lauren lunged for the smaller rib eye and sealed it in the cooler.

"Mission accomplished," declared Detective Banks proudly.

In keeping with her earlier explanation, Amanda assured Priestess Julia that with the dental impressions she would prove Tutu innocent of biting Ms. Adell. That was secondary to her more devious plan.

As she explained to Lauren earlier, Amanda successfully secured the bite impression that she planned to compare with those attributed to the Dead of Night killer.

****

Lauren asked permission to tour the rest of the house. No amount of anticipation could have prepared them for what they encountered. The home was like none that the two women had ever seen. Multicolored symbols, outlined in thick black edging, were painted upon otherwise white walls. The symbols were as difficult to interpret as hieroglyphics for Lauren and Amanda. It was hard to determine the composition of the furniture as most of it was covered with colorful fabrics of various textures and animal-skin prints. Without touching the material, it was impossible to know whether the animal prints were manufactured from cloth or came from animal hides.

The central piece of décor on the family room coffee table was the skeleton of an enormous snake, laid out artistically. Initially, it appeared to be ceramic, but closer examination revealed that it had once lived and breathed. A series of skeleton heads decorated the mantel of a huge fireplace made of coral. Neither Amanda nor Lauren wanted to know how they came to be there.

On the kitchen counter, where most people would have a cookie jar, sat a large glass Ball mason jar full of assorted teeth. It caught the attention of both visitors. They resisted discussing the origin of the contents of the jar.

However, when they entered Julia's bedroom, they found it to be surprisingly ordinary. A photograph of a lovely young woman wearing a cap and gown was displayed in a silver frame on the nightstand next to the bed. It appeared to be a high school graduation picture.

When Detective Banks inquired about the photo, Julia proudly explained that it was the graduation photo of Justine, her daughter.

"What's she doing now?" asked Lauren.

"She's a dental technician" replied Julia. The pride in her voice was obvious.

"A dental technician. That's fortuitous," exclaimed Amanda.

"Why would you say *that*, Detective?"

"The key to solving these Dead of Night Killings might lie in dental evidence. Do you think we could speak with Justine? Would you give us her contact information?"

"Of course, I'll call her first myself to tell her to expect to hear from you and to help in any way possible."

After getting Justine's mobile phone number, the two women thanked Julia and headed for the front door. Julia walked them outside. Amanda asked to take a closer look at some of the skulls in the yard. Julia went one step further, giving her permission to borrow any of them that she desired.

Julia had been remarkably cooperative. Strangely so. Amanda couldn't figure out why she had been so agreeable about their requests. As she opened the door to the car, Amanda promised to get back to Julia after having Tutu's bite impressions analyzed and following up with Ms. Adell.

The entire encounter seemed surreal to Lauren. Between the appearance of the exterior of the house, the contents in the interior, and Julia's accommodating behavior, Lauren didn't know what to think.

"Amanda, what's going on? What just happened?"

"It might not seem so now, but I think our house tour might have given us a much-needed breakthrough. That jar of teeth on the kitchen counter and her daughter's job seem more than a coincidence. Handy that Justine is a dental technician, don't you think?"

"Amanda, are you saying that Julia and Justine are somehow connected to the Dead of Night killings?"

"It's a distinct possibility that needs to be checked out. I also want to speak with the neighbor again. I'll pick you up around nine tomorrow."

****

When Amanda took the steak from the cooler, she looked critically at the teeth marks. For the first time in a long time, she felt reasonably optimistic about the case. The teeth marks on the victims were in an elongated oval pattern. Wolfhounds possess an elongated jaw. Had she and Lauren discovered the DON killer?

CHAPTER 69

Charlie Post, captain of "Team Nerd," was surprised when he received a call at 7:30 a.m. from Elliot Cook. Of all the nerds in high school, Elliot had always been the most reclusive, even among his peer group. Charlie often wondered whether some of Elliot's behavior had been fabricated to portray himself in a more romantic manner as a man of mystery.

"Elliot, even if it's way early, it's great hearing from you. I can't remember the last time we spoke on the phone. How're you doing?"

"Pretty good, Charlie. I still live with my folks, but I expect that to change, hopefully soon. I'm working on a new app."

"Good for you. What does the app do?"

"Can't say. I need to play this close to the vest."

"Okay, I get it. So why the call?"

"It's about the reunion and the chess match."

Charlie first thought was that Elliot was about to back out of the chess match that he championed with Lauren. If he lost even one of his players, the match might have to be cancelled. If he lost Elliot as a player, they might as well concede defeat without playing.

"What about it, Elliot? You aren't backing out, are you?"

"Absolutely not. It's just that this cyber chess just isn't going to do it. I'm sure that the four of us want to win desperately. How about we forget these simulated practice games on our computers and play face-to-face? It would be great to reconnect with each other before we quash the high school seniors."

"Elliot, I know you. You're a deep thinker and a planner. What's your *real* motive?"

"Okay. Okay. You got me. Maybe you know me better than most. You weren't valedictorian for nothing. If I tell you, you've gotta keep it a secret."

"I'll take your secret to my grave. If you were here with me, we could pinky swear."

"Okay, funny man. It's Jaclyn Struzer," said Elliot.

"Jaclyn? What about her?"

"I had a crush on Jaclyn since freshman year but was too shy to act on it. Despite my confidence issues, I think if the four of us are together I might find the courage to say something to her."

Charlie, like Elliot, had a limited circle of friends, the members of the chess team among them. He appreciated Elliot's honesty and saw no reason to deny his request.

"Elliot, I like the idea. Any thoughts about where to play?"

"Yeah, Domino Park."

"Domino Park in Little Havana?"

"That's the one. It's the perfect place. We'll find a table in the shade and play some chess," said Elliot. Evidently, he had given his idea lots of thought.

"Why the hell not? I'll call Ron and Jaclyn. On second thought maybe you want to call Jaclyn?"

"No, you call her. I'm still working up my courage."

"Well, get with the program, Elliot. Before you change your mind, I'm putting your plan into action. Three o'clock today works for me. Is that good for you? Assume it's all set with the others if you don't hear back from me."

"Perfect. Thanks, Charlie. I'll bring some tres leches for dessert. Little Havana has the best cafecitos in Miami. Would be a shame to not take advantage."

CHAPTER 70

Maximo Gomez Park at the corner of Southwest Eighth Street and Fifteenth Avenue in Little Havana is better known as Domino Park. Maximo Gomez was a soldier who fought in the war with Spain for Cuban independence. Players have gathered in this park for more than half a century for a game of Cuban dominoes, conversation, and camaraderie. The park has multiple gazebos that offer shade, seating, and a table. Most players are older men of Cuban heritage.

The park is no longer a gathering place for locals only. Domino Park, like the delights of the area's Cuban restaurants and cafes, has been discovered by tourists. Little Havana offers the most authentic Cuban experience available outside of Cuba. Some tourists arrive on their own, while the majority arrive in buses offering tours and a taste of the Latin experience. The park has benches for spectators who flock to watch the games or tourists busily snapping photos of the cigar-smoking players. The clacking of the tiles and the aroma of cigars are what most visitors remember from their trip to Domino Park. Bars, cafes, art galleries, and shopping are close by on Calle Ocho, known in English as Southwest Eighth Street.

In anticipation of seeing Jaclyn again, Elliot was the first to arrive. As promised, he had stopped at a local cafecito window and ordered slices of the sweet dessert known as tres leches. Elliot left nothing to chance, arriving forty-five minutes early because it might be difficult to get a table where his group could practice. For insurance, he brought a folding table and four chairs from his spare bedroom and loaded them into his car earlier that morning.

With the help of two young men and a generous tip, they set up the table and chairs in a shaded area under a mature live oak tree. This was a little unconventional at Domino Park, but Elliot was motivated to practice chess; he wasn't concerned about the optics.

He wondered how Jaclyn would look and worried about how she'd think he looked. As always, he carefully protected himself from the sun, but this time in stylish attire. Self-conscious about his hair that grew low on his forehead, he wore a cap, a gift from his sister that was embroidered with the name Breckinridge, a popular Colorado ski resort. In truth, he had never been west of the Mississippi River, nor had he ever gone skiing. His long sleeve sun-protective shirt, a purchase from a thrift shop, was emblazoned with the L.L. Bean logo. His black sun-safe driving gloves with maximum UV protection covered his hands. The sunglasses he wore had the Prada designation on the frame. The glasses were borrowed from his dad since Elliot, still living at home, had little disposable income. His insecurity made him dress to impress with recognizable brands.

It was 2:50 p.m. when Charlie Post and Ronald Martella arrived simultaneously. They had chosen to drive together.

Charlie spoke first. "Elliot, you haven't changed a bit. You look just like your yearbook picture. I'd recognize you anywhere. I see you're still careful about the sun." When Elliot's facial expression conveyed his displeasure, Charlie added, "Don't take it the wrong way. It's a compliment."

"I can't same the same about either of you," Elliot responded. "Charlie, you've beefed up considerably. I mean that as a compliment as well. You look and dress like a jock now. Are you taking steroids?"

"No, absolutely not. What you see is the result of working out. Thanks for noticing."

"And what about me, Elliot?" asked Ronald, anxious to hear Elliot's evaluation.

Ronald was wearing a long-sleeve shirt with French cuffs and cufflinks. This was odd attire for Domino Park.

"You look great, Ron. Perhaps a little overdressed but it makes you look very classy and prosperous."

"Thanks for saying that. It would make my dad proud. He was always the best dressed man in the room. Love that you used the word 'prosperous,' since I've successfully created and marketed two popular apps and a video game."

"Impressive, Ron. I have an idea for an app," Elliot added. "Perhaps you can give me some pointers later."

"Glad to."

"Oh, by the way, I'd like to be paired first with Jaclyn." Elliot attempted to sound nonchalant, but inwardly, he was nervous about making this request.

"No problem. Charlie filled me in on the drive here."

Almost on cue, Jaclyn arrived. She hated the traffic especially during tourist season and came by taxi. Thrilled that she didn't have her own car, Elliot was hoping to offer her a ride home later.

When Jaclyn stepped from the vehicle, she looked even more beautiful than Elliot remembered. Thinner than in high school, she had the physical appearance of a runway model. At least, that's how Elliot perceived her. Jaclyn's long brown hair was now cut in a short pixie style that suited her small frame and accentuated her bone structure.

"Remember guys. Make me look good to Jaclyn."

"Not a problem. Ron and I will be your wingmen."

Jaclyn recognized her classmates immediately.

"Hey guys," she said. "Kind of crazy that it took a reunion and a chess match to get us together. Seriously, we should have kept in touch after graduation. Kudos to whoever chose this spot. It's historic and charming. I always wanted to check out this park."

"Jaclyn, you look terrific," gushed Elliot. "By the way, it was my idea to get together to practice in person and to meet here."

"Well, good job." Glancing at the table and chairs, she commented on the setup. "Looks like you thought ahead, bringing your own table and chairs. None of these old guys look like they plan to vacate their spots anytime soon. Do I also detect treats?"

"That would be a yes. We're in Little Havana so what could be better than a serving of tres leches?"

"Can't argue with that."

Elliot was thrilled with Jaclyn's responses to his efforts. Everyone took a place at the table. As the men arranged before her arrival, Jaclyn was paired to play the first few matches with Elliot.

Charlie, as team captain, was glad to see that after ten years the four still seemed compatible. Explaining his strategy, Charlie said that the results of the cyber chess matches they had been playing in addition to today's games would determine their rankings. The results would enable him to pair his team's best with the best player from the current senior class. His plan was to demoralize the younger people early.

No one objected to Charlie's strategy. Anxious to begin, Charlie signaled to Elliot and Jaclyn to take their seats at the table. Once seated, Elliot addressed his teammates with some unexpected comments and suggestions.

"First, let's talk about how we were treated in high school and how we want to be treated from now on," Elliot stated.

"What do you mean?" questioned Jaclyn.

"I suspect that if any of us didn't live locally we probably wouldn't be attending the reunion. We were all ostracized in school, teased by jerks and ignored by students with different interests from ours. My high school experience wasn't a positive one and I often felt excluded. I like the idea of the reunion chess match both for the challenge and for the opportunity to get together again with you guys. That said, let's not let a bigger opportunity get away from us."

"Elliot, I agree with all that, but you lost me when you mentioned this 'bigger opportunity.' What're you talking about?" asked Ron.

"The opportunity to belong. It's time to be part of the alumni, not only identified as members of the chess team. The way the reunion activities are set up, everyone will be at the beach volleyball game except us. We'll be in the library, reinforcing the stereotyping we suffered from in high school."

"Elliot, you make a good point. Are you suggesting that we don't play the chess match?" asked Jaclyn.

"No, not at all. Let's play the match one week before the reunion. We all live locally. The members of the senior class live locally. Should be easy to arrange."

"Maybe I'm dense, Elliot, but what does that accomplish?" asked Ron.

"If we play one week earlier, we'll be free to attend the volleyball game with the rest of our class, cheering with them, bonding with them. By missing the volleyball game, we're the outsiders again."

Smiling at him, Jaclyn said, "I love your idea, Elliot."

As captain, Charlie said he'd bring up the suggestion to Lauren Mandich. She had been his contact concerning reunion activities.

"Now let's play some chess. That's why we're here. Elliot, you pair up with Jaclyn, while I pair up with Ron," directed Charlie.

"Sure thing, captain," said a grinning Elliot.

Each team member got to play two games with the other three players. During his games against Jaclyn, Elliot sensed that she showed interest in him beyond that of an opponent in a chess game. While they played, Elliot detected an effort on her part to make or rekindle a connection with him. Shy in high school, she was awfully chatty today. And she seemed enormously interested in what he had been doing in the ten years since graduation.

After the "Round Robin" mini tournament among friends. Charlie announced that he had all the data he needed to rank the players on his team. Elliot was the clear choice for number one.

Charlie again promised to contact Lauren to reschedule the tournament for a week earlier. "I'll let you all know if there's a new date and time."

They helped Elliot with the table and chairs, depositing them back in the trunk of his car. Then Charlie and Ronald left together in Charlie's vehicle.

Elliot and Jaclyn walked to dinner on Little Havana's Calle Ocho. They left the restaurant holding hands. As he hoped, Elliot drove Jaclyn home.

CHAPTER 71

Lauren slept poorly after yesterday's visit to Julia's home. For her, it had been a disturbing experience. So much of what Lauren saw was just plain creepy. She could only wonder what she might see today. She and Detective Banks would pay a visit to Veronica Adell's home and to the lab where Julia's daughter worked.

Detective Banks cleverly obtained bite imprints from Tutu, Julia's wolfhound, on a steak; the plan was to compare them against the wounds on Ms. Adell's thigh. The confluence of Julia's daughter being a dental technician and the macabre jar of teeth on the counter in Julia's kitchen was unsettling. No wonder Lauren slept fitfully. She awoke several times during the night. At best, she slept five hours in total. At 5:30 a.m. she forced herself back to the bedroom after reading a book on the couch. It was the third time that night she had resorted to reading.

Finally, in a solid sleep, Lauren's phone jarred her awake. It was 7 a.m.

"Hello, Lauren?"

Still sleepy and in a daze, Lauren didn't recognize the voice.

"Speaking. Who's this?"

"It's Charlie, Charlie Post."

"Charlie, do you have any idea what time it is? What's the emergency?"

"Sorry, Lauren. Sometimes I forget that not everyone's a morning person. Do you want to call me back later?"

"Now that you woke me, just tell me why you're calling."

"I'd like to change the schedule for the chess tournament."

"Everything's been arranged already. Why the change?"

"When the team got together to practice, we were talking about the reunion weekend. We'd like to be able to join the others at the volleyball game.

"Thanks for bringing that to my attention, Charlie. Frankly, when the principal suggested the date, I didn't think that the chess players would care about the volleyball game. I'm sorry I made that assumption. Terribly sorry. I'll contact Principal Towney and try to reschedule with all the original arrangements, but one week earlier. Same location in the school library, same time at noon, same format, just the prior week. Does that work for you?"

"Perfectly. I'll let the others know. Thanks, Lauren."

"I'll text to confirm that it's all set."

Lauren hung up the phone. Contemplating the eventful day ahead interviewing Julia's neighbor, Veronica Adell, and Julia's daughter, Justine, she decided against even a short catnap before preparing for the day. Instead, she showered, dressed, ate a leisurely breakfast, and lingered over her coffee and the newspaper.

As previously arranged, Amanda Banks arrived punctually at nine in a squad car. Anxious to get started, Lauren greeted Amanda before she could unbuckle her seatbelt.

"Look like you're ready to roll," said Amanda. "I've already contacted both Veronica Adell and Justine. Both are expecting us. We'll check out Julia's neighbor first. She has some photos of her wounds that I'm going to send to Dr. Wirth, the forensic dentist. It's likely that Tutu's bite impressions on the steak will match those on Ms. Adell's thigh. What really interests me is the comparison of Tutu's bite impressions and the markings on the victims of the DON killings."

"That would be something, wouldn't it?" remarked Lauren.

"The other thing I hope to get from speaking with Veronica Adell is her observations about Julia and her dog. Maybe she can alert us to any peculiar comings and goings from Julia's house, any conversations she might have overheard Julia having in the yard, anything out of the ordinary. Or, in this case, out of the ordinary *for Julia*, since her lifestyle is anything but ordinary."

CHAPTER 72

Lauren looked in the back seat of the squad car for the cooler that Amanda used the day before. It was missing. Yesterday, before her shift ended, Amanda delivered the rib eye steak containing Tutu's bite impressions to Dr. Wirth's office. He wasn't in, so Amanda left the cooler and its contents with his assistant, requesting that Dr. Wirth compare the impressions from the steak with photos taken from the victims of the Dead of Night killings. She asked that Dr. Wirth call her immediately with his findings. The assistant promised that he'd relay their conversation to the forensic expert.

"If you're looking for my cooler, I no longer have the steak. After I dropped you off, at the end of my shift I delivered it to Dr. Wirth's office. I'm waiting to hear back from him."

Detective Banks pulled out of the driveway and repeated the route they had taken the day before, this time to speak with Veronica Adell. Like yesterday, cars occupied all the street parking except for the small swale in front of Priestess Julia's house. Adept at parallel parking, Amanda maneuvered her car into the empty spot.

As they approached the front door, Veronica Adell was already at the doorway, pleased that the police were taking her case seriously.

The introductions made, Veronica led her guests to her living room. Although the home was rather small, the lack of clutter gave it a larger and roomier impression. Amanda judged Veronica to be a woman in her middle-to-upper sixties. She was on the plump side with curly gray hair that framed her face. She wore a long pleated gray skirt and a top with a peach, aqua, and gray paisley design. Her pride in her home was apparent from its immaculate condition; the glass coffee table sparkled, and the area rug showed signs of having been recently vacuumed.

Eager to tell her story, Veronica got right to the point of the visit.

"Let me show you my bite."

Seated on the couch, she lifted her skirt, removing an Ace bandage that was wrapped around her right thigh. The wrap protected expandable gauze that was firmly secured to the area of the wound with adhesive tape. After removing the tape, Veronica then lifted a nonstick Telfa pad from the wound site. Lauren recognized the Telfa pad from a supply in her medicine cabinet. It paid to be married to a dermatologist. Under the pad, the wound was covered by a viscous clear ointment that Veronica said was an antibiotic. The bite marks were still clearly delineated.

From the appearance of her thigh, Veronica had to have been petrified and in excruciating pain when the dog attacked her. The emergency room doctor had given her a set of photos of the wound which she now presented to Detective Banks. She duplicated several sets of these at CVS in case she decided to sue.

Immediately, both Amanda and Lauren realized that Veronica was bitten in an uncommon area, high on her thigh. Most dog bites are below the knee. Tutu, however, was not your average dog. A wolfhound, Tutu was much taller than dogs of other breeds. It made sense that the injury would be on the thigh.

Amanda had taken photos with her phone of the rib eye steak bitten by Tutu that was now in Dr. Douglas Wirth's possession. A person without Dr. Wirth's extensive training, Amanda made an educated guess about the results of a comparison of these photos with the bite marks on Veronica's thigh. It seemed to her that Tutu was the culprit. With Ms. Adell's permission, Amanda photographed the wounds as they now appeared. She'd send them to Dr. Wirth for further analysis, expecting that he'd confirm that the dog that had bitten the steak was the same dog that had also bitten Veronica Adell.

"What do you think, Detective Banks?"

"I'm not an expert, Ms. Adell. To me your wound seems to match the pattern on the steak Tutu bit. But we'll have a forensic dental expert officially provide confirmation. One thing is certain; if I ever have an injury, I'd like you to be my wound-care person."

"Thanks. Guess I haven't lost my skills, after all. As a younger woman I worked with emergency medical services."

"Well," Lauren added, "if you're ever looking for part-time work, my husband's a dermatologist. He'd probably be thrilled to hire a person with your abilities."

Veronica rewrapped her wound, applying the ointment, pad, and bandages with efficiency. It appeared likely that Tutu was guilty of biting Ms. Adell, but was Tutu involved in the DON killings? Amanda was leaving no stone unturned. Only Dr. Wirth could provide the answer.

"Ms. Adell, could you tell us about the howling you heard?" inquired Lauren. She recalled that detail from her conversation with Amanda about the police reports Veronica filed.

"Of course. It's not every night," Veronica explained, "although when I get woken up out of a sound sleep, it seems like it is. That dog is big and loud. I think Julia ties Tutu up on a short leash staked in the ground in her backyard. She probably can't stand the noise in the house, but it seems cruel to the dog."

Although the dog had viciously bitten her, Veronica still had empathy for the animal.

"How'd you get bitten?" asked Amanda.

"The dog was in Julia's backyard. I went out to pick mangoes from my tree. Out of nowhere, this monster of a dog leaps over the fence between our houses and is racing toward me.

I have no idea how the dog got free. I'm not a dog person, and frankly, I was petrified. So, I instinctively tossed one of the mangos I picked at Tutu. Probably like waiving a red cape at a bull. Tutu charged at me, and before I could run into the house, she opened her enormous mouth and bit me in the thigh.

"What an awful experience," said Lauren.

"You can say that again," Veronica responded. She then directed a question to Detective Banks. "Do you now have enough evidence to prove that Tutu bit me? What are you planning to do going forward?"

"As I explained before, I'm going to send your photos to the forensic dentist and when we get his results, we'll go from there. I promise to keep you in the loop. In fact, I'll get the process started right now."

Detective Banks used her cell phone to photograph the copies of the pictures taken at the emergency room that Veronica had given her. She texted those pictures to the forensic dentist as well as the ones of Veronica's thigh that she had just taken.

"Ms. Adell," Amanda asked, "within the last few months, did you ever see Priestess Julia go out a night with Tutu?"

"You call her 'Priestess' Julia. I don't believe that she's a priestess of any kind. As far as I'm concerned, I think she's a complete weirdo. Her house and yard are a blight on the neighborhood. Everyone fears her and her dog and they avoid her. No one dares to park in front of her house. I can only imagine what it looks like on the inside, but it can't be normal."

"Let me just say that you are a much better housekeeper," interjected Lauren.

"To answer your question about her going out at night with Tutu, I've only seen them leave the house together in the early evening, and they usually return by eight o'clock. Usually, they are on foot. I think she takes the dog for a walk at that time.

However, Julia has gone out multiple times alone late at night. I think her muffler needs fixing because I hear her car when she leaves."

"How do you know that Tutu hasn't been with her on these late-night outings?" Lauren asked.

"Simple," said Veronica. "Tutu howls in the yard more frequently than normal each time I hear the car muffler. Guess it disturbs the dog as well or Tutu is expressing displeasure that she's not going along for the ride."

This line of questioning seemed alarming to Ms. Adell. Wrinkling her brow, she said to Amanda, "You're asking a lot of questions about my neighbor's activities, particularly at night. Why does that matter? Do you think she and her dog are connected to the Dead of Night murders? Am I living next to a murderer? Oh my God! Do you think she's the DON killer?"

"It's not likely, Veronica, but we're being thorough."

Wishing her a speedy recovery, the team of Amanda and Lauren excused themselves and returned to the squad car.

****

On their way to SCA Dental Lab, Amanda's phone rang. It was Dr. Wirth, the forensic dentist.

"Hello, Detective Banks, this is Dr. Wirth. I've checked the photos of the bite on Ms. Adell's thigh you just texted me. Very nasty bite, I might add. It is a match to the impressions on the steak that you left yesterday with my assistant. That must have been some trick to retrieve that steak from the dog's mouth. That must be one very big dog."

"That's for sure," said Amanda. "It's a wolfhound."

Amanda and Lauren were not surprised that forensic evidence had shown that Tutu was guilty of biting Veronica Adell. But had Tutu bitten anyone else?

"What about the bite marks from those earlier photos that you have of the victims of the Dead of Night killer? Were any of those a match to the impressions on the steak?" asked Amanda.

"Sorry. Wish I could say otherwise, but not a match."

"I appreciate your time, Dr. Wirth. Guess we're back to square one."

Tutu had bitten Veronica Adell but was not connected to the Dead of Night killings.

At least, not yet.

CHAPTER 73

During their drive to SCA Dental Lab, Amanda and Lauren discussed their disappointment that Tutu's bite pattern did not match that of the DON killer.

Amanda's earlier research indicated that Julia was a scam artist. She had never been to Haiti and had been booked on check fraud in Georgia. This did not make Julia a killer, but Amanda could not shake her distrust of Julia. There were too many things about her that didn't add up. The coincidence of her daughter Justine working as a dental technician added another layer of suspicion to the detective's evaluation of the woman.

"Guess I'm not entirely surprised, but somewhat letdown by what Dr. Wirth said," Amanda remarked. "I thought we were onto something with Julia and Tutu."

"Maybe we'll catch a break at the dental lab," Lauren offered. "I'm anxious to see what Julia's daughter looks like and how she dresses."

The dental lab occupied a large suite in a one-story office complex. The company logo was mounted above the doorway, the lettering "SCA Dental Lab" formed by various dental tools. Alerted about their arrival by Justine, the receptionist was expecting a visit from the police today.

After Amanda and Lauren introduced themselves, the receptionist walked with them through the main working area of the lab, stopping at Justine's workstation. A petite version of her mother, Justine had Julia's almond-shaped eyes and eye color and the same skin tones, the color of burnished mahogany. Lauren was disappointed that she was dressed in scrubs embroidered with the name "SCA Dental Lab"; she would have like to have seen whether Justine dressed in the same flamboyant style as her mother.

From her forthright attitude, Julia's daughter didn't appear to be hiding anything. She offered her visitors a tour of the lab which they gladly accepted. They passed by stations where technicians were shaping dentures, implants, and crowns amidst a constant grinding sound. A potent chemical smell permeated the area.

"You get used to the smell of the lab. I hardly notice it at all anymore," Justine volunteered. Pointing to her earbuds, she said, "I drown out the noise with music. But you didn't come here about working conditions in a dental lab. My mom told me that you have some questions about the work I do. What can I help you with?"

"Before I explain, I need your assurance that our conversation will go no further. Not even your mother should be told about our discussion. Can I have your word?" asked Detective Banks.

"Why are you asking me to keep this from my mother?"

"It's just a precaution to avoid any leaks which might compromise our case," Amanda explained.

"All right, you have my word."

"I'm sure you've heard of the Dead of Night murders. Except for the two most recent deaths, all the victims had bite marks; in each case the bites were made by the same set of teeth."

While Amanda spoke, Lauren was observing Justine's body language. She was attentive, showing no signs of sweating, rapid breathing, or downcast eyes.

"That's where you come in, Justine. We need someone with your expertise, someone who creates dentures, implants, and crowns. I want to pick your brain about dental appliances as they relate to this case."

"Fire away. What do you need to know?"

"According to a wildlife specialist, the bites appear to have been made by a wolf. However, the victims seem to have been deliberately selected. That would be beyond the capabilities of a wolf," Amanda reported.

"I don't know anything about wolves. Where do I fit in?"

"Yesterday Detective Banks and I visited your mother's home," volunteered Lauren. "She was kind enough to give us a tour. In her kitchen she had a jar filled with teeth; as you can imagine, the contents struck us as somewhat unusual. I assume they weren't your baby teeth," Lauren said to lighten the mood.

"We both began to wonder whether someone could use teeth or a cast made from dental impressions of teeth to create an artificial jaw. Could that be used to produce bite marks that resemble the bite from a wolf? When your mother told us that you were a dental technician, it seemed like serendipity at work," explained Lauren.

Justine appeared shaken, for the first time concerned about the visit. "Am I in trouble? Is my mom in trouble?" she asked, her voice quivering.

Wanting to get as much information from her as possible, Amanda reassured her by replying, "No, you're a source, not a suspect."

"I guess it's possible to make an artificial jaw that could leave animal bite marks, but it's not something we do here," Justine stated. "A licensed dentist sends us a mold or casting from an actual patient, and we manufacture a crown to order. Sometimes we get an order for a full set of dentures which are made of acrylic resin with a metal base. We never use real teeth. By the way, I never understood my mother's collection of teeth.

Most of hers are not human, just like the skulls in her front yard."

Amanda wondered about the possibility of a special order of a peculiar nature; her question sounded as if she were inquiring about producing a prop for a horror movie.

"Is it at all possible that someone at this lab created a full set of dentures that would fit into a person's mouth, but could leave the impression of a wolf bite?"

Justine stared at the detective with her eyes opened wide, wondering if Amanda would break into a smile at the ridiculousness of the question. When that didn't happen, Justine replied.

"Pardon me if I say that your question is the most bizarre question that I've been asked in my professional life. I don't think it's even possible. There's no way anyone here at SCA Dental Lab could have made a mold like that. All work is carefully supervised; a project like that would be noticed."

"Any chance it could be done after business hours?" Lauren asked.

"No way. The bosses are exceedingly concerned about personal security in the building and theft of materials. They run the place like a military base, making sure everyone leaves punctually at closing time. No one would have the opportunity to work on something like that."

There was nothing more to be learned from Justine. Thanking her for her time and her expertise, Amanda and Lauren returned to the squad car.

Frustrated, Amanda wanted the investigative team working on the DON case to keep a close watch on both mother and daughter. She wasn't quite ready to declare their innocence.

CHAPTER 74

Exhausted, Amanda Banks sat at the dinner table in the one-bedroom apartment that she shared with her fiancé, Andrei Draca, a handsome man with thick jet-black hair and deep-set green eyes, the color of emeralds. They had not set a wedding date, planning to first build up some savings. While Amanda rarely discussed the cases she was working, the Dead of Night Killings were different. For weeks, she had been unburdening her frustrations to Andrei. Tonight, she was looking forward to a quiet evening without shop talk.

Attuned to Amanda's feelings during the last several weeks, Andrei decided to surprise her by preparing a candle-lit dinner with delicacies from Romania, his homeland. The menu consisted of cabbage rolls, polenta, and a desert made of cottage cheese and semolina that is shaped like a donut, fried, and covered in sour cream and jam. He chilled a bottle of Kendall Jackson chardonnay, Amanda's favorite, hoping it would help her relax. Despite numerous efforts, he had not yet turned Amanda into a fan of Romanian cooking; of all the recipes he tried, these dishes seemed to have pleased her the most.

Working as a plumber, Andrei recently became fully licensed and went out on his own. He developed a clientele in neighboring Broward County in the city of Hollywood, where a large population of Romanian immigrants resided. After making the move to work independently, he saw his income more than double.

The dinner and the wine accomplished Andrei's goal of helping Amanda unwind. No mention was made of the killings. Between the two, they had almost finished the bottle of chardonnay. The romantic dinner, Andrei's solicitous behavior, and their ever-growing bank account coalesced into Amanda's suspicion that Andrei wanted to set a date for their wedding. With that thought in mind, she was unprepared for the astonishing words that came out of his mouth.

"Amanda, I've been happy to be your sounding board about this case that's been consuming you. I've hesitated to give you my opinion, but I'd like to share what I'm thinking. Please don't laugh or dismiss my theory before giving it serious thought."

Not quite what Amanda expected or wanted him to say.

"I must say, *this* is not the conversation I was anticipating," she said with a sigh. "Okay, fire away."

"Many people in Romania, especially those living near a forest, believe in werewolves. These creatures transform from wolf to man and back again. They roam at night and howl at the moon. The only way to destroy these aggressive killers is with a silver bullet. My Uncle Ivantie and his neighbors abandoned their homes in the village of Brasov in the Transylvania region of Romania not too many years ago because of werewolf sightings. He now lives in Bucharest."

"Where are you going with this? *You're not in Romania anymore.* Are you suggesting that the killer is a werewolf?"

Although he detected some skepticism and sarcasm in Amanda's tone and her words, Andrei wasn't finished.

"Consider this. Your working theory is that the bodies have been mutilated by an animal, most likely a wolf. You also told me that the poor souls were tranquilized first, clearly by a person. What if the wolf and the person are one and the same? What if the killer *is* a werewolf?"

"Andrei, please don't misunderstand. I hate to mock your tradition and beliefs, but there's no way in hell I can present this idea to my superiors. They'd question my sanity."

"I understand, but maybe you can plant the seed."

"How would I do that? I'd lose all professional credibility."

"Go to your sergeant and tell him about your fiancé's bizarre theory. Say it in a laughing manner, so that it's clear that it's my theory, not yours. Any ridicule will be directed at me."

"What do you think that will accomplish?"

"Your colleagues will outwardly dismiss my theory, but maybe just one of them will give it some credence. You always say that you try to think outside the box. Well, if this doesn't qualify as outside the box, I don't know what does."

"Okay, okay. If I agree to talk to Sergeant Hernandez, can we finish the wine?"

"Right after my next surprise."

This time Amanda was certain Andrei would bring up a wedding date. She was wrong again.

"I've written to my uncle in Bucharest. He's ordering you a box of silver bullets. You still use a Glock 9-millimeter pistol, don't you?"

CHAPTER 75

Ever since signing Hoyt Stark as a client, Hamilton Davies began activating his plan. Stark's arrest was big news. A hometown celebrity and local football hero, Stark was charged with two murders. Not only was there speculation that he was copying the crimes of the Dead of Night killer, there was also speculation that he might be associated with the DON killer as well.

Craving media attention, Davies had chosen the steps of City Hall for a press conference, without the knowledge or permission of his client. He instructed his assistant to call the local papers and news stations, hoping that nationally syndicated writers and reporters would attend. Davies was confident that he could create enough of a buzz that the content of his press conference would circulate nationally.

Crowds had been gathering for more than an hour before the scheduled starting time. Like the celebrity he aspired to be, Davies arrived in a stretch limo. He was wearing his tallest Stetson hat and tooled leather cowboy boots in a rich shade of brown. His belt buckle, a huge metal ornament in the shape of Texas, glistened in the sun. A thick pearl handle adorned his briefcase. He looked as if he had been outfitted by a costume designer for a movie production, dressed to portray a prosperous businessman from Texas.

Two burly bodyguards cleared the way for him. Each wore nonfunctioning earpieces that were clearly visible solely for the purpose of stressing the importance of their employer.

Exiting the limo, Davies strode to the podium that his assistant set up earlier. He mounted the stepstool that the assistant placed there and tapped on the microphone to verify that the speaker system was operational. Flanked by his two bodyguards, he made quite the impressive figure. Dressed as he was, he was sure to be photographed by the reporters. It was all part of his plan.

"I have some statements to make after which I can entertain a few questions. Let's keep the question period short as I have important work to do. A man's life is in my hands." Observing that the crowd hung on his every word, he paused for effect. He was using his tried-and-true courtroom skills, timing his statements and his pauses for the maximum impact.

"My client is innocent. I understand that the District Attorney's office plans to waste *your* money on two trials. Of course, Mr. Stark knew his teammate, Sam McKay and his wife, Shannon Stark. He admits to owning a fishing knife. There are literally thousands of such knives in Miami-Dade County. According to the medical examiner, the wounds on the poor victims, may they rest in peace, were compatible with such a knife."

Similar to the way he plead his case in trial, he admitted to many of the facts that the prosecutor would use against his client, diffusing their effect. "The only DNA found on the knife was that of my client and some fish that he and his buddies caught. All the evidence is circumstantial. They're grasping at straws. Just because Hoyt Stark knew the victims and owns a knife that is the identical style as the murder weapon doesn't make him a killer. From where I stand, Mr. Stark is the victim here. He lost his wife and his teammate. This is America, folks. What happened to the presumption of innocence? Is my client, Hoyt Stark, being treated as if he is 'innocent until proven guilty'?"

Utilizing his theatrical skills, Davies employed a dramatic pause before he continued, allowing the crowd to digest his words. The audience was buzzing with indignation about how Hoyt Stark was being railroaded by the criminal justice system. The crowd played right into his hands.

Davies then looked at his watch. He apologized that he had time for only one question. In the third row of spectators, his prearranged shill was strategically placed and prepped with a question. It was the best fifty dollars Davies spent in a long time. He pointed to the man who had his arm raised.

"Mr. Davies, I heard you might be suing the city of Miami. Is that true? Also, are you petitioning the National Football League to change the venue of the Super Bowl?"

By design, the question was unrelated to Stark's innocence, the ostensible reason for the press conference. Davies had a grudge to settle with Miami and he set up the media event for that purpose. A pitchman for the city of Dallas, Davies was unsuccessful at convincing the selection committee to choose Dallas over Miami as the venue for the Super Bowl. His personal and professional setback fueled his antipathy to Miami.

Oozing sincerity, Davies responded, "I would never sue the good people of Miami or the State of Florida. I have roots here. However, sir, I do believe that certain individuals from the Florida contingent who presented the case to host the game in Miami slandered and besmirched my good name. They falsified and released my juvenile records. Maybe some of the reporters here should investigate *that*. All I hope to do is correct an injustice."

Davies stepped away from the podium, satisfied that his press conference would make things uncomfortable for the National Football League and the members of the committee who secured Miami for the game's venue. That had been his sole motivation for taking on Stark as a client. Only as afterthought did he consider how his response to the planned question might impact Hoyt Stark. If, by coincidence, the diatribe helped his client, that would be icing on the cake.

****

District Attorney Stanley Burns and Howard Cantwell, lead prosecutor in the two murder cases against Hoyt Stark, weren't present at the steps of City Hall. However, the press conference came to their attention quickly. The local television stations rebroadcast Hamilton Davies professing the innocence of his client and his claims that the evidence against Hoyt Stark was purely circumstantial. The tangential portion concerning the Super Bowl interested them equally. Both Burns and Cantwell recognized the true motivation for the public spectacle. What Davies cared about most had nothing to do with the defense of Hoyt Stark.

It seemed clear to both men that Hamilton Davies had an agenda. His name was familiar to them from stories about the competition between Dallas and Miami as prospective locations for the Super Bowl at the time the decision was being made. The press conference revealed the intensity of the grudge Davies still held.

Pursuing that line of thinking, Burns said, "Mr. Davies can't afford another failure or embarrassment in Miami. If we can demonstrate to him that we have airtight cases against his client, I suspect that he will plead them out. Davies won't want the negative publicity that will follow him if he loses at trial."

"I agree," said Cantwell. "This morning's press conference was an attempt to embarrass the NFL and the members of the South Florida promotional team. The operative word is 'airtight.' Do we have sufficient evidence that our cases *are* airtight? If so, can we successfully convince Davies that jury trials aren't in *his* best interest?"

Stanley Burns and Howard Cantwell worked well together. People often mistook them for father and son, Stanley in his late fifties and Howard in his late thirties. Both dressed conservatively, rarely wearing anything other than a solid white shirt and a diagonally striped tie in various color combinations under a black suit. Colleagues joked that Howard could predict how he'd look in twenty years simply by looking at Stanley. Their minds operated similarly as well. Both meticulous, they researched every avenue when assembling the prosecution of a case, leaving nothing to chance.

Burns responded to Cantwell's question to determine how to best proceed in dealing with Hamilton Davies. Ever methodical, he started from the difficulty of proving Stark's culpability in Sam McKay's murder. He withheld a communication he received before Cantwell's arrival, despite the explosive nature of that information. He would get to that in due time; he would build up to it. The same way he presented his prosecutorial cases.

"Since DNA evidence was lacking on the knife found in Hoyt Stark's tackle box, we might have difficulty with prosecuting the murder case involving Sam McKay. We can develop the theory that revenge against the Steelers and jealousy of McKay prompted Stark to kill his former teammate," Burns said. "We could interview everyone associated with the Steelers to determine any overt hostility by Stark, but that would be a time-consuming process that might not yield tangible results."

After tossing around other scenarios, neither man felt that proving a desire for revenge against McKay would be enough to get a conviction.

"On a more positive note," Burns added, "I think we can get Hoyt on the murder of Shannon Stark. There's a strong motive and we now have the evidence to convict."

"Did something new turn up? Run it by me."

"Hoyt Stark had a history of physical abuse against Shannon. The publicity caused by her restraining order against Hoyt cost him his career playing football. If that didn't create enough resentment and hatred for her, their living arrangements might have put him over the top. While she remained in their magnificent home, he rented a cheap apartment," Burns stated.

"I get the motive angle. But no DNA from either victim was found on the knife. That leads me to believe that Stark had a second knife that he tossed. But we can't prove that. You must know something that I don't. Spill it. What are you considering the damning evidence?" asked Cantwell.

"The footprint," Burns declared. "Just before you walked into my office this morning, CSU informed me about the boot print on the door that was kicked in at Shannon Stark's house. The size and tread pattern of the boot print match the soles of Mr. Stark's work boots. Lucky for us, the soles had dried blood on them when Stark was arrested. And if that's not enough, to drive home Stark's guilt, I saved the best for last. The DNA testing at the lab identifies the blood on the boots as Shannon Stark's blood."

"Let's see Stark wiggle out of this one, even with the illustrious Davies representing him," Cantwell commented.

"The way I see it," Burns explained, "Stark was drunk out of his mind when he went to his house after his fishing trip with his friends. That was the night Shannon was murdered. Apparently, Shannon either didn't hear him at the door or refused to open it to him. Obviously angry at being denied entry, Stark kicked in the door leaving a footprint that matches the work boots that Stark was wearing when he was arrested. The alcohol and his anger were a lethal mix. We don't know all that transpired in that house, but we do know one thing. Hoyt Stark killed her."

Smiling, Cantwell enjoyed his imagined scenario of presenting Davies with the harsh reality of his client's prospects in court. He couldn't wait to see the attorney's face.

"Sounds like we may be able to get Davies to go along with a plea agreement," Cantwell stated. "That should get him out of town. Nothing would please me more."

CHAPTER 76

As lead prosecutor, Howard Cantwell was anxious to speak with Hamilton Davies. He dialed the attorney's office in Dallas, identifying himself as the prosecutor in the cases against Hoyt Stark, Mr. Davies's client. Lorna, his secretary, promised to contact Mr. Davies to return the call.

Within two minutes Davies was on the phone. Howard Cantwell identified himself and told Davies that he wanted to speak with him in person about Hoyt Stark.

"What about Stark?"

"I'd like to meet with you concerning your client. Where are you staying while you're in town? I could meet you there."

The two men arranged to meet at four o'clock in the bar of the Intercontinental Hotel in downtown Miami, where Davies was registered. They both arrived simultaneously. Since he had seen clips of Hamilton Davies's press conference, Cantwell had the advantage in recognizing the attorney. He walked toward the man dressed in Western garb and extended his hand. After the perfunctory handshake, they both entered the bar and selected a table in the back corner.

Davies snapped his fingers to get the attention of a female server, addressing her in his usual vulgar manner. "Hey sweetheart, how about you shake your ass and bring me a Johnny Walker Blue on the rocks."

Using great restraint, the server rolled her eyes, pursed her lips, but said nothing before turning toward Cantwell.

"What may I get you, sir?"

"I'll have an iced tea with lime, please," Cantwell answered.

"Of course, sir. My pleasure."

As she walked away, she could hear Davies say to Cantwell, "Nice ass."

Cantwell did not respond.

Hamilton Davies was proving to be the sleazy excuse for a man that Howard Cantwell was expecting.

Davies addressed Cantwell snidely, "So, Mr. Prosecutor, what's the emergency? My gal said you wanted to meet urgently. She's a pretty little blond thing, if you know what I mean."

Ignoring the demeaning comment, Cantwell said, "The district attorney and I caught some of your performance on the steps of City Hall on television this morning. Let's ..."

Davies interrupted him, saying "I hope that you liked it. I thought that it went quite well."

"I prefer not to comment. Let's get down to business. You obviously hold a grudge against the city."

"Am I supposed to be grateful?"

"Well, the truth is, I don't give a damn about you. I've got a backlog of cases. Advise your client to plead guilty and take a plea agreement. Then take the next plane out of town."

"Why would I do that? Like I said this morning, the evidence against my client is circumstantial. When he's acquitted, I'll be in the headlines as a winner and you'll look like a fool."

"Guess you've been too busy planning that press conference and haven't kept up. There's now indisputable evidence that Hoyt Stark was at the house the night Shannon Stark was murdered. We have boot prints."

"What boot prints?"

"The boot prints on the door of the Stark house. When a neighbor walking his dog the morning after the murder noticed the severely damaged front door, he called the police. As you know, they found Shannon Stark's dead body inside. It was obvious that someone had repeatedly kicked the door until it splintered. The CSU team was able to get several clear boot prints from the front door. They determined the size and the brand of boot from the tread. The murderer kicked in the door. Then he strangled and stabbed Shannon Stark."

"That doesn't mean that my client is guilty," Davies argued. "Hundreds, maybe thousands of men must wear the same boot in the same size. If that's your new evidence, you've got nothing," Davies said, still believing the prosecution didn't have enough to convict his client.

Like an unexpected upheaval of the earth under him, Davies suddenly found himself and his case on shaky ground. Cantwell delivered incontrovertible information in the magnitude of a 7.0 earthquake on the Richter scale.

"If we didn't have more than that, I wouldn't be here right now, Mr. Davies. Stark's boots were meticulously examined. Dried blood was found deep in the crevices of the tread. Do I really need to tell you the DNA results? I doubt that you can explain away Shannon Stark's blood on your client's boots."

Davies knocked back a long swallow from his glass of scotch. Clearly, this was the first he heard about the blood evidence.

"Mr. Davies, you're a smart man," Cantwell said. "This is a slam dunk for the prosecution. You know that the death penalty is legal in Florida. Convince your client to plead guilty to the Shannon Stark murder. We'll drop the charges in Sam McKay's case. To sweeten the deal, we'll even take the death penalty off the table. Advise your client that in exchange for a guilty plea, I'm offering a life sentence with no chance of parole."

Davies was thinking about how this new turn of events would affect *him*. If the case went to trial, he would suffer an embarrassing loss in the courtroom.

Cantwell's deal would bail him out of an untenable position. The impact on Hoyt Stark's future was of no consequence to Davies; he only thought about the outcome as it related to him.

"If I agree, what do I tell the people back home? I bragged about getting Stark off. How do I protect my reputation?"

"Tell them that your client panicked at the possibility of a death sentence and demanded that you make this plea deal. Tell them that you had no choice but to yield to his wishes."

That explanation appealed to Hamilton Davies. He could work with it. No one would fault him if his client was running scared. Of course, he could have won, he'd say, but he had to accede to the wishes of Hoyt Stark.

"Cover Your Ass" was one of the guiding principles for Hamilton Davies throughout his life. Cantwell's suggestion would help him do just that.

CHAPTER 77

Hamilton Davies prepared for his final evening in Miami in his luxury suite at the Intercontinental Hotel. Room service delivered a meal with a Caesar salad, crab cakes, rack of lamb served with steak fries, and a large slice of white chocolate cheesecake with raspberries. He laughed to himself that he was like a prisoner on death row, eating all his favorite foods prior to his execution. Little did he imagine the truth in that thought.

Earlier, he had no problem convincing Hoyt Stark to accept a guilty plea for the murder of Shannon Stark. When Davies related his conversation with the prosecutor to his client, stressing that he could get the death penalty if found guilty, Stark saw the merit of accepting the plea deal. Not only did Hoyt agree to pleading guilty for killing Shannon, he thanked Davies for getting the charges for the murder of Sam McKay dismissed. Of course, Davies took credit for negotiating that part of the agreement, never mentioning that the idea came from the prosecutor. The Dallas attorney was proud of how he could spin the facts like a child spins a top.

Satisfied, Davies regarded his trip to Florida a success. He had gotten his fifteen minutes of fame. His face was in the national news.

In the style to which he was accustomed, he directed his secretary to book him a seat in first class on the first flight out in the morning and to arrange a limousine to take him to Miami International Airport. Upon retiring for the evening, he anticipated a comfortable three-hour flight to Dallas.

That night he went to bed for the last time. He would never again see daylight.

****

Sergeant Emilio Hernandez burst from his office. His face was grim as he made his announcement.

"DON is back. We have a body."

"Dammit," shouted Detective Brad Mandich, hurling rapid-fire questions at his superior. "Have you identified the deceased? Where's the body? Why do you think it's the Dead of Night killer?"

"It's that Texas lawyer from the press conference. Killed in his bed at the Intercontinental. Like the others, there are deep teeth marks on the body. His liver and stomach are missing."

Here we go again, thought Brad. Already he could foresee the impact on the department and on the people of Miami.

"Brad, I need you out there with Dennison," Hernandez said. "I just alerted CSU and they're on the way. Also, if I remember correctly, the wildlife expert from the zoo and your nephew wanted to be called to the scene of the next murder. I was hoping it wouldn't come to this. Ask them to meet you at the hotel. We could use some fresh eyes."

"Will do. Lew and I will call them from the car."

CHAPTER 78

With lights flashing and the occasional use of the siren, the two detectives navigated through the early-morning traffic. They had deliberately taken a squad car to afford them these perks in rush hour to save driving time. The Intercontinental Hotel was near Bayside, a popular tourist attraction. Even at eight-thirty, tourists were filling parking spots, eager to breakfast by the water, board a sightseeing boat, or browse through the kiosks.

Entering the lobby of the Intercontinental Hotel, the detectives were approached by a smartly dressed man in his early thirties. He had been waiting for their arrival, pacing anxiously as he repeatedly peered at the entrance.

Wearing a tailored navy suit with his nameplate pinned to the jacket, Felix Acosta introduced himself. With a somber look on his face and shakiness in his voice, he said, "Thanks for coming so quickly. I'm the hotel manager, Felix Acosta."

Brad and Lew introduced themselves, presenting their badges and identification to the nervous hotel manager. Rather than merely providing the room number, Acosta volunteered to escort them to the suite of the recently deceased Hamilton Davies.

As they headed to the elevator, Brad asked, "What can you tell us? Who found the body?"

"Actually, I did. At four this morning a limo driver arrived at the front desk asking for Mr. Davies, who was to meet him at our main entrance for a ride to the airport. When Mr. Davies failed to show and didn't answer his cell phone, the driver came inside. After the desk clerk was advised of the problem, he called Mr. Davies on the hotel phone. There was no answer. At that point, the desk clerk buzzed me. I advised the driver to wait in the lobby. Because of the prominence of Mr. Davies, I personally went up to his room, expecting that he had overslept. After knocking and getting no response, I entered."

Acosta's voice broke and tears filled his eyes. "I called out his name, but he didn't answer. I walked to the doorway leading to the bedroom of the suite and again called out to him. No answer. Then I looked over at the bed. I never saw so much blood. For as long as I live, I'll never be able to get over what I saw. It was all I could do to keep from puking. I ran out and locked the door to the suite. Avoiding the lobby, I went to my office and called the police."

Retelling the sequence of events seemed to have had a cathartic effect for Felix. Involuntarily, his entire body shook, his longish straight brown hair resettling on his head. It was as if he had cleared all the disturbing images from his brain. The detectives gave him a moment before continuing their questions.

"Did you move or touch anything?" Lew inquired.

"No. Not a thing. I left the room just as it was."

"We can take if from hear, Mr. Acosta," said Brad. "My nephew, Dr. Clifford Mandich, and Dr. Adam Crowe from the Miami Metro Zoo should be arriving shortly. When they arrive, please direct them to this suite."

"Of course, Detective Mandich. I'll be on alert at the front desk. I'll recognize Dr. Crowe from watching his interviews on the news and some of his nature specials. How will I recognize Dr. Mandich?"

"Don't worry, Mr. Acosta," said Brad. He laughed to himself as he responded, "I'm sure you'll know him when he starts pumping you for information at the front desk."

Handing each detective his business card, Felix said, "If there's anything else you need, call me directly."

With Cliff, Adam Crowe, and the Crime Scene Unit expected to arrive momentarily, Brad and Lew were glad to be the first in the suite, fortunate to be looking at an undisturbed crime scene. Before proceeding with their investigation, they donned gloves and disposable booties to avoid contamination of the evidence within. The hotel manager had not exaggerated the amount of blood at the scene.

Both seasoned detectives gagged when they saw Davies's face. The nose had been torn off. The abdominal cavity had been slit open. The liver, stomach, and intestines were missing. Lifting the mutilated head from a pool of blood on the pillow, Lew discovered a puncture wound on the back of the neck. They speculated that this may have been from a tranquilizer gun, but more likely from a syringe, because of the close quarters in the room. This was the work of the Dead of Night killer.

Confirmation of the time of death would come later once the autopsy was completed. However, they worked on theories about how the killer gained access to the room, speculating that the murder took place late in the evening like the previous DON killings.

My uncle's theory was that the killer gained access to the room while it was being cleaned. Lew added that he might have duped a maid with a story of having lost his key. Both agreed that the killer probably hid in the room for hours waiting for Davies to return.

As I arrived at the Intercontinental Hotel and was speaking with Felix Acosta, Dr. Crowe approached the front desk, carrying what appeared to be a large camera bag. Acosta advised us of the room number and directed us to the elevator. When we entered the suite, we were greeted by my uncle and Lew Dennison who handed us gloves and booties and advised us that CSU would be here in minutes.

While I was surveying the scene with my eyes, Adam Crowe was sniffing the air throughout the suite, particularly in the bedroom. At first, I was baffled by what he was doing. The scent was overwhelming; I tried to avoid it as much as possible by breathing through my mouth. I couldn't understand why he was focusing on such a sickening aroma.

It soon became clear when he reminded us that in addition to his work at Metro Zoo, he had taken countless camera safaris. To locate his photographic subjects, he often tracked animals in the wild and had become an experienced tracker. Olfactory clues often pinpointed the location of the species he sought.

"Try to forget the overpowering smell of the body. Do you notice the scent of urine?" Crowe asked, still walking around the room and sniffing the air.

"Now that you mention it, I do," said Brad. "Although, that's not that uncommon at a murder scene."

"I'd agree with you, but this is different. The urine smell isn't just near the body. Walk through the entire suite and take a whiff of the carpeting. The scent is along the entire perimeter of the suite. It's like an animal marking its territory," explained Crowe.

Adam Crowe approached the bed. For a few moments, he stared at Davies's face, particularly the mauled nose. He also noted the condition of the abdomen, now emptied of the liver, stomach, and intestines. Asking the detectives to turn the body on its side, he looked at the lower back and the buttocks. As he suspected, there were teeth marks in those areas. He pulled his camera from his bag and snapped photos just like a trained crime-scene photographer.

What I'm seeing is very strange," Crowe commented. "At first glance the bite marks on Mr. Davies *appear* to be made from a jaw of a wolf, Canis rufus."

"Would you mind explaining your use of the word 'strange'? What do you mean by 'at first glance'? And why did you say the bite marks 'appear' to be from a wolf jaw?" I asked. From only one statement, I had three questions that perplexed me.

"The pattern of the bite marks corresponds to the shape of the jaw and the spacing of the teeth of the Florida wolf. However, the teeth marks on the body are too perfect to have been made by a wolf as it attacked its prey. Also, I see no tearing where the bite marks appear. It seems to me that someone wants the authorities to *believe* that these wounds were inflicted by a wild animal. A genuine wolf would tear at the flesh, thrashing its head and neck from side to side as it devoured the internal organs. That's not what I see here. Whoever did this created the impression of a wolf attack. I think the opening to the abdominal cavity was made with some sort of knife, probably serrated. In my professional opinion, I don't believe that a wolf killed Davies."

"You're a wealth of information about wolf behavior," I said with admiration. "What you've explained is fascinating. Anything else you can tell us?"

"Yes, the perpetrator was familiar with the behavior of wolves," Crowe stated. "When a wolf chases four-legged game, it bites the hind quarters to wound and catch its quarry. Extrapolating that behavior to two-legged prey, that would explain bite marks on the lower back and buttocks of the victims. After a successful catch of its target, the wolf may grab the nose of its prey to render it defenseless. Often the attack on the face delivers the death blow."

"Three of the victims were close friends in high school ten years ago," I stated. "Two had bite marks on the face. Could you provide any explanation as to why the third did not?"

"Not all prey is bitten in the exact manner on the face. The wolf will do only what is necessary to apprehend its prey. The killer is mimicking wolf behavior."

"Was there any reason that the killer removed the abdominal organs?" I asked, intrigued by the killer's thorough planning to simulate wolf behavior.

"Again, the killer is emulating the actions of a wolf. While we humans prefer the muscle of an animal for our dinner, a wolf prefers the organ meat. If you've seen photos or watched videos of a wolf kill, you'd see the animal feasting on the soft underbelly of its prey."

The detectives listened attentively to Adam Crowe as he gave us reasons to suspect that the Dead of Night killer was familiar with details about wolves far beyond what the average person knows. Desperate for suspects, Brad and Lew brainstormed out loud. Hoyt Stark was immediately eliminated since he was in custody. His friends, the Augusta brothers, were also imprisoned. Stark's other friends, Iggy and Rollo, had a possible motive. They probably held Hamilton Davies responsible for convincing their buddy to take a plea deal. Thinking about their friend locked up for life could have made them furious. Especially if they had been drinking. Their rap sheets included many entries for drunk and disorderly behavior.

Because they weren't the sharpest tools in the shed, Iggy and Rollo were unlikely suspects. While it appeared that they lacked the capacity to devise this intricate plan, my uncle and Lew thought it would be best to leave no stone unturned. They would check out the pair but didn't have high hopes about the outcome of their investigation of the duo. Again, they were out of credible suspects.

That is, until Adam Crowe shocked them with his suggestion.

"I hesitate to propose a more likely suspect," Crowe said regretfully. "He's someone with a comprehensive knowledge of the behavior of wolves. Don't forget the urine smell in this room. I'd recognize the odor of wolf urine anywhere. This is the real thing. My assistant Pete Ward would know that wolves use urine to mark their territory. He'd have access to the real stuff as well."

Pete Ward had just become suspect number one.

CHAPTER 79

Just after Adam Crowe made his rather startling accusation against his assistant, my uncle's phone rang.

"Hello, Detective Mandich," said Dr. Murphy. "The DNA results are back. I think you should come to the lab. You're going to want to see the report for yourself. Can you bring Dr. Mandich and Dr. Crowe as well? I know they'll be interested."

"They're with me right now. We're just finishing up at a crime scene. The victim, the attorney for Hoyt Stark, will be delivered to you after CSU finishes its work. We'll see you shortly."

Brad filled in Murphy's side of the conversation. "That was Dr. Murphy. He got the results of the DNA tests and wants us to come to the lab immediately."

****

Dr. Murphy's pace mirrored his eagerness to share the test results with us. He led us to the lab area, taking large strides. He handed us copies of the lab report so we could review it while he spoke.

"Gentlemen, I'll get right to it. If you recall, I sent out samples for DNA testing to my colleague, Dr. Don Pinkney, director of the lab in Tallahassee, of all bite wounds. Initially baffled at the results, he sent those DNA samples to a second lab for confirmation. The results are back, and they are *bizarre*."

"In what way?" I asked.

"There are two perplexing oddities in the findings. The first one is the lack of saliva from *any* wound. Any bite wound should have some residue of saliva. The second peculiarity is the issue of DNA transfer among the victims."

"Can you elaborate further on 'DNA transfer'?" I asked.

"Dr. Pinckney tested the DNA of the victims in the chronological order of their dates of death. The only DNA in the bite wounds of victim number one was his own. DNA found in the wounds of victim number two was his own DNA plus the DNA from victim number one. The DNA found in the wounds of victim number three was again his own and the DNA from the previous two victims. You see where this is going. This pattern continued as the victims continued; each subsequent victim had trace amounts of DNA in his wounds from *all* previous victims. How did this DNA transfer occur? And why was no saliva identified? Any theories?"

While Dr. Murphy spoke, I had been perusing the lab report. I think I'm more a visual learner rather than an auditory learner. Seeing the data on the paper made me think about Dr. Crowe's evaluation of the bite marks on Hamilton Davies's body. Suddenly, I was able to connect the dots. There *was* a logical explanation for both oddities that Dr. Murphy described.

"While examining the body of Mr. Davies at the hotel," I said, "Dr. Crowe suggested that the bites were consistent with the jawbone and teeth of a wolf, but the markings seemed *too* perfect. Therefore, he believed that no *living* wolf had done the biting. Someone appears to be using a jaw and teeth, trying to simulate a wolf's bite. That would explain the absence of saliva; no saliva because there is no live animal."

Dr. Murphy listened attentively, nodding his head in agreement. I continued, "With an intact wolf skull, someone could manipulate the jawbone and the teeth to produce bites that would be identified as coming from a wolf."

Lew interrupted, "What about the DNA transfer?"

"My best guess is that the perpetrator never considered either hygiene or the fact that the teeth would retain the DNA from the previous victims. If he didn't use any cleaning product between kills, that would account for the transfer of DNA from one victim to the next; each subsequent bite would carry the DNA from all the prior victims."

"Makes good sense, Dr. Mandich," agreed Cecil Murphy. "I'll contact Dr. Pinkney. I'm sure he'll appreciate a logical explanation for such an illogical finding. Out of curiosity, where would a person obtain such a skull with a wolf jaw and intact teeth?"

"Red wolf skulls would be a scarce commodity, but as we all know, where there's a will, there's a way," I said. "No doubt, internet searches were instrumental in the acquisition of the skull. Like the buyer, *we* can also use the internet to see if anyone recently sold a red wolf skull. If we can figure out who obtained the skull, we'll find the killer."

At every turn, this case seemed to get more and more bizarre. Finally, logic and science confirmed that we were dealing with a man, not a beast. This conclusion made me more uneasy than I had been before.

Our killer was not an animal, operating on instinct. He was a human, utilizing highly evolved intelligence. An extremely troubling thought.

Not surprisingly, it has been said that man is the most dangerous predator.

CHAPTER 80

Back at the station, Brad and Lew were anxious to share the morning's events with Sergeant Hernandez. Stopping at Detective Banks's desk, Lew invited her to join them.

"Hey, Amanda, come with us. We're on the way to Hernandez's office. You'll want to hear this."

Detective Banks pushed back her desk chair and stood up. The trio headed to the sergeant's office; the two men were so elated about what they learned that morning that they neglected to knock. Startled by the three detectives who had just materialized unannounced, Hernandez peered at them over his reading glasses and said, "This better be good."

"Better than good, it's incredible. And great call when you suggested that we bring my nephew Cliff and Adam Crowe from the Metro Zoo with us when we went to investigate the murder of Hamilton Davies."

"So, what did you find?"

"There's no doubt that this was the work of the Dead of Night killer. Hamilton Davies was the first victim that Dr. Crowe got to see in person," Brad stated. "Crowe's observation of the pattern of the bites and the depth of the wounds indicate that someone was manipulating the jawbone of a wolf to give the impression that the bites were inflicted by the animal. They aren't bite marks from a *live* animal."

"Interesting," commented Sergeant Hernandez.

"What threw us off all along," said Lew "is that the bite marks were strategically placed on the bodies of the victims, in areas that a wolf would choose to bite its victims. The killer knows a helluva lot about wolves."

"What about the missing organs?" Hernandez asked.

"I was getting to that," Brad responded. "Dr. Crowe thinks that a serrated knife was used on Davies. The organs were removed as part of the subterfuge to frighten people into thinking a vicious wild wolf was killing people. Wolves consider abdominal organs a delicacy."

"Anything else I should know?"

Brad recounted their visit with the medical examiner and the second set of DNA results regarding the bite marks. Both Hernandez and Amanda found that information game changing.

"The lack of saliva and the DNA transfer from victim to subsequent victim open up a new line of approach," Amanda said. She looked as if she had much more to add to that topic. Before she was able to continue her train of thought, Hernandez interrupted her. Directing his question to the male detectives, he asked "Any suspects?"

"Brad and I were tossing around a few names earlier. Iggy and Rollo, friends of Hoyt Stark, are still on the list. They probably were angry that the attorney advised Stark to take a plea deal and end up with a life sentence. Anything's possible. Adam Crowe suggested a third suspect who is now our prime suspect. Pete Ward, the assistant wildlife expert at Miami Metro Zoo, is well-versed in information about red wolves."

The results of the lab report certainly provided invaluable data.

Naming Pete Ward as a credible suspect provided a potential killer never before on their radar.

However, Amanda's next statement provided the most consequential piece of information of the entire meeting.

CHAPTER 81

"I believe I might know where the wolf skull and jaw with a full set of teeth came from."

"Holy Shit!" was the first response that came out of Emilio Hernandez's mouth.

"When were you planning to mention this, Amanda?" he asked, glaring at her.

"Gimme a break, Sarge. Until Brad said that someone seemed to be using the *jaw* of a wolf to simulate the bites on the victims, I had nothing to tell."

"Don't keep us in suspense, Amanda," Brad suggested. "Let's hear it."

Practically running to her desk, Amanda shouted, "Be right back."

It took her only seconds to locate a report of a robbery filed by Clyde Haney near Big Cypress Swamp. Like many small business operations in the area, the store fulfilled various purposes in the community. The store proprietor, Clyde Haney, sold soda, beer, cigarettes, coffee, snacks, and live bait. However, the main business of his establishment was taxidermy. When she was a young girl, Amanda accompanied her dad on many fishing expeditions in the nearby canals. She remembered visiting the shop frequently with her father, drinking root beer soda while he purchased live bait. Clyde mounted several of her father's trophy catches which were still proudly displayed on the wall in his den.

The robbery report initially attracted Amanda's attention due to her connection to Clyde Haney. The report had been filed just two days prior to the discovery of the initial victim of the Dead of Night killer. Then all hell broke loose. As a result, it was categorized as low priority, taking a back seat to law enforcement efforts directed to solve that case. After her cursory review, she placed the report near the bottom of the pile of unsolved cases that littered her desk. She'd get to it later. Much later, as it turned out.

Ironically, it might now be at the epicenter of the investigation.

"Got it!" Amanda exclaimed, clutching the folder with the robbery report in her hand. "Almost a month ago, this robbery report was assigned to me. There had been a breaking and entering near the Everglades, but I haven't had the time to investigate further for obvious reasons."

"What's so important all of a sudden?" Hernandez asked.

"The owner of the place that was robbed sells fishing supplies and is also a taxidermist, kind of like one-stop shopping when avid fishermen have a successful day on the water. As a kid, I used to go to Mr. Haney's shop with my dad. Haney had lots of fish hanging on the walls and stuffed raccoons, birds, and snakes. I also remember he had some animal skeletons as well. His store was like a museum to me. Seems like a logical place to go to find a wolf's skull."

"It's worth a look, Amanda. Go for it," Hernandez told her.

With the police report in her hand, Amanda headed to her squad car, destination Ochopee, Florida, home of the Big Cypress Welcome Center on the Tamiami Trail. She observed the changes in scenery and population density as she drove. She began her journey on U.S. 41 (also known as the Tamiami Trail) in downtown Miami on Brickell Avenue, a financial district densely populated with banks, insurance companies, hotels, and high-rise apartment buildings. Continuing her drive on the Tamiami Trail, she passed through the heart of the Miami Cuban community along Calle Ocho (its English translation SW 8th Street). This section of the drive was teeming with both residents and tourists enjoying the restaurants, art galleries, cafes with walk-up windows serving Cuban coffee, all with a unique vibrancy from its Latin American roots. Once she departed these heavily populated areas, she marveled at the wide-open spaces as the Tamiami Trail headed into the Florida Everglades.

This had been familiar territory to Amanda. Just off the Tamiami Trail she spotted a weather-beaten wooden sign in the shape of an arrow announcing, "For live bait, turn here." She immediately turned onto an unpaved road leading to the shop known as Clyde's Place, about forty yards down the road. The advisory sign on the road and the appearance of the shop hadn't changed in over twenty years, other than normal signs of aging. The door frame was still splintered, the hinges on the door were still rusted, and the base of the door was still scuffed, only more so. To the left of the wooden door, Amanda remembered the sign advertising worms and shiners, a popular bait for bass fishermen, on a deep blue background to resemble water. It was now bleached pale by the sun. On the right side of the doorway, she recognized a large black chalk board listing the goods and services available at Clyde's. From years of erasures and regular updates, the background color was more gray than black. Amanda felt as if she were in a time warp.

Not surprisingly, hers was the only car in the makeshift gravel parking area; serious fishermen would have filled the lot earlier at the crack of dawn. The silence, interrupted only by the sound of birds and insects, was typical of the Everglades. She had forgotten how peaceful this part of Florida was, so close to Miami yet feeling as if it were in rural America. Nostalgic as she approached the doorway of the shop, she tried to imagine how Clyde would look to her. When she was ten years old, Clyde seemed ancient to her. Most likely he was in his late forties or early fifties at that time, his skin prematurely wrinkled from the intense Florida sun, adding to his appearance of being old to Amanda as a child.

Her arrival dispelled the quietude that she just observed. When she opened the rickety wooden door, its hinges creaked loudly, badly in need of lubrication. The next disruption of the peaceful atmosphere came from her footsteps on the original tongue-and-groove flooring made from local hardwood trees; when she entered the shop, the wooden floors squeaked just as she remembered. The shop, or shack as she might have described it, was frozen in time, but in a good way. It belonged in the Florida Everglades, typifying the history and unique flavor of the area.

The shop's owner had been working in the back room. Hearing the creaking hinges and the squeaking floorboards, he came out to greet his customer. It was as if the past twenty years hadn't gone by. The shopkeeper stared at the young woman, a puzzled expression on his face, until recognition turned his facial expression into a smile. Although Amanda had the advantage of knowing that Clyde Haney was the owner, she grinned at him, happy that he didn't appear to have aged much beyond her recollection of him. For a moment, both froze in place, waiting for the other to speak.

"Oh, my goodness, you're the Banks girl, Amanda, aren't you? You used to come in here years ago with you father and have a root beer soda. You'd examine all my displays, asking questions left and right. It's like it was only yesterday. Tell me I'm right."

"You sure are, Mr. Haney. You and your place haven't changed a bit either, except for the wood boarding up the side windows."

"The side windows were busted from the break-in. That's probably how the robbers got into the shop. I'm still waiting for the glass company to replace them. How's your dad? He hasn't been around in a while."

"Thanks for asking about him, Mr. Haney. When he retired, dad moved to one of those adult communities in Palm Beach County. He traded in his fishing pole for a golf club. He's doing well, golfing with the same enthusiasm that he had for fishing."

"Say hello to him for me when you see him. I get the feeling this isn't a social visit, and you're certainly not dressed for fishing. So, how can I help you?"

Amanda stated that she drove to the store to see him on official police business, telling him that she was a detective with the Miami-Dade police department. Apologizing for the delay due to the Dead of Night killings, she explained that she was assigned to look into the police report from Clyde's call about a break-in at his shop.

"No need to apologize about not coming sooner. I know the importance of the Dead of Night investigation. This is small potatoes. As much as possible, I've been trying to leave everything the way I found it after the burglary."

"That's helpful, Mr. Haney. Please describe for me what was taken. The report, unfortunately, is short on details."

"You've seen my place, Amanda, or should I call you Detective Banks? Congratulations, by the way. Makes sense you'd become a cop after all the questions you always asked."

"Amanda is just fine, Mr. Haney."

"Anyway, Amanda, money couldn't have been a motive. You see the shop. I don't keep a lot of cash around and my sales are nothing to write home about. Mostly, I sell the bait and supplies so I can interact with the people going fishing. It's my way to socialize. I earn most of my income from taxidermy, stuffing and mounting trophies for hunters and fishermen. I keep some stuffed snakes, raccoons, and birds in the shop as examples of the lifelike quality I can produce. I'm the one who killed most of the display samples that you used to find so intriguing as a little girl.

"Occasionally, I mount a full skeleton upon request. Since some are fragile, I keep those in the back room out of harm's way. I also have a collection of skulls of various animal species back there."

That got Amanda's attention. "By any chance, do you have a wolf skull in the back?" Amanda asked eagerly.

Sighing, Haney replied, "Interesting that you should ask. I did. That is, until the robbery. That's the one thing that the bastard or bastards took during the robbery. Just the skull of a wolf."

"Was there something special about it? Was it valuable?"

"It's valuable in the sense that it came from the Florida wolf, also known as the red wolf. Now it's an endangered species. Personally, I think stealing it was a prank, but I don't know why anyone would pull a prank like that on me."

"Sounds like a pretty sick sense of humor," Amanda said, commiserating with Clyde. "Were the teeth intact on the jaw of the skull?"

Her question seemed strange to Clyde, but he was used to Amanda having unusual questions from his interactions with her as a child.

"Yup, the teeth and jaw were intact."

Barely containing her excitement about his reply, Amanda said, "Please tell me that you still have the surveillance tapes from the evening of the break-in. I noticed you have cameras mounted outside."

“Sorry to disappoint you, but the cameras haven’t worked in a decade. Now they’re just for show. Same as my ‘Beware of Dog’ sign in the yard. There is no dog.”

Although disappointed that there was no recording of the robbery, Amanda was proud that her instincts and perseverance uncovered a major clue in identifying the DON killer. She thanked Clyde Haney for his help, promised to keep him informed about the case, and said she’d give his best wishes to her father.

“I’m going to arrange for a Crime Scene Unit to come out here to investigate your break-in and make some sense of the robbery. In the meantime, leave the wood on the windows, don’t walk on the grass outside by the broken windows, and don’t let anyone into the back room.,” advised Amanda.

Amanda never did inform Clyde of the potential significance that his little establishment might play in Miami’s most gruesome crime spree of the decade. It had not crossed Clyde’s mind to inform Amanda that the thief had removed the skull from a fully mounted skeleton of the wolf.

Clyde still had the bones of the body and trunk that were left behind.

CHAPTER 82

While Amanda was checking out Clyde's bait and tackle establishment, Detectives Mandich and Dennison headed out on I-95 to question Hoyt Stark's cronies, Iggy and Rollo. Brad and Lew found themselves in a depressing neighborhood. Garbage littered the streets, broken toys and rusted bicycles were scattered on the small lawns which had turned brown from an infestation of chinch bugs, and the houses were badly in need of painting.

They located the address for Iggy's house. It was a typical Old Florida small one-bedroom home, with jalousie windows that probably hadn't been washed since the house was constructed. Bent green metal awnings hung over the front windows, only partially attached to the stucco wall. It was hard to determine the underlying paint color of the house due to extensive rust stains from using well water on the lawn. The once white roof was black with mold. Like the other yards in the neighborhood, the lawn was brown, except for the hearty green weeds that seemed to thrive. They appeared to be the closest thing to landscaping. The lawn was littered with beer bottles and bags from takeout food that had fallen out of the overflowing garbage cans that sat at the curb.

Lew noticed an old-model gray pickup truck in the carport. The metal was corroding, and it looked as if it had been in one fender bender too many. The truck had been backed into the carport, hiding the license tag of the vehicle, a red flag for the detectives.

"This place is much like I expected. Not exactly the Taj Mahal. Since the truck is here, I suspect that Iggy is home," said Lew. Not surprisingly, even the doorbell suffered from neglect. Its plastic plate was barely attached to the door, and when Brad pushed on it, no sound was heard. Brad rapped on the door forcefully.

Unshaven, Iggy opened the door holding a beer in his hand. Another male voice could be heard from deeper in the house. The loud voice from inside shouted, "Who's at the door?" Not waiting for a response from Iggy, a bare-chested male with a hairy chest came to the doorway. The detectives assumed correctly that the second male was Rollo. It was as if these two dimwits were attached at the hip.

Confident that they could outwit the duo of Iggy and Rollo, prior to their arrival Brad and Lew devised a plan to get them into the stationhouse. They hoped that Iggy and Rollo would incriminate themselves during their interview. As part of their introductions, the detectives flashed their badges and IDs at the men. Having the experience of multiple encounters with the law, the pair knew not to antagonize the cops.

"What can we do for you, officers?" asked Iggy. While the words sounded accommodating, the tone was less than sincere.

Brad, however, delivered his fabricated story with as much sincerity as he could muster.

"We know how close you both are to Hoyt Stark. Although he already pleaded guilty to murdering Shannon, some new evidence has come up. It's possible that he's been framed. It's also possible that he was given poor legal advice when he was advised to plead guilty in exchange for a life sentence. You might be able to help your friend by answering some questions for us."

"Anything for Hoyt," said Iggy.

"I'm in," said Rollo.

"We need to conduct the interview at the station so that we can officially record your responses," Lew advised.

Iggy said, "Let me get the keys to my truck."

Rollo grabbed a stained T-shirt that was rolled up into a ball on the floor, sniffed the underarms, and decided it was clean enough to wear. The two pillars of society slammed the front door shut and headed to the gray Toyota pickup.

Concerned that the two men might choose to flee, Brad followed closely behind the truck, ignoring the rules of a safe following distance. The ride was especially unpleasant for the detectives, trailing behind a vehicle that spewed smoke from the exhaust pipe. Not only blinded by the smoke, they were nauseated by the smell of the exhaust fumes.

They regretted that Florida no longer required testing for vehicle emissions.

****

The four men entered a room formerly known as the interrogation room. It now had a kinder and gentler designation, referred to as an interview room. Sergeant Hernandez could secretly observe from another location that was equipped with a computer and video feed.

Iggy and Rollo were offered coffee, water, or a soft drink. Like the two detectives, they selected black coffee. The two friends were still unaware that they were murder suspects. They were informed that the interview was being recorded.

"Remind me why we are here again, detectives," requested Iggy.

"You're here because we believe you can help us help your friend. None of us trusted his attorney, Hamilton Davies. We believe that Davies was never interested in your pal, Hoyt Stark. He had his own reasons for advising Hoyt to make a plea deal. All we want is the right man behind bars," explained Brad.

"Yeah," Rollo agreed. "Hoyt shouldn't have listened to that cowboy guy from Texas. We tried to tell him that, but he wouldn't listen. Hoyt thought he was a good lawyer. Guess he sees he wasn't so good now that he's sitting in Raiford State Prison. I could kill that guy for how he messed up Hoyt's life," Rollo volunteered.

"Did you?" Lew asked.

"Did I *what*?" Rollo had no idea where Lew was going with his question.

"Did you kill Hamilton Davies, Hoyt's attorney?"

"He's dead? Hoyt's attorney is dead?" Rollo's shocked facial expression and the surprise in his voice were genuine. Iggy seemed equally startled by the news.

"Why are you looking at *us* for this?" Iggy asked. "We didn't even know the lawyer was dead until you just told us. I thought we were here to help Hoyt. I'm confused. What's going on?"

Not only did the detectives believe that Iggy and Rollo had no knowledge of the murder of the attorney, the detectives couldn't imagine them being capable of engineering the murder to replicate the DON killings in such elaborate detail. Abruptly, Brad ended the interview.

"Thanks for your cooperation," the detective said, as he lifted himself out of his chair.

"What about helping……?" Rollo asked, unable to finish his question because Iggy punched him in the shoulder. Iggy realized that they should leave before the cops changed their minds about their involvement.

He whispered to his friend, "Let's get while the getting's good."

CHAPTER 83

Sergeant Hernandez observed everything from the video feed, his frustration evident when he summoned the two detectives to his office.

"That was a whole lot of nothing. Total waste of time," Hernandez declared.

The two detectives defended themselves saying that they were just being thorough. Fortunately, they still had their prime suspect to interview.

"As I mentioned earlier, when Dr. Crowe examined the crime scene at the Intercontinental Hotel, he told us that the murderer had an expert's knowledge of the behavioral patterns of a wolf. It shocked us that he implicated his own assistant, Peter Ward, as a prime suspect," said Brad.

Lew added, "I bet the DON killer had been marking his territory all along. But since the other killings were outdoors, no one detected wolf urine. The smell probably had time to dissipate before they those crime scenes were examined."

"Too bad no one noticed that before. But Ward as a suspect sounds promising. Contact Dr. Crowe and make sure he's available when you interview his assistant." Hernandez then added, "Report back afterwards."

Realizing that they had been dismissed, they returned to their desks. Brad called Adam Crowe to set up a meeting with Pete Ward at a time convenient for Dr. Crowe. After their conversation at the Intercontinental Hotel, Crowe anticipated the call.

Combing the newspapers and the internet, Crowe familiarized himself with the salient details of the police investigations. The DON killer had special knowledge of wolf behavior and had access to tranquilizers. Immediately, two such people in Miami came to mind.

Thinking like a cop, he named himself as the first person to meet these criteria. He knew that *he* was innocent, and the police knew that he was out of the country when the DON killer was at his most active. The second person was his assistant, Peter Ward.

The more he thought about it, the more concerned Crowe became that Ward was the Dead of Night killer. It made sense logically, but was alarming, nonetheless.

Hiring Ward as a favor to his wife, whose best friend was Ward's aunt, irritated Crowe. Although Ward had the proper credentials for the position for which he was hired, his work ethic and attitude were less than stellar. Crowe was aware of Ward's shortcomings but retained his services because of the connection to his wife. Dismissing Pete could only cause problems at home. He'd rather deal with Pete's failings than his wife's wrath.

Brad's call interrupted Crowe's musings about Pete and why the man was still in his employ.

"Just to give you a heads up, Dr. Crowe, before we see you later today, your theory about the bites being simulated using a wolf jawbone and teeth proved invaluable." Brad then added, "We learned that a wolf skull with the jawbone and full set of intact teeth was stolen from a taxidermist. Hopefully, our CSU unit will be able to gather evidence to identify the person who robbed the shop. If they can recover the skull, we'll be able to confirm your theory."

"I can have Pete in my office in about an hour. Does that work for you?" asked Dr. Crowe.

"Perfect," responded Brad. "If he wants to know why, be vague. We'll handle him. Take your signals from me."

Following Brad's instructions, Dr. Crowe contacted Pete Ward on his walkie talkie, ordering him to be in his office in one hour. He disarmed Pete by lying about the true purpose of why his presence was required.

"I just got a call from Detectives Mandich and Dennison. You met with them in my absence. Guess you impressed them. Seems that they require more of your expertise."

CHAPTER 84

When Detectives Mandich and Dennison arrived, Adam Crowe and Pete Ward were already waiting in Crowe's office. With four men present, the office was cramped; the detectives saw this as an advantage. Being questioned by two large detectives in a confined space would intimidate Ward.

Acknowledging their arrival, Crowe pointed to two folding chairs that were leaning against the back wall. He sat in his desk chair. Pete sat across from him in another folding chair. They were both drinking Gatorade while waiting for the detectives.

"Grab a seat, detectives. You, of course, remember my assistant, Pete Ward."

"Thanks for seeing us, gentlemen," said Brad. "Dr. Crowe, I hate to commandeer your desk chair, but if you don't mind, may I sit in it? I've been having backaches and would appreciate having a padded cushion."

Brad had no back issues. He wanted to sit directly across from Pete Ward; he concocted his backache on the spur of the moment.

Pete had reservations about the true purpose of the meeting. His boss was the person with the expertise. His suspicion was aroused.

"What's really going on?" Pete asked. "Dr. Crowe told me you need my 'expertise,' but I don't buy that. If you really want expert advice, you only need Dr. Crowe. Am I in trouble? Do I need a lawyer?"

"Wait a minute, son. You're jumping to conclusions. Or is there a reason that you think you need an attorney? Of course, it's your right to have an attorney present if you feel that you need one. At this stage, I don't see why," responded Lew.

"Look, I didn't do anything wrong. So, no lawyer for now. Just answer my question. Why am I here?"

Brad looked across the desk at Pete, relieved that he wasn't terminating the interview by requesting an attorney. Pulling out his dog-eared notepad from his pocket, Brad flipped a few pages before he continued.

"Pete, we recently spoke with Dr. Crowe at the Intercontinental Hotel and at the morgue after the murder of Hamilton Davies. If you're not familiar with his name, Davies was the attorney for Hoyt Stark. What we're interested in now is your take on things."

"Could you be more specific? My 'take'? What 'things' are you talking about?"

"When Dr. Crowe was in India, you viewed the bodies at the morgue. In fact, you stated that the victims were bitten by a wolf, probably the Florida wolf."

"Yeah, that's right. So what?"

"When Dr. Crowe returned from his photo safari in India, the bodies that you examined had already been released to their families. He was only able to see the marks from photos, but he felt that there was something odd about them. There were puncture marks from the teeth but no tearing of the flesh. When Hamilton Davies was found in his hotel room with similar markings, Dr. Crowe examined his body firsthand. He concluded that the bite marks were definitely artificially induced, probably manipulated by a human using a wolf's jaw to produce teeth marks."

"So, I was wrong. What's the big deal? He's the one with the doctorate, not me. I'm not about to refute the opinion of my boss."

"Look, Pete. I admire your respect for Dr. Crowe. What I need to know is whether your inexperience missed the lack of tearing of flesh on the victims' bodies or whether you attempted to mislead us. Let me give you this piece of advice. Be very careful before you answer my question," Brad warned.

"Detective, you're scaring me. I'm embarrassed at what I missed due to my inexperience. There was no intention on my part to mislead. What would I gain from that?"

"Beats me, but since you're being truthful with us, let me be truthful with you," Brad said.

Not only Pete was intent on hearing Brad's next statement, but Adam Crowe and Lew Dennison were eager to listen to what Brad would reveal next. Without realizing it, both pulled their folding chairs closer to the desk.

"The killer had access to both an elephant tranquilizer and curare."

"I won't deny that I use the tranquilizer on occasion for large animals," Pete admitted. "However, other employees also know where it's kept and how to use the syringes. And, for your information, we don't have curare here. Where would I get that? Guess that puts me in the clear, wouldn't you say?"

Pete's relief about his innocence was short-lived. Brad's response to Pete's defense was just two words.

"South America."

"What are you talking about?"

"If you recall, when we last met in Dr. Crowe's office you told us that you had been to Peru and the Amazon. Native hunters in that region have been known to use curare to paralyze their game during a hunt. Therefore, as far as I can tell, you had access to curare."

"I never used curare in the Amazon or brought any back to Florida," Pete insisted. "You seem to be building a serious case against me with purely circumstantial evidence. Is there anything else I should know about?"

Listening attentively to Brad's buildup of the case against Ward, Lew decided to respond to his question.

"There is one last thing, Mr. Ward. Your knowledge of wildlife far exceeds that of the average citizen. You have access to tranquiller guns. I also believe that you have access to the drugs used in the killings. After reconsidering all of this, I have changed my mind."

"What do you mean when you say that you have 'changed your mind'?"

"You should hire a lawyer," answered Lew.

CHAPTER 85

Lauren and the reunion committee were on edge, but despite some cancellations from alumni, they decided to go forward with the reunion activities. The police kept the recent murder of Hamilton Davies under wraps; otherwise, fear might have generated enough alumni withdrawals to terminate the festivities. Today's activity, the chess match between the alumni of her graduation class and the current high school seniors on the chess team, would be taking place in a few hours in the school library. It was cleared with the principal and school administration to open the school at 9:00 a.m. Saturday morning in anticipation of the match scheduled one hour later.

The four alumni prearranged to meet in the school parking lot to enter the school together one hour before match time. Charlie Post, the chess team captain, and Ronald Martella arrived separately, while Jaclyn Struzer and Elliot Cook rode together in Elliot's car. The afternoon get-together at Domino Park evidently sparked a romance.

All players seemed tense beyond the normal anxiety of the competition. The foursome had been plotting strategy for more than just a chess match. Two weeks prior to the match they obtained the names of the teachers on staff. All four were delighted that some of their former teachers, especially the gym teachers, were still employed at Miami Senior High.

Charlie approached the couple who were holding hands.

"Did you bring them?"

"Mine is in my backpack," said Elliot.

"Absolutely," responded Jaclyn, pointing to her purse. "Can we do this quickly? It's freaking me out."

"Okay, Elliot, you take care of the boys' side. Jaclyn, you take care of the girls' side. Ronald, you know what to do. Hopefully, maintenance and security won't be a problem," said Charlie, the ringleader of the plot.

The outside of the school hadn't changed since their graduation ten years before. At the main entrance was a round-about encircling a statue of Chief Osceola in full ceremonial garb. Watching from the window inside, Mr. Nunziato, the maintenance man, was prepared for their arrival. After unlocking the front door, he recognized the former students and they recognized him as well.

Evidently, the school administrators felt that beyond Mr. Nunziato, no additional staff or security would be necessary. After all, few people were expected to attend the chess match other than the participants and perhaps a handful of spectators. All players were excellent students. There was no anticipation of misconduct.

Mr. Nunziato greeted each of the four by name. His appearance had changed little; his hair was now thinner and grayer and the slight curvature at the top of his spine was now more pronounced. He was delighted to see them. Similarly, they recalled him as a kind man and were pleased he still worked at the school.

Concerned that the prank that the quartet planned might cause problems for Mr. Nunziato, (whose first name they never knew), Jaclyn whispered to Elliot that perhaps they should abort their plot. Elliot assured her that if everything went as planned, no one would know they were the guilty parties or that what they were about to do occurred under the maintenance man's watch. Elliot convinced Jaclyn that Mr. Nunziato would be blameless.

Charlie set the plan in motion.

"Great to see you, Mr. Nunziato. For old times' sake, could we take a tour of the school? We have about an hour before we need to be at the library. Do you think we could visit our old haunts? Take a little trip down memory lane, if it's okay with you."

"Since it's you four, I don't have any objections. You were always good kids. I have work to do and I need to watch the door for the seniors from the chess team. Make sure you're not late for the tournament in the library or I'll have my head handed to me," he joked.

Things couldn't have been going better. With Mr. Nunziato out of sight they made their way to the gymnasium. The three men entered the office of Todd Howell, the male gym instructor. Their memories of him were nowhere as fond as those of Mr. Nunziato. He turned a blind eye to the bullying that the jocks subjected them to while they were students. From within Howell's office, Ronald Martella pried open the large window to the outside, leaving it in the open position. Elliot reached into his backpack and placed a special treat in Mr. Howell's desk drawer.

While the men were busy at Mr. Howell's desk, Jaclyn was occupied depositing her gift into the top desk drawer of the female gym teacher's desk. Jane Cosby had also been on staff during Jaclyn's high school years. Like her male counterpart, Jane ignored the bullying directed at Jaclyn by the cheerleaders and popular girls.

After making their respective "deposits," the four reconnected in the gymnasium and headed to the library. The four members of the senior chess team had already entered, looking much younger than the alumni.

****

I accompanied Lauren to cheer on her classmates. Since it was a Saturday morning, I wanted to support my wife and the effort she expended into making the reunion a success. As an outside observer, I found it interesting to watch them study each other with the same critical looks they probably exhibited at high school dances: the females comparing themselves to their perceived competition and the males assessing the females as potential dance partners.

Okay, so I'm prejudiced, but Lauren was in a class by herself as compared to this group. Jaclyn looked at her with envy. Two of the men ogled my wife with interest, more than I found acceptable. The other male seemed smitten with Jaclyn and barely looked at Lauren. That was perfectly fine with me.

Lauren and I were the only spectators from the reunion class. The parents and siblings of the high school players were the only spectators rooting for their team.

The team representing the current senior class seemed to be a homogenous group, reminiscent of the chess team from my high school. They dressed alike in T-shirts specially made for the competition and were in a huddle, probably discussing their strategy like football players discussing their game plan.

From their clothing alone, I couldn't help but observe the idiosyncrasies of the alumni team, all unique individuals. Lauren whispered their names to me, identifying them by how they were dressed. Charlie Post wore a tight sleeveless athletic shirt, looking more appropriate for a workout at the gym than for a chess tournament. Ronald Martella sported a navy three-pierce suit complete with vest. With his thick eyeglasses and professional attire, he looked like he was on his way to a business meeting. Jaclyn Struzer looked prim in a light pink cotton dress with long sleeves and a white lace collar buttoned to the neck. Elliot Cook dressed as if he were expecting snow. His jacket had long sleeves. He wore a faded red baseball cap and a scarf. As if his attire wasn't odd enough, he wore sunglasses much like the professionals in a Las Vegas poker tournament. Perhaps he thought the dark glasses would intimidate his opponents.

I was certain that there would be no snowstorms in the library. Perhaps Mr. Cook had a cold. I kept my distance from him and warned Lauren to do the same.

There was no way I could refrain from commenting to Lauren about my impression of her former classmates. The words "motley crew" popped into my mind, but what I said was kinder.

"Your chess team is something else, Lauren. They look like they dressed for four vastly different events. Hopefully, they coordinate their chess strategies better than their clothing," I added.

"Shush," she said. "It's about to start. You're going to eat your words when they win."

The players of each team were introduced, the rules of the tournament were announced, and the matches began. Elliot, the best player on the alumni team, beat the top seeded player on the Miami Senior High team in the first game. While his opponent appeared confident at the outset, he looked both surprised and bereft after Elliot beat him handily. As Charlie Post had strategized, the initial loss in such record time had a profound psychological effect on the rest of the young and less experienced chess team. It was all downhill for them from that point.

Elliot, Charlie, Ronald, and Jaclyn walked away, triumphant in their success. After shaking hands with the high school team, they high fived each other. Whispering together, their facial expressions appeared more serious than I expected from a victorious group. I shrugged off my observation and approached the team with Lauren as she ran to offer her congratulations to her classmates.

"That was amazing," Lauren said. "You nailed it! Those kids have a lot to learn about chess from you guys. Really great job. I'm going to put out an e mail to all the reunion attendees to brag about your success."

From their smiles, you could see that they were touched by her gesture. I couldn't be prouder of my wife.

"You're coming to the volleyball game next Saturday, right?" Lauren asked.

"We'll be there, and at the reunion dinner," said Jaclyn, answering for the group.

Lauren and I had no idea what they had done prior to the beginning of the chess match. We knew nothing about what they deposited in the offices of their former gym teachers that morning.

We didn't find out anything until several days later.

CHAPTER 86

Cynthia Kravitz, the force's top crime scene investigator, had been out with a cold when Phil Demarco, the director of the forensic lab, personally requested that she process the scene at Clyde Haney's shop near the Big Cypress Swamp. Detective Banks was anxious for her findings concerning the break-in. Learning that Cynthia had taken ill, Detective Banks requested that Clyde voluntarily close his business until Kravitz recovered. Since it was Amanda who did the asking, Clyde cooperated.

Now fully recovered, Cynthia headed to Clyde's Place. Bored since he had no customers to greet, Clyde peered outside, awaiting the arrival of Cynthia Kravitz who called earlier to make sure he was on the premises. Ever the proprietor, he greeted the crime scene investigator warmly, offering her a soft drink or water. She held up her water bottle in response, eager to get down to business.

Agreeing to call each other by their first names, Clyde addressed Cynthia with a question he couldn't help asking, based upon her gender and her slight frame. Her blond, hair pulled into a ponytail, peeked out the back opening in her CSU baseball cap. The hairstyle and the cap added to her appearance of youth and Clyde's concern for her safety.

"Cynthia, no disrespect intended, but as a small young woman, I'm kinda surprised that you don't appear to be armed. As for me, I'm never without a gun close by," Clyde added.

"Well, Clyde, by the time I arrive to investigate, the crime has already been committed and the perp is long gone. As you might have noticed, the official signage on my van makes it clear to anyone that it's police vehicle. A person would have to be incredibly stupid to try anything. I don't see the need for a gun."

While speaking, she donned gloves and was scanning his place both visually and by walking the perimeter of the store portion at the front of the building, observing the set up. Clyde rightly assessed that she wasn't interested in small talk.

"How can I help you with your investigation?"

"Clyde, just tell me what *you* think happened. I've been briefed that you reported a break-in several weeks ago."

"That I did. When I called about it, someone from the police department took a few notes and said he'd get back to me. I never did hear back from the police until Detective Banks showed up. I knew her when she was a little girl."

"She mentioned that when I spoke with her. If I had more time, I'd ask for the scoop on her as a child. Detective Banks indicated that a skull was taken. Are you sure that nothing else was missing after the break-in? No money was missing? Nothing of value from the shop like fishing rods, reels, or other equipment?"

"Nope," Clyde answered. "Just the skull. Damned if I can understand *that* either. It came from a wolf that used to live in the wild in Florida. I got some Native American friends out here who located the bones of a Florida red wolf a few years ago. They found them in the Everglades when they were hunting gators and asked me if I had any interest in them. With their help, I excavated the bones and brought them back to the shop. It was like putting together a jigsaw puzzle, positioning the bones to be anatomically correct. The skull was remarkably intact, all the teeth in the jaw in place. It's remarkable how a body works. The wolf skeleton was one of my favorite display pieces. Funny, I've had multiple inquiries about it, but there's no way I'd sell it."

Her interest piqued, Cynthia asked, "Was one of those inquires recent?"

Suddenly, it was as if a light bulb flipped on in Clyde's brain. "You betcha. Now that I think of it, it was a guy. I didn't put it together before now, but I think he asked about it a day or two before that break-in and robbery. I would've thought he'd want the whole skeleton. But he was clear that he only wanted the skull. Makes no sense."

Trying to get Clyde to focus, Cynthia asked, "Anything unusual about the man?"

"You could say so. He was wearing one of those hunting camouflage face masks. We see a lot of those around here but most everyone removes them once they're in my store."

"By any chance, did you notice his vehicle?"

"No, sorry to say. Unless I'm expecting someone like today when you came, I never look at the parking lot."

"Clyde, think hard. Is there anything you can tell me to help identify the person who was interested in the wolf skull?"

"You'll know better than me, but I think he left some of himself behind."

"What did he leave?" She wasn't prepared for how literal his response had been.

"Let me show you," Clyde said. He walked toward the back room with Cynthia trailing behind him. The skeletal body of the wolf, sans head, occupied a place of honor in the room.

"Look here," Clyde said as he pointed out the blood that stained the cervical spine of the specimen. "That blood wasn't there until after the robbery. The thief must've cut himself on his hand when he removed the skull. Serves him right," he added.

"I'm curious, Clyde. I know you spoke with Detective Banks. Didn't you show her the blood on the skeleton? Didn't you mention it?"

"Didn't think to do it. All she asked about was a wolf skull. Guess I should've mentioned the skull was removed from the full skeleton."

"Clyde, if it's okay with you, I'd like to transport the entire remaining skeleton back to the lab so we can get a sample of the blood and any other trace evidence that we may find on the bones. I promise it will be treated with care and will be returned to you as soon as we've completed our testing. In the meantime, I'm going to dust for fingerprints in the front office as well as this back area and outside by the broken window. Did you happen to notice any footprints outside by the windows after the break-in? Maybe I could make a plaster mold of the footprints."

"I did think of that, Cynthia. Unfortunately, there must've been a heavy rain after the break-in because the ground was all wet the following morning. Any footprints that might have been there washed away from the downpour. Take your time and do what you gotta do. I'll let you take the skeleton to the crime lab, but make sure they know how rare it is."

"One more thing, Clyde. I'll need to take a set of your fingerprints. It may be a bit intrusive, but with your permission, I'd also like to take a scraping from inside your mouth for DNA testing. That way the lab technicians can eliminate any fingerprints or DNA on the skeleton that match yours."

"Not a problem, Cynthia. I watch a lot of forensic shows on TV. Now I'm living one. Can't wait til I can tell my customers. Can I reopen the store?"

"Sure, Clyde. Once my van pulls away, you're open for business again."

"That's great news. I'm dying of boredom and loneliness out here. Tell me the truth, Cynthia, this much attention can't be about a robbery of a small place of business like mine. What's really going on here?"

"Unfortunately, Clyde, this is an ongoing investigation and I can't tell you much more. For now, let's just leave it at that, with us trying to figure out who robbed your wolf skull. I appreciate your cooperation and will be in touch about returning the skeleton."

Clyde had to satisfy himself with her response. After locating a box large enough to contain the skeleton, he helped her out to the van. Watching her pull away, he turned around the sign on the front door from "Closed" to "Open."

He pulled a root beer out of the small fridge and sat down on a rickety folding chair. He smiled as he thought of Amanda Banks as a child, drinking her root beer and sitting in the same chair.

Cynthia had a smile on her face as well. The crime lab would certainly find fingerprints from multiple sources, most likely from Clyde and from customers who touched various surfaces in the store. Possibly, there might also be fingerprints from the person who stole the wolf skull.

More importantly, she expected that the blood sample from the skeleton would be from a single individual. That DNA would identify one person - the Dead of Night killer.

That was her hope.

CHAPTER 87

After winning the chess tournament, the four pranksters waited for school to open on Monday morning. The student athletes comprised the largest portion of their tormentors throughout their high school years. The two gym teachers did nothing to stop the bullying they endured. By remaining silent and looking away, they were complicit in the emotional damage caused to these four young people. Considering their actions as payback, the chess players targeted only the gym teachers who could have put a stop to the merciless teasing and taunting. The team never could have imagined the collateral damage that was about to unfold.

****

The four handled the wait for Monday differently, with guilt, confidence, indifference, and eagerness describing how they individually spent the remainder of the weekend after the tournament.

Jaclyn, a former "goody two shoes," was plagued with guilt over what she and her chess team conspirators left in the gym teachers' desk drawers. Only hours after their dirty deed, Jaclyn phoned Elliot. He tried to allay her fears.

"Jaclyn, chill out. You're overreacting. Remember, Charlie had Ronald leave the window open in Mr. Howell's office. It will look like a break-in. No way they'll connect us to what they'll find. You'll see."

Elliot believed the reassurances he gave to Jaclyn. He slept soundly the entire weekend. If anything, he was eager to see the reaction to their prank.

Ronald focused on a new computer app that he was developing. He put their activities in the gym behind him. He lost no sleep worrying about what might happen when school reopened.

All weekend, Charlie Post had been imagining the startled looks on the faces of the teachers, Todd Howell and Jane Cosby, when they opened the drawers in their desks Monday morning. He wished he could have set up cameras in their offices.

****

Early on Monday, Charlie drove to the Krispy Kreme Donut Shop across from Miami Senior High. From a table at the window he could observe the happenings at the school.

He arrived just in time to see students and faculty as they streamed out of the building. Then the police arrived. With the arrival of law enforcement, teachers and students huddled together, trying to make sense of the evacuation.

Seeing the police, Charlie realized that the consequences of their prank had become serious, beyond what he and his friends had foreseen. The donut Charlie was enjoying just moments before was now making him nauseated. He tossed it in the garbage.

****

Unaware of what was happening inside the school, Charlie could only speculate. The one certainty was that the gym teachers found the "gifts" that the chess team left for them.

When Todd Howell, the male gym teacher, entered his office he noticed his window was in the open position. That alerted him to a potential problem. After examining the top of his desk and his electronic equipment and finding nothing amiss, he began opening drawers in his desk.

Curled into a ball was a snake, sitting on top of some office supplies. He hoped that it was rubber, a silly prank. When it moved, Howell realized that it was alive and possibly venomous. Slamming the drawer shut, he immediately headed to Jane Cosby's office. She hadn't arrived yet, but Howell decided to check her desk as well. In the female gym teacher's desk Todd located a similar serpent in one of her drawers. After shutting the drawer and locking the doors to both offices, Todd headed to Principal Lowell Towney's office to inform him of what happened over the weekend. They paged Jane to warn her to not enter her office.

Towney, a decisive man, considered student safety his preeminent function. To clear the building, Towney pulled the fire alarm. Teachers immediately organized their students to vacate the school. Towney was taking no chances that other potentially dangerous animals could be within the building in other offices or classrooms. He then called the police to investigate a possible act of vandalism. Or worse. When he contacted animal control, he alerted them about the snakes. In addition to removing them, he requested that they sweep the building to possibly locate other uninvited reptiles.

Todd Howell provided an additional helpful suggestion. He volunteered to call his friend, Adam Crowe from the Miami Metro Zoo, to assess the threat that the snakes presented.

****

From the donut shop Charlie continued to observe the pandemonium outside the school. When teachers noticed the police presence, they herded students toward the bleachers in the football stadium. More police squad cars sped into the parking lot, sirens blaring and lights flashing. The next arrival at the school was a large van identified as belonging to Miami-Dade Animal Control Services. A half dozen uniformed employees exited the vehicle, carrying cages, poles, nets, and bags of various sizes. They congregated together in the parking lot with their equipment. No sooner had they unloaded their implements when they heard tires screeching as a small van with Miami Metro Zoo identification barreled into the parking lot and abruptly braked. Charlie recognized the occupant from his multiple television interviews. It was Adam Crowe from the Miami Metro Zoo. At first, Charlie experienced a perverse sense of pleasure witnessing the school's evacuation. But now, seeing all the agencies called to the high school, he was becoming increasingly anxious.

****

Jaclyn, Elliot, and Ronald, Charlie's co-conspirators, found out shortly that their little prank unexpectedly blossomed into a major news event. Jaclyn had been watching reruns of old episodes of "The Big Bang Theory" when her show was interrupted with local breaking news. Scenes of students outside Miami Senior High School, police cars, a van from animal control, and a van from the Metro Zoo filled the television screen. Panicked, she sent a group text to Elliot, Ronald, and Charlie, telling them to tune into WPLG Local 10 news.

Elliot and Ronald seemed unconcerned. They tried to calm her down by replying that nothing could be traced back to them. At least, that was their hope.

Charlie surprised them all with his response to the text, "I'm sitting at a table at Krispy Kreme across from the school. I have a bird's-eye view of all the excitement. It's bedlam out there. I was just about to let you know. I'll call you all back in a second."

The four connected via a conference call. Charlie reported his observations from his vantage point across the street. His version included some additional editorializing.

"The police haven't entered the building yet. Looks like they're conferencing about their next steps. Two cops on the perimeter are examining the window we left open. I think we're safe. They'll think it was a break-in. The animal control people are still outside talking with Adam Crowe from the Metro Zoo. Seems like he's giving them instructions," Charlie said, sounding relatively calm.

Wait, now everyone's on the move. Oh, crap!" Charlie uttered. "They're heading to the front door. They're going in."

CHAPTER 88

When Adam Crowe and the staff from animal control entered the high school, they were directed to the gymnasium and Todd Howell's office. Like a popular Broadway show, it was standing room only, with people lining the walls. With the newest arrivals the office now held Todd Howell, Principal Towney, four police officers, the six employees from animal control, and Adan Crowe. The window to the office was in the open position, exactly as Howell found it when he arrived that morning.

"Principal Towney, with your permission," Crowe suggested, "I'd like to ask everyone to step outside the office except two animal control people so we can have the office to ourselves. Let's have the other four from animal control search the school, room by room, to check for other unwanted visitors, if that's okay with you."

Towney and the others were happy to oblige, less than eager to be up close and personal with a snake. Pointing to the two closest employees from animal control, Crowe ordered, "You two, with me. What are your names?"

After identifying themselves as Jennifer and Chad, they remained in Howell's office with Crowe. Donning thick suede protective gloves, Crowe opened the drawer slowly. Peering inside, he saw a snake coiled in a ball, out of place among various office supplies. He reached in and pulled out the multicolored snake with tan, brown, black, and white markings. While holding it behind its head, Crowe inspected it further. Prepared for Crowe to place the snake into a bag, Jennifer quickly stretched the opening of a bag she was holding, expecting him to deposit it inside. Instead, as she and Chad looked on, Crowe deftly placed the snake around his neck. She and Chad gasped in horror; Dr. Crowe was enjoying their startled reaction.

"Don't worry, it's a ball python, also known as the royal python or Python regius. It's a non-venomous snake, native to Africa. Here are some interesting facts about out little friend for your edification. They've been called royal pythons because legends tell of African royalty wearing live ball pythons as adornments. In fact, it's said that Cleopatra wore them as jewelry, a living necklace, if you will. The name ball python refers to a defense mechanism exhibited by this species. A timid creature, when frightened it's capable of coiling its body into a ball and rolling away. Ball pythons are harmless and make popular pets for snake aficionados. They're sold at some pet stores in Florida."

Jennifer and Chad followed Crowe out of Howell's office, the ball python still coiled around Crowe's neck. The principal, observing the wildlife expert, commented, "From seeing that creature wrapped around your neck, I assume that it's not venomous. So, we're safe. Is that correct?"

"Let's look into Ms. Cosby's desk before I confirm that," Crowe responded. "If the snake in her desk is a ball python like this one, it's harmless." Despite Crowe's description of the snake as 'harmless,' there wasn't one other person present who would have draped a snake around their neck with such a lack of concern.

The entourage of astounded law enforcement personnel, Principal Towney, Jennifer and Chad from animal control, and the two gym teachers followed Crowe to Jane Cosby's office. Jane was glad she was running late that morning and wasn't alone in her office to find the snake. The findings were much the same. A snake with similar markings, looking like a thick crocheted decorative pot holder, rested in the top drawer. One of the policemen noted that the only difference between the two offices was that Cosby's window was closed. He surmised that the vandal hadn't gained entrance to her office through the window.

Withdrawing two sacks from one of his jacket pockets, Crowe first placed the snake from Jane Cosby's desk into one of them. Next, he carefully uncoiled the snake from around his neck, depositing it into the second sack.

"If no one minds, I'll be leaving with these. We'll give them a good home at the zoo. I was in the middle of a meeting and I need to get back. When animal control finishes their search of the entire premises and school grounds, they can call me if they locate any additional snakes, other reptiles, or questionable wildlife. I'd appreciate their photographing additional critters they turn up and text them to my mobile phone. If necessary, I can return to consult with them if they have any serious concerns."

After providing his cell number, Crowe departed. The law enforcement officers and the animal control personnel remained behind to continue their respective investigations. A thorough search could take hours. Principal Towney sent teachers and students home.

****

At the donut shop, Charlie was getting antsy. He observed Adam's Crowe's departure, the only activity outside the school he witnessed in over an hour. Crowe carried two cloth sacks which Charlie correctly assumed were the two snakes they placed in the gym teachers' desks. He worried about arousing the suspicion of the employees at Krispy Kreme; he had lingered over his coffee an inordinate amount of time. Out of guilt, he headed to the counter and ordered a large iced coffee. That should give him reason to continue to occupy his table.

His nerves on edge, Charlie needed to change his environment. All the caffeine was taking its toll. Charlie called

Ronald Martella. "Hey, Ron, it's Charlie. I'm still at Krispy Kreme driving myself crazy. Can you get down here ASAP and replace me? I've been here so long that I'm worried they'll think I'm loitering."

Not terribly happy about Charlie's request, Ronald realized they needed to get a head's up about the developing situation at the school. Ronald appeared at the shop, ordering a cream-filled donut and decaf coffee. He decided to forego the caffeine; his nerves were jittery enough. While Ronald placed his order, Charlie departed, neither party showing any sign of recognition of the other.

Thinking ahead, Ronald brought the morning paper and his laptop computer, both signals that he'd be camped out at his table for more time than the usual customer. From his seat by the front window, he had an excellent view of what was happening outside the school building. Like Charlie, he could only speculate about whatever was taking place on the inside.

During Ronald's watch, he observed an officer outside Todd Howell's office dusting for fingerprints on the exterior of the window and carefully examining the grass below, hoping for footprints under the window. Unfortunately for the police, it rained Sunday afternoon and no footprints were found. Nor did they find cigarette butts, soda cans, candy wrappers, or other tangible evidence that could have helped identify the intruder. Since he was the one to open the window from the *inside,* he knew that the police wouldn't find his fingerprints on the outside of the glass or his footprints in the grass, even without the rain.

The fact that the police seemed to be focusing on the window gave Ronald hope that they might escape unscathed. Surely, law enforcement would think it was a break-in from outside; he had been careful to wipe down his fingerprints when he was in Todd Howell's office Saturday morning.

****

Inside the school the police developed a theory. The current thought was that, sometime between school closing on Friday afternoon and reopening early Monday morning, someone entered the school through the opened window and planted the ball python in Mr. Howell's desk. Once inside, the same person then placed a snake in Jane Cosby's desk as well. After targeting these two teachers, the perpetrator exited the premises through the window from which he entered.

Concentrating on the offices of the two gym teachers, the police thoroughly dusted all surfaces for fingerprints. They printed the two teachers as well as the secretarial staff and other personnel who normally accessed their offices; that way they could eliminate their prints from those of outsiders who weren't employees of the school. If need be, students could be fingerprinted at a later time. Their job at the school completed, the police departed.

Once the police left the scene, Ronald saw no need for him to remain at the donut shop. If none of his group had fingerprints on file with the police, the consensus was that the open window deception would save the pranksters.

Gathering his newspaper and laptop, he exited the Krispy Kreme shop thinking that at least for now the chess nerds were in the clear.

CHAPTER 89

Dr. Philip Demarco, director of the Miami-Dade Crime Lab, anxiously awaited Cynthia Kravitz's arrival with the evidence she collected from Clyde's Place. Weeks earlier, Demarco was furious about being bypassed when Dr. Murphy, the Medical Examiner for Miami, sent DNA evidence from the cadavers of the Dead of Night victims to his crony, Dr. Donald Pinkney, in Tallahassee.

The crimes were committed in Miami-Dade County, Demarco's jurisdiction. As a matter of pride, he wanted *his* laboratory to be instrumental in solving this high-profile case. He had great confidence in his team.

Demarco gave Roberto Flores the assignment of analyzing the DNA from the blood samples obtained from the wolf skeleton. Flores, who formerly worked with the FBI crime lab, was highly respected in his field.

Ruth Maglione, a fixture in Demarco's department, was assigned to process fingerprints from the skeleton. Other than Demarco, she had the most seniority in the department. A grandmotherly-type, Ruth's gray hair worn in a bun and her granny glasses belied her sharp intellect and impressive technical skills. Her job would be a herculean task.

From what she was told, the wolf skeleton had been on display for years at Clyde's Place. Even if he discouraged handling it, Clyde couldn't have prevented all curious customers from touching it to verify whether it was plastic or an actual skeleton. Working from the police theory that the Dead of Night killer removed the skull from the skeleton, the killer's prints should be retrievable. However, they would be found amidst prints of all the innocent visitors to the shop who also touched the display.

As Ruth prepared her tools, the overworked fingerprint analyst attempted to dismiss potential problems from her thoughts without much success. What if the killer's prints might not be in any law enforcement data base? What if the killer wore gloves?

Fortunately, Cynthia Kravitz from CSU had the forethought to have taken prints along with a DNA sample from Clyde Haney. At least Maglione would be able to exclude Clyde's prints. Regarding gloves, hopefully it wouldn't be an issue.

****

Ruth Maglione performed a meticulous examination of the skeleton, retrieving fingerprints from all sites. After the retrieval of the prints, she utilized AFIS, the Automated Fingerprint Identification System, to try to identify them, hoping for a hit. In a secondary search, she then checked into the FBI fingerprint database, known as IAFIS, or Integrated Automated Fingerprint Identification System, which also includes the criminal history of the individuals with fingerprints in its files.

Sergeant Emilio Hernandez sent prints to Ruth from Hoyt Stark, Iggy, Rollo, as well as a water bottle Pete Ward was drinking from during questioning. There were no matches.

Out of ideas, and disappointed by the time expended with no fruitful outcome, Ruth had no choice but to report to Demarco.

"I suspect you have some news for me," said her boss.

"Well, the only fingerprints I got from the skeleton that I could positively identify belong to Clyde Haney, the taxidermist. No surprise there, since it's his skeleton."

"What was the problem?"

"There were multiple prints. Despite a painstaking search of AFIS and IAFIS, I couldn't match any to law enforcement data bases. None of the suspects that Sargent Hernandez was interested in left any prints either," Ruth explained.

"The best that I could do was catalog them and hope that by a stroke of luck, they'll show up again elsewhere. Then perhaps we can make an identification. I'm really sorry, Phil, that I don't have better news."

"Not your fault, Ruth. The science is the science. Hopefully, Flores will succeed with a DNA match from the blood sample."

****

Roberto Flores began processing the blood left on the cervical spine of the wolf specimen. The sample was sufficient for testing, but the results of DNA testing would not be immediate.

Pressure from the top contributed to Demarco's pacing back and forth in front of Roberto's work area. Chief Alberto Santiago was feeling mounting pressure from the police commissioner and the mayor. He subsequently passed the pressure down the chain of command to all those working on the Dead of Night murders.

Wanting a status report from all departments, Santiago scheduled a meeting for the following morning at 9:00 a.m. at police headquarters.

As director of the Miami-Dade crime lab, Philip Demarco was instructed that his attendance at the meeting was mandatory. He wasn't looking forward to being in the hot seat.

CHAPTER 90

Chief Santiago chose the briefing room as the meeting location due to the size of the group: law enforcement people, political figures, forensic specialists, medical experts, investigators, and ancillary personnel. I was included as part of the illustrious group. The purpose of the meeting was to bring everyone up to speed and to brainstorm ways to apprehend the Dead of Night killer.

As the organizer of the meeting, Chief Santiago approached the podium, eyeballing the assembled group. Standing at the back of the room, Police Commissioner Inez Vargas had her arms crossed over her chest. Her body language didn't bode well, nor did the frown and stern expression on her face. Mayor Robert Diaz, standing close to the commissioner, seemed only slightly more relaxed as he sipped from his Starbuck's cup.

Over the years Santiago had become somewhat of an expert at reading people's state of mind. Philip Demarco, director of the crime lab, appeared nervous, repeatedly glancing at the door. Having taken an end seat nearest the exit, he looked prepared to make a hasty departure.

Sergeant Emilio Hernandez sat with detectives Brad Mandich and Lew Dennison, lead detectives on the case. My uncle Brad looked at his watch several times, as if he had more important things to do than attend this meeting. Not far from the sergeant and the two detectives, I was seated next to detective Amanda Banks. I was honored to have been invited to attend the high-level meeting. Amanda sat with her pen poised over her notepad, prepared to jot down important information.

In the farthest corner of the room, Cecil Murphy, the medical examiner, chose to sit alone. With his face down, he made no eye contact with any of the other attendees. When Chief Santiago spotted him, Murphy looked away. He didn't want to be noticed or called upon.

Clearing his throat to get everyone's attention, Santiago began a gloomy recitation of the state of our city.

"Excuse me if I dispense with the niceties. Let's get right to the purpose of our gathering. The Dead of Night murders have terrorized residents of Miami and have frightened people throughout the country and around the world concerning our fair city. Of course, our main concern is to arrest the killer and prevent further deaths in our community. However, the economic impact is also devastating. Snowbirds have been cancelling hotel reservations left and right. Several European countries have warned their citizens to avoid traveling to Miami. I don't need to tell you that tourism has taken a hit we can't afford. There are rumors circulating that the National Football League may call an emergency meeting to discuss changing the venue of the upcoming Super Bowl. Am I getting through to you? Do your jobs!"

Santiago's picture summarized the past weeks of the dire situation in Miami. He had everyone's attention.

"Some of you are familiar with all the details, but some are not. Let's get everyone on the same page. Most of the local victims have been young people with active lifestyles, mostly in their twenties. The out-of-town victims, a couple from New Jersey, and an attorney from Dallas, have been older. We're not sure what that means. Upon questioning, people who reside near the site of the murders often report a howling sound that they believe is from a creature of some sort. To make things even stranger, most of the victims appear to have been bitten or mauled and are missing their abdominal organs. Recently, with the help of wildlife expert Adam Crowe, we determined that the bite marks were made with *the skull of a wolf*. Let me repeat that. The bite marks were made with the *skull of a wolf;* the victims were not bitten by a live wolf."

That piece of information was new to many of the attendees of the meeting. Santiago continued.

"The young victims who lived locally and attorney Hamilton Davies were paralyzed with curare. Just imagine their terror. They were awake when they were cut open. The New Jersey couple endured a more merciful death. A large animal tranquilizer rendered them unconscious before their attacker carried out his mutilation. Nevertheless, because of the teeth marks, I am convinced that we are dealing now with only *one* killer; for some reason did not want the tourists to suffer."

Everyone was squirming in their seats.

Chief Santiago went on. "At least we have our copycat killer behind bars. Hoyt Stark was never the brightest bulb. Although his victims' stomachs were opened, Shannon Stark and Sam McKay were never sedated or bitten."

Santiago's eyes pierced Philip Demarco like a skewer piercing shish kebab. "I understand that your lab recently received fingerprint, blood, and DNA evidence, Dr. Demarco. What can you tell us?" demanded Chief Santiago.

The crime lab director knew his response wouldn't be well-received. "We have no fingerprint matches, other than the prints of the owner of the shop, Clyde Haney. My DNA analyst has been working with the blood from the wolf skeleton from which the skull was removed. Our best guess is that the person who stole the skull cut himself in the process. We postulate that the blood sample we're testing belongs to the killer. Unfortunately, I can't provide you with anything confirmation today. The DNA results aren't completed yet."

"Not what I was looking for," Santiago said as he looked around the room. "Anyone here with something *valuable* to add?"

"What happened with the fabric samples that you gave the Haitian Voodoo Priestess? Was she any help?" asked Inez Vargas.

"Don't you think she'd be here if she had anything? Total waste of our time. The woman's a complete fake, considering she's *not* Haitian, *not* a Voodoo Priestess, uses an alias, and has a record for fraudulent check writing. Seems like she wanted to advertise on her website that she was a police consultant, promoting herself for her psychic skills to boost her online sales. She was using us. As far as I'm concerned, she's persona non grata," Santiago snapped.

"Until this bastard is caught all police personnel in this room will meet here daily at six a.m. That includes weekends. I expect you to think outside the box and come up with some fresh ideas. We need results, people, not excuses. That's it. Get back to work."

The audience remained silent, not wanting to contribute further to Santiago's ire. The mayor and police commissioner stormed out. Knowing that they'd be waiting for him as a hostile reception committee, Santiago took his time walking back to his office. He expected a reprimand, but not an ultimatum.

Holding nothing back, they laced into him for his handling of the Dead of Night case. They threw his words back at him.

"Results, Santiago, not excuses!"

There was no question that the chief's reputation and any future promotions were on the line.

CHAPTER 91

I left police headquarters after attending the morning meeting with all the bigwigs involved in the DON murder case. After the palpable tension in the meeting room, returning to my office seemed relaxing. I didn't envy the people whose presence was mandated daily at six o'clock in the morning until the killer was caught.

Lauren and her business partner Eve were attending a conference in Las Vegas. During their absence I was enlisted to babysit Eve's finicky canine, Teacup. Although I never considered myself a "dog person," I somehow bonded with Teacup and enjoyed my evening walk with the miniature yorkie. It was a beautiful time of day. The sun was setting, and a temperate breeze was blowing. The tranquility was restorative.

It didn't take long for that to change. My phone rang, the ring tone alerting me to my uncle's call.

"Hi, Uncle Brad. Didn't get enough of me today? What's up?"

Without any preamble, Brad gave me an order as if I were one of his underlings. "Get yourself over to Miami Senior High. Meet me at the football field."

"Whoa! No explanation? What's going on?"

"You need to see it to believe it."

Brad disconnected the call before I could ask further questions.

With no choice but to take the dog with me to save time, I picked her up and did my best to strap my companion and her wicker basket into the doggy car seat mounted in the rear. She didn't stop barking as I fidgeted with the straps and the car seat.

However, as soon as I turned the radio station to country music, Teacup ceased her yapping.

Dusk turned to darkness by the time I arrived at the high school. Parking the car in the lot adjacent to the football stadium, I could see that the action was clearly at the center of the field. Multiple law enforcement officers were shining flashlights at the ground.

After I unstrapped Teacup, leaving her in her cushioned basket, I carried her toward the commotion on the field. Initially, Teacup was calm, but as we approached the scene, Teacup became agitated. She yelped, jumped from her basket, and ran back toward my car. I chased after her. Reaching the rear door, she clawed at it as if asking to be let in. Following her lead, I opened the door and watched the tiny ball of fur throw her body into the doggy car seat, trembling uncontrollably. She didn't even wait for me to place her basket inside. Clearly, Teacup was fearful of something she sensed as we were approaching the center of the field. I had no time to play dog psychologist, so I cracked open a car window for her. I headed to the fifty-yard line where the commotion was ongoing.

Squeezing through the two young police officers as well as my uncle and Lew Dennison, I peered at the ground, startled by the scene; what I saw appeared to be some type of performance art awaiting an audience.

A scarecrow stuffed with straw lay on the ground, dressed in a Miami Senior High football uniform. There was a large gash and gaping hole in the abdominal area. When I leaned down to get a closer look, I detected a powerful odor of urine. No doubt, Teacup, had a more sensitive olfactory sense; evidently, she smelled the urine at a much greater distance.

I yelled out to my uncle, "Uncle Brad, call Adam Crowe and get him out here. Let him know it's an emergency. I'll be right back. I'm just getting something from my car."

One of my most strongly held credos is that "timing is everything in life." Today further confirmed that belief. Earlier that afternoon, I was asked to see a consult for a patient at Jackson Memorial. To diagnose his condition, I brought a handheld Wood's lamp, often called a "black light." It helps diagnose certain fungal infections that fluoresce. After my visit to the hospital, I didn't bring the lamp back to the office. It was still in my trunk. That's what I mean by timing.

The same lamp is used in crime scene investigations, after spraying the site, often with Luminol, to check for body fluids. Truthfully, I watch way too many crime shows that deal with forensics and medicine. And if you ask my wife and my uncle, they'll confirm that I get a kick out of thinking of myself as an amateur sleuth.

I retrieved the lamp from the car. Turning on the battery-operated Wood's lamp, I pointed it downward and circled the body on the ground. When I focused on the areas where the odor seemed most intense, I noticed something peculiar; a fluorescent pink glow encircled the body. Not that I had any idea what I was expecting from my use of the lamp, but *this* wasn't it.

When I looked up, Adam Crowe was peering over my shoulder, with my uncle and Lew flanking him. Crowe heard earlier about the activity on the field and had arrived in the school's parking lot when my uncle called him.

"That's pretty cool, Doc. The way the urine encompasses the body appears to be the way an animal marks its territory," Crowe explained. "What's causing the pink glow?"

"I'm not one hundred percent sure. By the way, do you notice a strong smell of urine?"

"Sure do. It's wolf urine," Crowe replied. "However, a wolf didn't place a scarecrow in a high school football uniform in the center of a football field. Whoever did this likely purchased dried wolf urine on the internet. Many South Floridians spread it around the perimeter of their pools to scare away pests like raccoons."

"Wolf urine? Makes sense. That's what must have spooked the yorkie that I brought with me. The closer Teacup got, the more agitated she became. Only thing that bothers me is that urine from a wolf or a person shouldn't fluoresce with my Wood's light, unless......"

"Unless what?" My uncle interrupted.

"Unless the person who did this has porphyria, a metabolic disorder that exhibits distinctive skin manifestations. Many believe this condition is the origin of the vampire and werewolf legends. Like vampires and werewolves, people with this disease have severe light sensitivity. I've used a Wood's lamp as a diagnostic tool to test urine when I suspect porphyria. The urine exhibits a pink fluorescence just like this," I explained.

"So, you're saying that there's wolf urine *and* human urine from someone with porphyria around the mock character in football attire? Why would the person leave his own urine sample?" Lew asked.

"The scarecrow is symbolic of the killer's victims. I guess what he did is an act of revenge and humiliation. Urinating on a victim disgraces that victim even further."

An anonymous phone call, probably placed by the Dead of Night killer, alerted the police to investigate what was described as "a brutal murder" on the football field. Most likely he arranged the staged scene a short time earlier, after the school grounds were vacated for the day.

"We better find this psycho. And fast. Lauren's returning from Vegas in a few hours. Her ten-year reunion begins in earnest tomorrow morning with a volleyball game at the beach, followed by a dinner in the evening. I don't mean to be an alarmist, but I'm uneasy, especially because this simulation is on school grounds. The way I see it, this reenactment of the previous murders is a warning."

CHAPTER 92

Lauren's flight home arrived at Miami International Airport on time at 10:55 p.m. Ordinarily, I would have questioned her about her convention when I picked her up, but I was anxious to fill her in on what had been going on during her absence. I described the meeting at police headquarters as well as the alarming scene at the football stadium only hours before. She couldn't help but notice that I was keyed up, fearful of the reunion activities and what might transpire at them. The traditional beach volleyball game pitting current high school seniors against returning alumni from Miami Senior High was scheduled for the following morning at ten o'clock at Crandon Park Beach.

****

Neither of us slept well that night. That was unusual after being apart for several days. Lauren was anxious about the reunion going as planned; I was anxious about Lauren's safety. As an organizer of the volleyball game, Lauren wanted to arrive at Crandon Park early. To save time, we munched on granola bars and sipped our coffee from Styrofoam cups in the car.

The ride out to Key Biscayne lulled us into a false sense of security. As we drove on the Rickenbacker Causeway, we observed people getting an early start in the morning as they unpacked their car trunks, preparing for a day of picnicking, swimming, fishing, and relaxing. Sailboats were already out on the sparkling water of Biscayne Bay. After crossing the Rickenbacker Bridge, we passed the Miami Seaquarium, its multifaceted roof glistening in the sunlight. Although we're Florida residents, we continue to appreciate the beauty of where we live. Nothing from this scenic drive suggested the horror that was to transpire within the next hour.

We arrived at the designated site for the beach volleyball game with plenty of time to spare. My organized wife confirmed that the volleyball net had been planted in place and the court playing field marked in the sand. Participants and spectators were beginning to arrive, many toting coolers.

"So far, so good," Lauren commented. "I was worried that the news of the Dead of Night killer would have caused us to cancel the reunion. Looks like we're a motivated group."

By ten o'clock, team participants and fans of the senior class and the ten-year alumni mobbed the area. Lauren estimated a crowd of close to two-hundred people, an impressive number considering the negative publicity during the prior month. Lauren pointed out the arrival of the chess team, happy that they came to support the alumni athletes. Secure in the belief that they outsmarted the police regarding the pythons and break-in incident at the high school, the chess team staked out an area in the sand under an umbrella one of them carried.

I was happy to see my uncle Brad and his partner Lew. They thought their presence was advisable after I reminded them that several of the first victims had been athletes from the alumni class.

****

Lauren announced the rules of the game to the participants who had already assembled on the sand. Despite the ten-year age difference, players from both teams took the game seriously and exhibited a similar degree of athleticism. In an almost reckless disregard for the health and safety of their own bodies, the players repeatedly spiked the ball as their opponents threw themselves onto the sand to make a save. Joey Bell, one of the high school students, dove to his left to prevent a ball from landing on the back corner of the makeshift court. His chest landed on something hard that was hidden in the shallow portion of the sand. Dislodging the sand to see what he landed on, he screamed and leapt up in horror.

Joey had just uncovered a human head.

CHAPTER 93

Recoiling in fear, Joey Bell looked down one more time before retreating, running backwards, and tripping over a beach chair. He recognized the head. It belonged to one of his teachers.

The other players couldn't see what Joey found. Anxious to resume the game, they yelled to him, "Let's go, Joey. Shake a leg."

Barely able to process what he saw, Joey vomited. After wiping his mouth, he shouted, "It's Mr. Howell. He's dead."

The crowd instinctively pulled back from the volleyball court, everyone talking at once. Like rubberneckers slowing down to witness a traffic accident, they remained close enough to ogle the gruesome sight. While shouting above the din, Brad instructed Lew to summon CSU. He quickly drew a circle in the sand establishing a crime scene perimeter, advising the onlookers to stay clear of the circumscribed area.

As he brushed away sand covering the head, Brad took a closer look; the head was still attached to the body which was buried within a deeper layer of sand. The colorless corpse indicated to Brad that the blood had drained from the victim, yet no blood appeared in the surrounding sand. About to order everyone to clear the area, Brad remembered the adage that the criminal "always returns to the scene of the crime." He'd wait until he had the chance to observe the onlookers before taking that step.

I was doing my own scan of the crowd. Everything came together in that moment.

I could identify the person who killed Mr. Howell.

I recognized the Dead of Night killer.

CHAPTER 94

What I hadn't been able to connect earlier now materialized like an oasis in a desert; my identification of the killer was as sudden as it was welcome. I headed to the victim and his sandy grave. Excited, I pulled my uncle close and whispered in his ear.

"Take a look at the guy over there with the sunglasses, sun shirt, and broad-brimmed hat. The one carrying an umbrella. Not only did he kill Todd Howell, but he's the Dead of Night killer," I declared authoritatively. "He's the guy," I insisted.

"What makes you sure *he's* the killer? That's quite the accusation. Was he acting suspicious?"

"No," I admitted. "However, I got a glimpse of his face a moment ago when a gust of wind blew off his hat. When he chased it down, I noticed excessive hair growth. Also, I thought I saw some scarring on his forehead, but I need a closer look. I think I've seen him before, but only at a distance."

"When was that?" asked Brad.

"I think he's one of the alumni chess players who competed against the current seniors. By the way he was dressed at the tournament, I thought he had a cold. So, I erred on the side of caution and suggested to Lauren that we sit in the back of the room away from him. His choice of clothing for the beach today makes me think he's the same guy. I've got a hunch that there's a medical component to why he's all covered up. If I can get close to him, I'll know for sure."

"Cliff, I hope I'm not going to regret this, but I'll give you the benefit of the doubt. Can you at least give me probable cause? I need some reason to detain this guy."

"What do you mean?" I asked.

"Since I don't have an arrest warrant for him, I need probable cause."

Repeating the identical words didn't make Brad's statement any more explicit to me. "English, please, Uncle Brad."

"There needs to be a high probability that he's *been* involved in or *will be* involved in some sort of criminal activity in order for me to detain or arrest him."

I felt as if I were on safe ground. "Uncle Brad, it just so happens that I can help you there. Remember last night when we saw that the urine at the athletic field glowed pink? I suspected that it came from a person with porphyria cutanea tarda (PCT). The guy I pointed out to you has excessive hair growth typical of porphyria. I'd like to check his face for scarring, another indicator of this condition. If he has porphyria, he was probably the one who orchestrated the scene at the football field last night. It seems more than coincidental that he's also at this crime scene. Is that enough for probable cause?"

"It works for me," Brad said. "Let's get him."

My uncle approached the man as I followed behind. He began to walk away but froze in place when Brad flashed his credentials and yelled for him to stop. He appeared too frightened to move.

"We've got a few questions for you. What's your name?"

"My name is Elliot Cook, officer."

"Just for the record, it's "detective." Mr. Cook, please remove your hat for me."

Begrudgingly, Cook yanked the hat off his head. At close range, the scarring and unusual hair growth were quite noticeable.

"Where did you get those scars?" I asked.

"I had acne as a teenager," he explained.

My eyes were then drawn to the suspect's hands.

"What's with the driving gloves?" I asked him.

"Just a fashion accessory," he answered without hesitation. It seemed as if he had been asked similar questions repeatedly. His answers seemed credible and were probably rehearsed.

Understanding the reason behind my question, my uncle ordered him to remove the gloves.

What I noticed was exactly what I expected. "You exhibit the manifestations of a severe sun sensitivity. That explains why you're all covered up, even at the beach, just like you were at the chess tournament," I stated. "The backs of your hands are scarred because of this sensitivity. As a dermatologist, I'm familiar with your medical condition. I'm sure it's no surprise to you that you have porphyria cutanea tarda," I said with authority.

My uncle became tired of the medical evaluation. Eager to bring Cook to the police station for questioning, he said, "Sorry, Mr. Cook, but as your bad luck would have it, we're looking for someone with *that* condition."

Dumbfounded, Elliot Cook remained silent. Since it seemed that an arrest was likely, Brad read him his Miranda rights. Given permission to make a call, Elliot phoned his parents who said they would contact an attorney and meet their son at police headquarters.

Brad secured Cook in the back of the squad car. I rode shotgun in the front, next to my uncle. Once Elliot placed the call to his parents, he became combative, shouting threats that Brad was all too accustomed to hearing from suspects.

"I'll have your badge, detective. You've got nothing on me."

“Your best bet is to remain quiet,” suggested Brad in response. “Remember the Miranda warning. You might not want to say too much,” Brad admonished.

Elliot Cook decided to take the advice.

CHAPTER 95

Before the official interview with Elliot Cook, my uncle wanted to hear my reasons for declaring that not only had Cook killed Todd Howell, but he that he was also the Dead of Night killer. Although he trusted my instincts, part of him was uneasy; Brad needed reassurance that I wasn't just blowing smoke. His reputation was at risk,

"Okay, Cliff. What do you know that I don't? I hope this isn't going to backfire on me."

"It all came together for me only minutes after Howell's body was uncovered. Last night when I mentioned the connection between urine turning pink under black light and porphyria, I didn't have anyone in mind with that condition. When I spotted the chess team on the beach seated under a large umbrella, I became curious about Cook. He was the only person dressed so protectively in long sleeves, long pants, a hat covering a good portion of his face, and those gloves I asked about.

"Then I remembered that most of Elliot Cook's body was similarly covered at the chess match Lauren and I attended last week. When I asked Lauren if he dressed the same way in high school, she recalled that he did. She mentioned that other students, especially the athletes, teased him mercilessly and called him 'Wolfman' because of the unusual hair growth on his face. She expressed disappointment with the gym teachers who ignored Cook's predicament."

"What was it today that made you put it all together?" Brad asked. "What's different now?"

"I guess I began thinking about porphyria last night at the football field. Seeing the way Elliot was dressed today made me suspect his sun sensitivity. Gloves would cover blisters and scarring that often appear on the backs of the hands. A large hat would hide facial scarring and excessive hair growth in abnormal areas on the face. When his hat blew off, I verified that he did, in fact, have the hair growth associated with PCT. At closer range, I confirmed the scarring on his face when you had him remove his hat. All the physical manifestations were there," I explained.

"Everything just fell into place. If you consider Cook's mindset, it all makes sense: porphyria, suffering intense bullying, being taunted as 'Wolfman.' Lauren's recollection of how he was treated in high school provides a strong motive to carry out a vendetta against those who were cruelest to him. If you remember, the earliest victims of the Dead of Night killer were athletes. They were all from Cook's graduating class."

My uncle was listening attentively, sporadically asking questions or making comments. "Do you think that being called 'Wolfman' influenced him to kill his victims the way a wolf would kill its prey?"

"Exactly what I'm thinking, Uncle Brad. Mimicking the mannerisms of a wolf must have given him a degree of perverse pleasure after being taunted with the derogatory nickname. For him, it must have been a very satisfying method of killing. Cook used a paralytic agent on the athletes who offended him. Unable to move, they were conscious when he opened their abdomens and removed their internal organs. I have to believe that he relished their suffering. To maintain the wolf pretense, I suspect Cook obtained dried wolf urine and placed it around the bodies like a wolf marking its territory. Seems that he gave considerable thought to the wolf pretense."

I had my uncle's full attention, so I continued with my theory.

"According to Lauren, Elliot was reclusive, with few friends beyond the chess team. He studied the grandmasters. His proficiency at chess was apparent at the chess tournament. Cook seemed to be able to predict the plays of his opponents and the outcome of the game from just a few moves. I think that his study of chess strategy served him well in planning and executing the killings, Uncle Brad."

"You make a good case, Cliff, especially regarding the murders of the athletes from his class. I'm going to extrapolate from what you said that it might also explain his killing Hamilton Davies, the attorney staying at the Intercontinental. In keeping with Cook's hatred for athletes, by extension, he must have hated Davies for defending Hoyt Stark, the popular football player fired from the NFL because of spousal abuse. I suspect that didn't sit well with Cook."

My uncle's comment made sense. Elliot Cook certainly had an antipathy to bullies. Hoyt Stark repeatedly beat his wife; he was a bully of the worst kind.

"I think you're right, Uncle Brad," I said.

"What puzzles me is the tourist couple from New Jersey. There seems to be no motive. Anything you can think of to explain why Cook killed them, Cliff?"

"He changed his pattern for sure, but I think that was the point, Uncle Brad. I suspect the tourists were in the wrong place at the wrong time. Cook chose *them* to deliberately confuse law enforcement, as if he were playing chess and using psychological ploys against his opponent. I'm speculating that because Cook had no specific grudge against the couple, he killed them in a more humane manner; they were unconscious when he cut out their organs. He wasn't trying to punish them the way he did with the athletes and the attorney, making them watch but powerless to protect themselves."

"You know, Cliff, this case has all these people and scenarios interwoven. Interestingly, Hoyt Stark tried to cover his tracks by mutilating his victims like the Dead of Night killer. However, without the proper equipment, he left no bite marks or puncture wounds from a tranquilizer gun on the bodies. His work was a poor imitation. That didn't work out too well for him. He didn't do a particularly good job as a copycat killer."

I kept circling back to Elliot Cook and the intensity of his quest for revenge against his childhood bullies. The emotional scars he carried might have been hidden from view, but they were more severe than the physical scars from his medical condition. My uncle interrupted my musings.

"Any thoughts about Todd Howell, Cliff? You believe that Cook killed him as well. Why would he do that? What can you tell me about his motive?"

"According to Lauren, when Elliot was being taunted by the athletes, Todd Howell turned a blind eye to the bullying. I'm sure that the members of the chess team put snakes in Howell's desk drawer and that of Jane Cosby, the female gym teacher. It was retribution from Elliot and the other chess players for their teachers' inaction against their tormentors. Evidently, Cook wasn't satisfied with the snake prank, wanting a more grandiose punishment for Howell. He chose the time and place to disrupt and destroy the reunion by ruining the volleyball game. Probably seemed fitting to carry out his revenge at a *sporting* event."

"What are you basing that on, Cliff?"

"When Howell's body was discovered buried in the sand, there were no blood stains discoloring the ground, even though his body was drained of blood. Cook killed Howell elsewhere and moved his body from the murder scene to the beach. When I examined Howell's body, I noticed a lack of decomposition. The medical examiner can confirm the time of death more accurately, but I think it's safe to assume that the murder took place only hours ago. Cook would have timed it so that he could bury the body before the volleyball game began. Howell's body was meant to be discovered this morning as the game was being played. Cook would have the satisfaction of an audience witnessing his retribution against Howell, even if they had no idea that he was the killer. However, the other chess players would probably connect the dots."

"That certainly goes along with Cook's motive for the murders," Brad stated in agreement. "With his intelligence Cook could easily have researched wolf behavior and become a self-taught expert. Now that he's our prime suspect, we can trace his steps to get his hands on the chemicals and a tranquillizer gun." Brad concluded.

"Elliot Cook is clever and resourceful," I said. "Sometimes people as smart as he is are also cocky. That cockiness can lead to carelessness. Call it a gut feeling, but I think you'll find evidence at his house to connect him to these killings. Check for tranquilizers and curare. I bet that you'll also find the knife and the wolf skull."

"What a waste of his talents. A damn shame. In a way, I feel sorry for him to be that haunted by his past."

"Sometimes you amaze me, Uncle Brad. Under that gruff exterior, you've got a compassionate heart."

"And one last thing that should seal the deal, Uncle Brad. Get a DNA sample from Cook. I bet it will match the blood from the wolf skeleton that was brought to the DNA lab," I said knowingly.

"Just for fun I will take your bet, Cliff. FYI, that's one bet I'll be happy to lose. In fact, if you're right, and Cook's DNA is a match, your Aunt Ellen and I will settle up by treating you and Lauren to a meal at your favorite restaurant in Miami."

"Get ready to shell out some big bucks, Uncle Brad. I'm going to tell Lauren to make a reservation for four at a new place she's been dying to try." I was that confident.

*****

Lauren had just finished putting on her lipstick when the doorbell rang. It was Brad and Ellen picking us up for dinner.

ABOUT THE AUTHORS

Married almost fifty years, Garry and Sheila Gewirtzman have resided in South Florida since 1977. Garry, a dermatologist, and Sheila, a retired accountant, have had extensive law enforcement training, including graduations from the FBI and DEA civilian academies.

The two main characters, Cliff and Lauren, are loosely based on the authors' lives, their relationship, their professions, their personalities, and their unusual experiences. Their familiarity with life in South Florida contributes to the sense of realism of their books.

"Miami Madness" is the fourth book in their Cliff Mandich mystery series. They have authored a total of seven books, several of which have been translated into Spanish and Chinese, a testament to their wide appeal.

Made in the USA
Columbia, SC
16 January 2021